Sweet Victory

She lunged at him, holding back on the *flèche*. He met her foil with a blandly nonchalant beat. "That arm should be straight," he informed her. She drew back, took the *en garde* position, wishing she could see his eyes. Then she had a notion. She half-turned away from him, as if in disgust.

"Perhaps we should just call it a day," she began, "since you are so determined to find fault with my"—And then she sprang at him, extended in the *flèche*. He hadn't even time to raise his blade before her tip struck him square in the chest. Filled with glee, she failed even to attempt to check her momentum; she smacked into him head-on. There was a thud. The chair he sat on tumbled over, leaving her sprawled atop him in the grass.

"Oh, darn," Nichola said, caught in a tangle of blades and chair and limbs. To her astonishment, Lord Boru was laughing. She could feel it, seeing as she was splayed atop his chest.

She let go her foil. The hand he'd put up belatedly to shield himself was hard against her breast. "*Touché*, Miss Hainesworth," he declared, their faces so close that except for the mesh, they might have been embracing. "That was an excellent *flèche*!"

Hurriedly she rolled to the ground beside him—but the imprint of his glove on her breast seemed somehow to linger, imparting warmth despite the February dawn.

Praise for Sandy Hingston's
previous novel

THE LOVER'S CHARM

"*The Lover's Charm* has an ingenious plot. Ms. Hingston's heroine develops like the proverbial butterfly, and you'll be fascinated by her emerging beauty. This author clearly defines the difference between lust and love."
—*Rendezvous*

"Sandy Hingston weaves a sensual tale in *The Lover's Charm*. Jack is very real, and Priscilla is enchanting."
—*Affaire de Coeur*

"Likable characters, solid conflict, good emotional development—all there and done well."
—*Valley Times* (Pleasanton, Ca.)

"Sensual . . . with a tangled plot, a fine cast of characters and a dramatic Gothic ending, *The Lover's Charm* will keep readers glued to the page. Sandra Hingston's fine storytelling skills come to the fore in her second long historical Regency."
—*Romantic Times*

"*The Lover's Charm* made my day! . . . A knock-your-socks-off read from page one to the end. Jack's free-loving spirit, his fairness, intelligence, and full-blown sense of humor are the heart and soul of this book. What a hero! I can't say enough nice things about this fabulous book except whatever you do, don't miss this superb story, and start early or you'll be up all night."
—*The Belles and Beaux of Romance*

"*The Lover's Charm* is a leisurely paced Regency historical peopled with a vast array of characters. . . . Ms. Hingston does a very fine job of slowly peeling back the layers of the characters' pasts, and this makes the novel enjoyable and worth reading."
—*Under the Covers Book Reviews*

School for Scandal

How to
Kiss a Hero

Sandy Hingston

A Dell Book

Published by
Dell Publishing
a division of
Random House, Inc.
1540 Broadway
New York, New York 10036

Cover art copyright © 2000 by Jon Paul

ISBN: 0-440-23534-0

Printed in the United States of America

Published simultaneously in Canada

February 2000

10   9   8   7   6   5   4   3   2   1

OPM

For Liza Hatcher Dawson,
with love,
in memory of our days as schoolmates

*'Tis safest in matrimony to begin with
a little aversion.*
—Richard Sheridan
THE RIVALS

Prologue

Kent, England, April 1811.

"I must say, Christiane, you look simply splendid," Mrs. Treadwell declared as the waiter held her chair for her—*nearly* managing to keep any hint of envy from her tone as she glanced across the table at the Countess d'Oliveri. "Such a charming hat, and your gown, and those gloves— why, you have gone quite continental on me."

The countess smiled back at her, cocking her head, with its stunning mass of auburn ringlets beneath a confection of tulle and crepe and dainty silk roses. "What else would you expect, Evelyn? I *have* been abroad for the past twenty-odd years."

"You even have an *accent*!" Mrs. Treadwell trilled, enthralled. The waiter was attending patiently; she noticed, and looked down at her menu. "Oh, dear, I haven't the least idea of what I want. Christiane, do go ahead."

"I should like," the countess began, "an omelet *aux fines herbes,* very soft, accompanied by bread and green salad, dressed *very* lightly, and a glass of champagne."

Mrs. Treadwell raised her eyebrows. "Champagne? At luncheon?"

"The only proper toast to raise to my reunion with you, Evelyn."

"Well . . . I'll have a glass then as well. And the chicken loaf, please. So long as it is not too salty."

"Very good, ladies." The waiter withdrew. The Countess d'Oliveri removed the long, lacy gloves that Mrs. Treadwell had admired, laying them beside her knife. There was a brief silence. Then Mrs. Treadwell began, a trifle nervously:

"I was surprised when you wrote you would be here in Kent on your visit, instead of in London."

"It was solely to see you that I returned, Evelyn. And I thought perhaps you would not care to be seen out and about with me in the city," the countess said steadily.

"Oh, Christiane! How can you imagine such a thing?"

"I am not exactly *de bon ton.*"

"You are my oldest and *dearest* friend," Mrs. Treadwell said fervently, "and I should be proud to be in your company anywhere." She paused. "Well. *Nearly* anywhere."

The countess burst into a delighted laugh, reaching across the table to grasp her hand. "Oh, Evelyn! I am so very glad to find you haven't changed! I've missed you so."

"As I have missed you," Mrs. Treadwell confessed. "When I look back to the happiest moments of my life, they were all spent with you. Do you recall that picnic we went on with the Wentworths, when you fell in the duck pond?"

The countess winced. "I think of it occasionally."

"And then you pulled in Robert Carston when he went to help you—"

"*Grope* me was more like it."

Mrs. Treadwell was laughing. "In his new coat and breeches! He was so furiously angry!"

"He was an utter ass."

"Oh, you are right about that. He married the Caddleby girl, you know—Amabel. Then went about wasting all her fortune in record time. I feel quite sorry for her. Living out in Hampstead Heath, of all the forlorn places, with a whole passel of children and no staff to speak of, and the house impossible to keep up, while he gallivants about to every boxing-bout and gaming hell around in an effort to recoup—oh, but listen to me running on! Tell me about your life. Tell me *everything* you have done since I saw you last!"

"You've had my letters," the countess pointed out, as the waiter set their flutes before them.

"Yes, but it was so difficult sometimes to make out what you meant! This Maison de Touton in Paris, where you resided for so long—what sort of place was that, exactly? It seems a very odd name for a hotel."

"It was a gambling hell," the countess told her, raising her glass. "Cheers!"

"Cheers." Mrs. Treadwell returned the toast absently. "But you cannot mean . . . you had an apartment there?"

"I owned the house."

"I see," Mrs. Treadwell murmured, taking a gulp of champagne.

"Dear Evelyn. Are you shocked?"

"I must confess, I am. Just a tad. To think of you amongst that rough company . . ."

"That rough company earned me an average of thirty thousand pounds a year."

Mrs. Treadwell spurted out champagne. "Good heavens!" Hurriedly she mopped her mouth with her napkin. "No wonder you are looking so well! Did you find it—exciting?"

"Rather depressive, actually. Men can be such fools. I don't believe there's a woman alive who'd lose five thousand in a night at the tables and keep playing, just because her luck was *sure* to change."

"Is that why you removed to Italy?"

"Oh, no. I removed to Italy after Jean-Baptiste died."

"Yes, now I think of it, I do recall you writing of him.

He was a—a close friend of yours, was he not? A general in the campaigns?"

"He was my lover for more than a decade." The countess's fine dark eyes narrowed. "Surely, Evelyn, you must have understood that."

"I—perhaps I did. I know you wrote most movingly of his death in the war. But—you will forgive my asking—why did you never marry him?"

"He was already married."

"Oh!" Mrs. Treadwell saw, with some relief, that the waiter was approaching with their meal. "My, doesn't the chicken loaf look delightful!"

"I have shocked you now, haven't I, Evelyn?"

"No, no! Not at all. I presume his wife was somehow incapacitated—"

"She was a thoroughgoing bitch who wed him for his money."

"There . . . there is a lot of that going around, isn't there?" Mrs. Treadwell said helplessly. The countess laughed her wondrous laugh again, and at the sound of it, her old friend softened and smiled. "I suppose I seem hopelessly provincial to you."

"Oh, Evelyn, no. You are the epitome of all that's right and true in this world. It's what I've always treasured in you. Of *course* I would have preferred it had Jean-Baptiste been free to marry me. A mistress's life, even the most treasured mistress's life, is never so fulfilled as that of lawful wife."

"But you did marry," Mrs. Treadwell pointed out brightly, "after he was killed."

"Yes. To the count."

"He was quite a bit older, I gather?"

"God, he was ancient," the countess said frankly. "But the most charming—and the *richest*—man I've ever known. I don't know if you can understand me, Evelyn. But it came as a great relief, once Jean-Baptiste was killed, to be taken in hand, to be taken care of. . . ."

"And to be made an honest woman of."

"Yes. I was grateful for that."

"What did you think of Italy?"

The countess giggled. "I love the way you make it sound as though I'd gone there on holiday, instead of as wife to a man three times my age! Italy was ravishing. That's yet another thing for which I am most grateful to Paolo. No one should die without having seen Italy." She took a bite of her omelet and winced. "*Fines herbes* indeed! Nothing but parsley and onions. I ought to have known better."

"I imagine the cuisine was quite good in France and Italy. Still, you don't seem to have gained an ounce since we came out." Self-consciously, Mrs. Treadwell tugged silk down over her own ample bosom.

"But you must tell me about *your* life," the countess said warmly. "I read in the overseas *Gazette* about Vanessa's triumph. The earl of Yarlborough—and in her first season! Quite the coup!"

"Ye-es." There was an undercurrent to the word that did not escape the countess, even after so long an absence from her childhood friend.

"Dear me, Evelyn. There's no . . . no trouble, I trust?"

"No, no trouble to speak of." Then Mrs. Treadwell's gentle voice turned bitter. "Not unless you count two babies within two years, and a philandering husband."

"I see." The countess stabbed at her salad. "Is she terribly unhappy?"

"No!" Mrs. Treadwell burst out. "That is the most aggravating thing! She's not unhappy at all, the silly chit! She goes on having his babies and making apologies for him!"

"Well, if she loves him—"

"That little fool wouldn't know true love if it kicked her in the rear," Mrs. Treadwell said indignantly. "I tell her and *tell* her—stand up to him! Don't let him treat you so shabbily! But it's as though she doesn't even hear. 'I have everything I want, Mamma,' she tells me. 'I have a new

gown every week! I have more jewels than I can count!'
And I want to grab her and shake her and shout at her: *You
have nothing if you don't have love!"*

The countess delicately turned over a lettuce leaf. "Too
much dressing," she sighed. "I must confess, I am surprised
to learn any daughter of yours could be so blind to those
things that matter most in life."

"I've no one to blame but myself. I set her no example
in my own marriage. Mr. Treadwell behaved every bit as
badly as the earl of Yarlborough does."

The countess glanced up sharply. "You don't mean
he . . ."

"Oh, yes. Indeed he did. Right up until he died in Lady
Southerton's bed."

"Oh, *mon Dieu! Ma pauvre petite!* But you never gave
any *hint* in your letters that you were unhappy."

"There's little sense, is there, in carping on what is
one's own fault? You were right, Christiane, when you
counseled me to hold out for better than Everly. I was so
terribly timid, though, in that year we debuted. So afraid
that no one else would make an offer . . ."

"At least Vanessa did not make *that* mistake!"

"No. No. But it might have gone better for her if she
had. It was young Edwin Blessings that offered for her first.
Not much money to speak of, and no title, of course. But
he *was* very fond of her." Mrs. Treadwell pushed at the
chicken loaf. "Do you know, Christiane, I really *am* the
guilty party. In preparing Vanessa for the *ton,* I focused on
such superficial matters—dress, manners, flirting, dancing.
No wonder the poor girl is silly and flighty and has no
backbone."

"What would you do differently," the countess asked
curiously, "had you to do it again?"

"I would teach Vanessa to read books, and think, and
prepare herself for life," Mrs. Treadwell said firmly, "and
not merely to become an ornament on a rich man's arm."

The countess took a sip of champagne. "What an
amazing coincidence, Evelyn. I myself have been giving a

great deal of thought lately to just this situation. Women on the Continent have so much more personal freedom than those here in England. Why, take Caroline Lamb, Lord Byron's erstwhile lover, who is so scorned by the *ton*. In France, a woman of her verve and character and originality would be appreciated—nay, honored! And she has considerable literary talent as well. It is a dreadful shame that English society demands you bring your daughters up to be no more than baubles, and ostracizes them when they refuse to succumb."

"So it is," Mrs. Treadwell agreed mournfully. "But what can anyone do?"

The countess's dark eyes gleamed. "I believe, Evelyn, that you and I could do a great deal to remedy this sad state of affairs."

"You and I? What on earth can you mean?"

"I have it in mind to open a school. A school for young ladies."

"A *school*? For heaven's sake, Christiane, what mother in her right mind would send her daughter off to be educated by the likes of *you*?"

The countess's laughter rang out again—so loudly that the occupants of the neighboring tables looked at her askance. But the elegance of her costume and bearing set their minds at ease, and they were able to return to their meals in peace. "None," she agreed with her old friend cheerfully. "That is precisely why I need your assistance. I propose we create a school for the uplifting of the hearts and souls of England's young women. It would need to bear *your* name rather than mine, of course. I would be a—a silent partner. Provide the money and such, but remain discreetly behind the scenes."

Mrs. Treadwell was silent for a moment, considering. "What would we teach them?" she asked finally.

"Just what you said. To think for themselves. To act for themselves. To be more than baubles on rich men's arms."

Mrs. Treadwell nibbled her lip. "If Vanessa had attended such a school . . ."

"She might not have married so well," the countess acknowledged gently. "Or perhaps she would have. But she surely would have married more fulfillingly."

There was another lengthy pause. "I will confess to you, Christiane, I have been at loose ends," Mrs. Treadwell said then. "I feel myself neither wanted nor needed in Vanessa's household. Not to mention how it torments me to be there, watching as she makes an idiot of herself. But still . . . to go into business! It is not, I believe, *bon ton*."

"God knows there are few enough respectable occupations for women," the countess agreed. "But I don't see how anyone could argue that you mean anything but the best by founding such an establishment. You are, after all, the mother of the set's most astonishing success."

"So I am," Mrs. Treadwell acknowledged dryly. "You are likely quite right. England's mammas would flock to have their girls taught what I taught Vanessa. Any number of them approach me every time I make an appearance and beg my advice."

"There, you see?"

"But what you are proposing . . . teaching them to think independently, giving them the true benefit of my experience—not to mention *yours*—why, it sounds like a school for scandal!"

"The perfect name!" the countess declared—then winked. "But only between you and me. To the world, I propose our school be known as 'Mrs. Treadwell's Academy for the Elevation of Young Ladies.'"

Mrs. Treadwell reached for her champagne. "I don't know. It seems a dreadful trick to play on mammas who expect offerings in pianoforte and dancing."

"Oh, we shall offer pianoforte and dancing."

"And what else?" Mrs. Treadwell asked suspiciously.

"Whatever the young ladies entrusted to our care require," the countess said solemnly, "to achieve their potential in life. Oh, Evelyn, imagine! If we are able to save even one of our charges from poor Vanessa's fate—"

"Or from yours," Mrs. Treadwell noted, with a sudden

flash of the shrewdness her matronly figure and placid manner so adeptly hid. "What assurance do I have that your preposterous scheme is anything more than an attempt to wreak vengeance on the *ton* that behaved so badly to you— forcing you into exile, making your very name a caution to its misses?"

"I can only tell you," the countess declared, "that I harbor no resentment toward those who did me ill—for in doing so, they effected a favor." And she leaned forward again. "My life, Evelyn, has been impossibly rich. I had Jean-Baptiste. I had Paolo. I had money of my own, that I'd earned, to jangle in my purse. I used my wits, but I never lost sight of my heart. When I die, I know I shall look back upon my time on earth and be able to say, with complete conviction, 'I was happy.' How many Englishwomen do you know who will do the same?"

"I could count them on one hand." Mrs. Treadwell's champagne glass was empty. The countess gestured to the waiter. "Oh, no. I couldn't."

"Why the devil not?" her friend demanded. "What's to stop you?"

"Why—I'm not really sure."

"Two more glasses of champagne," the countess said definitively. "No, wait—bring us the bottle."

"Oh, Christiane . . ."

"Your chicken loaf is growing cold."

"I detest chicken loaf."

"Why did you order it, then?"

"It is considered a genteel choice for ladies dining alone." And Mrs. Treadwell giggled. "God, how stuffy I sound!"

"Not at all," the countess assured her. "It is precisely that sort of knowledge the young ladies of our school will be required to absorb if they are to flourish. I am under no illusions as to that. English society is a formidable foe." The waiter had arrived with the champagne bottle. Mrs. Treadwell's hand floated up to cover her glass, then wandered back to her lap.

"Foe, Christiane?"

"Foe," the countess said firmly. "But, Evelyn, do think of this. The nation's young men will benefit as well by our labors."

"Will they?"

"Naturally. The end result will be happier, stronger marriages—marriages based on mutual respect, on shared endeavor, even—dare I say it?—on *true* love, love that is equally fulfilling to both parties, secure and joyous, loyal by choice, reaching far beyond the conventions of the *ton*."

"My goodness. When you put it that way . . ."

The countess raised her glass. After a moment, so did Mrs. Treadwell. The handsome flutes touched with a bright clink.

" 'To achieve their potential in life,' " Mrs. Treadwell murmured thoughtfully. "I cannot *imagine* what such a curriculum might consist of."

"Nor can I," said the countess. "But I *shall* know, once I meet our girls."

Chapter One

Nichola Hainesworth slumped against the side of the coach, arms folded across her chest, her face beneath her poke bonnet positively mutinous. Her mother, who was sitting opposite her and busily knitting, sighed in exasperation. "Nichola, do sit up. You will ruin your posture slouching about that way." Nichola muttered under her breath. "I didn't *hear* you," said the baroness, needles clicking.

"I *said*, what bloody difference does my posture make?"

"Nichola! Do mind your language! I can only imagine what Mrs. Treadwell will make of you if you resort to such coarseness!"

Nichola muttered something that sounded very much like "To bloody hell with Mrs. Treadwell."

Her mother blinked. "I beg your pardon?"

"You heard me."

The baroness set her knitting aside, glaring across the

coach. "You do understand, young lady, this is *precisely* the sort of behavior that impelled me to enroll you in Mrs. Treadwell's academy." Nichola, facing the window, was mimicking her, mouthing the words, her wide lips drawn up to imitate her mother's prim expression of distaste. "Oh, you are the *height* of cheek!" the baroness declared in frustration. "I don't know *what* I could have been thinking of, to neglect your education so atrociously. It's this dreadful war is what it is. If I hadn't been so sick with worry over darling Ollie, and then Spence, and poor dear Daniel and Jody, and now Tommy, my sweet baby Tommy—"

"I'm younger than Tommy," Nichola pointed out.

"Yes, but you are only a girl." The baroness shivered prettily in her elegant Norwich shawl. "I declare, every time I think of Tommy facing the guns of that atrocious Sicilian—"

"Napoleon is Corsican."

"Don't be cheeky." The baroness squared her shoulders. "At least I can do my *utmost* to make certain his poor toes are not chilled." And she held up her knitting. "Do you think this sock long enough?"

"Try it on me," Nichola offered, sticking out her foot. "We wear the same size boot, Tommy and I."

"Nichola, that is nothing to boast of!" The baroness, her own petite shoes tucked daintily against the seat, surveyed her robust daughter with despair. "I don't for the life of me know how you ever got so big. And to think that you are only sixteen!"

"Eighteen," Nichola corrected her.

"Eighteen? No, no. That's quite impossible. Were you eighteen, Oliver would be twenty-five. And that would make *me*—"

"Forty-two," Nichola noted complacently. "Which is what you are."

"Hush!" the baroness said sharply. "What if the coachman overhears?" Nichola, turning to the window again, rolled her eyes. "Besides," her mother noted perplexedly, "were you eighteen, you would already have come out."

"I don't *care* to come out," Nichola declared firmly. "I want to stay at home and ride and wrestle and shoot, just as I always have."

"Don't be ridiculous. Such preoccupations are unsuitable for a young lady of six—"

"Eight—"

"Your age," her mother amended, blazing right through the interruption.

"Not," Nichola added sadly, "that there's anyone to ride and wrestle and shoot *with,* since Tommy's gone to war. The lucky bastard."

"Nichola!"

"What?"

"Oh, I have been remiss with you, haven't I? Just look at you! Not a whit of style or charm or polish—and you are *slouching* again! Don't you know that if you go on like this, you never will attract a husband?"

"What's so bloody wonderful about a husband?"

"And you are *far* too defiant! Let us hope Mrs. Treadwell is able to instill some submission and humility in you, for I have certainly failed!"

The coach had rattled up to a pair of intricate iron gates. Nichola, heart sinking, saw the scripted sign mounted upon them and sighed from the depths of her soul. *Mrs. Treadwell's Academy for the Elevation of Young Ladies* . . . "We're here," the baroness declared, fluttering into activity. "Have you your reticule? Your face is smudged, there right below your chin—no, no, do use your *handkerchief!* Gracious sakes, I shall be glad to be quit of the responsibility for you. Please, don't *clump* when you exit the carriage. You have the most unfortunate tendency to clump. A *lady* . . ." Baroness Hainesworth gathered her voluminous skirts as the coach rolled through the gates and then came to a stop. "A lady *floats,*" she declared serenely, and did so, alighting with impossible grace as the coachman pulled down the step.

Nichola followed, her boot heels making a clank that caused her mother to wince.

A small, round-figured woman with brown hair going gray and a warm, welcoming smile came through the front doors to greet them. "Lady Hainesworth!" The woman dropped a curtsy that contained just the proper sense of deference; the baroness's responding curtsy was equally calculated. Then the two embraced, lips brushing cheeks. "You are the peak of fashion, as always," the little woman declared, still holding to the baroness's arm.

"I hardly imagine so," Lady Hainesworth demurred, "after that lengthy ride!" But she preened at her bonnet, pleased by the compliment.

"And you must be Nichola!" The woman came forward as though to embrace Nichola as well. Nichola shrank back in alarm—then noted with interest that their greeter instantly perceived her reluctance and extended her hand. "I am Mrs. Treadwell. Welcome to my academy! You may put Miss Hainesworth's bags inside," she directed the coachman, "and the servants will see to them. Won't you join me for tea, ladies?"

"We would be delighted." Nichola's mother shoved an elbow into the ribs of her daughter, who was staring up at the walls of her new home. "Come along," she hissed. "And *do* mind your manners!"

"It doesn't look like any school *I've* ever seen," Nichola noted dubiously, contemplating the two-story structure of weatherbeaten gray stone.

"It was a Cistercian monastery in the time of Henry the Second," Mrs. Treadwell declared, ushering them through the stout doors and into a dim, tile-floored vestibule in which her voice echoed spookily. "Since then, it's been largely abandoned. My staff and I had a great deal of work to bring it up to snuff."

"Ah, yes. I'd been meaning to speak to you on that matter of staff, Mrs. Treadwell. At the date of our last correspondence, you had not yet entirely fixed on your faculty."

"I am delighted to inform you, Lady Hainesworth, that my fondest dreams have come to pass in that regard. For stitchwork, I've engaged Madame Papillion."

"*The* Madame Papillion?" the baroness asked, awe-struck.

"Indeed. And for dancing, Monsieur Alphonse Albert."

"How amazing! Monsieur Albert instructed *me* in the year of my debut!"

"He must be awfully old, then," Nichola put in curtly.

Mrs. Treadwell turned to her with a smile. "Your mother and I, you might be interested to discover, made our debuts within months of each other. And we both had our instruction from Monsieur Albert. He is extremely experienced." Nichola flushed. The rebuke had been mild and largely unspoken, but richly deserved. She started to stammer an apology, but Mrs. Treadwell shook it off, with a completely unexpected twinkle in her blue eyes. "For Latin," the headmistress continued, "I—"

"*Latin?*" the baroness said in alarm.

"Why, yes. Have you some objection to Latin?"

"Well . . . I cannot see exactly what good Latin might serve in a young lady's education."

"I'll admit," Mrs. Treadwell confessed, "I had my own doubts. But Professor Hallaby was so convincing in his argument that I—"

"You don't mean Professor Augustus Hallaby!" The baroness turned to her daughter in excitement. "Oh! I have been to every one of his speeches at the British Museum! He is an utter *genius* at gardening nomenclature!"

"Precisely," Mrs. Treadwell confirmed. Nichola, whose spirits had briefly soared at the prospect of tackling the Latin language, sank into a funk. Gardening nomenclature! Dancing and stitchwork! God, she would go out of her mind! She scanned the parlor they'd attained, noting with dismay that the windows were barred and distressingly narrow. No doubt the monks had been just as eager to escape as she.

"Then we have Mrs. Caldburn for household management," Mrs. Treadwell continued, gesturing them to seats.

"Nichola, you must pay special attention to her lectures," the baroness decreed, nodding for two sugars in her cup. "Nothing is so much a challenge to a wife as proper household management."

"And Mr. Jonas Saliston for riding." Nichola perked up—riding? "Sidesaddle only, naturally," Mrs. Treadwell added, deflating her hopes again.

"Naturally," the baroness acknowledged, accepting a marmalade cake. Nichola was scowling as the platter was offered to her. Mrs. Treadwell noticed, and smiled.

"My dear. I pray you, give us a try," she urged. "If you find the curriculum is not to your liking, you can always write to your mamma and tell her."

"The curriculum," Lady Hainesworth said dauntingly, "sounds exactly what my daughter requires. *Do* sit up straight, Nichola; you look a common sight!" Depressed beyond caring, Nichola scrunched farther down in her chair. Beneath lowered lashes, she glared balefully at the tormentor who was to replace her heretofore blessedly neglectful mother—and saw, to her astonishment, that Mrs. Treadwell's blue eyes were unexpectedly bright with tears. Why, she looks almost . . . almost *sympathetic,* Nichola thought—and then dismissed the notion as absurd.

"You may even find you like it here," the headmistress said very gently.

"I sincerely doubt *that,*" Nichola retorted.

"Nichola! Where are your manners? Oh, I tell you, Mrs. Treadwell, young folk today are so impossibly headstrong!" Her mother dabbed powdered sugar from the corners of her tight, hard mouth. "Why, in *our* day, we would have been downright *grateful* had our mothers seen fit to prepare us so completely for what the future held for us, wouldn't we?"

"Indeed we would have." There was an undercurrent in the headmistress's voice of something like bemusement.

But—no, Nichola thought. I must be mistaken. Her mother certainly had noticed no such thing.

The two older women chatted on interminably then about the splendor of the old days and acquaintances they had in common—practically the entire English population, so far as Nichola could tell—and the weather and the war and which girls to be brought out that season seemed most promising. Nichola sat and fidgeted and ate six cakes and plucked at her skirts and cleaned beneath her fingernails with the handle of her teaspoon and finally, bored beyond bearing, yawned, hugely and with relish. The baroness shot her a look of utter horror and drained her cup. "Well! I must say, Mrs. Treadwell, I have no great hopes or expectations for this daughter of mine in this or any other season. You can see she is gawky and unmanageable; she has no culture or learning to speak of, and her manners are intolerable. I blame only myself. You know I have five sons, all of them older than Nichola. I have no doubt been neglectful of my duties toward her. But young men *must* take precedence, mustn't they? Nonetheless, you inspire me with newfound confidence. Perhaps your academy will succeed where I so decidedly have not. And now I must be going. I hope to reach St. Peter's, at least, before sundown; there isn't a decent hostelry between here and there."

"We are a touch remote," Mrs. Treadwell acquiesced. "But I trust that will prove all for the best. Let me just make certain that your coach is ready." She rose from the sofa and bustled through the doors.

"Nichola!" the baroness hissed once she was gone. Nichola ignored her, reaching for a tart. "Nichola! By St. George, you listen to me! That woman managed to marry her daughter to the earl of Yarlborough in her very first season—and Vanessa Treadwell wasn't much to look at, either! Not to mention that she hadn't any fortune whatsoever. So there is hope for you. Mind you do as you're told and work hard and acquire some pretense of polish. Otherwise, you will certainly turn out an old maid!" Nichola bit into her tart lustily. "Oh! I wash my hands of you, you impossible child!"

Mrs. Treadwell appeared again in the doorway. "Your horses have been watered and fed, Lady Hainesworth. Any time you are ready—"

"I'm *more* than ready." Nichola's mother glared at her daughter in fury.

"Good-bye, Mother," Nichola said absently.

The baroness hesitated for a moment, then embraced her. It was the first movement she'd made that was lacking in grace. "Nichola. *Do* be good for Mrs. Treadwell, won't you? There is so *very* much she has to teach you that's worthwhile."

"I'm sure she'll be as good as gold," Mrs. Treadwell said warmly. "Won't you, Nichola, my dear?"

Nichola belched. Too many cakes.

"Nichola!"

"Never mind," Mrs. Treadwell reassured the baroness, steering her toward the door. "I promise you, we shall take very good care of her. Do have a safe journey to St. Peter's. And set your mind at ease. Nichola is in *very* good hands."

"You would have to be a miracle worker, Mrs. Treadwell, to accomplish anything with *that* one."

"I'm a great believer in miracles," Mrs. Treadwell said complacently. "Come and wave farewell to your mamma, Nichola, and I shall show you to your room."

The carriage rattled off through the gates. Nichola stood beside Mrs. Treadwell on the portico, wondering what she *ought* to be feeling. Sadness, she supposed, and regret, and homesickness. What she was actually contemplating, though . . . "How far are we here from Dover?" she asked of the headmistress.

"Only about twenty miles."

Nichola perked up considerably. "Really? Imagine that!"

"Have you friends in Dover?"

Time will tell, Nichola thought, but said only, "No. It's simply a place I've never been."

"Perhaps we might arrange a visit there," Mrs. Tread-well mused. "The cliffs are quite a splendid sight. And of course there is a wealth of history in the town itself."

"It's to the southeast, I suppose?" Nichola asked airily.

"I suppose. Geography was never my strong suit." The headmistress took Nichola's arm and gave it a pat. "Now, let's go meet your classmates in the upper form, shall we? I just know you are all going to get along famously!"

She led Nichola back into the vestibule and up the stairs, then along an echoing corridor. "This wing houses the girls in the lower forms, from ages ten through twelve." The hallway made a sharp turn, and Nichola saw through a set of clerestory windows to her left that the abbey was built in a square around a central courtyard. These inner windows, she also noted, had no locks or bars. "Here are the girls of the middle form, up through age sixteen," Mrs. Treadwell announced, nodding at the rooms they passed. The hallway turned again. "And here you are—your new home! We have three other girls your age, so I've grouped you together. They've only just arrived as well. I know you are going to be such *special* friends." She paused and knocked on a door to her right. "Ladies!" she trilled cheerily. "The last of your classmates is here!" She turned the knob and, nodding encouragement, gestured Nichola inside.

In the light of a pair of oil lamps, three faces turned to Nichola—two looking timid as mice, and the third as haughty as a Spanish queen. Mrs. Treadwell made the introductions: "Miss Nichola Hainesworth, Miss Gwendolyn Carstairs." The smaller of the mice bobbed nervously in a curtsy. "Miss Elizabeth Boggs." That was the second mouse, rather heavyset and plain, with masses of wavy red hair and eyes that shied hurriedly away. "And Miss—"

"Lady," the third girl announced in a voice as haughty as her looks. "*Lady* Katherine Devereaux. How do you *do*?"

"I'm an Honorable," Nichola said bluntly. "But I don't stand on it."

The Spanish queen's crystal-blue gaze surveyed her coolly. "Odd. You don't *look* like an Honorable. Or even a lady."

"You *all* are ladies, naturally," Mrs. Treadwell said smoothly. "But as I have already explained to Miss Dever—"

"Lady—"

"—eaux, here at the academy we make no distinctions as to rank."

"Obviously," said Lady Katherine. "I really must insist, Mrs. Treadwell, that I be assigned private quarters. I'm quite sure that had my parents, the duke and duchess, known I was to be forced to share accommodations, they never would have consented to enroll me here."

"Really? You must make sure and write them, to tell them of your displeasure. Perhaps they will see fit to remove you." Nichola glanced down at the little woman in surprise. Her words were pleasant enough, but they were spoken with an edge of steel she never would have expected from the headmistress.

"You may be certain I intend to do so at the earliest opportunity," Lady Katherine countered, just as indomitably.

"I—I find the room entirely to my liking," the littlest mouse piped up unexpectedly.

Lady Katherine favored her with a withering glance. "Oh, I've no doubt *you* would." The mouse blushed and retreated to the trunk she'd been unpacking. There was a moment of silence. Then the plain mouse stepped forth.

"I've taken this bunk here, Miss Hainesworth, and left you that one." She pointed to a bed beside the window. "But if you'd rather, I'd be happy to exchange with you."

"This will suit me well enough, Miss—Boggs, was it?"

"Aye." The red-haired girl giggled. "Dreadful name, isn't it? But what can one do?"

"Marry and assume another," Katherine Devereaux

noted, then looked her up and down. "Although in *your* case, that may prove quite difficult."

Mrs. Treadwell cleared her throat. "I'd suggest, Nichola, that you begin settling in. Dinner is in less than an hour; you will hear the bell. Now I'll leave you all to your unpacking." She withdrew, closing the door behind her with a smart, crisp click.

Katherine Devereaux sniffed. "I really can't *think* what Mamma and Poppa were imagining, to consign me to this dreadful school." She turned her back on Nichola and the others, moving to the single looking glass hung by the door and primping at her amazing golden ringlets.

Nichola made a face at her, then crossed to where her own trunks were waiting. The little mouse—Miss Carstairs—was humming beneath her breath. Nichola took the opportunity to examine the window fastenings. She might have made it through the casement, but it was a sheer two-story drop to the ground below.

The plain mouse had followed her. "I've already unpacked my things. Do you need any help with yours?" she inquired politely.

"Oh, I don't intend to unpack," Nichola said idly, sticking her head through the window and checking for vines or footholds. It did not look promising.

"Why ever not?"

"Because I'm not staying."

"*There,*" Lady Deveraux declared, "is the first sensible thing I've heard anyone in this miserable hellhole say."

"I don't see why not," Miss Boggs protested. "It might prove very pleasant, being away to school."

"I am looking forward to it," Miss Carstairs mentioned quietly, breaking off her song. "It makes a change from home."

"At home," declared Lady Devereaux, "I had eight *personal* servants. *And* an entire wing of the estate to myself."

"What is it, Miss Hainesworth," Miss Boggs asked curiously, "that you so miss about home?"

"I?" Nichola was startled. "Nothing at *all* about home."

"Mm. No. Nor I either." Miss Carstairs's voice was thoughtful.

"I miss my cat," Miss Boggs put in.

"How positively *pathetic*," Lady Devereaux observed.

"But if you don't miss your home," Miss Boggs pressed Nichola, "then why are so anxious to go back there?"

"Oh, I'm not going *home*." Nichola paused. "I say. You're not the sorts, are you, to go bearing tales? To Mrs. Treadwell, I mean."

The two mice stared at her, round-eyed, shaking their heads. Lady Deveraux snorted and said, "Hardly likely."

"Well, then." Nichola took a breath, relishing the opportunity to impart her plan. "I am going to the Continent."

"I've been," Lady Devereaux said in a bored voice.

"To be a soldier," Nichola added.

That brought Lady Deveraux's elegant head whipping round. "How utterly absurd. Girls can't be soldiers."

"Why not?" Nichola demanded, hands on hips. "I can ride and shoot and wrestle just as well as Daniel, and *better* than Ollie and Spence and Jody. Tommy, though, can best me—sometimes."

"Who," Miss Boggs demanded, wide-eyed, "are Daniel and Ollie and Spence and Joey—"

"Jody," Nichola corrected her. "He and Spence are twins. They're my brothers."

"Good Lord," Miss Carstairs said. "Five brothers? Are they older or younger, or what?"

"Older. Except for Tommy. He and I are twins as well. Though he is two minutes older—as if that counts."

"And are they soldiers?" Miss Boggs wanted to know.

"Well—all of them except Spence. He's a clergyman. But he is posted overseas with the army."

"Five brothers," Lady Devereaux murmured, almost to herself. "What's your father, then? He cannot be a duke or earl, or I would know the name. Is he a viscount?"

"Baron," said Nichola briefly.

"Only a baron. Pity."

"What is it like to be a twin? If you don't mind my asking," Miss Boggs said apologetically.

"Oh, it is splendid! Or *was*, rather, until Tommy went off to war. Until then, we always did *everything* together. Swam, and hunted, and broke in Papa's horses—"

"That," said Lady Devereaux, "would explain your physique."

"My what?"

"Your *build*."

"I think Miss Hainesworth has a *lovely* build," tiny Miss Carstairs said enviously. "So big and tall and—and strong!"

"I am strong as an ox," Nichola declared proudly. Lady Devereaux turned back to the mirror, rolling her eyes.

"Do you do exercises?" Miss Boggs queried. "Mamma is—was—always after me to do exercises. I do hope we shan't have exercises here."

"There's to be dancing," Nichola told her, with an echoing frown. "Mrs. Treadwell said so. With some antique instructor. And horseback riding. But only sidesaddle."

Katherine Devereaux craned her lovely neck. "How else do *ladies* ride?"

"You can't get up a proper gallop going sidesaddle," Nichola informed her.

"I'm afraid of horses," Miss Carstairs said. "But being a soldier—how will you go about it?"

"I brought a set of Tommy's clothes with me. I'll put them on tonight and climb out the window, make my way to Dover, and take ship for the Continent."

"You *won't*," Miss Boggs said, agog.

Miss Carstairs was frowning. "I don't think you can just 'take ship' for the Continent any longer. You have to join up with a regiment first. They train you somehow, make you fit to fight. And I don't see how, being among all those men, you are going to conceal the fact of your sex for very long. They all live together in barracks, don't they?

Change in front of one another? And what about using the—the facilities?"

"Oh, please!" Lady Devereaux was highly offended. "I find this entire conversation in most questionable taste!" Miss Boggs giggled, then hid the fact behind her hand.

"England needs every soldier it can get to fight Napoleon," Nichola said stoutly. Hadn't she heard her father say that often enough?

"Still . . ." Miss Carstairs was far from convinced. "There's the matter of uniforms as well. They'd have to fit you for one. I just don't see how—" She was interrupted by a resounding gong

"Suppertime!" Miss Boggs brightened. "I wonder if it will prove as tasty as the tea cakes. Those were *lovely* tea cakes, didn't you think, Miss Carstairs?"

"Please," the smallest mouse said, coloring, "call me Gwendolyn. That is—Gwen."

"I will be pleased to, if you'll call me Bess."

"And I am Nichola," Nichola put in. They waited for a moment, expecting Lady Devereaux's invitation. It was not forthcoming. Nichola shrugged and headed for the door. "I may as well eat. It could be a long time before I have another meal. It is twenty miles, Mrs. Treadwell said, to Dover. And I'll be walking, of course. Unless . . . unless I can steal a horse from the stables! Where are the stables, does anyone know?" Gwendolyn and Bess shook their heads, perplexed.

"Follow the scent of manure," Lady Devereaux suggested rather nastily. "I imagine you are well acquainted with it."

If Nichola had intended to remain at the academy for even a single night, she would have smashed the blonde's face in. Since she did not, however . . . "Excellent advice," she noted calmly. "Shall we go and dine?"

Chapter
Two

Later that night, Nichola lay in her bed beneath the window, watching clouds scrim across the half-moon and through the darkened sky. She was wearing Tommy's trousers and shirt and coat, and had his boots and hat at the ready. She'd dawdled on the way back to the room long enough to ascertain that while the outer walls of the abbey were too sheer to climb down, those giving onto the courtyard were simply slathered with ivy. She trusted ivy; that was what she'd used to climb out of her bedchamber at home. Now she was only waiting until it grew so late that she could be certain everyone belowstairs would be asleep.

Supper had been rather amusing, really. The younger girls—there were twenty or so—all looked so wan and frightened. Miss Boggs—Bess—had been wonderful with setting them at ease; she'd told jokes and made puppets out of napkins and put on a very witty play. Nichola had thought the food quite splendid, though Lady Devereaux had sniffed that it was horrid and plain. Gwendolyn Carstairs had been almost entirely quiet. Only when Mrs. Treadwell mentioned something about having procured an instructor in the sciences had she come to life, bubbling out with so many questions about what they might be taught that the headmistress finally laughed and waved her hands and suggested that she wait and ask the good gentleman himself.

It was odd to be in the company of so many females. Nichola was accustomed to a dinner table overflowing with her brothers and their friends, to talk of horses and hounds and boxing matches, loud jests, grabs for bread and slabs of meat. Since the boys had gone off to war, the baroness took most of her meals in her rooms, and because the baron stayed mostly in London, Nichola ate in her own rooms. She hadn't minded—her mother only nattered about her table manners and dress and posture on those few occasions when they did dine together—but she was intrigued by how different eating here at the academy had been. All those timid faces seated about the tables! The precise unfolding of napkins, Mrs. Treadwell's murmured corrections at the misuse of a knife or fork, the dainty appetites of the students . . . she felt she'd caught a glimpse into another world. And though it wasn't one she planned to stick around for, she couldn't help but wonder drowsily what other revelations might have lain in store.

"What are you waiting for?" a voice whispered out of the darkness. Nichola, on the edge of sleep, sat up with a start. It was Bess who'd spoken, her green eyes glinting in the moonlight as she hung over the edge of her bed.

"She isn't going," Lady Devereaux said flatly. "It was nothing but talk. All talk."

"I most certainly *am* going," Nichola announced, sliding into her boots. "I was only waiting to be sure everyone was asleep."

"How can we possibly sleep when you are on the verge of such an adventure?" Bess demanded.

"Come with me, if you like."

"I? Oh, good heavens, no. I'd be a reprehensible soldier. I hate getting up in the mornings. And I can't stand the bang of guns."

"You know," Gwendolyn Carstairs put in quietly from her pillow. "Mrs. Treadwell is bound to send out search parties in the morning, once she finds you are missing."

"I've already thought of that." Nichola jammed on her hat. "She'll send them toward home, naturally. In quite the opposite direction from Dover. *Unless,* of course, one of you tattles on me."

"*I* never would," Bess said fervently.

"Why bother?" Lady Deveraux declared through a yawn.

"There will be hoofprints," Gwendolyn noted. "If, that is, you really mean to steal a horse."

Nichola frowned. "I hadn't thought of that."

Bess sat up eagerly. "You know what you do? You cut a branch from a tree. One with leaves. And you trail it behind the horse along the ground. That wipes out the hoofprints."

There was a moment's silence. Then, "That might work," Gwendolyn said thoughtfully. "However did you think of it?"

"Oh, I didn't. I read it in a novel. *The Saracen's Revenge.* It is all about a Moor who kidnaps the princess of Jerusalem and holds her for ransom during the Crusades. That's what he did to get away from her father. Only he used palm fronds. Still, I imagine a tree branch would serve as well."

Lady Devereaux let out an inelegant snort. "How utterly absurd. You won't get away with it, you know. It is just *like* something from a cheap novel."

"*I* think it's wonderful," Bess protested with a romantic sigh.

"You would."

Gwendolyn clearly had been pondering Nichola's planned absconding at some length. "I've been considering about the uniforms. If you only had some bandaging or gauze, you could wrap that tight around your chest. To hide—you know."

"I have a gauze scarf," Bess offered, and bounced up to fetch it. She brought it to Nichola with the air of an acolyte attending the altar.

"Oh, I couldn't," Nichola protested.

"I insist. I hate scarves, anyway. They always seem to tangle around my throat." In the moonlight she clutched at her neck, making highly convincing choking sounds. Gwendolyn giggled, and so did Nichola.

"You ought to be an actress," she told the girl in admiration.

"How could I be, when I'm so plain?"

"Actresses paint themselves," Gwendolyn observed.

"Some things even paint cannot hide," Lady Devereaux said tartly. "If you are going, then for God's sake go, and let a body get some sleep." She turned over in her bed with a flounce.

"I suppose it's late enough by now." Nichola nibbled her lip. "Well. It's been quite pleasant meeting all of you." Was this, she wondered, what it might have been like to have a sister—whispering and giggling in the night, sharing secrets, hopes, dreams?

"Best of luck," Bess said solemnly, and to Nichola's astonishment embraced her in a quick, clumsy hug.

"Be careful," Gwendolyn warned, and she, too, rose from her bed, to shake Nichola's hand. Lady Devereaux began pointedly to snore. Nichola slung the pack she'd brought over her shoulder and started for the door.

"Make sure the branch has leaves!" Bess called after her.

"I will."

"How are you going to get out?" Gwendolyn wondered.

"Climb the ivy down into the courtyard."

"And from there?"

"I'll find a way," Nichola vowed.

"The horses in the stable won't be saddled," Gwendolyn pointed out.

"I can saddle a horse with my eyes shut."

"Can you really? Imagine that. Oh, but wait! You said Mrs. Treadwell told you there would be only sidesaddle riding here. If all the saddles are sidesaddles, you'll look rather peculiar, won't you? Since you are dressed as a man."

Nichola shrugged. "I'll go bareback if I have to."

"You can ride *bareback*?" Bess was awestruck.

"Of course I can."

"Will you just *go*," Lady Devereaux said crossly, "so the rest of us can sleep?"

"I beg your pardon," Nichola apologized. "Well! I am off, then!"

"I shall remember you always," Bess said devoutly.

"When you get to the Continent, you might write us," Gwendolyn put in.

"I'll be certain to do that. Farewell!" Nichola opened the door and crept out into the hall, with a strange pang of loss. As she carefully pulled the portal to behind her, she heard Bess sigh enviously:

"God, what I wouldn't give to be so brave!"

"So stupid, rather," Lady Devereaux snapped. "Now do shut up and let me sleep!"

Smiling to herself, Nichola made her way along the corridor to the north side of the square, where the ivy was thickest. She wound the casement out slowly, fearful the old wood and iron would creak. They didn't. Much encouraged, she crawled through, tested the nearest vines, found two that clung especially tightly, and clambered to the ground. Then she stood in the courtyard, catching her breath.

The silvery moonlight showed a fountain in the center of the square, but otherwise the space held nothing but rather sparse grass. Nichola made a silent circuit of the perimeter, staying in the shadows, searching for a way out. Her efforts were rewarded. On the far side, beneath what she judged to be the back stairs, the walls opened in an arch and gave onto a low wooden door.

She was reaching for a hairpin—her brother Tommy had been a whiz at springing locks and was generous with his knowledge—but the latch lifted readily in her hand. She'd just given the handle a tentative yank when a voice at her shoulder seemed to stop her heart. "I beg your pardon," it said, with a faint hint of foreign accent. "I don't suppose you have got such a thing as a match about you?"

Nichola turned and saw in the faint argent glow a woman—not a girl, definitely a woman, though of what age she could not tell. She was dressed very handsomely in a high-waisted, low-cut gown, with a shawl over her slim shoulders, and in her hand she held what looked to be a very slim cigar—a fact that so astonished Nichola, she forgot for a moment what she was about.

"A-a-a match?" she stammered. "No, I'm afraid I don't. So awfully sorry."

"Ah. Pity. Evelyn—Mrs. Treadwell—says I must not smoke inside the building, so I came out here. Only I seem to have forgotten a match."

"You smoke cigars?" Nichola asked dubiously.

The woman made a moue. "I know. Dreadful habit. But what can I say? I picked it up on the Continent."

The mention of her destination yanked Nichola to her senses. "I suppose you'll have to go back inside to fetch one," she noted, reaching for the door handle again. "Now, if you will excuse me—"

"You are one of the students, are you not? Let me guess. Are you Miss—I mean, Lady—Devereaux?"

Nichola couldn't help laughing. "God, no!"

"But surely you are in the upper form." The woman pursed her lips. She had, Nichola saw, a very lovely face. "I watched you climb down the wall. A commendable display of courage."

"Oh, no. Not at all. My room at home is ever so much higher, and I climbed down from it all the time."

"Really? To what purpose?"

"Oh—just to get out. To get away."

"Is that what you are doing now?"

Nichola hesitated. She did not want to risk this woman raising a hue and cry over her departure; on the other hand, so far the stranger had made no move to try and stop her. And she smoked cigars. That pointed to an open mind. "As a matter of fact, I am."

The woman had been patting her gown; now she reached into a pocket and triumphantly brought forth a small silver box. "Ah! I am not losing my wits after all! Most reassuring." She took a wooden match from the box, ran it along a strip of rough folded paper, and held the resultant flame to the tip of her cigar, inhaling deeply. The sting of phosphorus mingled with the pungent odor of tobacco as she let out her breath. Then she cocked her head at Nichola. "Are you so unhappy here as that?"

"I'm not unhappy here at all, I don't think. I have only just got here. It's just that I've made plans."

"What sorts of plans?"

Again Nichola paused. But the woman didn't look alarmed or upset, merely curious. "Well—I am going to the Continent, if you must know."

"Oh, the Continent is *lovely*!" the woman said warmly. "Where are you headed, then? Italy? Austria? France?"

"I'm not certain. Wherever I'm most needed, I suppose."

"Needed?" the woman echoed, drawing on her cigar. Its tip was a beacon of orange char.

"Yes." Nichola took a breath. "I intend to become a soldier." She waited for the inevitable ridicule. But it did not come. The woman merely nodded thoughtfully.

"A noble profession, soldiering. But difficult also. Demanding."

"I am very hardy."

"Yes. I could see that by the way you came down the wall. Still . . . what do you have to offer in the way of soldierly arts?"

"I can shoot extremely well," Nichola said proudly.

"And as you can see, I am strong and tall. As strong and tall as most men. Indeed, I think sometimes that I ought to have *been* a man."

The woman flicked ash from her cigar. "Do you? How so?"

"Well, it's certainly what Mother and Father were expecting. I have five older brothers, you see. And my name—" She stopped. She hadn't given her name yet.

"Five brothers!" the woman marveled, seeming to take no notice of her hesitation. "And are they on the Continent?"

"Yes. All of them. My brother Tommy went a year ago last May. It's been horribly dreary for me since he did. We—we're twins."

"Twins! How fascinating! Do you know each other's thoughts?"

"And finish one another's sentences." Nichola laughed, a bit hollowly. "Mother says I should knit socks for him. But I think I'd be more use at his side. I'm terrible at knitting."

"I tried it once," the woman said, exhaling a cloud. "Found it quite deadly."

"Exactly!" Nichola cried. "All that counting and keeping track of stitches—I am just not *made* for that sort of stuff."

"But you think that you are made for soldiering. You shoot, you say. Have you any skill with the sword?"

"No," she admitted sorrowfully. "Tommy had fencing lessons. But I wasn't allowed. Mother said it wasn't proper. Because I am a girl."

"Nonsense," the woman said crisply. "I have had quite a few years of fencing instruction. There is nothing at all unladylike about it. On the contrary, it is a most graceful art."

"If it's graceful, I should be dreadful at it," Nichola said self-consciously, pulling up her breeches.

"I don't see why you say that. You showed extraordinary grace climbing down the wall."

"Oh, well, *that*. That's different. And besides, no one was watching—or, rather, I *thought* no one was watching. I am fine when nobody is watching. It's in drawing rooms and ballrooms that I have trouble. Mother says I clump. And I do."

"In that case, I should think fencing instruction would prove most valuable to you. If you like, I would be more than happy to teach you what I know."

"Really?" Then Nichola recognized what the woman was up to. "You are only trying to keep me from running away," she said accusingly.

Her companion drew herself up. "Not at all. But if you are to prove useful as a soldier, these are skills you will require."

Nichola yawned. She hadn't meant to, but it had been a dreadfully long day, what with rising at dawn to finish packing, and the tedious coach ride with her mother, and meeting all the girls, and minding her manners, and forcing herself to stay awake in order to escape.

"We could begin our lessons in the morning," the woman offered.

Another yawn was coming. Nichola clamped it down firmly. "That's very kind of you, but—"

The woman was looking her up and down. "I have padding and a mask I believe will fit you. And extra foils, of course. Even a single lesson will make you more likely to be accepted into a regiment."

The yawn broke through despite Nichola's best efforts. God, but she was weary! What difference could one more day make? Especially if the woman's offer was sincere . . . "You really would try to teach me?"

"Absolutely. I have an instinct that you will prove a most adept pupil. Shall we say at dawn, here in the court-yard?"

"Dawn?" Nichola said faintly.

"I think it best we pursue this privately. Before the rest of the girls are awake. You and I, we are both willing to flout convention. But Mrs. Treadwell . . ."

"Oh. Yes. I quite see what you mean. Very well, then. At dawn." Nichola, suddenly dog-tired, started toward the ivy.

"You might just go in that door there." Her new fencing instructor pointed with a wave of her cigar.

"Through the door . . . yes, I believe I'll just do that. Good night."

"Bon soir, ma petite."

Nichola, yawning again, dropped a negligent curtsy. "And thank you very much, Miss—Mrs.—"

"Madame," the woman said. "I am just called Madame."

"Thank you very much, Madame," said Nichola, and made her way back to bed.

The countess d'Oliveri finished her cigar, ground the stub out with the tip of her kid boot, then went inside herself, to the parlor, where Mrs. Treadwell was seated at her desk with a glass of sherry and a pile of papers. "Just looking over the crop," Mrs. Treadwell explained.

"Ah." The countess poured herself wine at the sideboard, then came and stood by her shoulder. "I've just met one of them. In the courtyard."

"The *courtyard*! Whatever was she doing there?"

"Running away."

"Dear heavens! Not already? Did she say why?"

"She was heading for the Continent. To become a soldier."

Mrs. Treadwell's wide face puckered in an expression of utter bewilderment. "Well! I never! Which one was it?"

"She didn't tell me her name. But she is quite the tallest girl I've ever seen."

The bewilderment transposed to something very like alarm. "I do hope, Christiane, that you managed to dissuade her!"

"Stalled her, rather. By promising her a fencing lesson."

This news, which ought to have soothed Mrs. Treadwell, only served to heighten her trepidation. "Oh, my. No. Not fencing, Christiane. Not that one."

"Why ever not? Who is she, anyway?" The countess reached for the registration papers Mrs. Treadwell had been examining, and was taken aback when her old friend clamped her hands down firmly on the stack.

"Evelyn!" The countess's dark eyes glinted. "What are you hiding from me?"

"Nothing! Nothing at all!" But Mrs. Treadwell was a dreadful liar and knew it. She sighed, relinquishing the papers. "Oh, dear. I had hoped she wouldn't actually attend. But her mother was so terribly insistent . . . and just seeing the way she wrote of the girl made my heart quite go out to her. Not the mother. Nichola," she clarified, as the countess paged through and finally found the sheet of vellum she sought.

" 'Hainesworth, Nichola,' " she read out, and raised her gaze.

"Emily Hainesworth's daughter," Mrs. Treadwell confirmed nervously. "Emily *Madden* Hainesworth." And she gulped her sherry.

"Really?" the countess said. "You never would imagine it, would you, to look at the child?"

"Now, don't pretend with me, Christiane! You cannot tell me you don't despise Emily Madden Hainesworth after what she did to you! Why, it was thanks to her you had to go abroad! That dreadful trick she played on you—more than a trick, though, wasn't it, to have that scoundrel Weatherston tell you Harold Hainesworth was wild to elope with you, and take you to that iniquitous tavern, with the full knowledge of half the *ton,* when all Weatherston meant was to dishonor you himself! And then, when you spurned his advances, to spread such horrid *lies* about you, claiming you had given in to him! He *ruined* your good name—and all at Emily's instigation, because she'd been on the shelf for two entire seasons and her pursuit of Lord Covington came to nothing when he proposed to Millicent

Winthrop and so all that was left to her was Harold, and she was determined to have him come what may!"

The countess had listened to this breathless recitation of the scandal that had sent her to France with a bemused half smile. "Surely, Evelyn, you don't believe I harbor any animus toward Emily Madden. It was thanks to her intriguing that I've led a life of such remarkable fulfillment."

"But what she did to you was so *awful*!"

"It was also more than a quarter of a century past. Am I to understand you harbor some qualms I might revenge myself against her daughter?"

"Well . . ."

"*Zut alors,* Evelyn! What sort of woman do you think I am?"

"Never mind what sort," Mrs. Treadwell declared. "You *are* a woman. And women don't forget such things— nor forgive them, either."

"Some women do," the countess noted, and turned over the page. "Now, let's see. What else have we here? Gwendolyn Carstairs—and look! She is mad old Admiral Carstairs's daughter! Poor thing, what a heritage to live up to! Whatever did you make of her, pray tell?"

Chapter
Three

The sky was still shrouded with a thin blanket of darkness when Nichola returned to the courtyard, this time using the stairs. A chill north wind blustered down over the walls, and she shivered inside Tommy's shirt and breeches, wondering if the woman from the night before had been some sort of chimera. The entire episode, in retrospect, took on the quality of a dream. But—no. There was Madame coming toward her, arms piled with a most intriguing mix of stuffed canvas and wire and steel. "I half expected you to miss our appointment," the woman cried cheerfully, dumping her burdens onto the grass, "after you were up so late last night!"

"I don't need much sleep," Nichola explained. "I never have. My mother says I was a dreadful bother as a baby because of it."

"Ah, well, the French say sleep is a waste of life's opportunities." Nichola started. That was just what *she* had always felt about it. "And I am glad to see you dressed appropriately."

Nichola glanced down self-consciously at her attire. "I didn't know quite *what* to wear. But I couldn't imagine fencing in skirts." Madame, she noted with relief, was also in breeches, though they were far more elegant and fitted on her dainty figure than Tommy's on Nichola.

Madame glanced at the sky. "Let's suit up, shall we, before we run out of time? Here is your *plastron*." She handed Nichola a folded pile of thickly quilted canvas. "Over your head—there, you see the hole? And then it buckles on each side." Feeling simultaneously excited and foolish, Nichola slipped the garment on. Madame had to help her with the buckles, adjusting the straps. "You want it snug, so that it offers protection, but not so tight that your motion is restricted. That should do. Now, over that you wear your *cuissard*." This was another padded piece, that fit over the *plastron* but buckled between the legs as well as at the sides. "And your bib, across the throat, and cuffs, and gloves, and mask . . ."

Nichola couldn't help giggling with each successive layer of cotton and bunting. "I must look as fat as the regent."

"I doubt it. I hear Prinnie's grown quite enormous. No, you look like a fencer." Madame quickly donned her own gear. Her instructor cut quite a dashing figure, Nichola concluded, even if the mask gave her the aspect of a giant white grasshopper. *"Eh bien."* Madame bent down and retrieved one long, gleaming blade from the lawn. "Your foil." Nichola reached for it eagerly, entranced by its deadly beauty. "Not so fast!" Madame reproved her. "This is a dangerous weapon. You must learn something about it before you start whacking away." She held it and pointed. "This is the pommel, and then the hilt. The bell guards your hand. Together, they are called the 'mounting.' Then comes the forte—the thicker part of the blade. Then you have the foible, which is slimmer—more flexible." She demonstrated, showing how that section sprang to and fro

when snapped. "And, of course, the button—the tip.
Blunted for practice. But do not make the mistake of thinking it cannot wound, even through your padding. It can."

Nichola was *itching* to take the foil. At last Madame
allowed her to, and she clutched it tightly. "Not like that,"
Madame told her, turning Nichola's wrist so that her palm
was upward. "*Comme ça*. And gently, gently. As you would
hold a fishing rod. Just let it rest between your thumb and
forefinger. Elbow well away from the body. Yes. Yes, that's
it. Take a step forward with your right foot. Bend your knee
toward me—your opponent. Oh, that's very good! And
raise your left arm . . . curl it . . . point the fingers at
me." She took a step back, surveying Nichola from behind
her mask. "Chin down a bit. Your left leg is too stiff. Bend
your knees. Bounce on them."

Nichola complied, making a series of awkward pliés.
"It doesn't feel as though I have any grip at all on this foil,"
she noted dubiously, as the blade wobbled in her fingertips.

"Never mind the blade. Believe it or not, the blade is
not the sine qua non of fencing."

"It isn't?" Nichola was most disappointed.

"No. The blade is simply an extension of the body. To
make the blade do what you desire, the body must be in
place."

"Oh." Nichola's left arm, still curled over her head,
was getting tired. "I say. Why must I have this hand stuck
up here?"

"In the olden days, you would have had a dagger in it,
for when you closed in for the kill. Now"—the countess
shrugged in her cocoon of canvas—"an affectation, perhaps. But the art of fencing has a long and noble history
which must be respected. So we raise our left hands when
we assume the stance." She took up her own weapon and
struck an effortless pose that made Nichola breathless with
admiration.

"Where did you ever learn to fence?" she demanded
curiously.

"It was a favorite interest of one of my . . . lovers."

Behind her mask, Nichola's amber eyes widened. "You have had lovers?"

"I have. Does that offend you? Make you want to run and tattle to your mamma?"

"Oh, no! Not at all! I think it would be *wonderful* to have lovers! Much better than having a husband!"

"And why is that?"

Nichola pursed her lips. "A husband means nothing but children and drudgery. A lover, though—a lover is *freedom*!" And she flashed her foil wildly through the air. "*En garde!*"

Madame laughed. "No, no! Flex the knees! Bounce, I said! And let the rapier *float*!"

Simply holding the foil as Madame directed was much more difficult than Nichola had anticipated. And what her teacher called "bouncing" seemed very strange. The baroness's instructions in comportment and dancing had always been accompanied by despairing entreaties for her daughter to control herself, get hold of herself, straighten up, stiffen up, until the mere act of making a curtsy turned Nichola's muscles to knots. Now here was Madame urging her to relax, be less rigid, let movement flow from her toes through her legs and arms. . . .

"Feel!" Madame cried, pushing on Nichola's shoulders, forcing her knees down. "The feet—the feet are where it must begin!"

"I am sorry," Nichola said abjectly. "I am hopelessly clumsy."

"Nonsense. You aren't clumsy at all; you are just wound tighter than a harp string. Do you swim?"

"Oh, I love to! Mother never would allow it, but I used to sneak out to the river with my brothers, even so."

"Well, then! Why do you love it?"

Nichola considered. "Because when I swim, I don't weigh anything."

"Ah-hah! You *float*! Close your eyes." Nichola complied. "Imagine you are swimming. It is August, very hot. You jump into the river. Your feet hit the bottom." Instinctively Nichola crouched down. "And you push off—up! Back up to the air! Yes! Yes! You are bouncing now!"

Put that way, Nichola thought, it wasn't so hard. She opened her eyes and tried again. "That is really very good," Madame told her.

"You are a very good teacher," Nichola said humbly.

"I *had* a very good teacher," Madame corrected her gently. "Let me see you bounce once more."

Nichola did. And if at first she felt foolish, clad in these outlandish garments, pretending she was jumping into rivers or holding a fishing line, by the end of an hour she was nothing but proud. She and Madame never did get to the point of crossing foils, but it hardly mattered when there was so much to try to get right. When Madame pushed up her mask and declared, "*Eh bien,* that is enough for our first day," Nichola's disappointment was keen.

"I'm not a bit tired!" she protested.

"I believe that. You are a very hardy young lady. *I* grow weary, however. And besides, the other students will be awakening."

"Damn," Nichola muttered. Then she caught herself. "I beg your pardon. It's only that I've had the most marvelous time!"

"As have I. It's been ages since I fenced with anyone. Not since Jean-Baptiste . . ." Her voice trailed off, recovered. "Shall we meet again this afternoon?"

"I suppose we had better," Nichola said ruefully. "I never thought this would be so complicated. I'm not exactly ready for a regiment, am I?"

"You show great promise at fencing."

"Do you honestly think so?" Recklessly Nichola made another swashbuckling feint with her foil—and, dismayed, saw the older woman knock the blade straight out of her grip.

"Promise, yes—but unfulfilled promise!" Madame said, and laughed. "I must have some breakfast, though, to build up my strength! And I have other duties . . . other girls to attend to. But if you like, we could meet again at two o'clock."

"I'd like that very much," said Nichola, sounding almost subdued.

That evening, in the room she shared, Nichola undressed with delicious weariness. Her second bout of instruction had been far more strenuous than the first, and she ached from her toes to her hair. When she reached down to unbuckle her boots, she groaned, causing Bess to look at her anxiously. "I say, Nichola. Are you all right?"

"Sore muscles," Nichola explained.

"I'm not surprised. I saw you in the courtyard this afternoon. Whatever were you doing?"

"I am learning fencing."

"Why?"

"So I can join a regiment."

"Oh." Bess digested this for a moment. "That makes sense."

"Nothing about this place makes sense," Katherine Devereaux sniffed from in front of the mirror, where she was braiding up her glorious hair. "It's like some sort of— of bedlam!"

"Oh, I disagree," Gwen piped up, pulling her nightshirt over her dark head. "I had the most fascinating lesson in science today, from that woman called Madame. We discussed the elements. And we did an experiment. Did you know that if you mix potassium with vinegar, you get a great bubbling mess?"

"Can't say I did," Katherine said squelchingly. "Nor, I might add, that I care." She looked down at her elegant hands. "Good God. I've broken a nail."

"She promises to teach me to make gunpowder," Gwen said in a dreamy voice, and Katherine Devereaux shuddered.

"I had a lesson from Madame too," Bess told them shyly. "In literature. We are reading *The Canterbury Tales* together. She must know everything there is to know about poetry."

Nichola saw Katherine grimace into the mirror. "What were your lessons today in?" Nichola asked curiously.

"Mine?" The blonde hesitated. "Well—if you *must* know, your sainted Madame showed me how to milk a cow."

Bess gasped. Gwen giggled. "Milk a cow?" Nichola echoed, nonplussed.

"Aye. Filthy disgusting creature! It *spurted* all over my skirts. And I muddied my best boots. Not to mention that the smell in that barn was indescribable!"

"But why—"

"I assure you," Katherine snapped, "I haven't any idea! I *told* her milking cows could not possibly be of use in securing the hand of a gentleman of the *ton*! And do you know what she said? 'It would be a fallacy, Lady Devereaux,' she told me 'to imagine that the current social structure of England will continue indefinitely. There may come a time,' she said to me—the daughter of a duke!— 'when our nation will cast off the chains of arbitrary class distinctions and require every citizen to pull his or her own weight, just as France and America already have.' "

"Did she really?" Bess marveled.

"She did. You may rest assured I've already written to Mamma and Poppa of it. Even if my previous letter regarding the *impossible* conditions here does not move them to remove me, I am quite sure such treasonous utterances will!"

"Seems to me," Nichola noted, "that she has a point."

"Oh, *you*! You would say that! You with your lessons in athletics . . ." And she looked Nichola up and down very nastily. "I should hardly think you need more instruction in *that* to catch yourself a husband!"

"Perhaps," Nichola said with a grin, "I am preparing to ward suitors off."

Gwen giggled again, and Bess guffawed—then quickly hid the fact behind her hand.

"If so," Katherine Devereaux declared archly, "you might spare yourself the exertion. It is certain to be wasted."

The day before, Nichola would have been intimidated by her form-mate's bland cruelty. Now, however, she merely eased her weary limbs onto her bed. "When you are done doing whatever nonsense you're about with your hair, would you put out the lamp?" she inquired politely. "I have another fencing lesson at dawn."

"God," Katherine said with feeling, "I can't *wait* to be quit of this place!"

Chapter Four

A month later, alone—for the moment—in her rooms, Nichola was perusing a letter from her mother that chastised her for her own failure to write. "If you are so angry and resentful at me for having consigned you to the academy," the baroness had penned in her elegant but nigh-illegible hand, "that you intend to punish me by this long silence, *do* kindly say so. If you are miserable there, I suppose I must fetch you home."

Nichola laughed out loud. *Home?* Why in God's name would she want to go home? Mrs. Treadwell's already felt more homelike than Hainesworth Hall ever had. True, there were occasional lessons in the most useless matters, like embroidery and music and dancing. But she always had her fencing instruction to live for, once she'd untangled her skeins or pounded out her scales or tripped over her skirts in a waltz. She had two new friends—Gwen, who despite her quietness was slyly funny and sharp as a tack, and Bessie, whose good nature endured the most brutal attacks by

supercilious Katherine, who still had not been rescued by
the duchess and duke from her exile in hell. And the supper hour held the most fascinating opportunities for discussion with Madame.

Still, she considered, reaching unwillingly for a quill, if
she did not write to her mother soon, the baroness might
very well take it into her head to come and fetch her off—
which had at all costs to be prevented, at least until she had
learned to execute a passable *passata*. "Dear Mother," she
penned, and then sat without the slightest idea what to say.

She certainly couldn't mention her fencing lessons—
nothing could be surer to bring the baroness to Mrs. Treadwell's academy instantly! Poor Mother, she thought idly,
making a little sketch of a foil in the margin. You ought to
have had Katherine for your daughter. She cares about all
the same things you do—clothes and rank and comportment.

Catching a husband was all Katherine seemed to think
about—besides, of course, getting sprung from Mrs. Treadwell's, and her glorious hair. Oddly, Nichola hardly gave
any consideration to the subject of marriage at all. Oh,
she'd had a terrible crush on Daniel's best friend, Joshua
Biddle, back when she was twelve. But since then, she
could honestly say she'd never met a boy to whom she was
attracted. Or, more accurately, who showed any signs of
attraction to *her*. She was jolly good pals with loads of
Tommy's friends, and used to shoot and ride and hunt with
them whenever she could. But she knew, had always felt,
that the way they treated her was very different from the
way they behaved toward young ladies who had caught
their eye. She was just Nicky, always good for a laugh or a
stomp through the fields. They didn't ask her to dance,
though, on those occasions when the baroness roused herself to put on a rout. They asked dainty little Olivena
Hutchings, or Pamela Spenser, or Annabelle Proffitt, or any
of the other simpering misses who batted their lashes and
spoke in winning whispers and never, ever clumped when
they walked. Which, when Nichola considered it, was really

quite unfair. Tommy's friends were far happier riding to the hounds than waltzing. So why on earth would they prefer girls who didn't know a courser from a nag?

She'd covered half the page now with doodles. Impatiently she thrust it aside and took a clean sheet. This was no time to ponder life's impenetrables. If she wanted to remain at Mrs. Treadwell's—and against all odds, she did, very much—she had to quell the baroness's fears. "Dear Mother," she wrote again. "I pray you forgive my long silence. It is just that I have been so awfully busy settling into my new—" She almost wrote "home," but then realized her mother might take offense. "Quarters," she finished. "It is quite pleasant here." That would sound suspicious, seeing as she'd argued with every ounce of her breath not to be sent to the place! "Despite the fact," she continued, "that the lessons in comportment and 'broidery and dancing are ever so dreary." Nichola nibbled her lip. If that was so, why, her mother was bound to wonder, was it pleasant? "I have made new friends," Nichola put down, very honestly, "and I like the food." Damn. Now the baroness would fret that she was putting on weight—which, actually, she wasn't, what with all the exercise she was getting at fencing. "I have riding lessons, too," she wrote in mitigation—then chewed on the pen. She'd been paired with Katherine for those—sidesaddle, and excruciatingly boring. Katherine's seat was continually praised by their instructor, whereas Nichola's—well. No more to be said about *that*.

God, writing letters was dreary! "In short," Nichola concluded, "I find myself quite contented, and assure you that you need not fear for my happiness." That was so far from either the baroness's or Nichola's expectations that she felt obliged to add, "all things considered, that is." She had the distinct impression she was digging herself into a hole, and added hurriedly, "My love to you and to Father. Best wishes, Nichola." She folded and sealed the letter before second thoughts could deluge her. At least the damned thing was done!

She really ought to write to Tommy. It had been ages

since she'd done so. He'd surely be wondering how she was faring at this "academy for young ladies"! But if she wrote him, she couldn't bear not mentioning her fencing, and there was always the danger he might let word slip to the baroness. Tommy was wonderful, of course, but he could be an awful idiot.

She realized she'd bitten the quill down so far that ink was leaking onto her chin. Quickly she swiped at it with her handkerchief, just as the door opened and Gwen came in.

"I hope I'm not disturbing you," the dark-haired girl murmured shyly.

"Not a bit. I've just finished a letter to my mother." Nichola grimaced. "Trying to explain why I haven't written before. She'd sent one threatening to come and fetch me home if I didn't."

"You don't want to go home?" Gwen inquired, perching on her bed.

"God, no! I like it much more here."

Gwen traced the patterned carpet with the toe of her shoe. "I like it here as well. I am lonely at home. There's no one there but Father. And half the time he is away."

"You haven't got a mother?"

"She died when I was small."

"I'm sorry," Nichola said automatically, then laughed. "Though perhaps I wouldn't be, if I were you. Or you were I. My mother and I do not exactly see eye to eye. Just between us, I'd be happy if I *never* had to go home again."

"You will, though." Gwen's small face was troubled. "So will I. Mrs. Treadwell just announced it. For the Christmas holidays. She is going to visit her daughter. The academy will be shut down."

"Really?" Nichola pondered that glumly. "Pity." Then she brightened. "But what about Madame?"

"She has plans of her own, Mrs. Treadwell says."

Nichola shrugged. "Well, if I work hard enough, I *might* be ready to leave for the Continent by Christmas anyway."

"You're so brave."

"Not really," Nichola confided. "It is just that I'd far rather confront Napoleon's armies than listen to my mother natter at me to sit up straight!"

They laughed together. Then Gwen said wistfully, "Perhaps something will come up by Christmas, and we'll both of us be spared."

"I hope so," Nichola told her, even as she determined to make certain they would.

"And *lunge,*" Madame urged Nichola, watching her pupil closely. "And *step—feint*—keep that elbow up! Better, better. Follow through—there!" Their foils clinked in the early morning air. Nichola had come to love that sound of steel against steel. "Mind the left shoulder; it is dropping again. Remember, your sword—"

"Is an extension of my body," Nichola finished for her, and deftly sidestepped her instructor's attack with a quick swivel of her hips. Madame stopped short, her elegant staccato interrupted.

"Oh, that was very nice!" she declared, falling back into a parry. "You are learning to *wait,* to see what I am up to instead of just barging in."

"I was born a barger," Nichola said cheerfully.

Madame laughed. "Indeed, I think you were. But you are tempering it." The hard November wind swept through the courtyard, sweeping dead leaves up against the north wall. The older woman shivered inside her padding. "God, there is nothing so cold as an English winter! I think perhaps we'd better go in now. We can't have you catching an ague for the holidays."

Nichola raised her mask. "Would you say I have learned enough to escape to the Continent?"

"Still determined on that, are you?"

"Absolutely," Nichola said stoutly. "*You* escaped to the Continent, didn't you?"

"Not to be a soldier. And anyway, not until I had more experience with the *ton* than you have. Besides, even wars wind down in the winter. You'd do better to wait until spring."

Nichola held open the door for her. "I think it's best I go now. Especially since the academy is shutting down for the holidays. I don't want to lose my edge."

"I hardly think three weeks will cause you to forget all you've learned." In the warmth of the kitchen, Madame gratefully stripped off her padding.

"Three *weeks*?" Nichola echoed in horror. "Is it to be for so long as that?"

The cook had brought Madame a cup of hot tea. "A million thanks," she murmured, then looked at Nichola, who was struggling with her buckles. "Most of the girls are quite eager to return to their families."

"Gwen's not. And neither am I." Nichola took a deep breath. "If I'm not ready for the Continent, then perhaps could I . . . stay with you? Go wherever you are going?"

"Oh, Nichola." Madame's lovely face was downcast. "I'm afraid that's not possible. If I could take you, I would."

"It doesn't matter," Nichola muttered, even though it did.

"You *must* want to see your parents again. Don't you?"

"Not especially. I don't imagine any of my brothers will have leave. And Mother—Mother will have all sorts of plans for me. Balls and fêtes and such . . ." Her expression at the prospect was so woebegone that Madame smiled.

"I should think you'd enjoy the chance to meet some young people . . . perhaps some nice young men?" she ventured gently.

"I'm not the sort young men go for. At least, not at balls and fêtes." Nichola frowned. "Perhaps I could stay and exercise the horses? Surely you'll need someone for that."

"And what would Mr. Saliston say when he returned after the holiday to discover you had spoiled them for sidesaddle by riding them astride?" Nichola smiled, but her heart wasn't in it. Madame sipped her tea for a moment in silence. "There *is* a possibility," she said then.

"What?" Nichola demanded.

"You could, perhaps, go with Mrs. Treadwell to her daughter's. You and Gwen."

"I can't imagine her daughter would want us."

"From what Evelyn tells me," Madame said wryly, "Yarlborough House is such a press at Christmas that no one would likely even notice you."

"Even so . . . her daughter is a countess, isn't she? It would just be the same sort of thing as at home. Balls and teas and formal dinners."

"True. But with this one advantage—your mother wouldn't be there."

"I should still have to worry about disgracing Mrs. Treadwell."

"Surely you've realized by now that Mrs. Treadwell is not easily disgraced."

Nichola considered. While the academy's headmistress was just as much a stickler for propriety and decorum as the baroness—and while she'd had plenteous opportunity to offer Nichola correction—the manner in which she did so was markedly different. "I think you'll find," she would murmur when Nichola took too large a mouthful of meat, or sprawled gracelessly in her chair, or laughed too loudly, "that a more socially acceptable method of accomplishing your purpose would be . . ." Most of all, she made sure no one but Nichola ever heard the remonstrance. After so many years of her mother robustly pointing out her tactical errors to everyone present, Nichola was unspeakably grateful for that. And, curiously, minus the fear of having her social failings called into prominence, she found it far easier to remember to sit up straight, take small bites, keep her voice suitably low. Still . . .

"I imagine Mrs. Treadwell is only too eager for a holiday away from all of us," she said wanly.

"She *might* welcome the distraction," Madame countered with a smile. "She's very fond of you, Nichola, you know. As am I. I'm inclined to believe you are going to prove one of our great successes."

"You *are?*" said Nichola, who harbored no such inclination herself.

"Absolutely. You are an original, *chérie*. And nothing is so refreshing to the jaded *ton* as an original."

Nichola's cheeks went red. "An original *what* I can't imagine," she muttered.

Madame laughed. "I'll speak to Mrs. Treadwell about it. Now go and dress, or you'll be late for your dancing lesson."

"Wouldn't *that* be a pity," said Nichola, and Madame laughed again.

Chapter
Five

Much to Nichola's surprise, Mrs. Treadwell embraced the notion of having her and Gwen accompany her on the holiday with great enthusiasm. "A splendid idea!" she exclaimed. "I ought to have thought of it myself." Even more gratifyingly, Katherine Devereaux's nose had been put severely out of joint at the news her form-mates were to visit Yarlborough House. "If *anyone* here is worthy of such an honor," she sniffed, "it certainly is me!"

"Is I," Bessie amended her grammar absently.

"You!" Katherine declared in horror. "Surely not you!" Which only made Gwen and Bessie and Nichola dissolve in giggles. "Still," Katherine went on grandly, "I should not care to miss Christmas at the estates. And once I have the opportunity to explain to Mamma and Poppa face-to-face how absolutely *wretched* this so-called academy is—well! Let us only say you three will have more room in here for your meager belongings."

"And perhaps a shot at the mirror every now and again," Gwen said.

That was how she and Nichola found themselves ensconced for a fortnight and more at Yarlborough House, a vast sprawl of gray stone along the coast of Dorsetshire. Nichola had been severely cowed by the pomp and circumstance of their arrival—*dozens* of the most elegantly liveried servants scurrying about, and a brace of heralds, of all things, brassing out a fanfare, and the countess of Yarlborough coming to greet her mother, all smiles and lacquered hair and beauty patches as the girls bobbed nervous curtsies. "So *charmed* that you could join us!" she'd exclaimed, eyes sparkling bright as her diamonds, her voice a thrilling purr. She was such complete *perfection* that Nichola's heart sank down to her shoes—until Mrs. Treadwell, her mouth turned down at the corners, declared, "For heaven's sake, Vanessa! *Heralds?* Don't you think that is a bit de trop?"

And the epitome of style that was the countess of Yarlborough had pouted sullenly, in an expression Nichola recognized instantly as having crossed her own countenance countless times in dealing with her own mother, and said curtly, "Oh, Mamma. Must you be such a wet rag? I *like* the heralds. And Jonathan does, too."

"Well, we must by all means bow to Jonathan's taste," Mrs. Treadwell had replied with equal curtness, and brushed through the throng to the doors.

"My!" Gwen had breathed at Nichola's side. "Our Mrs. Treadwell takes no prisoners, does she?"

Nichola, to her relief, discovered that since neither she nor Gwen had officially debuted, they were excused from most of the countess's busy social schedule—and it was unspeakably busy. Vanessa left the house by eleven in the morning and was gone straight through till midnight, and often later; Nichola was awakened by carriage wheels on the drive at two in the morning more than once. Mrs. Treadwell rarely accompanied her daughter; she preferred to spend her time with her little grandsons, two-year-old

Peter and one-year-old James, who were looked after by a formidable nurse named Pears. As for the earl of Yarlborough, Nichola and Gwen never caught so much as a glimpse of him the entire first week they were there.

"It's a very odd sort of life, don't you think?" Gwen queried as she and Nichola settled into the grand bed they shared in their very large chamber one night.

Nichola was examining a nasty bruise on her shin where Peter had kicked her. "How do you mean?"

"Why, everyone is always exclaiming over Vanessa's conquest of the earl of Yarlborough. But she never goes anyplace with him. And neither of them seems to see much of their boys."

"We were brought up by governesses," Nichola countered, "my brothers and I. Weren't you? And my father was always up to London for Parliament. Mother spends her time much the way the countess does—calling on friends, shopping, going to dinners and balls."

"But what is the sense of a glorious conquest if there is nothing to share?"

"You sound as romantic as Bessie."

Gwen grimaced. "Goodness, I hope I am not such a fool as that!"

"Marriage among the uppermost classes," Nichola said, echoing what her mother had frequently told her, "is by necessity founded on more practical bases than mere infatuation. Bloodlines. Political alliance. The enlargement of estates."

Gwen gave a shudder. "You make it sound so cold! I am glad I am not of the uppermost echelon." Then her small face screwed up in the candlelight. "Still. Neither was Vanessa Treadwell. And so there must have been something once between her and the earl less . . . practical than that. Don't you think?"

Nichola yawned and fluffed her pillow. "Who's to say? But you needn't worry. Whatever Vanessa used to snag the earl is precisely what is Mrs. Treadwell's job to teach us.

Why, next Christmas, I may very well be visiting *you* and your new husband, the earl."

"Or I you." The notion made them both giggle. Nichola snuffed out the candle, and they lay for a time in the dark. Then Gwen spoke up again: "Do you know what is even more strange? I don't believe Mrs. Treadwell even *likes* her daughter very much."

"There's nothing strange at all about that to me," Nichola noted wryly, thinking of her own mother.

"In which case," Gwen mused drowsily, "why on earth would she have founded an academy to make us all turn out just like her?"

Nichola hadn't any answer to that—which was just as well, since Gwen had fallen asleep.

In the nursery the very next morning, between pulling James off Peter and Peter off James, Mrs. Treadwell informed the girls that their attendance would be expected at a rout the countess was throwing the following night. Both their faces fell.

"Must we?" Nichola asked faintly. "My understanding was that since we have not debuted—"

"That rule is quite properly relaxed when the affair is put on in one's own home—or, by extension, the home in which one is staying," Mrs. Treadwell explained, and sniffed at Peter's gown. "Pears. I believe the young master needs his nappy changed."

The nurse took him, screaming, in hand, and led him off. "What—what sort of rout is it to be?" Gwen asked nervously.

"Large. Very large. You will not be expected to dance." Nichola sighed with relief. "Though if you should be asked . . ."

"There's not much danger in that," Gwen noted.

Their chaperone frowned. "You two have a dreadful habit of downplaying your attractions. Why, you have every bit as much to offer a young man as any girl I know!" Their dubious faces stared back at her. "You do!" she insisted. "You are very clever, and witty, and amusing. . . ." Their expressions never faltered, and she heaved a sigh. "But on to more practical matters. What have you brought to wear?"

"I . . . I have my white organdy," Gwen said hesitantly.

"Splendid! White suits you very well. I'll dress your hair myself. What about you, Nichola?"

Nichola was peering through the window, from which she had a tantalizing view of a company of hunters setting off through the woods, baying hounds at their horses' heels, shotguns over their shoulders. What she wouldn't give to be going with them on this crisp winter day!

"Nichola?" Mrs. Treadwell said again.

"She has her gold brocade," Gwen offered helpfully. Nichola shot her a grimace.

"That should do nicely." Mrs. Treadwell paused. "There's just one thing I must say. While it is true neither of you has officially debuted, you should be aware that a great many highly eligible young men will be attending tomorrow evening. I expect you, naturally, to be on your very best behavior. First impressions are so vitally important— and what is more, they can never be erased. Flippant words or coarse actions or any sort of moral laxness on this occasion could very well spoil your future chances of success." Gwen colored furiously, and Mrs. Treadwell smiled at her. "I see you are aware of what I mean. Once a young lady has lost her reputation, it can never be regained. And yet the plain fact is, men can be terribly persuasive."

One of the hunters, Nichola noted, was atop a remarkable roan with a lovely high step. Mrs. Treadwell caught her looking and sighed again. "Nichola. I do hope you will pay more attention to protocol than you are paying to me."

Nichola laughed. "You needn't worry about me, Mrs. Treadwell. I've never met a man worth glancing at twice, unless you count my brothers."

"You will someday," the headmistress said knowingly.
"Not I," she retorted with great certainty.

Nichola was sitting on the sort of slender, gilded chair
that always made her nervous about breakage, well away in
a corner of Yarlborough House's exceedingly grand ballroom, half hidden behind a providential stand of potted
palms. The gold brocade itched terribly at her armpits, but
every time she went to scratch, Gwen, seated at her side,
gave her a nudge. Her form-mate, Nichola thought, looked
very pretty in her demure, high-waisted white gown, with a
string of pearls at her throat and her dark hair swept back
into a chignon. Nichola herself, she knew, looked ridiculous. She shifted her bared shoulders self-consciously, willing the chair not to crack.

"The music's very fine, don't you think?" Gwen whispered. She had a white feathered fan in her hands and kept
opening and closing it nervously. A small band of glorious
female creatures swept past them, their voices high with
excitement, their eyes wide and alluring as they scanned the
crowd. Their gazes passed over Nichola and her companion
as though they weren't even there.

"This is dreadful," Nichola muttered.

"Oh, no, this is Mozart!"

Nichola couldn't help laughing. "You really are too
good for words, Gwen. No. I mean us—or rather, me—and
all of this. I don't belong here."

Gwen's small face crumpled. "No. Neither do I. But it
is what we are doomed to endure, isn't it? So I suppose we
may as well accustom ourselves."

"Never!" Nichola declared. "I am sorry for Mrs.
Treadwell, but there's no sense in her trying to make a silk
purse out of *this* sow's ear. God, I am starving."

"There's to be a supper. . . ."

"At *midnight*. It is only a quarter to ten." Nichola
stood up abruptly. "I am going to find something to eat.
Coming?"

"I don't dare! Mrs. Treadwell said—"

"Mrs. Treadwell said we should mind our manners. She didn't say we had to stay planted like oaks. Besides, I have a horror of these silly little chairs. One of them shattered quite to pieces beneath me at one of my mother's receptions. She's never let me forget it. Are you coming?" Gwen shook her head. "Suit yourself." Nichola stood, stretching to her full height, impossibly relieved to be moving. The band of girls, who'd paused by the palms, noticed her at last, with a great deal of surreptitious elbowing and giggling. Nichola flushed and strode defiantly away, telling herself she did not care.

She could feel herself *clumping*, knew that she made a sight—taller than most of the men in the room, and taller by far than any of the ladies. She felt exactly as she always did in social situations—large and awkward and conspicuous. Lucky Gwen, who could at least fade into the mass of guests! But Nichola stood out no matter how hard she wanted not to. And suddenly, as she skirted the dainty dancers and their elegant partners, she was consumed with rage—at Mrs. Treadwell, for putting her in this position; at her mother, for having birthed her so monstrously huge; at God, for creating her a female instead of the male she was so clearly intended to be. In her wake she heard an astonished titter, and *knew* those bloody girls were laughing at her. *If only I could,* she thought viciously, *I'd mop the floor with all of you. I'd—*

She paused in mid-vituperation. Sprawled before her in a chair—not a dainty gilt one, but a good, solid armchair upholstered in red velvet—was the biggest human being she had ever seen, a great hulk of a fellow with thick red-gold hair pulled back in a tight queue. He was simply *enormous*—his neck was thick as a bull's, his arms were like tree trunks, and his legs, in slightly faded black evening attire, were broader still. And he was staring straight at her with deep-set eyes the high blue of an October sky.

Hurriedly she glanced away . . . and then let her gaze wander back, after a suitable interval. God, but he was big!

He reminded her of portraits of Henry the Eighth that she'd seen. He had a wineglass in his hand, and as she watched, he snapped his fingers for a servant hovering at his elbow to refill it. Slothful creature, she thought with distaste—too lazy to make his way to the wine tables himself! She brushed past him, then turned—to see with dismay that though he hadn't moved a single muscle in his massive body, his clear blue eyes were following her. Coloring, she hurried on.

She'd just managed to locate a spread of hors d'oeuvres against the opposite wall when Mrs. Treadwell appeared at her elbow. "Where is Gwendolyn?" their chaperone inquired.

"I left her over by the palms," Nichola confessed rather guiltily. "I just—I just felt the need to be up and about."

Mrs. Treadwell considered her with that wounding gentleness. "Poor Nichola. It is hard on you, isn't it, simply to sit and watch the world go by? We must make a dancer of you; then you will have something to occupy you at these affairs."

"You might as well try to make me a bird."

Mrs. Treadwell tapped her with her fan. "You may sprout wings yet, one of these days!" Then she winked. "Do try the pâté; it's quite remarkable. But not too much on your plate at one time." The headmistress waved gaily and made her way across the floor.

Nichola took a smaller scoop of the pâté than she ordinarily would have, then dipped crisp rounds of toast into it as she leaned against a wall, slumping slightly, as usual. She watched Mrs. Treadwell cross in front of the big sloth in the chair and nod to him brightly. He scarcely inclined his head, and Nichola bristled on her headmistress's behalf.

Stealthily she maneuvered closer to the red velvet chair, intrigued by the man's boorish manners. One might think he was royalty, the way he half reclined while one after another of the guests paused to pay him tribute. From her angle, she saw him in profile, saw the surly curl of his mouth and how he barely acknowledged the constant stream of folk stopping by his chair. She could hear his voice now, and it was just what she'd imagined—pompous and self-important, with some absurd affectation of foreign accent. That anyone could be so lazy as he! She watched in utter disgust as the cigar he was smoking slipped from his fingertips and he signaled again to the poor servant to fetch it up from the floor. What was the matter with him? Did all that great bulk of body make him suppose himself above other mortals? He personified everything she detested in life—uselessness and pretentiousness and, above all, indolence. She found herself hating him with a surprising passion, had to fight an itch to go and slap his broad, complacent face.

Then she saw Mrs. Treadwell approaching the velvet chair with Gwen. And—damn!—the bastard lord, whoever he was, didn't even deign to stand, but simply stayed splayed in his seat as Gwen, the poor thing, blushing furiously, was presented to him, exchanged a few halting words, and withdrew. This snub to her friend was the final seal on Nichola's fury. She strode straight up to the stranger and planted herself before the red velvet chair.

"You know," she said, her mind a muddle of fierce resentment at the tittering girls, the unheeding men, but most of all this despicable idler, "it is considered polite for even the loftiest lord to stand when a lady approaches!"

The man in the chair looked her up and down very slowly, scowling. "Is it? And is it considered polite for an utter stranger to rebuke another so rudely?"

Nichola was seething. "By God, if I were only a man, sir, you would have my challenge for that remark!"

"Were you a man," he drawled, flicking cigar ash to the floor, "perhaps I might accept it."

"Were you a *man*," she shot back, "I would expect you to."

His wide face flushed suddenly, unexpectedly, and Nichola felt a surge of triumph, glad that her barb had struck home. Head held high, she strode—*clumped*—back across the ballroom to the potted palms, and took great care not to so much as glance in his direction again.

Her sense of exaltation endured straight through to midnight, when Mrs. Treadwell came to fetch her and Gwendolyn off to bed. "The company is becoming altogether too risqué for the likes of you," she said, clucking her tongue. Nichola and Gwen were only too relieved to follow their chaperone across the ballroom. "By the by," Mrs. Treadwell noted as they made their way up the stairs, "I believe I saw you exchanging conversation with Lord Boru, Nichola."

"Lord Boru?"

"Aye. The big man in the velvet chair."

Nichola sniffed. "Boru, eh? A most appropriate name for such a disagreeable sort."

"Well," Mrs. Treadwell said charitably, rounding the landing, "it is very difficult for him—a man once so strong and athletic—to have been made a cripple."

Nichola, stumbling on the step, felt the blood drain from her face. "A—a cripple?"

"Oh, my, yes. He was badly wounded at Dresden. A cannonball took out his knee. But prior to that, he was the very *soul* of manliness. Champion boxer, wrestler, horse-racer, duelist—you name it, Brian Boru excelled. Hard to imagine he will never again stand on his own now," she added, with a sad little sigh. "War is a dreadful thing, is it not?"

Mortified beyond imagining, Nichola followed her up the stair.

Chapter
Six

Only the great unlikelihood of ever again encountering Lord Brian Boru enabled Nichola to rise from her bed the following morning. She was overcome with shame each time she recalled the harsh words she'd spoken to the crippled soldier, and the flush that had spread across his cheeks when she'd insulted his manhood. That she'd had no way of *knowing* his misfortune proved no consolation whatsoever. As always, she had barged in, with typical results. She had dishonored Mrs. Treadwell *and* the academy with her thoughtless effrontery—and really, why the devil had she bothered? What business was it of hers if Lord Brian Boru made himself comfortable in a red velvet chair?

She was so unaccustomedly quiet and withdrawn all morning that Gwen inquired more than once if anything was wrong. Nichola considered confiding in her, but found she couldn't. Her offense was too great. She simply sat and squirmed in silent misery, turning over the horrible encounter in her mind, wishing she could roll back time and leave her cutting words unsaid.

At tea, Mrs. Treadwell took note of her charge's odd demeanor and drew conclusions of her own. "Both of you comported yourselves with much aplomb last evening," she assured Nichola and Gwen. "I was very proud of you." Gwen smiled, but Nichola turned deep red. "I'm quite sure," their chaperone went on, "only the knowledge amongst the company that you had yet to debut kept the young men from showering you with attention." Nichola slumped further down in her chair. Mrs. Treadwell looked at her, nonplussed. "Whatever is the matter, Nichola?"

"Nothing," she muttered, her appetite ruined for the tasty ham sandwich upon her plate.

From her expression, Mrs. Treadwell clearly intuited that something had gone amiss at the rout. But the conclusion she jumped to next was almost worse than the truth. "If some young man has caught your eye, Nichola—"

Nichola yanked upright in her seat. "Certainly not!" she declared, so forcefully that the corners of Mrs. Treadwell's mouth turned upward in a knowing grin.

"Well! We'll let you keep your secret—*for now*. Won't we, Gwendolyn?" Gwen, who was staring at Nichola in amazement, nodded. Mrs. Treadwell pushed back from the table, laying her napkin aside. "I'll excuse you now, ladies, as I'm sure you'll want to dress for this evening."

"This evening?" Nichola echoed in alarm.

"The theater, dear. Didn't I mention it? Vanessa has given us her box for the night."

Gwen perked up. "Has she really? How lovely! What is the play to be, do you know?"

"Shakespeare, I imagine. That's what the Dorsetshire players do best. I only hope it isn't too ribald and raw."

Nichola was aching to ask for assurance that Lord Brian Boru would not be in attendance. But in light of the assumption Mrs. Treadwell had drawn—that she had lost her heart the night before—she didn't dare. Instead she feigned a headache—which her chaperone dismissed completely. "I'm sure the divertissment will do you good," Mrs. Treadwell said crisply. "Now get yourselves into evening attire." Nichola did so, with a leaden heart only slightly lightened by common sense. What, after all, were the chances that a man she'd never seen before in her life would be thrust into her sphere on two nights in a row?

Despite Nichola's qualms, the aura of excitement at the playhouse in Dorset was infectious. Exquisitely dressed gentlemen and ladies crowded the entrances, and a swarm of commoner folk pressed for space in the pit. "Oh, *Hamlet*!" Gwendolyn breathed excitedly as she saw the signs in the lobby.

"And with Mr. Burton," Mrs. Treadwell noted in delight. "I've seen him perform many times. We are in for a treat!"

But Nichola did not truly relax until she and her companions had climbed the long, tight steps to the countess of Yarlborough's box. Lord Brian Boru, she decided, could never manage that staircase with a shattered knee. Thus it was with great relief and even some anticipation that she parted the long velvet curtains at the rear of the box and entered, eyes widened in adjustment to the dim light—

And saw with horror a familiar burly figure already sprawled in one seat.

She faltered, nearly tripping, so that Mrs. Treadwell, close behind, caught her elbow to steady her. "Touch of vertigo?" she inquired worriedly. "We *are* rather high up."

The man in the chair had half-turned at Nichola's stumbling entrance. Their eyes met; Nichola, her worst fears realized, hurriedly glanced away. "Why, Lord Boru!" Mrs. Treadwell declared happily. "What a most pleasant surprise!"

"You'll forgive my not rising, I trust," Lord Boru said in his deep, strange voice.

"Of course we will! Gwendolyn, Nichola, I believe you both have the acquaintance of our companion for the evening? Miss Carstairs, Lord Boru, and Miss Hainesworth." Gwendolyn made her curtsy; Nichola, after a nudge from their chaperone, did so as well. She was petrified with chagrin. She had taken note, in the glow of the gas lamps, of the twin canes set discreetly behind His Lordship's seat, and of the same manservant she had seen the night before hovering by him, to attend to his needs.

"Naughty Vanessa," Mrs. Treadwell declared, making her way to the front of the box, "not to tell me she'd invited you to join us!"

"I find myself the recipient these days of any number of offers of unused seats at theaters," Lord Boru said thoughtfully. "Not to mention boxing bouts, edifying lectures, concerts, readings, and the occasional opera or ballet."

"Your friends know what you need is entertainment and distraction," Mrs. Treadwell noted cheerily.

"My friends," Lord Boru retorted with a touch of bitterness, "have no idea what I need." Then, with a visible effort, he shook off his mood and trained a smile at Gwendolyn. "Sit here by me, won't you, Miss Carstairs?" Alarmed, Gwen turned to Mrs. Treadwell, who nodded encouragement. "Are you fond of Shakespeare?"

"I—I—" Whatever Gwen managed to reply was lost on Nichola, who settled into her own seat in a fog of dismay.

What a bloody *awful* twist of fate! she thought, cringing into a ball, attempting to make herself as inconspicuous as possible. Mrs. Treadwell glanced at her curiously. "Do you feel all right, my dear?"

What she felt was wretched. But she managed to nod, and even to resign herself to this torture as penance for her idiocy the evening before. The gas lamps hissed, guttering low, and in the gathering darkness she heard Lord Boru murmuring conversationally to Gwen. She gave some whispered reply, and he laughed—a strong, bold laugh that reverberated through the theater and made more than one female head incline their way. Then, blessedly, the performance began, and she could lose herself in the misery of the prince of Denmark, whose tribulations seemed not a whit more profound than her own.

The lights came back up at the close of the third act, with Hamlet stuck in the tightening coils of his uncle's plotting and his mother's perfidy and his own compulsion for revenge. Nichola's head was spinning, but this much the play had clarified: Her only hope for peace lay in complete honesty. When Mrs. Treadwell started out to the lobby to greet acquaintances, beckoning to her charges, Nichola lingered behind. With great trepidation, she approached Lord Boru. His manservant, a grim, unsmiling fellow, was pouring him wine. "Milord," Nichola began, and had the word stick in her throat, so that she had to begin again: "Milord. I believe I owe you an apology."

His heavy head, crowned by that mass of red-gold hair, swiveled toward her, his expression politely blank. "Do you? I cannot imagine what for."

She took a deep, deep breath. "When I rebuked you last evening, I was unaware that you were . . ." She paused, looking down at him, at the massive muscles of his neck and chest and arms, and for a moment she could see in her mind how splendid a figure he must have cut before tragedy struck him. *Crippled.* For the life of her, she could not speak the word. In the lamplight, his blue eyes were dark and unreadable. "Unaware of your . . . circumstances," she amended at last.

He raised one red-gold eyebrow. "I've no idea, Miss—Hainesworth, is it?—what circumstances you might refer to," he said coldly. Then he turned his back on her, leaving her to scurry after Mrs. Treadwell and Gwen.

She had to bite back tears as she stood with her chaperone, being presented to a seemingly endless stream of friends and acquaintances. Gwen glanced at her, her dark eyes filled with concern. "Is something wrong, Nick?" she asked worriedly. "You know that you can tell me."

But Nichola couldn't. Lord Boru's rejection of her stammered apology had only made things worse.

It was with great reluctance that she returned to the box—only to see Lord Boru greet Gwen with delight, offering his field glass so she might inspect the players more closely, pressing a cup of his wine on her with his splendid laugh. Mrs. Treadwell was purring with excitement. "I do believe our Gwendolyn has made a conquest!" she whispered to Nichola.

Grimly, Nichola trained her attention on the stage.

Despite her humiliation, she could not help but be caught up in the action unfolding there. She mourned for poor, disgraced Ophelia with, perhaps, unusual vigor; she felt Laertes's demands for his sister's vindication to the depths of her soul. That was what Tommy would do if he only knew how Lord Boru had treated her, she decided—and then shriveled to recall that his boorishness was no more than she deserved. But in the final act, it was the swordplay that caught her attention. She watched in fascination as Laertes and Hamlet dueled, then both died as a result of Claudius's poisonous treachery.

When the lamps came up for the final time, Mrs. Treadwell mopped her eyes with her kerchief. "Shakespeare can be so *very* affecting," she murmured. "I take it you enjoyed the play?"

Nichola nodded. "Oh, the language was marvelous. But the fighting in that last scene was *appallingly* done! Did you see how clumsily Laertes handled his blade? Why, I don't think the fellow knows a *passata* from a soufflé! And as for Hamlet, someone ought to teach him to keep his staccatos in line! He—" She broke off abruptly. Mrs. Treadwell had her brows raised in alarm. Gwen was staring at her. So, for that matter, was everyone within earshot; the ladies in the neighboring boxes were positively agog.

Nichola wished devoutly that a hole would open in the earth and swallow her up. Since, alas, it did not, she ducked her head, reaching for her wrap, knowing that she had committed another dreadful faux pas. She hurried toward the exit, only pausing to wait for Mrs. Treadwell and Gwen, who were exchanging niceties with Lord Boru. Desperately she looked back, willing them to hurry and deliver her from this latest misery.

To her surprise, her abashed eyes met the gaze of Lord Boru, who was contemplating her with an expression of what might almost have been respect.

Chapter
Seven

All through the seemingly interminable ride home from the countess's to the academy, Nichola had the pleasure of listening as Mrs. Treadwell teased Gwen about Lord Boru's attentions to her at the theater. Gwen blushed and made disclaimers: "Really, Mrs. Treadwell, he was no more than suitably polite!" But their headmistress was relentless, and finally Gwen declared she was exhausted and drifted off to sleep. Mrs. Treadwell nudged Nichola and winked. "Nothing could better boost Gwendolyn's opinion of herself than an evening such as that!" she murmured happily, then sighed, gazing out the window. "Pity he's entirely unsuitable material for marriage."

"Is he?" Nichola said a bit too quickly.

"Well, of course, now that he is incapacitated. What girl would give her heart to a man who cannot walk?"

"He climbed all those stairs to the box," Nichola pointed out.

"Not without that manservant. And I imagine it took

him *hours,* the poor soul. You notice he took care to be in place long before we arrived, and not to leave until everyone was gone."

Nichola pondered that with a glimmer of hope. If Lord Boru were the sort to care so much about his public image, perhaps she could stop tormenting herself. "I imagine he is a very *proud* man," she ventured.

"And well he should be," Mrs. Treadwell said with complacence. "He would be king of Scotland if not for a few quirks of history."

"He is Scottish?" Nichola asked in surprise. That would explain his odd manner of speech.

"Scotch-Irish, actually. His ancestors controlled most of Strathclyde and Annandale and Ulster, before the time of the Bruce." It was on the tip of Nichola's tongue to point out that the time of the Bruce had been half a millennium earlier. But Mrs. Treadwell had plunged on: "I often wondered, in the old days, if that accounted for his recklessness. Trying to prove himself, you know, against the Saxons who'd taken his birthright. He was renowned all over Britain for never once having refused a challenge." That made Nichola swallow hard, remembering the one she had presented him. Mrs. Treadwell's face had turned dreamy. "I recall so clearly watching him best Gentleman Jackson when he was no more than a mere pup!"

Gwen, the faker, blinked awake. "You attended a boxing match, Mrs. Treadwell?"

"An impromptu exhibition," their chaperone said hastily, "arranged due to a wager. Oh, Brian Boru was always up to such mischief in those days!"

"I suppose," Nichola said sourly, "his war injury was due to some such mad caper."

Mrs. Treadwell turned instantly solemn. "Not a bit. By all accounts, his wound was the result of a valiant attempt to protect the soldiers under his command. They'd been holed up by enemy fire, and the only escape route was feared to be commanded by French cannon. Lord Boru rode forth and drew the artillery's attention to himself, quite boldly and openly. The company was then able to rejoin the line."

"My!" Gwen breathed.

Mrs. Treadwell beamed at her. "So you can see, my dear, how great a heart your charms have conquered!" That embarrassed poor Gwen so much that she promptly fell asleep again.

Nichola, meanwhile, sat and stewed. A war hero—just the sort of soldier she had always imagined she herself would be—and she had as good as called him a coward! Mrs. Treadwell's heartfelt caution about the importance of first impressions rang in her ears. Well, she'd spoiled any chance of Lord Brian Boru ever thinking her aught but an utter fool. *But why should I care?* she asked herself indignantly. *It was a simple, honest mistake. If he hadn't been so haughty and proud—if he hadn't beckoned so regally for that manservant to retrieve his cigar—I would have kept my mouth shut. So what if he is—was—a hero?* So, she supposed, was Hamlet—and yet she would not want to befriend him, either. Look at what he'd done to poor Rosencrantz and Guilderstern!

"Back in '07," Mrs. Treadwell began, with that same dreamy tone to her voice, "he played whist against Lord Powellton and Lord Hammermill at White's for three days straight, they say, until Hammermill, in despair, with his fortune gone, offered up his wife as a wager!"

Nichola's mouth curled. "I assume Lord Boru accepted."

"Not at all," said Mrs. Treadwell. "He laid down his hand and went home."

"So," said the countess d'Oliveri, pouring sherry for her business companion, "how went the visit to Dorset?"

"Quite well," Mrs. Treadwell declared, accepting the glass gratefully. "If, that is, you do not take account of my daughter's advancing idiocy. I tell you, Christiane, every moment I spend in Vanessa's company makes me more glad you convinced me to found this academy."

The countess smiled. "No untoward behavior by our wards, I trust?"

"They were as good as gold." She sipped, then reconsidered. "Though I am not entirely certain that Nichola did not form some sort of—well, attachment."

"Really?" the countess asked in surprise. "To whom?"

"That, I could not say. But little Gwendolyn appears to have won herself a swain."

"You *have* been busy, Evelyn!"

"Alas, he's quite unsuitable. Lord Brian Boru."

"Brian Boru!" The countess stared. "Good Lord, I haven't seen him in a dog's age! Is he still so wild and reckless?"

"Hardly. He was crippled, you know, at Dresden. Took a cannonball in the knee."

The countess d'Oliveri paled. "Dear God. I hadn't heard."

"Yes. It is very sad. He cannot so much as stand. Still, that did not stop him from being exceedingly attentive to Gwen when we shared a box with him at the theater."

"Lord Boru—crippled. It seems impossible." The countess poured another cup of sherry, very tall.

Mrs. Treadwell considered her for a moment in silence. Then her brows contracted. "Christiane," she said. "If I am not mistaken, Lady Chumford mentioned to me once that she encountered you and Lord Boru in Paris quite a few years past. He was your escort at an embassy ball."

"Boru and I were quite close at one time," the countess admitted.

"You mean you—Good God, Christiane! He is ever so much younger than you!"

"Only ten years," the countess said. Her dark eyes had a curious, excited expression. "Where is he staying, do you know?"

"With Lord and Lady Dalton, I believe." Mrs. Treadwell pursed her mouth. "You don't intend to run off with him, do you? I should never be able to manage all these girls on my own!"

"How little faith you have in me, dear Evelyn," the countess observed, going to her writing desk and reaching for a quill. "I should have thought by now you would recognize I am not the sort to leave a job half done."

Chapter
Eight

Nichola battled her shame with an absolute frenzy of
fencing. So intense did her swordplay become that a fortnight after her return from Yarlborough House, following a
particularly hard-fought bout in which Nichola mentally
superimposed Lord Brian Boru's head over Madame's
mask and nearly decapitated the poor woman, her instructor tossed her foil aside and said, "Congratulations, *chérie*!
We have arrived at that happy point where the pupil has
surpassed the teacher."

"Oh, no!" Nichola demurred.

"Oh, yes. I have nothing more to teach you."

"But that's not possible! You tell me I am still over-
eager and wild; that my lead from my *cinque* is graceless;
that my parries inevitably are misjudged. Why, you are ever
so much better a fencer than I!"

Madame, breathing heavily, raised up her mask. "No, I
may be more practiced, but I am *not* a better fencer. You

were made for this sport, Nichola. Even with the awkward-nesses that remain, you make your foil *sing*."

Nichola blushed at the compliment. "Anything I am, you have made me."

"Anything you are," the countess responded, "already lay within you. I only brought it to the fore." Then she rubbed her ribs ruefully. "Frankly, *chérie,* I do not think I dare continue to cross foils with you. When you touch, you truly *touch*. What you require now is a more worthy opponent."

"What I need now is to go to the Continent."

Madame considered her. "Still harboring that dream?"

"I am," Nichola said stubbornly. "Why not? What else is there for me? I showed well enough at Christmastide how utterly unsuited I am for civilized society."

"Did you? How so?"

Nichola flushed, unwilling to admit that dreadful incident with Lord Boru. Instead she scuffed her toe in the grass and gazed across the yard. "Mrs. Treadwell told me she was very proud of you and Gwendolyn both," the countess pressed.

That only shows how little Mrs. Treadwell knows of what went on, Nichola thought, and bit her tongue.

Madame guided her to the kitchen door. "Nichola, pet," she said gently. "Were you to go off to the Continent to fight Napoleon, you would be cold and lonely and as miserable as any human soul could possibly be."

"I would be a *soldier,*" Nichola began, but the countess shook her head at her:

"You would be an impostor. False to yourself and to those around you. And an impostor . . . is a very difficult thing to be."

"Tommy would welcome me!" Nichola said hotly.

"Would he? You think it would be an honor to him to have you appear outside his tent in a foot-soldier's gear? It would improve his performance in battle to have you to look out for?"

"That wouldn't matter to . . . ." But Nichola stopped.

She'd never really considered what impact her scheme to join her brother might have on his chances for survival. But she knew suddenly, with a sinking sensation, that Tommy would be mortified should she show up in France. As much as he loved her, as similar as she and her twin might be in looks and temperament, there had always been this un-bridgeable gulf between them—that she was female and he was male. He'd send her packing off home in an instant, she realized—and have to put up with unending jibes and teasing from his mates to boot. "Oh, God, I *hate* being a girl!" she cried in fury.

To her surprise, Madame nodded sadly. "I know," she said, as Cook smiled at them and put the kettle to boil. "Life is dreadfully unfair. Men have all the better part of it, don't they? They get to ride to the hounds, and carouse till they're cockeyed, and wench and gamble and smoke, and what do we get? Childbirth and household accounts and worrying whether our stockings have ladders or the roast is dry."

Despite herself, Nichola giggled. "Oh, you understand *precisely*," she said, and for the first time in her life did not feel a complete contradiction to the ways of the world.

"Of course I do. No intelligent woman could look at the divisions of labor and pleasure as they exist and not find fault with God's great plan."

"*I* says," Cook declared, bringing them both steaming mugs, "there's no sense in fightin' the Almighty. What is, is, 'n' always will be, at that."

"Thank you, Cook, for that insight," Madame replied with a twinkle. She drew Nichola down beside her at the broad kitchen table, then lowered her voice. "Change is possible," she murmured discreetly. "But it must be *slow* change. At times, agonizingly slow. We must work within the boundaries if we ever hope to change them."

"Do *you* hope to change them?" Nichola asked breathlessly.

"With all my heart."

"Does Mrs. Treadwell?"

"Well. You have met her daughter. What do you think?"

Nichola pondered that. "Surely *any* woman would be extremely gratified by a success such as the countess of Yarlborough's."

"There is a vast difference," the countess d'Oliveri noted, "between success and happiness." Cook was leaning close. Madame reached for the sugar bowl. "So. What I am thinking is that I must find you a new fencing master."

"I don't see why," Nichola muttered, "if I'm never to go off and fight Napoleon. God knows no man is ever going to consider my adeptness with the foil a positive."

"One of the dangers of viewing the world from the vantage point of the oppressed," Madame said, stirring her tea with a delicate wrist, "is that it tends to make one despise the oppressor. Men are every bit as much victims of the current schema as we." Nichola's surprise betrayed her disbelief. Madame laughed. "You doubt that? Well, you are young. When you have lived to see as many unhappy husbands as I have, you may reconsider. Meantime, our only choice is to make the most of what we have. In your case, I am much inclined to think that includes further instruction in fencing. I'll put my mind to it, shall I?"

"If you like," said Nichola, a little dazed by this conversation. That men might be disgruntled with their lot— why, what stuff and nonsense!

"Are those scones, Cook?" Madame asked amiably of the tray being taken from the oven. "Do you suppose we might trouble you for a pair?"

Three days later, the countess appeared in the upstairs parlor to rescue an extremely grateful Nichola from a lecture on bleaching linens with the redoubtable Mrs. Caldburn. "Thank God!" Nichola cried when they'd withdrawn down the corridor a discreet distance. "Why in heaven's name anyone would care if the sheets go gray is absolutely beyond me. When I have a household of my own, I shall order them gray in the first place, and never, ever bleach!"

Madame laughed. "It is amusing to contemplate what sort of household you might someday have, *chérie*!"

"They only go gray anyhow the moment the dogs get up on them," Nichola said matter-of-factly.

The countess suppressed a faint shudder. "Your mother allows dogs in the beds?"

"Oh, no. She'd have a conniption. But I always managed to sneak one up to my bedroom with me. It's very pleasant to have a good, big hound stretched out beside you."

"I shall have to take your word on that."

"Are we to have a lesson, then?" Nichola struck a fencing pose, imaginary foil at ready.

"You are. Be in the courtyard tomorrow at dawn."

"You found me an instructor? So quickly as that? Who is she?"

"He," the countess corrected her.

Nichola stared. "I could not *possibly* take lessons from a man."

"Why ever not?"

Remembering how the countess had held her arms and waist and even her buttocks to teach her proper positioning, Nichola went scarlet. "It simply wouldn't be proper!"

"You need have no fear. He is *ages* older than you. I know him quite well indeed, and he has always shown himself most trustworthy."

"But—but—" Nichola struggled to put her apprehensions into words. It was one thing to practice in the courtyard with the countess, whom all the girls at the academy— except for Katherine, of course—adored and respected. It would be quite another to suit up against a man!

The countess was considering her curiously. "Don't tell me you are afraid to cross foils with a member of the opposite sex!"

That snapped Nichola back. "Of course I'm not!" she said hotly. "I am not afraid of anyone or anything!"

Madame nodded. "That is what I told your new fencing instructor. So be ready to put on a fine show for him in the morning. I have written to him singing your praises, and I should hate for him to travel all this way only to be disappointed. Now, back to Mrs. Caldburn and those linens."

"*Must* I?"

Madame laughed. "Yes, *chérie*. You must."

Chapter
Nine

Dawn came late in a Kentish January, and this one, Nichola thought as she crawled from her warm bed, seemed particularly drear. The sky beyond her window was thick with clouds, and a few negligent scraps of snowflake drifted down through the air. Her teeth chattered madly as she yanked off her nightdress and pulled on Tommy's breeches and jacket. "What in the world are you doing?" Bessie asked sleepily from beneath her own covers.

"Fencing lesson," Nichola said briefly, trying to fit her cold hands into her gloves.

"Mmm." Bessie snuggled deeper in the blankets. "Better you than me."

For once, the looking glass was open, since Katherine was still sleeping soundly. Nichola cast a glance into the polished surface as she headed for the door. God, I look a sight, she thought, averting her eyes from the stuffed white image, all lumpen with padding, and hurrying out into the corridor.

The air there was even more frigid, and she snapped her mask down just for protection from the wind that howled between the stone walls, stomping her feet as she walked, wishing she weren't so stiff. There was frost on the handle of the door to the courtyard—the *inner* handle. Embroidery, she thought with a hint of wistfulness, really wasn't so dull as all *that*. . . .

She had to put her shoulder to the door to force it open against the outside gusts. The courtyard was blanketed in shadow, and she blinked through the eyeholes in the mask, hoping her new instructor might have reconsidered this appointment. But—no. There he was against the far wall, his own masks and pads already in place. He looks very *large,* Nichola thought, starting across the hoar-crusted grass, and then remembered—so did I, in the mirror. And any opponent would, compared to dainty Madame.

"Miss Hainesworth?" he growled from behind his headgear as she approached. Nichola considered curtsying, but the nicety seemed absurd under such conditions. Instead, she made a fencing salute. "Let's see what you've got, then," he muttered, snow swirling around him as he raised up his foil.

"Aren't you going to assume a stance?" Nichola inquired in confusion, having expected him to step out toward her.

"I *am* assuming a stance," he grunted impatiently, still leaning against the wall.

Nichola shrugged and advanced with some nervousness, foil at the ready. She was still trying to decide where to take her position when his arm, much longer than the countess's, flicked out with astonishing quickness and scored a touch. "I wasn't ready!" she protested.

"Get ready, then."

She did, starting from her best offensive posture, the *quatre*. She'd no sooner set herself than he scored again, the tip of his foil poking effortlessly against her pads. "Two," he noted blandly, and Nichola felt resentment boil up inside her.

"I am not very experienced," she told him, straightening, "and I have only ever faced one opponent."

"Three." Even as she spoke, he'd laid another touch.

Nichola gritted her teeth and paid attention. For a minute or two, they parried one another, the chink of their steels barely registering in the wild wind. He was, she noted, impossibly quick and outrageously strong; within his enormous glove, the foil looked to be a child's toy. Remembering Madame's lessons, she summoned up patience, fought her heightening anger, and nearly managed to score a touch against him, only to have it deflected at the last moment by a countermove so adept that she gasped. "Oh, that was very nice!" she told him excitedly, in the complimentary tone she and the countess used to acknowledge accomplishment.

"Are we having tea or fencing?" was his only response. Nichola was so flustered that she forgot to mind her guard, and his foil pricked her pads again.

Enraged, she took a step back, panting. "Why won't you come out from that wall and fight properly?" she demanded.

"Why should I, when I can outscore you from here?"

Bastard, Nichola thought grimly. But she bit her tongue and concentrated, checked her rapid breathing, forced herself to *wait,* watching his moves instead of rushing in. He was, she saw now, a trifle slower when approached from the right; he seemed to have trouble shifting his weight from leg to leg. God, it was so infuriating that he would not come out from the wall; it nullified all her favorite tactics. But Madame had taught her that fencing was a matter of adjusting to one's opponent, and so she would.

His eyes were unreadable through the mask; she had only the language of his body to work from. She feinted to the left, quickly, sharply, and he met the move with maddening ease. But that was what Nichola had intended. She struck again, thought she heard him sigh as though in boredom—

She whirled in a circle to the right, fast as fire, and thrust. Her tip struck his shoulder with gratifying strength.

"Well!" he said. "That was—"

But Nichola had moved again, back and then forward. This time her blade hit his chest. He started to laugh. Nichola lunged and landed another touch, low but solid, at his right hip. He staggered.

"Are we having tea or fencing?" Nichola demanded tautly, the blood racing in her head.

"Oh, we are fencing, now." Straightening up, he took a firmer grip on his blade.

She stopped talking then. It took all her energy to withstand his assaults, try to parry his movements, which were smooth and clean and so elegant that she was in awe. She did not score again, but neither did he. They fought fiercely for what seemed hours, while the sky slowly brightened above them and the wild wind howled across the courtyard and the sparse snow fell. He was so strong that her only advantage was speed; she darted about, searching for an opening, another lowering of his defenses. One never came. Everything she tried, he turned back on her, until her frustration finally boiled over. "It isn't *fair*!" she cried at last, cold and exhausted and angry. "You have the wall at your back! Why won't you come out and be a proper man?"

He dropped his guard, reaching to lift his mask. Beneath it, his red-gold hair was drenched in sweat. "I already have your assurance, haven't I, Miss Hainesworth, that I am something less than that?"

She stared in dismayed horror at his broad face, his startling blue eyes. *Lord Brian Boru?* Before she could think of anything to say, he swayed on his feet and slowly, slowly, like a sawn oak, toppled onto the ground.

Out of the shadows his manservant came running, glaring reproachfully at Nichola. "Dinna I tell His Lairdship this would prove too much?" the fellow snapped in a thick Scottish brogue, kneeling at his master's side, a flask already in hand.

"Can I—can I help?" Nichola faltered.

"Ye hae done eno' already!"

Completely disheartened, she turned and fled.

The moment she encountered Madame, on the way in to luncheon, Nichola drew her aside. "I have been searching for you all morning!" she hissed as they stood outside the dining room.

"Have you? Whatever for?" the countess d'Oliveri asked calmly.

"To tell you I have no intention of taking further fencing lessons from Lord Boru!"

"I very much regret to hear that, Nichola. He told me he was very much impressed with your performance."

"I find him most disagreeable!"

"Do you? And what, pray tell, think you of his fencing?"

Nichola paused, torn between fury and fairness. She'd seen flashes of true genius in his handling of the foil. There was so very much she might have learned from him. But still . . . "Clearly he is a master of the sport," she admitted. "Nonetheless, I *refuse* to fence with him again."

Gwen and Bess and even Katherine were staring from their table in the dining room, their attention drawn by Nichola's agitation. Madame shut the door, leading Nichola to a chair in the hall. "I feared as much," she murmured. "When one is young, one sees the world through such an exceedingly narrow prism. Youth can be so self-centered."

Nichola gaped. "I? Self-centered?"

"But of course. Lord Boru, you know, has been dealt a very rough blow by life. This wound to his knee . . . I have been in correspondence with His Lordship's physicians. They believe it is possible he might someday walk again—but not if he will not rouse himself to try. He has given up, Nichola. He has surrendered to the harshness of fate. As he sees it, he lost all that made life worthwhile when he lost the use of his leg."

"I am very sorry for that, of course, but I cannot see what it has to do with me!"

"That man *breathed* sport, once upon a time." Madame's fine mouth curved in a smile of recollection. "They say, you know, that he never once refused a challenge. Yet he is refusing the greatest of all challenges by refusing to attempt to walk again. He was always such a *proud* man, too proud now to allow his friends and companions to view his weakness. He slouches in a chair, looking so nonchalant, Mrs. Treadwell tells me. And yet I know from his physicians what it costs him to arrive at social affairs before anyone else does, in order to assume that negligent posture. Were he to put as much effort into his recovery as he does into denying it to the world, he would be much better served."

"I am, of course, sorry he has suffered such misfortune—"

Madame seemed not even to have heard her. "He would never deign to ask a man to exercise with him, in the state he is in. He has *uncommon* pride," she reiterated. "Yet I hoped it might not prove too humiliating for him to give lessons to you."

Nichola chewed her lip. "You think that teaching me fencing might somehow work toward his recovery?"

"I do. It will engage his mind, and, more, engage his body, or what is left of it. It pains me to see him grown so lazy and lax."

"You speak as though you know him well."

"We are old friends." Madame's mysterious smile as she said this, the light dancing in her dark eyes, sent the most ridiculous pang shooting through Nichola's heart. *I wonder if they were lovers once,* she thought, then wished she hadn't—and then was certain they had been. Beautiful, glamorous Madame was the sort of woman who would appeal to a man like Boru.

"Have you ever fenced against him?" she inquired.

"No. When I knew him, he never would have crossed

foils with a woman. Not even in jest, or for play." The countess was silent for a moment, lost in thought. Then she roused herself, with a little shake of her shoulders. "I suppose one might call it a victory for womankind that he did so today. Oh, if only you might have known him, Nichola, when he was whole and himself! He had more *joie de vivre* than any human soul I ever have encountered. It was a pleasure simply to stroll the streets of Paris with him."

Nichola's mind formed a sudden picture of the two of them, Madame and Lord Brian Boru, doing just that, arm in arm—Madame in an exquisitely elegant gown and a cunning little hat, Boru in the latest male fashion, walking stick in hand, that thick hair the shade of Scottish gold pulled back into a queue. "Perhaps," she proposed, with more bitterness than she'd intended, "he ought to give fencing lessons to *you*."

"Don't be foolish, child," the countess said in blithe dismissal. "I would not be a worthy opponent for him."

Perhaps, Nichola thought, I am reading more into what she says than is there. It could be they were merely friends. Still . . . that glint had reappeared in the countess's eye. *Joie de vivre*—she had not glimpsed much of *that* in Lord Boru.

Half of her—more than half—wanted to wash her hands forever of the sad mess she'd made upon meeting him. *First impressions* . . . And yet some stubborn scrap of will reared up and begged for the chance to prove that she could best him on the fencing strip, learn to land touches against him as easily as he had on her. It would not be so much of a victory, she argued to herself, to triumph over a man who could not even stand without a wall at his back. But that morning in the courtyard, he had awakened an absolute frenzy for mastery in her. God knows he hadn't seemed a cripple then.

"If you honestly believe," she said slowly, "that instructing me can in some way be helpful to Lord Boru, I shall, of course, bow to your will."

The smile the countess bestowed on her then was dazzling. "Oh, Nichola! I am so glad!"

It wasn't until Madame had embraced her and they'd gone in to luncheon that a discomforting notion popped into Nichola's head. Was the countess so anxious to restore Brian Boru to health because she longed to renew past intimacy with him?

Chapter
Ten

"Wrong, wrong, *wrong!*" Lord Boru bellowed from his chair in the courtyard. "That was abominable. Will you *never* learn?"

"I'm sure I'm very sorry!" Nichola shot back. "I was occupied with beating off your *coulé!*"

"You don't beat off a *coulé,*" he snarled. "You *deflect* it. And your front foot is pointing inward again."

Fuming, Nichola adjusted her toes so far that she stood like a duck. "Is that better!"

Lord Boru raised a hand, signaling for his manservant. "We may as well go, Hayden. Miss Hainesworth is affecting irony again."

"Oh, I *do* beg your pardon, great master!" Nichola made a sweeping bow of apology.

"*And* insolence."

Hayden, the gloomy servant, had stepped forth from the shelter of the colonnade, where the winter wind was not so biting. "Very gude, m'laird."

"Stay where you bloody are, Hayden!" Nichola shouted, turning her blade on him. He took a rapid step back.

From the chair, Lord Boru's masked head tilted upward to her. "Such language, Miss Hainesworth!"

"Go to hell," she muttered, angry at him, but even more infuriated with herself, for letting him get her goat again. She knew he was unpleasant—three weeks of lessons with him had certified that—but did he have to be so damned superior? *Nothing* she did ever earned her a kind word. And, by God, she thought she'd fought off his *coulé* marvelously, considering she'd been sailing in midair at the time. How like him to carp on the position of her left hand, which wasn't even involved!

She paused to catch her breath, took a somewhat less belligerent tone. "Besides my hand and my front foot, what else displeased you about that move?"

"That it so nearly succeeded," he grunted, shifting in his chair.

Nichola stared, her emotions undergoing an abrupt transformation. "You—you really think so?" she asked, much more humbly.

"I said *nearly*," he barked back. "Now try it again."

She did. She was attempting a *flèche*, a leaping attack in which she launched herself forward with her sword arm outstretched. The great danger in the *flèche*, Lord Boru had explained in his usual impatient manner, was that the extended position, coupled with the impetus of one's spring, left room for little or no defensive response should the move fail to land properly. So far, she'd missed on every try.

She did on this one, too, and went sailing past his chair. "Swing the back leg forward!" Lord Boru thundered. She tried a midair correction and ended sprawled on the ground with her face in the frost. "Get up, get up," he said curtly, and she clambered to her feet, red-faced beneath her mask, hating him with a passion. Easy for him to tell her what to do, while he sat like a damned pasha on his throne!

"You *told* me the value of the *flèche* lies in the element of surprise!" she cried furiously. "How am I to surprise you when you know precisely what to expect?"

"If you ever learn to execute it properly," he said with maddening calm, "you *will* surprise me."

"Oh! You are the most—most *aggravating* man!"

"I've been called worse." From behind the mask, there was a hint of humor to his voice. That was new, Nichola mused, as she dusted herself off and took her place once more. *Composed,* she told herself, forcing her breath to slow, willing her wild heart to cease pounding. *I will be composed. I will wait and watch. I WILL NOT BARGE IN!*

Through the mesh of the mask, her breath made clouds that the wind whipped backward. But she did not feel cold. She lunged, holding back on the *flèche*. He met her foil with a blandly nonchalant beat. "That arm should be straight," he informed her. She drew away, took the *en garde* position, wishing she could see his eyes. Then she had a notion. She half-turned from him, as though in disgust.

"Perhaps we should just call it a day," she began, "since you are so determined to find fault with my—" And then she sprang at him, extended in the *flèche*. He hadn't even time to raise his blade before her tip struck him square in the chest. Filled with glee, she failed any attempt to check her momentum; she smacked into him head-on. There was a thud, then a whoosh of his breath. The chair he sat on tilted back on two legs, hung for a crazy moment, and then tumbled over, leaving her sprawled atop him in the grass.

"Ooof!" said Lord Boru.

"M'laird!" Hayden screeched, leaping forward.

"Oh, damn," Nichola said, caught in a tangle of blades and chair and limbs. She cringed, expecting to be barked at. But to her astonishment, Lord Boru was laughing. She could hear it through his mask, and even more, she could feel it, seeing as she was splayed atop his chest.

She let go her foil. The hand he'd put up belatedly to shield himself was hard against her breast. "*Touché,* Miss Hainesworth," he declared, their faces so close that except for the mesh, they might have been embracing. "*That* was an excellent *flèche!*"

Hurriedly she rolled to the ground beside him, but the imprint of his glove on her breast seemed somehow to linger, imparting warmth despite the February dawn.

"I really think, m'laird, ye hae gone far eno'," Hayden chastised his master, bustling to retrieve Lord Boru's foil and set the chair upright. "Dr. Cohen said—"

"To hell with Dr. Cohen; *he* never made a *flèche* like that in his life." By now, Nichola had risen to her feet. She bent to offer him her arm, but Hayden waved her off, glowering. So she could only watch impotently as Lord Boru struggled to right himself, with the aid of the servant and chair. His mask was trained toward her; he grunted, heaving to his good knee and then pausing. "You might have the decency to look away," he said curtly.

"Why?" Nichola asked.

"That's what everyone else does. Pretends not to notice my . . . infirmity."

"It's rather hard *not* to notice it," she pointed out.

The strangest sound escaped him—a sort of *whoop*. He was laughing again.

With some effort, Hayden got him onto his feet—or onto one foot, rather—then handed him his canes. "That bae eno' fer t'day, m'laird," he announced sternly.

Lord Boru lifted his mask, and so did Nichola. Their eyes met—his, blue as the sky in autumn, and hers, warm amber filled with chagrin. "I suppose it is," he said with reluctance. "Still. That was one *hell* of a *flèche.*"

Nichola flushed. "Thank you, milord," she stammered.

He limped away awkwardly, pausing only to call over his shoulder: "Day after tomorrow, then! At dawn! Do you know, I think we might finally be getting somewhere!"

* * *

Nichola hurried back to her chambers, not even stopping in the kitchen for her customary cup of tea. Her face burned, and not entirely from the wicked winds. Lord Boru's praise had unsettled her somehow. She was so accustomed to gruffness and dissatisfaction that his accolades made her self-conscious. And yet, she thought, opening the door to the room where her form-mates still lay abed, how much a compliment meant when it came so hard-earned!

She had a sore spot on her thigh from when she'd toppled onto him. She paused to rub it, caught a glimpse of a face in the mirror. Katherine. She frowned, and the face frowned back. Shocked, she moved closer and saw she'd been staring at herself. But she looked so different, so— peculiar. The cold had brought a glow to her cheeks finer than any paint could ever put there. Her tousled hair gleamed in the young sunlight streaming through the windows, and her eyes were luminous, chatoyant, warm brown shot through with gold. She blinked, certain the image would vanish. When it didn't, she put a hesitant hand to her face.

"Are you hurt?"

Gwen's anxious voice made her whip from the glass in embarrassment. "No! Not at all. I just . . . thought that I might be."

Bess was rousing as well, swinging her legs over the side of her bed. "Lord, it's positively freezing!" She clambered into her robe. "I really don't know how you can bear to rise so early in this weather, Nick."

"Especially for anything so grotesque as swordfighting." That was Katherine, of course, gorgeous even in waking, her pale hair perfectly arrayed in wrapped braids, her flawless skin unmarked by blanket or sheet. *But I, too, was beautiful there, for a moment. . . .*

"You are only jealous," Gwen told Katherine.

"Jealous?" Katherine snorted. "Of her? That will be the day."

"You should be," Gwen went on complacently. "She has an extremely engaging young lord to give lessons to her."

Nichola shot her friend a warning glance, but the damage had been done. "I thought you had your lessons from Madame," Katherine said to Nichola, eyes narrowing.

"I—I did. But I learned all that she had to teach me, so she brought another teacher in."

"Surely any young lord worth his salt would have better ways to occupy his time than teaching fencing to you. Who is he, then?"

Nichola was thoroughly regretting having confided her instructor's identity to Gwen. "No one who moves in your set, I am sure," she said as she took off her pads, and shot the brunette a pleading look.

Gwen either missed it or chose to ignore it. "How can you say that, Nick? Why, all of England knows of Lord Brian Boru!"

"I don't," Bess noted. "Who the devil is he?"

"A great war hero," Gwen told her. "And a terrible rake."

Katherine had furrowed her brow. Now it abruptly cleared. "Good God. You don't mean *that* Lord Boru! I thought you said a *young* lord! He is positively ancient. Not to mention semi-impoverished."

"Trust you," Bess noted, "to know the financial standing of every unmarried man in England!"

"*And* a cripple," Katherine finished smugly. "No wonder he is stuck fencing with you."

Bess's eyes had gone wide. "He's a cripple?"

"He was wounded in the war," Gwen helpfully explained. "A cannonball took out his knee at Arden. Or was it Dresden? But before that, Mrs. Treadwell told us, he was the manliest man in the British Isles."

"God, how romantic," Bessie breathed. "Like something in a story."

"He is *fat,*" Katherine said.

"He is not!" Gwen sprang to his defense. "He is

merely huge. Everything about him is big." For a moment, Nichola wondered why Gwen should stand up for him so stoutly. Then she recalled His Lordship's attentions to her friend at the theater that night.

"Everything?" Bess asked with a giggle.

Gwen blushed. "Oh, you are terrible, Bessie! I'm sure I wouldn't know."

Katherine had appropriated the mirror again and was brushing her hair. "*You* are hopeless, Gwendolyn Carstairs. Imagine pining after a cripple—a man twice your age who cannot even stand on his two feet!"

"He isn't twice my age, surely," Gwen said dubiously. "Is he that old, Nick?"

"I haven't given it a thought," Nichola said airily, which was God's own truth. She pulled on her gown, and Bess obligingly came over to do up the tapes. "But he must have been one hell of a fencer before he was hurt." Before lowering her skirts, she glanced down at the sore spot on her thigh, which had become a bruise.

"Mrs. Treadwell," Gwen informed Bess, "said he was renowned all over England for never having refused a challenge."

"What does he look like?" Bess demanded.

"He is ever so handsome," Gwen noted. "Blue eyes and a ruddy complexion, and reddish-gold hair."

"He sounds a perfect *dream*!"

"I still say he's fat," Katherine put in from the mirror, turning so as to better examine her long lashes.

"What do you say, Nick?" Bess asked curiously.

Unexpectedly, Nichola colored, remembering the sensation of lying atop him, his palm cupping her bosom, their mouths nearly meeting except for their masks. His chest had been broad and warm, his thighs firm and strong. . . . "I say we are going to be late to breakfast," she announced, ducking her head to pull on her shoes. "And I, unlike you slug-a-beds, have worked up an appetite. So if you will excuse me . . ." She brushed past them to the door.

"Perhaps I ought to take up fencing," Bess noted

thoughtfully. Then she shivered, standing in her unmentionables. "But not if it requires such early rising. Do share the mirror, Katherine, you vain pig."

The question of Lord Boru's age occupied Nichola all through that day and the next, while she half-listened to Mrs. Caldburn's exceedingly tedious class on how to procure suitable household servants, and stitched away absently at the hideous chair cover she was being forced to embroider, and endured another sidesaddle riding lesson, and foundered through a session on the waltz with huffy little Monsieur Albert, and came exceedingly close to falling dead asleep during Professor Hallaby's lecture on Virgil's *Eclogues*. Only a thoughtful nudge from Gwen kept her from tumbling straight out of her chair. But she straightened with such a start that Professor Hallaby mistakenly assumed she was in the throes of intellectual fervor and made her scan the next section aloud, which she did very poorly indeed. Not that Nichola cared.

She didn't know exactly why it mattered how old he was. Perhaps her interest had been pricked by Katherine's blithe dismissal of him as a suitor—*not* that Nichola was considering him as such! Still, she could not stop wondering if he truly was twice her age. She could, of course, simply have asked Madame, or even Mrs. Treadwell. But the memory of the gleam in the former's eye when she'd spoken of Lord Boru stayed Nichola's tongue. And as for inquiring of the headmistress—well, Nichola had learned how very dangerous it was to show any sign of interest whatsoever in gentlemen in her presence.

At last, the day of her next lesson arrived. Nichola dressed hastily in the frigid predawn, and then found herself taking the time to brush her hair and braid it up becomingly. He was waiting for her in the courtyard, already seated in his chair. "You are late," he grunted as she hurried toward him.

"Quite late," the hateful Hayden put in dourly from

the shadows. "I should think that if His Lairdship bae willin' t' forgo his sleep t' tutor ye, ye might at least be on time."

"Sorry," Nichola mumbled, and pulled on her mask. "I overslept. It won't happen again."

"I should hope nae!" Hayden snapped. His master's head swiveled toward him for a moment, then turned back to Nichola.

"Let's have at it, then," he said, in what for him was nearly a gentle tone. "Footwork, to start." Nichola began moving from side to side in the curious foot-over-foot gait the sport required. "And *gagnez la mesure.*" Nichola obediently advanced, moving a step forward, taking care to land her weight on her heel and follow with the toe. Through his mask, Lord Boru watched intently. "And *rompez.*" She retreated, hind foot first. *"Gagnez! Rompez! Gagnez!"* He kept it up until she was dizzy—but proudly dizzy, for she gave him no cause to find fault with either of her feet. *"Engagez!"* he barked suddenly, and she lunged, her foil meeting his. He beat the stroke off readily, and she retreated to her *en garde,* awaiting his instruction. "Again! With point in line!" This was an overtly threatening action in which she advanced with her foil arm straight out. He met it with a neat, clean counterparry, no wasted movement or motion, just his foil turning hers aside. Nichola withdrew. "Why are you fading back?" he shouted. "You were in perfect position to use the *croisé!*"

"Your parry was too strong—"

"Nonsense! You have the leverage! Come in against me!"

Nichola gritted her teeth and engaged again, with a spirited thrust. He parried in answer—but laterally this time, which threw off all her mental preparations for the *croisé.* She barely managed to deflect his follow-up riposte. She was starting to get angry. "That was entirely unfair," she noted. "You had set me up to expect a counterparry!"

"A fencer who makes the same move twice in a row is a very poor fencer indeed."

He was, of course, absolutely right, but that merely added to the sting. She lunged at him, determined to execute the *croisé*. Instead he did so himself, sending her foil sailing across the yard.

"You *bastard*!" she cried.

"A fencer who makes—"

"Oh, do shut up!"

He leaned back in his chair, grinning—she was sure of it—behind the sheltering mask. "Don't you ever cry, Miss Hainesworth?"

"What?"

"I asked, don't you ever cry. Most women—nay, *all* women of my acquaintance would be reduced to tears by such frustration."

"No," she said curtly. "I don't cry. I get angry." She was so angry at that moment that her head was beginning to pound.

He nodded slowly. "I see."

"There isn't any point in tears, is there? I mean, crying is not likely to help me best you."

"No," he acknowledged. "It might, though, incline me to go easier on you."

She'd been headed across the frosted grass to retrieve her blade; now she stopped in mid-step. "Why in God's name would I want that?"

"I'm sure I don't know. But you must be wary of anger, you know. In fencing, you must never, ever let your heart overrule your head."

"What would you know of heart?" she muttered mutinously, picking up her foil.

"You're quite right," said Lord Boru, to her great surprise. "I am heartless and difficult and miserable and cruel. A cruel, miserable old bastard."

Nichola bent down for her foil. "How old?" she asked.

"Ancient," he grunted.

"How ancient?"

"Land that *croisé* and I'll tell you."

She came back to face his chair, took her *en garde,* then

hesitated, thinking. What counterparry might he use this time? They stared at one another through their masks, and she wished again that she might see his eyes. The foil lay perfectly balanced in her hand. She darted forward as though in attack, then at the last possible moment turned it into a feint. She had not fooled him at all; his blade remained stock-still. "You signaled," he commented.

"I did not!"

"You most certainly did. You lacked resolve."

"I'll show you bloody resolve." She retreated once more, to plot a move.

"Don't think too much," he cautioned.

"What do you mean? You just told me not to let my heart overrule my head!"

"Trust your arm and your sword. Trust your body to follow your instincts. Don't try to outthink me. Do what you will, and then react to my parries."

She hesitated, standing in the *en garde*. Then she lunged. He countered this time with a classic riposte. She counter-riposted. He feinted. And Nichola, her gaze trained on his sword arm, knew instinctively what he would try if she moved in—the low *passata sotto*. She came in perfectly to meet it, catching his foil at mid-foible, forcing it up and away. And this time, it was his blade that scuttered into the grass.

"How old?" she demanded.

He pulled off his mask, signaling to Hayden for wine. "Seventy-nine." She set the point of her foil against his chest. "Oh, very well! Twenty-eight."

"That's not ancient," she said in surprise.

"Oh, it must be, to a pert young thing such as you. Wine?" Nichola nodded, raising her mask as well, and Hayden, scowling, brought her a cup. "What is wrong?" Lord Boru demanded.

Now that she knew his age, Nichola had been trying to guess how old Madame might be. If she and Mrs. Treadwell came out in the same year, and Vanessa was now twenty, that meant—

"Nothing," she replied, immensely reassured by the recognition that Madame had to be at *least* nine years older than her fencing instructor, and more likely ten. Why, she was feeling downright cheerful! "Have at it again?"

"I believe, m'laird," Hayden said quellingly, "ye hae exerted yerself more than enough fer t'day." From the shelter of the balconnade, he brought forth Lord Boru's canes.

His Lordship grimaced. "I'd very much like to stay and play with you," he said in a high-pitched, childish voice, "but Nanny says I must stop now." Nichola was so surprised at the imitation—and the sad truth behind it—that she simultaneously giggled and blushed. Hayden shot her a truly vengeful look. His master heaved himself up unsteadily, his blue eyes trained on Nichola. And for the first time, she understood society's impulse to avert its gaze. Bess was wrong. There was nothing romantic in what had happened to Lord Brian Boru. She had a sudden grieving intuition of what his life must be like: helped from his bed, helped to bathe and dress, helped to the table . . . and then the long day stretching away ahead of him, leading into the no less lengthy night. God. It was a wonder he hadn't put a shotgun to his head. She would, in such a state.

"Day after tomorrow?" he asked, as Hayden led him away. Nichola nodded, not trusting herself to speak. There was a lump in her throat so large, it threatened to choke her. But he didn't want her pity; he had enough of that.

"Day after tomorrow," she confirmed, forcing her voice to be steady. He nodded, satisfied, and clumped off over the frozen grass. She wished, idly, hopelessly, that just once she might have seen how he walked before that cannonball took his future away. Like a god, proud as a peacock, she'd wager. And now to be reduced to this . . .

Hayden glanced back over his shoulder at her, eyes narrowed beneath his black brows. She realized she was staring and quickly turned aside. But the fleeting image that had formed in her mind of His Lordship in his glory stayed with her, haunted her, as she slowly went into the kitchen to drink her tea.

"I was watching this morning," Bess said excitedly upon Nichola's return to her rooms. "From the courtyard window. Gwen made me get up to watch you. And she was right—he is *exceedingly* handsome! Are you in love with him? I most certainly am!"

Katherine, who was sitting on her bed to pull on her stockings, made a moue of disgust. "How can you be in love with a *cripple*?"

"Especially a cripple you have never even met," Nichola noted dryly. She was not in the mood just now for Bess's wide-eyed wonderment.

"It was only his kneecap that was injured," Gwen put in, struggling with her ribbons. "Do these up for me, Nick? And given time enough, the bones of the patella might well bond again. It is good that he is active, insofar as he can be. That will keep the long tendons in his calf and thigh supple enough to—" She broke off, realizing that her form-mates all were staring at her. "I—I've been taking some anatomy lessons from Madame's friend, Dr. Caplan," she confessed abashedly. "They are ever so fascinating!"

Katherine shuddered. "Ever so inappropriate—just, I might add, like so much being taught at this so-called academy for young ladies."

"I don't see why you say that," Bess objected. "I'm sure if you showed some interest in something beyond your appearance and that of your future home, Madame would find a proper scholar to instruct you, just as she has with Gwen and Nichola and me."

"With whom are *you* studying?" Katherine asked very nastily. "Lady Caroline Lamb?"

"No," Bess retorted, "but Madame *did* send her one of my sonnets that she thought was good, and I got a very complimentary letter back."

"I'd keep that to yourself," Katherine noted, "if you've

any hope of prospering in this life. She is the most *shameless* female in all of England!"

"Tomorrow," Gwen said dreamily, hugging herself, "Dr. Caplan and I are to dissect a fetal piglet. The physiology of the pig, you know, is very similar to that of humans."

Katherine made a gagging sound and ran out of the room.

"Why," Gwen asked, after a bout of shared giggles, "does she *stay* here, if she detests it so?"

"That," Bessie declared, "is nearly as great a mystery as why Nichola isn't head-over-heels in love with her fencing instructor."

"You must be jesting," said Nichola. "He is old enough to be my father." But she knew better now, and found the knowledge oddly comforting.

Chapter
Eleven

In the quiet predawn, Lord Boru yanked the bell rope connecting his room at the inn with Hayden's quarters. Then he waited. And waited. After what seemed half an hour with no response, he groped for his canes, hauled himself to his feet, and crossed to bang at the adjoining door. "Hayden! Damn you, we'll be late!" he growled through the stout wood. His valet finally appeared, scowling, tucking his shirt into his breeches.

" 'N' wha' if we bae, then?" Hayden grumbled, going to light the lamp. "It bae nae way fer a man o' yer years t' spend his time, grapplin' wi' an English lass young eno' t' bae yer daughter."

"I'm not *grappling* with her. We are fencing." Lord Boru waited, again, while Hayden fetched water for him to wash. "And you exaggerate the discrepancy between our ages."

"Beggin' yer pardon, m'laird." The sneer came through

clearly. "But I recall a day when ye yerself would hae balked at hangin' about wi' a passel o' schoolgirls."

"For your information, Hayden, I am merely performing a favor for the countess, who imagines that fencing lessons will somehow improve Miss Hainesworth's self-esteem."

"A two-month favor?"

Lord Boru took the towel he was belatedly handed and wiped his face. "You know, most servants wouldn't dare question their master's comings or goings."

"One o' us needs t' keep an eye out fer propriety," Hayden muttered darkly.

"Propriety?" Boru stared. "As though there's been anything the least bit improper in my behavior toward Miss Hainesworth!"

"I suppose ye think her parents would approve o' wha' ye 'n' she bae doin'."

Exasperated, Boru flung the towel at him. "As Christiane has explained it, her academy is intended to provide its students with experiences they do not have the opportunity for in more . . . traditional circumstances." His pique burst through. "How the devil should I know what her parents would think? But why should they care? There's nothing wrong in it."

"In a lass wearin' breeches? Plyin' a sword?" Hayden was incredulous. "Against the greatest rakehell that e'er chased skirts in Britain?"

Boru gestured for his shirt. "All that is in the past."

"Oh, aye—'n' wi' women wha' had come o' age. Now ye bae snatchin' conquests out o' th' cradle."

"For your information, I have no intention whatsoever of making a conquest of Miss Hainesworth!" Boru roared, then lowered his voice, recalling the surroundings and the hour.

Hayden shrugged eloquently, turning away to bring His Lordship's breeches. "Aye, well, 'twould nae be much o' a conquest, would it, then? A babe such as that . . ."

Boru swore beneath his breath. "By God, Hayden, one

more such intimation and I'll give you your notice! I'll do it! On my honor, I will!"

Utterly uncowed, the servant knelt to pull the breeches on. "Ye cannae, though, can ye, m'laird?"

"If you mean that antiquated crap about yours being a hereditary position—"

"Four hundred 'n' seventy-eight years," Hayden said with complacence. "That bae how long the men o' my clan hae been aides-de-camp t' the Boru."

"Long enough," Boru snapped, "that I am ready for a change!"

"Yer father, 'n' his father, 'n' his, 'n' his, 'n' his afore him—"

"And I am sure none of your ancestors were so dour and pestilential as you!"

"I only seek t' serve ye as best I can, m'laird. Now that ye bae nae needin' my advice 'n' counsel on th' battlefield, I maun adjust my sights, as 'twere."

"Pray forgive," Brian said through set teeth, "any inconvenience my injury has caused you."

"Well, m'laird. Dinna my father tell me 'twar like a marriage, t' bae born t' serve th' Boru? 'Fer better or worse,' sae he said."

"If you ask me, you're damnably fortunate the post *is* hereditary. Otherwise no man in his right mind would keep you on." Boru glanced at the boots the manservant held. "A bit less meddling in my personal affairs and more attention to my blacking would make you more tolerable."

"I cannae see wha' difference it makes if yer boots bae blacked fer fencin' wi' a *lass*—a *Sasenach* lass." Hayden's disdain was palpable. Lord Brian Boru felt a familiar pounding at his temples as the servant eased him into his boots, first the left, then the right, very gingerly.

"It isn't *Sasenach* anymore, you bigoted prig. She is British. I am British. *You're* British."

"Tell that t' my cousin Feargus, wha' bae turned out o' his croft sae some bludy English laird can graze sheep on it."

The world changes, Boru started to say. *We must change with it. The Scotland you dream of . . .* But Hayden's obstinate expression made him curb his tongue. What use was there in argument? The aide-de-camp had a right to chafe. His ancestors had suited up their Borus for battle, and here was Hayden stuck arraying his lord for tomfoolery such as this.

But it wasn't foolery. Not entirely. Miss Hainesworth might be young, might even be a girl, but she had the makings of a glorious fencer. Brian could hardly believe himself the way she'd taken to the sport. The headlong manner in which she approached it reminded him, quite unexpectedly, of himself, when he'd been young and able. She had a hunger for sport, for competition, as broad as his own. In truth, he'd never met a female like her—and he had known a *lot* of females. He reveled in watching her attain each new step toward mastery, observing how her strong, lithe body responded to his commands—

God. *Was* there something in what Hayden said? Was his vicarious enjoyment sexually charged? *Of course not!* he told himself fiercely. *It is no more than a favor. For Christiane . . .* "Bring my gear," he said shortly, starting toward the door with his canes. He paused, seeing a letter propped up against the cigar tray on the mantel. "What's that?"

"Came fer ye yesterday."

Boru hastily hobbled toward it. "Why the devil didn't you tell me? Dammit, it's from Woffentin, in the regiment!" He tore the missive open. "Bring the lamp here." Hayden did so, and Boru tilted the page toward the light. "Oh, God," he muttered, scanning the first paragraph.

"Ill news, m'laird?"

"Oh, God. Oh, God." Boru was still reading, his fingers clenched on the paper. "Atworth . . . and Smith-Jones . . . oh, God, and Tarkville as well! Damn! Dammit all!" He smashed the letter into a ball and hurled it to the floor.

"Dr. Cohen says, m'laird, that ye maun nae get excited," Hayden murmured.

"To hell with Dr. Cohen. To bloody hell with the whole bloody world." He clenched his eyes shut. "Sweet, brave Tarkville . . ."

"P'raps, m'laird," Hayden said soothingly, "in light o' this sad news, 'twould bae best fer ye t' stay here this mornin', 'n' nae gae t' sae whimsied a pastime as a fencin' lesson wi' a mere bairn. Ye could mourn yer mates properly, wi' a wee dram o' whiskey, a cigar or two. Or better yet, ye could gae on home t' Scotland, 'n' leave bludy England behind ye once 'n' fer all."

Boru glanced up. "By Christ, Hayden, I'd swear you steamed the damned thing open yesterday and left it for me to find this morning just to keep me from that lesson! No! What's done is done. I'm no use to the regiment now, and I'm in no mood to sit in Strathclyde and have a lot of disgruntled Scotsmen calling on me to whine about the Forty-Nine and Bonnie Prince Charlie and what *could* have been. It's not, I'm not, and I may as well do *something*. I cannot *bear* to sit, always to be sitting doing nothing. Bring my gear."

"I still say, m'laird—"

"Bring my gear or I'll sack you, four hundred and seventy-eight years or none!"

Not one whit intimidated, Hayden fetched up the pile of fencing equipment and went to hold the door open for his Boru.

Nichola was in a quandary. The camaraderie she'd seemed to share with Lord Boru on their last outing in the courtyard had vanished completely; this morning, nothing she did pleased him. He shouted and blustered and found fault with her every move. "Supinate that sword hand!" he bellowed at her. "Extend! Extend! Are you a bloody turtle in its shell?" And even worse, with icy irony: "Was that meant to be a *froissement*, Miss Hainesworth? It had all the force of a huswife laying into an apple." She endured the abuse for as long as she could, bolstered by the warmth left over from their prior meeting. But when she executed what she thought was an impeccable low-line *septime* parry, only to have him carp about her footwork, she had had enough. She hurled her blade to the ground.

"There was *nothing* wrong with that parry!" she cried angrily. "Marozzo himself could not have performed it better! What the hell burr is beneath *your* saddle?"

There was a pause. Then he slowly raised up his mask. "I beg your pardon," he said, and the apology was so unexpected that Nichola blinked. "I received word this morning that my regiment—my *former* regiment—has suffered heavy casualties in a battle."

Now it was Nichola's turn to pause and lift up her mask. "I'm so very sorry!" she told him contritely. "What regiment were you with?"

"Crown's Twenty-Fifth."

Nichola went stark white. "Dear God! That is my brother's regiment!"

"Your brother?" Lord Boru stared. "Hainesworth . . . by Christ! You aren't—you must be Tommy Hainesworth's sister! Oh, don't blanch so—he is fine, never fear. My correspondent mentioned it especially."

"Are you sure?"

"Positive." He had not stopped staring. "I cannot believe I didn't make the connection before. You are very like him."

"You mean as tall as him." She went from white to red in an instant.

"Why do you color when you say that?" Lord Boru demanded. "There's naught to be ashamed of in a strong, firm body such as yours."

"Not for a man." She was thinking longingly of Madame's elegant petiteness.

"Not for *anyone*," Lord Boru insisted. "Personally, I am exceedingly nervous around dainty women. Feel like a bull in a china shop—worried I'll break them. But you . . ." He looked her up and down as she stood in her grotesque padding. "Nothing could break you. So you are Tommy Hainesworth's sister!"

"Twin, actually."

"You don't say! You have a number of other brothers serving on the Continent as well, do you not?"

"Five altogether." That, she spoke with pride. "Tommy and I are the youngest. I would be abroad as well, fighting Napoleon, if only I could."

"Oh, no, no. It must afford your poor mother a great deal of ease to know one of her children, at least, is safe from soldiering."

"She'd rather I had been a boy."

"Now, what on earth would make you say that?"

"Oh . . ." Nichola toed the grass. "It is plain enough, from what she named me. She expected a Nicholas. Instead, she got me."

"I think Nichola's a lovely name. Do you know what it means, in Greek? 'Victory of the people.' "

"*Nicholas* does," she objected. " 'Nichola' is just an afterthought."

Lord Boru considered her curiously, his blue eyes dark in the half-light. "I cannot believe any woman would not crave a daughter—for companionship, for comfort."

Hayden cleared his throat meaningfully. "M'laird. If th' lesson bae finished, ye hae best remove fro' this chill mornin' air."

"Shut up, Hayden. Beyond your name, what else makes you think she would have preferred another son?"

"Well . . . not another son, perhaps. But certainly not a daughter like me." She glanced up from beneath lowered lashes. "She is very good, you see, at dancing and fashion and needlework and that sort of thing. Whereas I . . . am only good at manly stuff. Hunting, riding, shooting—"

"Fencing," Lord Boru put in.

"It is kind of you to say so."

"I wouldn't if it weren't true."

"All the same," Nichola said rather plaintively, "I cannot see where it's to get me. I mean, amongst the *ton*. Madame says we are all to pursue what we are best at. But men prefer girls who are . . ."

"Yes?" he prompted.

"You know. Pliant. And dainty."

"Is that the height of your ambition, Miss Hainesworth—to procure a husband?"

"No!" she answered, startled. "I don't want a husband at all! I never have!"

"What *is* your ambition, then?"

"I don't know," she confessed. "For the longest time, it was to join Tommy in the regiment. I had it all planned out—had even borrowed the clothes. But then Madame . . . well, Madame pointed out that it would prove horribly embarrassing to him if I showed up in Flanders."

"Madame is a very wise woman."

Deep in Nichola's heart, a pea-green shoot of jealousy unfurled. "She is also very dainty."

"Christiane is the exception that proves the rule. I never worry about breaking her, either." He grinned. Nichola should have felt heartened. Instead she was discouraged to learn that they were on a first-name basis.

"M'laird," Hayden began again.

"I know, I know. I'll catch a chill if I stay out too long. Is it any wonder, Miss Hainesworth, that in my condition I admire the qualities of strength and robustness in you that you yourself deplore?" He said it jauntily, but she caught the undercurrent of bitterness in his tone.

"You," she said haltingly, "you . . . are everything I ever wished I could be. A great war hero—"

"A vastly overrated condition, in my opinion."

"M'laird—"

But Nichola paid no mind to the glowering Hayden. "Do you mean," she asked intently, "that if you had it to do over again, you wouldn't? Save all those men, I mean? Make the sacrifice?"

He sighed. "No. Of course I would. But that doesn't take away the sting. Especially not when I get word that three of the men I sacrificed my leg *for* are dead now any-way."

"But you're certain Tommy is safe?"

"Absolutely," he assured her, and shook his head, smil-ing. He had a great, blazing smile, and Nichola realized how seldom she had seen it. "Tommy Hainesworth's sister! Talk about your odd coincidence!"

"I shall have to write to him that we are acquainted."

His head jerked up in alarm. "Oh, no. I don't think you should do that."

"Why ever not?"

It was his turn to color. "When I knew your brother . . . I was somewhat roguish."

Nichola snorted. "And what, pray tell, are you now?"

"Somewhat monkish instead." His smile had turned crooked, rueful. "Let's have another go at it, shall we? And I profess my apology. There *was* nothing wrong with your *septime* parry. But you are holding your shoulders all wrong still on the counter-riposte. Come here. Let me show you." She moved to his chair, standing still as stone while he put his hands on her pads to adjust her stance. She clapped down her mask. His touch was as gentle as his voice was gruff, and she wondered suddenly, for no good reason whatsoever, what it would be like to be kissed by him. Beneath the protective muslin and swaddling, her flesh tin-gled under his hands. "There. That's better," he declared with satisfaction. "Do you feel the difference?" Behind her mask, Nichola nodded dumbly. "Good! Come in at me again, then, with that fine *septime*."

She did, but her limbs seemed all like jelly. She tried to summon up the anger she'd felt against him moments be-fore, but it had dissipated, sailed away on the wind like their frozen breath. "M'laird," Hayden began.

Lord Boru nodded. "Quite right. She's weary. Suppose we call it a morning?"

"I can go on," Nichola objected—though she wasn't sure how she would.

"Very well, then. *I'm* weary." He handed his foil to the

servant in exchange for his canes. "Another most rewarding lesson. But you really must not mention me to your brother."

"You could not have been so roguish as that."

"Oh," Lord Boru said, hobbling away, "you might be surprised."

Something odd and disturbing had happened to Nichola, and she could not fathom what it was. Her fencing lessons with Lord Boru had assumed an importance to her all out of proportion to their actual significance. Whatever else she was doing—dining, listening to Bess and Gwen chatter, riding beside Katherine—she found herself dwelling in ridiculous detail on everything that had occurred at their prior bout of instruction, playing over in her mind how he had touched her arm to correct her grip, laughed when she shouted in glee upon landing a touch, raised his wine cup to her in a mocking salute, his blue eyes bright with devilment above the brim. She counted the hours—literally—until her next session with him. And she had the most extraordinary dreams of him. They all began the same way: with the two of them engaged in a fencing bout, Lord Boru seated in his chair. But always, near the end, he would rise up and stand on his own, his mask raised to show his great, broad smile. Nichola would smile back at him, and they would walk toward each other—

Then she would wake up with a jolt, to the gentle sounds of her roommates' breathing and the sigh of the wind and the chill of her pillow pushed half to the floor.

She wished she could talk to someone about her strange feelings. Gwen was the obvious choice, but Nichola still had not forgiven her for telling Katherine her fencing instructor's identity. Bess was too inclined to see romance in everything, and Katherine—well, Katherine had made clear enough her opinion of Lord Boru. Nichola really longed to discuss the matter with Madame, who she was certain knew all there was to know about men and women and what went on between them. She still suspected, though, that Madame had reasons of her own for having sent Brian Boru her way. And Mrs. Treadwell was just out of the question. Had Nichola even broached the subject, the headmistress would have had her embroidering initials on bridal sheets.

Not, Nichola thought wistfully, sitting at yet another of Mrs. Caldburn's interminable lectures and making little sketches on the sheet of paper where she was supposed to be taking notes about the proper fermentation times for small and great beer—*not* that she had any hopes of ever marrying His Lordship. For one thing, he *was* a cripple. And the glimpses she'd had of all that fact entailed, the daily hardships, weren't to be taken lightly. Any woman brave enough to take them on would need to be a saint. When she imagined his life, she saw a daunting sequence of medicines and chamber pots and awkwardnesses over the most common activities. Not to be able to run up a staircase, saddle a horse, ride to the hounds, even stalk with a gun through the fields in autumn was impossibly sad.

There was also the point that she was not a girl he would likely *want* to marry. He must have had *droves* of women chasing after him before he was wounded, and Nichola knew very well the sorts of girls they had been. Dainty, of course—despite his bluster about breaking them—and gorgeous, and witty and clever. The belles of the ball. The kind who tittered at her when she stood up in their company, or whispered cruelly when she clumped across a drawing-room floor.

No. Lord Boru put up with her in the same way her brothers' friends had, because she was a sport, because she strove to beat them at their own games, because she had a keen eye and a reckless seat and could be counted on for fun. But he would no more think of courting her than any of them had, because—

"What *are* you writing?" Bess whispered from the seat beside her.

Nichola glanced down at the paper, upon which she'd

made a looping sequence of B's joined together. His initials:
Brian Boru. Brian Boru . . . "Nothing," she murmured
back, moving her arm to shield the page. "Just letters. Mrs.
Treadwell has been chastising me about my penmanship."
To drive the point home, she began a series of C's.

"Did you have a question, Miss Boggs?" Mrs.
Caldburn demanded from her podium.

"Yes, I did. It concerned what you'd said about the
percentage of hops affecting the fermentation cycle. But
Miss Hainesworth answered it."

"Very good, Miss Hainesworth! They say, you know,
that beer is the life's blood of an English estate. Why, I
recall one dreadful occasion when Lady Cuthbertson inad-
vertently failed to oversee the proper preparation of Tilbert
Manor's autumn brewing."

"What happened?" Gwen asked curiously.

"They were forced to import from Belgium—at *blockade* prices," Mrs. Caldburn confided, her arched brows indicating just how shameful this calamity had been.

Afterward, in the corridor, Nichola and Bess and
Gwen laughed together at their instructress's horror. "Oh,
it is easy enough for the three of you to sneer," Katherine
said tartly, glowering at a cluster of younger students running past them. "But I find Mrs. Caldburn's lessons highly
valuable. Of course, *I* intend to marry well."

"We all wish you would," Gwen said earnestly, "and
soon." Which launched the threesome into another burst of
giggles. Katherine glared and moved past them, with her
haughty-Spanish-queen mien.

"I cannot for the life of me figure her out," Bess whispered. "Why, if I had her looks and her money—not to
mention that impeccable social standing—I'd be relishing
the season in London, not sequestered here studying beer!"

"And why do you suppose," Gwen added, "those parents she adores so pay no mind to the tons of letters she
writes them, imploring them to remove her from our
plebian presence?"

They both were looking at Nichola, who'd been remembering how when Lord Boru had lifted his mask at the finish of their lesson that morning, a bead of sweat had hung just above his eyebrow, like a bright salt pearl. She'd had the most absurd impulse to put her tongue to it and taste it. . . .

She recollected herself. "I haven't any idea. But I think she must be terribly unhappy."

Gwen and Bess both hooted. "Unhappy?" Bess cried. "She has *everything*! Why on earth should she be?"

Nichola paused. "She hasn't got love," she said finally.

"She loves herself enough to more than make up for that," Bess said mercilessly.

"I only hope," Gwen put in, "she will procure herself a suitor at our visit to the countess of Yarlborough's, and marry him instantly."

"*What* visit to the countess of Yarlborough's?" Nichola asked, alarmed.

"Where on earth have you been lately, Nick?" Bess shook her head in amazement. "Mrs. Treadwell told us all at supper last night. We are invited for the Easter holiday."

Nichola groaned. "Oh, God. Not again!"

"And that's not all," Bess confided. "Our mothers are to be invited, too."

"Our *mothers*?" Nichola's voice was so horrified that Gwen laughed.

"Well, those of us that have them. I imagine Mrs. Treadwell will invite my father. He, of course, will be too busy to attend."

"I won't go," Nichola announced.

"Oh, but you must!" Gwen cried out. "How could I face all that without you there?"

"Besides," Bess added practically, "this time, I gather attendance is required. It's a sort of evaluation of our progress so far. To assure the parents their tuition monies are being well spent."

"So gird yourself," Gwen advised. "It will be our first real taste of battle."

"I ought to have gone to Flanders while I had the

chance," Nichola muttered, and headed down the stairs to tea in a true blue funk.

"Reprehensible," Lord Boru declared as Nichola attempted a *trompe*. "A child of four would not be fooled by that. Do it again." She did. He sighed. "Worse still. Whatever *is* the matter with you this morning, Miss Hainesworth?"

"Nothing," she muttered, but her posture and stance belied the words.

"You are *drooping*," His Lordship told her, sounding perplexed. "I have never seen you droop before. Are you ill?"

"No."

"In love?"

She jerked her head up. "Certainly not!"

"Well, other than illness or love, which is its own form of malady, I cannot imagine what else might turn a tigress into a slinking barn cat."

Nichola glanced away from him across the courtyard. The first soft fingertips of spring had been at work there, greening the dull brown grass, raising jonquil trumpets around the fountain, glazing the ivy on the walls with a fresh new sheen. The rough wind at moments bore a tantalizing hint of future balmy breezes, and the sky above them was cloudless, the dawn breaking in a great crest of undimmed gold. He waited patiently, his foil at rest. "Very well," she said at last, gracelessly. "If you must know, we are all going to Mrs. Treadwell's daughter's again at Easter. And my mother is to be invited."

"I see," he said, his voice deep and grave from behind his mask.

"No, you don't see at *all*. How could you possibly?"

"I do have a mother, you know."

"Not like mine. And anyway, you're a man. It is different for men."

"What is different, precisely?"

"*Everything*," Nichola said in misery. She floundered for an example. "Does your mother tell you that you *clump*?"

"Not these days," said Lord Boru with a wisp of humor.

Nichola blushed behind her mask. "I beg your pardon. That was thoughtless of me."

He lifted his blade. "Miss Hainesworth. Kindly execute an advance." Sighing, she did. "And retreat. Advance. Advance. Retreat. Now, double change! Retreat. Triple change!" She followed his instructions, and though her heart wasn't in it, footwork by now was such second nature that her motions flowed of their own accord. Lord Boru nodded approval. "I don't think even the most critical observer could accuse you of clumping just then."

"But fencing is entirely different."

"How so?"

"When I am fencing, it is only me and my opponent. I haven't got a ballroom full of people looking on!"

"Perhaps you might pretend the ballroom is a fencing strip."

"I should look even more ridiculous then."

"I don't mean literally. But figuratively. If you—"

"M'laird," Hayden broke in from the sideline. "Dr. Cohen says ye bae sure to catch an ague if ye—"

"Shut up, Hayden. I am talking to Miss Hainesworth. Let us imagine, Miss Hainesworth, you are approached by a gentleman."

"I never am approached by gentlemen."

"But if you should be. For argument's sake. And suppose he strikes up a conversation."

"Beyond the realm of imagining."

"Why do you put yourself down so? Here." He removed his mask and let it drop to the grass. "Take yours off as well." Dubiously, she obeyed. "Now. Close your eyes for a moment. Imagine we are in the countess of Yarlborough's ballroom. And I walk up to you—I said this would take imagination—and I say, 'How do you do?' What is your reply?"

"I—I don't know. 'How do you do,' I suppose."

He shook his head. "No, no. That's the equivalent of a straight parry and riposte. Is such a move likely to make your opponent think you worthy?"

"He isn't my oppo—"

"Of course he is! That is all social give-and-take consists of, Miss Hainesworth—a verbal fencing match. You want to keep your opponent guessing, off-guard, intrigued. What other response might you make to a straight parry?"

"Retreat," she said with a flash of irony.

"Come, come, Miss Hainesworth."

"The *gagner la mesure*?"

"Very good! To gain distance—to advance! Now, how might you do that?"

She contemplated it. "Perhaps—make some comment on the surroundings?"

"Such as what?"

Nichola put her arms behind her back, eyes downcast. " 'How do you do?' " she mumbled. " 'The music is very . . . musical, is it not?' "

"Miss Hainesworth." He glared at her ferociously. "A *worthy* opponent, I said!"

"Shall I say what I think, then? 'Have you ever in your life attended such a dreary gathering?' There—how is that?"

"Better," he acknowledged. "At least it shows spirit. And now I, your opponent, reply: 'I thought so, dear lady, until I found you here.' "

" 'Oh, for heaven's sake. What slosh.' "

"Very good, Miss Hainesworth!"

She stared at him. "You cannot be serious!"

"Of course I am! You just executed the verbal equivalent of a point in line! You are forcing your opponent—"

"I *do* wish you'd stop using that term."

"To notice you. To take you into account."

"But what I said was rude."

"What you said was what any thinking person feels at a large social affair."

"Really?" she asked dubiously.

"Of course! And your opponent's response will now tell you in turn whether *he* is worthy. Should I raise my brows—" He did. "And look offended—" He did, very much so. "And huff, 'I beg your pardon; I've mistaken you for someone else,' then you know perfectly well the match with him isn't going anywhere at all." She started to speak. He held up a hand to forestall her. "*If,* however, his reply is, 'God, isn't it the truth? But I was brought up to believe all ladies like hearing that sort of nonsense'—well! Then, you are getting someplace!"

"No gentleman would ever say that," Nichola protested.

"*I* would," he countered. "And anyway, how will you ever know if you don't even try? So, suppose I do agree with you that I've been talking nonsense. What would you say then?"

"I would say, 'What in God's name ever made you approach me in the first place?' "

"And I'd boldly advance. I'd say, 'I think you are the most beautiful girl I have ever seen.' "

" 'Oh, really!' " Nichola cried. " 'That is beyond imagining!' "

"And then I'd say, 'Would you do me the honor of dancing with me?' "

"And I'd refuse."

"Why?"

She tilted her head at him. "Are you in character now, as my opponent, or just asking?"

"Either way. The former, I suppose."

"I'd say I am a terrible dancer."

"I cannot believe that."

"It is true. You need only ask Monsieur Albert. He tells me so all the time."

"No, no. As your opponent, I say, 'I cannot believe that.' "

Nichola paused again to think. " 'Then I shall prove it to you.' "

"Oh, very good, Miss Hainesworth! Very good indeed!"

She colored at his praise. "Well. It seems to me the only honest thing to do. If this hapless, deluded gentleman truly does find me attractive, one circle of the floor ought to bring him up hard against reality."

"M'laird," Hayden said plaintively from the shadows, "th' ague—"

Lord Boru ignored him. "So! I lead you out onto the floor, and we dance. And you discover I am positively abysmal—clumsy beyond imagining. I tread upon your toes. I rip your hem. While effecting a twirl, I knock Mrs. Treadwell on her bum." Nichola burst out giggling. "I like that! Very natural, that giggle! All around us on the floor, I create havoc. The music, blessedly, ends. Then I, your eager swain, clutch your hands, unwilling to release you." He grabbed Nichola's wrists. " 'My sweetest dove,' " he murmured, pulling her closer. " 'That was divine. Shall we do it again?' " He looked up at her from his chair. "Your turn."

" 'Dear sir,' " Nichola began, still bubbling with laughter. " 'Clearly, we must leave for Gretna Green at once. It is obvious we are destined for each other.' "

Lord Boru nodded in satisfaction. "I signal for my carriage, and we elope, to live happily ever after. End of bout. *Touché.*" He gave her hands a little squeeze and released them.

Nichola stopped laughing. "It doesn't happen that way."

"M'laird, ye maun nae," Hayden began, with mounting insistence.

"No. It doesn't," Lord Boru acknowledged. "But you must keep in mind that everybody, everywhere, always feels just as awkward and uncertain as you do."

"Nonsense," said Nichola, thinking of Katherine.

"Well, almost everybody. Anyone who is a worthy opponent. Who is intelligent and sensitive and kind. Self-consciousness is part and parcel of the human condition. And those who . . . who laugh at others, make untoward remarks . . . they are only trying to fight down their own feelings of unworthiness."

She looked at him. His blue eyes were burning with intensity. *How does he know?* she wondered. *It was just such sensations that made me speak so unkindly to him that first night we met. . . .* "Were you always this wise?" she asked softly.

"I like to think so. But I used to hide it exceedingly well. Now . . ." He gestured to his knee. "Now there's no point in dissembling. That is the one—the *only*—gain I've found in having suffered this. Miss Hainesworth—"

"It bae time t' leave," Hayden announced in a brook-no-argument tone.

"Somewhere out there," Lord Boru went on, as the servant raised him up from his chair, "lies a worthy opponent for you. But you never will find him if you go on avoiding the fray."

Nichola bent down for her discarded foil. "Will—will you be there? At the countess of Yarlborough's?"

"Of course I will. What master would miss his star pupil's first real match?"

"I hope I won't disgrace you."

"As do I. Just remember, Miss Hainesworth—it is nothing but a fencing bout."

Chapter
Twelve

Upstairs at Yarlborough House, Nichola glanced over Katherine's shoulder to see into the pier glass. "You look positively radiant, Nick," Bess told her earnestly. "Do move aside, Katherine, so she can see. Is that a new gown?"

"Mother sent it," Nichola said with a grimace. "Madame helped me to remove about a thousand yards of frills and lace and artificial roses. She says I ought to dress like a Grecian—simple and plain."

"It *is* simple and plain," Gwen noted, "and it is also stunning."

Since Katherine wasn't sharing, Nichola turned around. "You both look lovely as well. Bess, I adore what you've done with your hair."

The redhead reached up self-consciously to pat her artfully arranged curls. "Madame says it is my best feature."

"She's quite right," Katherine announced. Her formmates goggled at her elegant back, wondering what might have impelled this unprecedented compliment. Then Katherine went on: "In fact, it is your only good feature."

"Thank heavens!" Gwen cried. "For a moment there, I feared you'd been taken over by a döppelganger."

"A what?"

"An evil twin. Only in *your* case, one would have to say a kindly twin." Nichola and Bess laughed outright. Katherine merely adjusted her gorgeous sapphire neckpiece to her satisfaction and at long last moved.

"Since there are certain to be a few fellows present tonight without either titles or fortunes," she said blandly, "I suppose all this bother you three have gone to won't be entirely wasted. If you'll excuse me now, the countess has requested particularly that I help her to receive guests." She waved her hand and glided toward the door in her breathtaking blue charmeuse gown.

"I don't wonder," Bess muttered when she was gone. "They are two of a kind, the countess and she. Hard to fathom how that Vanessa could be our Mrs. Treadwell's daughter." She took a deep breath, then a step toward the mirror. "Shall we?" The three girls joined arms and stood nervously before the looking glass.

"Could be worse," Gwen said cheerily, staring at their reflections.

"Could be better." Bess's voice was glum. "I look fat. I *am* fat."

"Nonsense!" Gwen assured her. "You are fleshy. Like a Rubens. Lots of men like a bit of meat on the bone."

"How would you know?"

"The admiral always says so. When he's trying to get me to eat. At least you have got a bosom."

"That's my corset," Bess confided. "Some contraption Madame lent me. Pushes them out and up, she said. I can scarcely breathe. Still . . ." She twisted for a side view. "I *have* got a bosom, haven't I? I shall have to make the most of that." She strutted across the room with her breasts thrust out like a figurehead.

"Men will be presenting themselves to *them* five minutes before they ever meet you," Gwen noted drolly. "You're awfully quiet, Nick."

"Mm? Oh. Just thinking." She'd been wishing, in point of fact, that the gown her mother had bought her hadn't been white. Lord Boru only ever saw her in white—the color of her pads. Still, the makeover Madame had effected was becoming. The diaphanous orange-blossom sarsenet was shirred at the shoulders and across the bodice, then fell away from the Empire bodice in a great snowy sweep over a satin underskirt. She wore simple gold hoops in her ears, and a gold chain with a rosy cameo; the burnished metal played up the golden gleam in her brown eyes. Her thick, fair hair was drawn back into a heavy chignon that left her throat bare. The image that stared back at her was surprisingly elegant and lovely—and impossibly tall. She sighed.

Gwen caught her hand. "Come along. We mustn't leave dear Katherine alone down there with the young men, or Mrs. Treadwell's academy will acquire a dreadful reputation for snobbery."

"May as well get it over with," Bess said philosophically. "Then we can all go home to the abbey and have some *fun*."

Naturally, the first person Nichola saw as they entered the ballroom was her mother, looking petite and polished, as always. "Yoo-hoo! Nichola!" she cried upon glimpsing her daughter, and waved her dainty handkerchief in signal. "Over here!"

"We'll come with you," Bess whispered in support, and together they surged forward across the gleaming parquet floor.

"Mother," said Nichola. "Permit me to present to you my friends, Miss Boggs and Miss Carstairs."

"Charmed," the baroness said automatically. "Where is the dress I sent you, Nichola?"

"This *is* the dress you sent me."

"It most certainly is not! That one had Irish lace here and here, and a cascade of roses—"

"I had it made over," Nichola said nervously, "on the advice of Madame."

"On the advice of *whom*? I'll have you know that lace cost ten shillings the yard! And the roses were—"

"Lady Hainesworth!" Nichola saw with relief that Mrs. Treadwell was rushing to their side. "How positively *divine* you look this evening!" the headmistress said swiftly. "Your gown *must* be the work of Madame Descoux. No one else in England has her hand with silk."

"Oh, you know me too well, Mrs. Treadwell! But I quite agree; she is a miracle worker. If only this wretched blockade did not prevent her from importing from Nice, as in the old days."

Mrs. Treadwell winked. "Now, now, you cannot fool me! That silk is French, or I'm a babe in arms!"

The baroness colored prettily. "Well, I must confess— for certain of her *longtime* clients, Madame has shown great resourcefulness in acquiring stuffs."

"Did you happen to notice," Mrs. Treadwell murmured, drawing Nichola's mother aside conspiratorially, "that Lady Despenser is here?"

"No! Really? Where?" The baroness brought up her lorgnette to survey the crowd.

"And you'll never guess with whom!"

"*Don't* tell me. Anthony Darlington. Am I right? Oh, I knew it! I heard rumors about them all winter in London! Do you know, they say she—" The baroness broke off, noticing Nichola and her companions listening avidly. "Do run along, girls, for heaven's sake, and amuse yourselves! Can't you see we are talking?"

"Yes, Mother," Nichola murmured—and saw Mrs. Treadwell drop her a sidelong wink as she rushed away.

"So that is your mother," Gwen observed, as Nichola practically dragged her to the opposite side of the room.

"That's the baroness," Nichola confirmed, but rather happily, now that she'd been sprung from her clutches.

"There is mine! And my father!" Bess cried, waving at her parents. "Do let me introduce you." Mr. and Mrs.

Boggs were quiet and well-mannered and seemed a bit adrift in the glittering crowd. It was plain to see where Bess had gotten her red hair—her father had a great shock of it, swept back from his brow—as well as her figure. Her mother was small and plump, just like her daughter. But there was undisguised warmth in their greeting of Bess, with hugs and kisses all around, and Nichola felt a pang, observing the cozy threesome they made. Bess was burbling tales of her lessons and life at the academy; after a bit, Mrs. Boggs laughed and said that Nichola and Gwen must have better things to do than listen to a recitation of events they had already lived through, so why didn't they mingle? Nichola was inclined to linger within that unfamiliar circle of familial bliss, but Gwen announced she was dying of thirst and tugged her off to the wine table, where she secured them each a glass of champagne.

"I've never had champagne before," Nichola said doubtfully.

"Nor have I. But Madame told me how they get the bubbles into it. Quite an amazing process. Its discovery is ascribed to a monk, Dom Perignon, who managed the cellars of the abbey of Haut Villers. It is said that he also invented the use of the cork as a bottle stop. He—"

"I do beg your pardon," said a smooth male voice at Nichola's back. She stepped to the side, assuming she was blocking someone's access to the table. But Gwen's eyes had widened, and she made a little motion of her head, indicating that Nichola should turn. She did, and saw standing before her the most elegantly got-up gentleman she had ever encountered in her life. He wore an olive-green superfine coat, well padded at the shoulders; close-fitting chamois pantaloons tucked into Hessians that positively gleamed; and a fine linen shirt finished off with a Belcher necktie in the most astonishing cascade. His black hair was cut in a Stanhope crop, and he had a short, pointed beard. His eyes were brown and close-set, his nose a perfect aquiline. He also barely came up to Nichola's ears. "I know we have not been properly introduced," he went on, his voice at once apologetic and winning. "But I trust you will forgive the impertinence. I simply *had* to learn the identity of the countess's most beautiful guest."

Nichola hurriedly stepped aside in the assumption he meant Gwen, who did indeed look very fetching in her copper-colored jaconet, with her dark curls tumbling around her small, winsome face. "This is Miss Carstairs," she pronounced, falling into the role of doyenne. "Miss Carstairs, I have the honor of presenting—"

"Lord Wallingford," the young man said politely, kissing Gwen's hand. "My great pleasure." But the rapidity with which he turned back to Nichola gave her pause. "And you are . . . ?"

"Miss Hainesworth," she confessed.

"Miss Hainesworth!" The kiss he lavished on her hand was lingering. "What a great, great delight to hear you speak your lovely name."

"Oh, really," she murmured in embarrassment—then realized with shock that *she* was the one he'd been so anxious to meet. Not sure what else to do, she took a heady sip from her champagne glass. The bubbles tickled so, she very nearly snorted the wine out through her nose. Keeping it in forced her to cough, quite heartily.

"Ah, champagne!" declared Lord Wallingford, taking a glass himself from the table and tipping it to hers. "What more perfect beverage to accompany an introduction to the girl of my dreams?" He touched the flute to Nichola's and gave her a dazzling smile.

"If you will excuse me," Gwen said brightly, "I was just on my way to find Lady Devereaux." Nichola shot her a look of abject alarm, but her friend simply smiled and extended her hand to Lord Wallingford again. "*Such* a pleasure," she cooed.

"Gwen," Nichola began, but she was off, disappearing amidst the throng. With a sense of dread, Nichola turned back to the young man at her side.

His dark eyes surveyed her from head to toe, with such attention that she wanted to die. "When last I was in Austria," he told her, "I read the stories of the Valkyries. You know of the Valkyries?"

"I cannot say that I do," said Nichola, and gulped more champagne.

"The warrior-maidens," he went on intently, "who ride through the air in the service of Odin, lord of all the gods. They determine the course of battles. They dress in full armor. You, dear lady, are a Valkyrie." He swept her a bow. "Honor me. Fulfill my dreams. Dance with me."

Nichola was struck dumb by his intensity, the fierce longing in his words—not that she believed them for a minute. Just then the music stopped. To gain a moment's thinking space, she gazed over his shoulder—over his head, actually—to the ballroom beyond. Her attention was caught by a familiar ruddy face contemplating her and her companion from a distance—Lord Boru, seated on the sidelines in his velvet chair. Of course. He must have arranged this somehow, convinced Lord Wallingford to court her in order to put her to the test, see if she could rise to the occasion. Why, even Wallingford's words—*the countess's most beautiful guest*—echoed their banter at their last fencing lesson. She flushed suddenly. What had he done—paid this Wallingford fellow off? *He never thought I had any hope of attracting male attention without his intervention,* she realized in humiliation. Was it a fencing bout he wanted to witness? Then, by Christ, she would give him one!

"I am not much of a dancer, Lord Wallingford," she said, meaning it to come out crisply, but her voice was made low and hesitant by her shame.

"I cannot believe it. How could that be so when you are a Valkyrie, handmaiden to the gods?"

Across the room, Brian Boru's blue eyes were still trained on her. Nichola threw caution to the wind. "But you must not say I did not warn you," she told Wallingford as she let him lead her onto the floor.

Within the space of five measures, Nichola had discovered a great truth: Dancing was relatively easy when one had an expert in the lead. And Lord Wallingford was without doubt the most accomplished dancer she had ever known. The difference between taking a turn with him and with, say, Gwen, in the person of the man, or even Monsieur Albert, was incalculable. His firm hand at her waist positively forbade mistakes; he signaled with his body precisely what he would do next, and she had only to follow. For the first time in her life, she did not feel a clod on the dancing floor. With him to guide her, she steered without mishap through an entire waltz—and even found herself, against all odds, enjoying the experience. "You are a most remarkable dancer," she told Lord Wallingford as he spun her about.

"I am inspired by my partner," he said, so gravely that she colored again. "God," he whispered, "I love it when you blush."

Nichola felt dizzy—and not only from the dancing. When the set was finished, Lord Wallingford bowed, she curtsied, and he proposed: "Another? Or perhaps you would care for more champagne?"

"I say, Wallingford." A tall, blond fellow in a tight blue coat had come up beside them. "How about an introduction?"

"Not a chance," Lord Wallingford replied, tucking Nichola's hand into his.

"Wallingford!" Another young man hailed them as they stood. "Would you mind presenting—"

"Go to hell," said Wallingford, his grip tightening on Nichola's arm. He gazed up at her, his dark eyes intent. "What will it be, then, Valkyrie? Champagne, or dancing?"

"Anthony Wallingford!" a voice cried eagerly. "Do share the wealth! Who is your extremely fetching partner?" This fellow, Nichola saw, had been dancing with Katherine, and had left her standing alone to accost them.

"That is for me to know and for you to find out," said Wallingford, his eyes still on Nichola.

"I think . . . that I should like some air," she said faintly.

He smiled. "My sentiments exactly." And he led her eagerly through the press to the French doors that opened onto the terrace. On their way, they passed close by Lord Boru's velvet chair. Nichola raised her downcast gaze to glare at him for his trickery. But the expression on his face gave her pause. He looked rather the way he was wont when she had deflected his best lunge. Raising her chin—perhaps he had not thought she would acquit herself so well?—she breezed past him and onto the terrace without a backward glance.

The night air was cold. Impulsively Nichola wrapped her arms around herself. "Take my coat," Lord Wallingford urged, and removed it to drape the cloth across her shoulders.

"Tell me," she said dryly. "Are you very good friends with Lord Boru?"

"Lord Brian Boru?" In the moonlight, she saw his perplexed expression. "Why—no. I scarcely know the man. Why do you ask?"

"No reason," she replied coolly. If he was a liar, he was a good one. His coat smelled of sandalwood and patchouli; she liked the fragrance. "Do you fence, Lord Wallingford?"

"I have some acquaintance with the foil." Now he looked even more nonplussed. Then his brow cleared. "Do you intend to incite me to a duel in your defense this evening? I should have to challenge any comer, you know, who tried to take you away from me."

Nichola laughed. "Of course I don't! But you must not be so possessive. We *have* only just met."

"I have been waiting for you for a lifetime, though," he said, so reverently that she caught her breath. He moved closer to her on the flagstones, and his arm tentatively encircled her waist. "Would you take offense, Miss Hainesworth, if I kissed you?"

She cocked her head, uncertain how to respond. She

never had been kissed, and she was naturally curious. At the same time, Mrs. Treadwell's warnings about the need for a girl to protect her reputation rang in her head. If this unlikely suitor *had* been put up to it by Lord Boru, she wouldn't want him telling any tales. Or would she?

As she hesitated, he stood watching her, his dark eyes burning. "You think me too forward," he said quietly. "You think rightly. Forgive me. You are so very lovely that you go to my head, like strong drink. Come, then. We'll go in. But you must promise to dance with me again."

Through the French doors beyond his shoulder, Nichola could see Lord Boru's chair. He had shifted in it, gazing out at them. What the devil did he expect to see? She wondered suddenly if he and this Lord Wallingford might have some sort of wager riding on her comportment this evening. She'd heard her brothers and their friends laugh and jest about such things often enough—and she had laughed and jested with them, secure in her knowledge that she would never be the victim of that kind of bet.

A gilded couple strolled past Lord Boru, obscuring his view of Nichola and Lord Wallingford. Impulsively she smiled at her companion. He had made her feel graceful and elegant and desired, even if it was only in fun, and she was grateful for that. "You ought not to have spoken up so quickly, milord. I was on the verge of submitting."

"You were?" He returned the smile. He was really very handsome, Nichola decided. "Damn my sense of propriety, anyway! Is it too late to recant?"

A fencing bout, Nichola thought giddily. This was rather amusing. "You should have to decide for yourself about that." She was rather proud of her riposte—it was sure to give him pause.

It didn't. He promptly caught her to him and touched his mouth to hers.

My first kiss, Nichola was thinking, even as the pressure of his arm around her tightened, as she felt his mustache tickling her nose. His lips were warm and eager, and he smelled even better close up. Pity he was so short. But, oh, the kiss was lovely! He was as accomplished at that as he had been at dancing. He put his hand to her cheek, cupping it, smoothing its softness, while he drank in the taste of her mouth with a long, low sigh. When he finally released her, Nichola's knees were trembling. And she had quite forgotten Lord Brian Boru.

"Angel," the man before her whispered. "Precious, precious angel. The way you looked just then . . . I will carry the memory with me to the day I die. It will be the last image in my conscious mind before I pass on. And I will meet death happy."

"Gracious!" Nichola said. Just then, she caught a glimpse of Mrs. Treadwell's worried face in the doors. The headmistress saw her, and her brows arched in abrupt alarm; she yanked for the knob.

"Nichola!" she cried. "Whatever are you—" Lord Wallingford turned, following Nichola's wide eyes, and hastily made a bow.

"Mrs. Treadwell! What a distinct pleasure. I had the immense honor of dancing with Miss Hainesworth, here— and may I add, she does your academy a great deal of credit—when she professed to feeling faint. I thought perhaps the night air might prove curative. And so it has." He gave Nichola a little nudge, and she started forward, still dreamy with the sensation of that silken kiss.

"I see! It is fortunate for you, Wallingford, that I know you as a gentleman! Nonetheless, Nichola, it is time you came in."

Lord Wallingford took his coat from her shoulders, his fingertips lingering for an instant against her bare neck, making her tingle. Mrs. Treadwell no longer looked alarmed; in fact, she seemed as complacent as a hen. "Shame on you, Wallingford," she scolded Nichola's escort, but gaily, teasingly. "Can you not even wait until the young lady has debuted?"

"How dare I?" Wallingford replied, his voice also light. But the hand with which he gripped Nichola's elbow was firm and forceful. "I simply could not risk her losing her heart to another fellow when she has so thoroughly captured mine."

Mrs. Treadwell bestowed on Nichola an altogether new look—one of unmeasured approval. "Come, both of you," she insisted, holding the door open for them. "It's plain I cannot in good conscience permit you to remain alone together."

"Nichola," Lord Wallingford whispered as they made their way past her into the brightness of the ballroom. "What an exquisite name."

"You cannot truly think so."

But he seemed to; he was trying it out on his tongue. "Nichola. Nichola. Nichola, will you?"

"Will I what?" she asked, startled.

"Dance with me again. Say yes now, before the vultures descend."

"The vultures . . ." With astonishment, Nichola saw that a thicket of young men was moving toward them, all with identical hopeful expressions. She bit back her laughter. "Of course I will."

"You have made me the happiest man on earth," he murmured in her ear. They took their places for the next set as the other gentlemen faded back, grumbling audibly. Nichola felt she must be in a dream.

And then she knew she was. For as Wallingford grasped her waist and set her hand to his, she saw Lord Boru signal to Hayden where the servant stood behind his chair. Hayden fetched the canes, and in the full view of all the assembly, Lord Boru struggled to his feet, teetered a moment, found his balance, and then hobbled awkwardly from the hall.

The remainder of the evening was a blur of delight. After their next set of dances, Lord Wallingford was required by etiquette—not to mention the clamoring of his competitors—to release Nichola. She waltzed and minueted and quadrilled with any number of young men, none of whom held a candle to Wallingford in expertise; several apologized to *her* for their deficiencies! There was a gratifying tussle over who would fetch her champagne when she expressed that she was thirsty, and another when supper was announced. Lord Wallingford proved victor in that one. He simply sailed up to her through the press and offered her his arm; she accepted it with a curtsy. And they strolled off to the tables, leaving protests of unfairness in their wake.

Lord Wallingford made sure she had everything she desired from the compotes and chafing dishes before settling in beside her. If Lord Boru *had* put him up to this, Nichola thought, he could not have made a better choice. Wallingford's attentions had instantly made her the object of envy; she could see it in the eyes of the girls around them. "Now," her companion said, moving his chair so close that his thigh brushed hers, "we shall have a chance to get to know one another, Nichola. Tell me about yourself. Tell me *everything*."

Nichola, eyes downcast, could feel herself blushing. "There really isn't much to say. . . ."

"What do you like to do?"

"Well . . ." She hesitated. This, of course, was where she would lose this wondrous young man's affections. She contemplated lying, going on about music or embroidery. But the way he looked at her, as though she were some magical, enchanted creature, gave her pause. If it *was* all to end, best get it over with now. "I am very fond of riding."

"*Are* you! Splendid!"

Taken aback, she blinked. "And—and hunting."

"Nothing I enjoy better than a good, hard ride to the hounds!" he declared, and took a bite of crimped cod. "There's to be a hunt tomorrow, you know. Are you riding?"

"I—I hadn't thought about it."

"Oh, we *must* hunt together, you and I! Say that you will. There must be something in Yarlborough's stables worthy of you. I'll see to it, shall I?"

Nichola hesitated. "I—no doubt this will shock you, but—"

"Shock me," he murmured, and his hand covered hers beneath the edge of the tablecloth.

"Well—at the academy, we are taught to ride sidesaddle. But I do much, much better astride. It is because I grew up riding with my brothers," she added hastily, certain he would be horrified. "And somehow I just—"

"In breeches?" Lord Wallingford asked, his dark eyes positively aglow. She confirmed it with an embarrassed nod. "God! How I should love to see you in breeches!"

"Lord Wallingford!"

"I beg your pardon. Too forward again. But see what it gained me the last time?" He grinned rakishly, and Nichola felt a flutter in her heart. Oh, it was too much to expect, that he might understand her! Farther up the table, she saw her mother staring at her—at *them*—with the most amazing expression on her face. It was so unexpected that it took Nichola several moments to identify it. *Pride.* That was what the baroness was feeling. Pride—in her. Under the table, Lord Wallingford's hand squeezed hers intently. "I was wrong. You are not a Valkyrie at all; you are Diana, the huntress. Tomorrow, you must ride astride."

"Oh, I couldn't. It would cause a dreadful to-do."

"It would in my heart."

Nichola blushed. "And I haven't any breeches with me," she added.

"I would be thrilled to have you borrow mine."

She looked at him—looked *down* at him. Didn't he realize they likely would be too small? She couldn't think how to explain her dilemma. Instead she said softly, "Mrs. Treadwell would never allow it. If I am to accompany you, it must be sidesaddle. I merely wanted to explain—I will not be at my best."

"You told me you couldn't dance," he pointed out. "Yet I found you a most devastating partner."

"That was all due to your prowess," she said truthfully.

"I prefer to think it is because we make a perfect

match." He shot her a devastating grin. "Are you not going to eat?"

Nichola glanced down at the plate he had so thoughtfully filled for her. She was very hungry suddenly. She speared a stuffed mushroom and brought it to her mouth, then realized with horror that she ought to have cut it up instead.

But Lord Wallingford's dark eyes never altered in their adoration. "I love a girl of appetite," he murmured, his fingers curling around hers. "Indeed, Miss Hainesworth, I fear I am utterly enamored of you."

"Well!" Gwen declared, as she and Bess and Nichola climbed wearily up to their rooms in the thin light of dawn. "Don't get me wrong, Nick—I always knew you were a wonderful catch for any man with sense in his head. But still—Lord Wallingford!"

Nichola's feet were aching, but it was a delicious ache. "I don't have the slightest notion who he is," she confessed.

They both turned to stare. "You must be joking," Bess exclaimed. "He is the most eligible bachelor in all of England!"

"Why?"

Bess waved a hand. "Where shall I begin? His exquisite manners? His irreproachable wardrobe? His cunning and wit?"

"Or," Gwen put in dryly, "his fifty thousand a year."

"No!" Nichola gasped.

"He is the duke of Strafford's only son."

"Then wouldn't he be called Strafford?" Nichola asked in puzzlement.

"Don't you pay any attention whatsoever to Mrs. Caldburn's lectures?" Gwen demanded.

"Of course not. What do I care about bleaching sheets?"

"She is also an invaluable source of information on eligible bachelors," Bess informed her.

"Your mother seemed happy with you at supper," Gwen interjected shrewdly.

Nichola yawned. "She did, didn't she?"

"I overheard her telling Mrs. Treadwell how exceedingly pleased she was with your progress at the academy." Gwen hesitated. "In fact, she said she didn't see any reason why you should finish out the term."

Nichola stopped in mid-step. "Oh, God! Why not?"

Gwen shrugged. "As I recall, her precise words were, 'If she can capture Wallingford now, best to strike while the iron is hot.'"

"I've only just met the man tonight!"

"He is exceedingly handsome," Bess said with a sigh.

"He is also short."

Gwen shushed them with her hand; they were approaching the door to the bedroom. "Katherine's already inside," she whispered. "Went up with a sick headache."

"If you ask *me,*" said Bess, "she went up with a hard case of the jealousies at Nichola's success." Gwen laughed, but quickly stifled it. "And anyway, Nick, so what if he is short? You are tall. Surely you of all folk wouldn't hold an accident of birth against him."

"No," she said slowly. "Of course not." Would she? Did it matter, when he had made her feel so cherished, so appreciated? Gwen opened the door, and they tiptoed in.

"I intend to sleep until noon at least," Bess mumbled wearily, as Nichola untied her tapes. "Or perhaps one o'clock. Kind of you, Nick, to steer your disappointed suitors toward us."

"I did no such thing." But she *had* suggested to the young men who kept clustering around her that they dance with Bessie and Gwen.

"Liar," Bess said happily. "But I don't care. It was the closest I shall ever come to being rushed. And it was delightful. Are you seeing him again, Nick?"

"We're going hunting. In the morning." Nichola turned so that Bess might return the favor and unfasten her.

Katherine raised her golden head from her pillow. "*Would* you all be quiet, please?"

"Sorry," Gwen whispered, and then giggled. "What did you think of the evening, Katherine?"

"A dreadful bore," the blonde pronounced, flopping over in her bed. "Just like the three of you."

Chapter
Thirteen

"I chose him especially with you in mind."

Nichola looked at the big bay Lord Wallingford had by the lead, her eyes narrowed with excitement. "Oh, he is splendid!"

"Up you go, then." He put his hands to her waist to hoist her into the saddle. Nichola, knowing she likely weighed more than he did, quickly grasped the pommel and hauled herself up. He stood below her in his red coat and jaunty black cap, his smile warm and intimate. "I still wish you were in breeches."

"Hush!" she said sharply, aware of the riders milling all around them.

"Why? It's true." He accepted a lift himself, from the groom, onto a dapple-gray with a swishing tail.

"That's a beautiful horse," Nichola observed.

He patted the gray's haunch. "Achilles. My favorite from my father's stables. He has a keen eye for horseflesh."

The groom handed him up a shotgun. "And one for the lady," he ordered.

"Oh, but—" Nichola began.

"My Diana must have her weapon," he insisted, and so she took the gun. The bay sidled, showing signs of restlessness. Nichola yanked him into submission, to an admiring glance from Wallingford. "You have a very firm hand."

"Oh, well, horses are like dogs, aren't they? They only want to be told what to do."

"Are you fond of dogs?" The gray was even bigger than the bay, so that Nichola and he were for the first time eye to eye.

"I adore them."

"I have a pack of hounds at home that are howling out just now for a mistress."

"You must get them a bitch, then."

He laughed. "Or get myself a wife." He reached to take her hand and kiss it. Nichola colored. The master blew a sharp staccato on his horn. "Off we go!" Wallingford cried, heels digging into the gray. The dogs were let loose, and the riders followed after them in a brilliant blur of color. Lord Wallingford, Nichola noted as she spurred her mount, had a most impressive seat.

They rode in silence for a time, concentrating on the hounds and the surrounding riders. The horses spread out gradually beneath the dense cover of the earl of Yarlborough's great oaks. "Splendid park, isn't it?" Wallingford called, urging his gray closer to Nichola.

"Lovely." And it was, with all the trees tipped in spring green, and cushions of violets crushed beneath the horses' hooves.

The dogs had got a scent; they circled for a moment, anxiously sniffing and snuffling, then took off through the forest with the riders in pursuit. Nichola raised her chin, with the wind on her cheeks and streaming back through her hair, and felt happy enough to burst. Lord Wallingford was studying her so intently that he nearly rode into a tree.

"God! I wish I were a painter," he said fervently, "that I could capture how you look just now."

Somewhere up ahead, the horn sounded. "Come!" Nichola cried, spurring the bay. "We are going to miss all the fun!"

She took off at a gallop, with Wallingford following. He rode as straight and erect as Katherine did, she noted, showing the same invincible elegance he had displayed at dance. But his gray was a tease, given to shying and starting, and she thought his hand might be a trifle soft. He looked so splendid, though, in his close-fitting pinks. The polish on his boots was blinding, and his riding shirt showed frivolous lace cuffs and a tumbling cravat. Still, there was nothing untoward in a man who cared about his dress.

He'd managed to ride up beside her, with some effort. "You were born to the saddle," he observed, trying to catch his breath. "You must be hell-for-leather going astride!"

"It is the horse," she demurred.

"Nonsense. It is the horsewoman." Achilles snorted, tossing his silvery head, jostling the gun Wallingford had laid across the pommel.

"Mind your—" Nichola cried, just as he grabbed for it. But it slipped to the ground, hitting stock-first, letting out a deafening report.

"Damn!" she heard him shout, just as her alarmed bay shot forward into the trees. "Nichola!" Wallingford's voice trailed after her. But all she could do now was wait until her mount had outrun his terror—and try her best not to tumble from his back.

The bay plunged on, deeper and deeper into the forest, while the sounds of the dogs and horn grew ever more faint. Nichola was beginning to think they must be halfway to Scotland when he finally eased his pace, brought up short by a wide, sparkling river. "Thank God!" Nichola murmured, reining him in. "Now, that's enough of that! We'll have a nice, sedate trot back to the others, shall we?" He was lathering and panting and seemed altogether ready to submit. "Best you have a drink first, though," she decided, and directed him down the bank to the stream. "You are a wicked horse," she told him as he bent to the water, "and you are lucky I don't take the whip to you. But oh, that was a lovely run! I suppose we won't be in time for the end. To tell the truth, though, I don't much like that part anyway. If *I* ruled the world, the fox would—" She stopped, her attention snagged by something bright and red-gold floating toward them from far off down the river. "Now, what in heaven's name is that? It looks almost like a . . ." The horse shivered beneath her. *A body.* That was what she'd been about to say.

"Dear God," Nichola whispered. The thing, whatever it was, was still hundreds of yards off, bobbing in the white-crested rivulets of a patch of rapids, but more and more, it resembled a man. Just as she started to nudge the bay into the current, a hand cut cleanly above the surface, followed by a hardy muscle-bound shoulder. Then the other arm rose and plunged. "A swimmer!" she breathed in relief. "Lord, for a moment there . . ." The man had reached the end of the rapids; now, in a wide, quiet pool, he stood in the waist-deep water—it must be positively *freezing,* Nichola thought with admiration—and brought his hands up to push back his hair. The spring sun sparkled on the clean, silvery streams coursing down his neck and his torso, which was broad and strong and crowned with a thatch of hair darker than that on his head, red-brown instead of red-gold. Nichola felt a stirring in her soul. He had the body of an athlete, a wrestler, a rider: he was the most magnificent specimen of masculine perfection she had ever seen, and she could not look away. Then she recognized him. It was Lord Boru there in the river. She sought to stifle her gasp, but he heard and raised his head, for the first time seeing the horse and rider downstream.

Their eyes met. It seemed for an instant that he would dive back beneath the surface; she glimpsed in the instinctive ripple of his muscles his urge to vanish, to hide. He must have thought better of it. Slowly—and time was moving so slowly—the tension flowed out of his tight-coiled shoulders, and he simply stood, buoyed by the water, his crippled leg of no consequence in its bolstering flow. Then he glanced behind him, along the bank, and Nichola knew with utter certainty what he was searching for: Hayden, trotting along with clothes and canes and cautions about this perilous expedition. But the river and his strong, sure strokes had carried him far past the servant's reach. They were alone.

A flush crept upward from her breasts to her face. She knew she ought to look away, or at the least to acknowledge him. But she was paralyzed, stricken numb by embarrassment and ripe confusion and something more: abject admiration, a desperate sense of want. He looked like a bloody god, with his sun-slicked shoulders and his torso gleaming and his hair smoothed back into a loose, water-bright cascade. She did glance off then—only to have her gaze return unbidden, like the point of a compass drawn inexorably north. And as she did, he stared implacably back at her, then reached above his head for the branch of an elm that stretched out over the river. Nichola released her close-held breath, and the sound traveled toward him across the water, magnified. As she watched, he raised himself up by one arm from the limb, effortlessly, inch by inch, his body climbing higher and higher, the water coursing off his waist to his loins. As the river relinquished him, his manhood came into view, bold and stark-hard, aimed at the sky.

Hurriedly she averted her eyes. It was something she had never thought of—that the part of him that made him manly had not suffered along with his knee. She stared down into the mud of the riverbank. A man who could not walk had no claim to such . . .

Magnificence. He was magnificent, like the statues in museums that mammas steered their offspring around in such a rush. She looked up again, against her will, furious with him for having brought this to her attention, having forced her to reckon with an image she knew she never would forget: him, and the river, and the wild, unconquerable force of nature that had made him erect.

"M'laird!"

The anxious cry resounded through the unbounded silence that had ensnared them. At the same time, in the forest at her back, Nichola heard the crash of hooves, and Lord Wallingford's plaintive calls: "Nichola! Miss Hainesworth! Are you there?"

For an instant longer, their gazes were locked. Then the world intruded, with unforgivable force. Wallingford came pounding down to the river. "Oh, thank God!" he shouted, catching sight of her riding habit. "I never would have absolved myself had you suffered any harm!" And he stretched up in the stirrups to touch her, caress her face.

Nichola, turning reluctantly, heard a splash from under the elm tree. "Are you safe?" Lord Wallingford demanded anxiously. "Are you whole?"

She did not know what to answer. He held her close against his coat and felt her shiver. "Diana," he murmured, stroking her hair. "My marvelous Diana, will you ever forgive me for my clumsiness?"

"Of course," she said, her own voice sounding very faint and far-off. "Of course. You know that I will."

Chapter
Fourteen

Though Nichola said again and again that she was fine,
Wallingford insisted on accompanying her back to
Yarlborough House rather than seeking out the rest of the
hunting party. It turned out not to matter; by the time they
retraced the bay's wild ride, the hunters were also trailing
back. A chum of Wallingford's noted slyly that no one had
seen much of Miss Hainesworth or her companion in the
course of the morning. Nichola blushed, but Wallingford
launched into the story of her horse's bolt and how amazing it was that she hadn't lost her seat. "I tell you, the
monster would have thrown any mortal," he declared
proudly, holding tight to Nichola's hand. "But not my Diana." And he gazed at her with such devout admiration that
she blushed even more.

In the great hall, there was a sumptuous hunt breakfast, allowing Wallingford plenty of opportunity to recount
Nichola's exploit again and again. The guests who hadn't
ridden joined them, and Nichola was touched by the care

her escort took to include Gwen and Bessie in his circle of friends. He went so far as to make an effort with Katherine, but apparently she had decided that even the heir to a duke was beneath her notice so long as he was paying court to Nichola. "Whatever has gotten Lady Devereaux's goat?" Wallingford asked as she coldly rebuffed yet another of his overtures.

"She is always like that," Bess said bluntly. "She despises us for a pack of plebians."

"Well, if you are plebians, you are extraordinary attractive ones."

"Oh, do go on, Wallingford."

"No, I mean it!"

Bess laughed. "Of course you do! And so do I. Go on—don't stop now!"

Their end of the long table was giddy and gay, and under Wallingford's wondrous solicitude, even Gwen dropped some of her shyness, in the process snagging the eye of one of His Lordship's many, many friends, all of whom were drinking copiously. Nichola ate her roast beef and sipped ale and sat quietly, basking in happiness. Not even her realization that Lord Boru had joined the company—she had not seen him come in, yet there he was at a neighboring table, with Hayden close behind him—could mar her contentment. It helped, of course, that he never turned to look at her.

"Now, tell me true," Wallingford urged, leaning close to her so that Bess, on her opposite side, could hear him above the buzz and chatter. "You know her best, as her schoolmate. Is there anything at all at which my Miss Hainesworth does not excel?"

"Oh, honestly!" Nichola cried. "Bessie, mind what you say!"

"Not unless you count most of the curriculum," Bess replied with promptness.

"She is hopeless at embroidery," Gwen noted helpfully.

"Pooh! Embroidery!" Wallingford dismissed it with a wave.

"And huswifery," added Bess. "*Any* form of huswifery."

"To think I counted you my friends!" Nichola said with a laugh.

"Honesty is best," Bess intoned, with a sly wink, "in matters of the heart."

"You do not discourage me at all," Wallingford said stoutly. "Though were anyone but the two of you to suggest she suffers any insufficiences whatsoever, I should call him out at once."

"You could have Nick do it for you," Bess told him— and then cringed. "Ouch! Someone has kicked me!" It had been Nichola, of course, who was trying to warn her off that subject. Bess, alas, was oblivious.

"Whatever do you mean?" Wallingford demanded.

"She fences," Bess explained. "Nick, why ever are you making those faces?"

But Wallingford had turned to Nichola with delight. "Do you really? So that is why you asked me last night if I did!"

"I have had a few lessons, that is all," Nichola mumbled.

"From Lord Boru, no less," Bess interjected.

"Really?" Wallingford's dark brows rose. "With such a master instructor, Miss Hainesworth, you must be very good indeed." He snapped his fingers. "Here, now! What do you say to a bout? You and I."

"What are you proposing, Wallingford?" a red-faced fellow across from Bess demanded, downing a pint of ale in one gulp.

"Miss Hainesworth fences! I have just challenged her to a match."

"I haven't brought my gear," Nichola tried to demur.

"Does she really?" the fellow asked, intrigued.

"She is very, very good," Bess assured him. "She takes lessons from Lord Boru."

He pursed his lips and whistled. "A force to be reckoned with indeed! You are a regular Boadicea, Miss Hainesworth, aren't you?"

"The queen of the Britons," Gwen explained to the puzzled-looking gentleman on her right, "who led their war against the Romans."

The ruddy fellow signaled for more ale, then called up the table: "Hear, hear! Miss Hainesworth and Wallingford are getting up a fencing match!"

"Against whom?" somebody shouted back.

"Against each other!"

"Huh! Are we taking bets?"

"Bess," Nichola hissed, beneath the mounting uproar, "have you gone daft? My mother would *murder* me!"

"Just now," Bess murmured back, "your mother could not possibly find fault with anything you did!" She made a little nod in the baroness's direction. Nichola glanced up fearfully. The baroness beamed at her and gave a wave like the benediction of a pope to the masses. Nichola was so astonished that she dropped her spoon.

Even so, the thought of what Lord Wallingford suggested made her rather nervous. "I—I have never really faced a true opponent," she said hesitantly. "And it is only a few months since I began my lessons." But the proposal had caught the fancy of the company. The red-faced young man had appointed himself cashier and, between gulps of ale, was taking wagers: "Wallingford by how many touches? No, no, we must give the lady her handicap!" Purses were plunked on the table as he scribbled down the bets. "Dead odds at a three-point advantage to Miss Hainesworth!" he announced.

Nichola tried to put her foot down. "I honestly don't think—"

"Here, we'll put it up to your instructor, shall we?" Wallingford, grinning, stood to shout over the throng of bettors: "Lord Boru!"

Slowly he shifted in his chair to face their table. "Aye?"

"I've challenged your Miss Hainesworth to a fencing

bout," Wallingford called. "They say you never once refused a challenge. Convince her to take on mine!"

"Frankly," said Lord Boru, his deep, rich Scottish burl cutting straight through the din, "I would advise her against it."

Nichola flushed. "On what grounds?" Wallingford demanded.

Boru's blue gaze searched Nichola's face for a moment. Her color deepened as she remembered the way she had seen him that morning, naked in the river, a potent, lusty god. "She's but a novice," he said then.

"We have given her a three-touch lead," the ruddy-faced lord overseeing the betting promptly noted. "But I could increase it."

"D'you know," the man beside Gwen drawled, leaning back in his seat, "I'll be damned if I've ever seen a woman fence."

Nichola's cheeks burned. If she was so wretched at the sport, why had he squandered so much time to instruct her? "Pay him no mind," someone farther down the table offered. "He's nothing but an old fud out to spoil our fun."

She looked at Boru again. His clear eyes held a definite warning. Well, to hell with him, anyway! What right did he have to stickle so for propriety's sake, when he'd behaved so shamelessly toward her in the forest? If she'd told Wallingford what he'd done, her suitor would have challenged *him* to a duel, bad knee or none!

"I accept your challenge, Wallingford," she said quietly.

"Did you hear that? She's accepted!"

"She is going to fight him!"

Business for the ruddy wager-taker increased in a rush. Amid the hubbub, Nichola raised her chin and stared defiantly at Lord Brian Boru. "Will you be there?" she called to him coolly.

"I think not," he replied, and turned back to his plate.

* * *

The earl of Yarlborough had, of course, a fencing strip, and a very well-groomed one. Nichola, attired in her borrowed pads and mask, toed the lush grass with her boot. She wasn't used to a lawn so fine. "Nervous?" Bess whispered at her side.

"Furious, rather! How dare you bring the bloody subject up?"

"I never meant it to turn into *this*." Bess looked in dismay at the throng of observers who had gathered along the edges of the strip.

"Did you bet?" Nichola asked, testing her foil's spring.

"No."

"I did," Gwen offered.

"On whom?"

"On you, of course!" her friend said proudly. "Straight at the handicap—which now, I believe, with Lord Boru's expressions of doubt, stands at five."

"I really don't know how I got into this," Nichola said, and sighed.

"He is certain to go easy on you," Bess assured her. "He is head-over-heels, you know. What precisely happened on the hunt this morning? Lord Turlington tells me no one saw hide or hair of the two of you for nigh on two hours."

"My horse bolted." Nichola swallowed. Lord Wallingford had stepped onto the strip. His black-trimmed-with-gold fencing outfit was as superbly tailored as the rest of his wardrobe, and he looked very dashing. He came toward her, mask raised, smiling enchantingly.

"Diana." He swept a bow, with a flourish of his blade. "How devastatingly lovely you are in your armor."

Gwen pushed Nichola forward. Lord Turlington, the ruddy-faced lord, who'd been appointed referee, clapped his hands for attention. The effort made him stagger a little. "The bout is to ten," he announced loudly. "Monsieur Angelo's rules, of course. Contestants are honor-bound to con-

fess points. No—uh—low touches permitted." He winked
broadly, and laughter rippled through the assembled ladies
and lords. Nichola scanned the crowd, wondering if Lord
Boru might have reconsidered his refusal to attend. Apparently he had not. She would show *him,* she thought, as
Turlington brought their two blades together, then raised
his arm. "And ready. Set?" Nichola nodded, pulling down
her mask. Lord Wallingford did the same. *"En garde!"*
cried Turlington, and blundered backward from the center
line. Wallingford executed a brisk *gagner la mesure.* His
footwork, like his dancing, was matchless. Nichola, feeling
the weight of all those eyes on her, hurriedly retreated. He
pressed forward and engaged. Their blades clinked as she
met his parry. Her boots felt oddly heavy, and she was
perspiring within her pads.

He'd made a *dégage.* Instinctively she responded with a
counter-parry, her blade moving in a smooth *contre de quatre* circle. His posture, she noted, was all Lord Boru demanded of hers: erect and alert, free hand cupped for
balance, with the thumb opposed. Now he followed with a
coulé, his foil running up against hers as he lunged. Graceful as the motion was, it lacked either surprise or force.
Nichola, impatient—did he truly intend to go easy on
her?—broke the engagement with a brisk parry from the
septime. He let his edge drop, and her momentum carried
her forward so far that her tip pricked his shoulder. There
was an *ooh* from the onlookers. Wallingford nodded to
Lord Turlington, who announced, sounding extremely surprised, "First touch to Miss Hainesworth!"

It had been so easy that Nichola *knew* he had allowed
it. He faded back, with impeccable crossover footwork. She
pressed, with a swift double-change. He countered it, but
not so readily as she had expected, and responded with a
coupé. Nichola disengaged adroitly, mentally forming her
next attack, gauging his weaknesses. The way he'd responded to the double-change gave her pause. Lord Boru
would have met that elementary move with a fast, shocking

une-deux, or perhaps a feint and then the *passato sotto.* But
Wallingford's play seemed far more restrained, more . . .

He'd reprised. Somewhat annoyed at the interruption
of her thoughts, she riposted and lunged. The force of her
stroke sent Wallingford's blade skittering into the grass.
The audience caught its breath, and so did Nichola. With
awful abruptness, she realized why Boru had advised
against this fight. She was an infinitely better fencer than
Wallingford.

Oh, damn. What the hell was she to do now? She
didn't dare fight him fairly; she'd land ten touches before
he placed even one! He had all the necessary moves, but he
seemed incapable of stringing them into any sort of coher-
ent attack. And as accepting as he'd been so far of her
prowess at masculine matters, she knew with absolute certainty that she must not win this match. Not in front of all
these people. But how in heaven's name was she to let him
triumph and have it look convincing? Nothing in her train-
ing had prepared her for this circumstance.

He'd retrieved his foil. Turlington summoned them
back to the center line, his expression as he beckoned to
Nichola altogether new and not a bit respectful—indeed,
openly resentful. Nichola glanced through her mask at
Gwen, who raised her fist in a salute.

"Your friends didn't lie about your prowess," Wallingford said, breathing heavily.

"A lucky blow," she answered, and set about allowing
him to win.

It wasn't easy. His picture-perfect posture and stances
disguised a positively abysmal sense of the sport. He lunged
when he ought to have parried, riposted with more style
than vigor, and had no feel for a sustained attack. Nichola
had to hold back on all that she had learned. Her constant
need to rethink did have the fortunate effect of disrupting
her own game, and Wallingford took advantage of her hesi-
tations to drive home a few touches. But her heart sank as
Turlington, much more cheerful now, recorded them. Four
to two—God, would they ever reach ten?

What made it all the more difficult was having to convince not only the crowd, but also her sweet-natured suitor that he was besting her. Even as his points tallied up, Nichola could not believe he wasn't aware of her shenanigans. That she would meet a low-line attack with a supinated stroke—he had to think her daft! He appeared to gain confidence, though, with each of her ridiculous responses. With him ahead eight to five—and her last three points had been absolutely unavoidable; he simply *would* not keep his guard up!—she went so far as to stagger and fall when he made a parry of prime. Instantly he threw aside his foil and rushed to her side, kneeling in the grass. "Nichola! Have I hurt you?" he asked anxiously, raising up her mask. "Turlington! Bring some wine and water!"

Nichola wanted nothing but to lie there and be spared any further dissembling. "My ankle," she whispered. "I believe I've sprained it."

"God, I shall never forgive myself! What madness made me incite you to this, my dear, sweet dove?" He stroked her cheek. Beyond his shoulder, Nichola glimpsed Bess and Gwen huddled together, their faces taut with concern. Why? she wondered, and had her answer when Wallingford had helped her limp to her room and, with profuse apologies and another of his sweet kisses, withdrew.

"What a bloody charade!" Gwen declared angrily. Nichola waved a hand to shush her, but Bess was equally irate:

"You could have beaten him with one hand tied behind your back!"

Nichola sighed. "You don't understand. It wouldn't be fitting for me to show him up in front of all that crowd!"

"Oh, Nick," Gwen said sadly.

"It was only a game!" she defended herself. "Besides, I like him! I like him very much. I did not want for him to be embarrassed."

"I'm not at all sure it's worth it," Gwen pronounced. Bess and Nichola both stared at her.

"What?" Bess asked finally.

"The academy. Madame. Finding what is best in ourselves and then pursuing it. Where will it get us, after all, if the world isn't ready for it?"

Bess screwed her face up. "I *think,*" she said slowly, "the idea is for us to change the world. A little bit at a time."

"And I did that!" Nichola noted heatedly. "I fenced a man in public! Surely that's a step forward!"

"You threw the match," Gwen said implacably.

"Oh, to hell with the match. It was all Bess's fault to begin with." Nichola was weary and grumpy and not at all in the mood to put up with her friends' second-guessing. And at the heart of her discontentment was knowing what Lord Boru was sure to think of her for what she had done. He'd recognized that Wallingford didn't stand a chance against her. That was why he'd sought to deter her. But she'd misread his motives, damn it. She'd been so sure he was jealous of Wallingford. Why else would he have made that gesture in the river, raised himself with his one arm, formed that tableau of puissance and desire she could not forget?

"Nichola?"

Oh, Christ. It was her mother, poking her head through the door with unaccustomed reticence.

"She's perfectly fine," Bess said impatiently. "She only—"

But this time Nichola managed to forestall her, with an expression of absolute despair.

"—turned her ankle," her friend finished reluctantly.

"Well! That's what *will* come, isn't it, from treading into territory that rightfully belongs to men?" the baroness asked fondly. "I trust you've learned your place, Nichola, my dear!"

Chapter
Fifteen

The excuse of her feigned injury allowed Nichola to spend the rest of that day in her rooms, for which she was extremely grateful. She needed time to think. Wallingford came by every hour, with wine and flowers and chocolates and fruit and sweetmeats and apologies so abject, she recognized in relief that he had no notion of what had really gone on at the fencing strip. The baroness was also much in attendance, fussing over whether the windows should be opened or not and if the fire should be built up and was there anything at all Nichola would care to eat or drink? Her solicitude was so out of character that Nichola grew cross. "For heaven's sake, Mother!" she exclaimed as the baroness tidied the coverlets on her bed. "You weren't half this kind to me the time I broke my arm jumping out of the barn into the haystacks!"

"Hush!" her mother hissed in alarm. "You don't want Wallingford to find out about that!"

Nichola sat up beneath the covers. "Frankly, I don't believe it would discourage him a bit."

"Perhaps not." The baroness perched beside her. "But oh, my darling, you must be so very careful now!"

"Careful? What of?"

"Why, of his affections! You do recognize, don't you, what a catch you have made?"

"How could I not, when everyone keeps telling me so?"

"I only wish your father and your brothers might have been here to see you. I tell you, Nichola, that Mrs. Treadwell is a positive *genius*! To think that only a few short months ago, I despaired of your future! And now you are the toast of the town! Wallingford singling you out has put the absolute stamp of approval on you amongst the *ton*. They are all saying, you know, that you are an original." She patted her daughter's hand.

"And what do you say, Mother?"

The baroness hesitated. "Well! It is hardly the avenue *I* would have had you take—all this athleticism. Still, that just shows how clever Mrs. Treadwell is, doesn't it? And heaven knows, it has done the trick with Wallingford. I simply *couldn't* be happier, Nichola." She leaned forward conspiratorially. "And you would not *believe* the number of mothers who have come up to inquire of me about the academy! Rest assured, Mrs. Treadwell is in for a great rush of new students!"

Her words reminded Nichola of something. "Gwen said you were announcing you saw no reason for me to finish out the term."

"Well, darling, I don't. I am heading off to London for the spring season, and you might as well, too. That's where Wallingford will be."

"I don't want to go to London."

"Oh, but darling—"

"Why *do* you go on calling me that? You've never in my life called me that before!"

"The academy is intended to prepare young ladies for

their debuts," the baroness said reasonably. "Clearly, you are well enough prepared."

"Because I happen to have caught the eye of one nice young man?"

"Wallingford is rather something more than simply one nice young man."

Nichola was suddenly exceedingly weary. "I'd like to sleep now, Mother."

"Of course, dar—of course, my dear. You go right ahead." The baroness tucked her in attentively, then bent to kiss her brow.

"Mother."

"Yes?"

"I want to finish out the term. If you don't let me finish out the term, I'll tell Wallingford—I'll tell him—I'll say he is too short for me."

"Nichola!" The baroness's voice had taken on that old, familiar steel. "For God's sake! How could you?"

"I mean it," said Nichola.

"You are making a *dreadful* mistake," her mother fretted. "What if some other girl should attract him in the meantime?"

"Then," Nichola noted dryly, "his attachment to me could not have been very strong in the first place. And I would not care to marry such a man."

The baroness's brows contracted; she poked Nichola's chest with a finger. "You had best watch out, young lady! You are hardly so attractive or gifted that you can afford to throw this opportunity away!"

At least their relationship was back to its usual footing, Nichola thought with rue. The difference was that Wallingford's besotted attentions had given *her* the upper hand. "Go away now," she murmured, lying back on the pillows. "I want to sleep."

The baroness was instantly the soul of compassion. "Of course, my darling. You must rest. You have so very much to look forward to!"

* * *

By suppertime that night, Nichola was grinding her teeth
from her enforced inactivity, and she insisted on dressing
and going downstairs for cards and charades. Her earlier
dissembling required that she affect a limp and remember
to sustain it—giving truth to Sir Walter Scott's epigram, she
thought regretfully, that one spins a tangled web when one
first starts to deceive. Wallingford was kindness itself,
planting himself by her chair and only leaving to fetch her
dainties and sweets he thought she might enjoy. He held
her hand as they watched the charades, and they laughed
together at Turlington's hapless imitation of a cow and
Bess's deft, sly rendering of a stalking tiger and Lord
Botheringly's hysterical evocation of a hunted mouse. From
time to time, Wallingford brought her hand up to kiss it. "I
have never in my life been so happy," he whispered to her.
God, if he'd been put up to this by Boru, he was the finest
actor in all of England, she thought wistfully.

Boru was playing cards, with Hayden hovering behind
his chair. The servant seemed, Nichola noted, to be bringing his master an awful lot of whiskey. She wished she
might have a word with Lord Boru; there was a great deal
that she longed to say to him about that morning's fencing
bout. But it did not seem likely she would have an opportunity; he was winning steadily at whist and never glanced her
way.

The charade game was fading as the hour drifted
toward midnight. "Let's go out to the terrace," Wallingford
urged her. She looked at him and saw his dark eyes gleam.
More of those lovely kisses . . .

"If you like," she said coyly. "But I shall have to lean
on your arm."

"There's nothing I wish more."

He helped her to the doors, ignoring the teasing comments from their companions. "Miss Hainesworth requires
some fresh air," he explained blithely, while Nichola dutifully limped along at his side. He shut the doors behind

them. "Here, we'll sit on the wall." He led her there. "I really cannot forgive myself for having hurt you, Nichola." His hand came up to her cheek. "I would rather die than ever cause you pain."

Sandalwood and patchouli . . . she drank it in. He put his mouth to hers, his arm tucked close around her. Nichola leaned against him, feeling so warm, so . . . appreciated. "Oh," he murmured in wonder. "My sweet, sweet Nichola . . . say that you love me."

"I . . . I scarcely know you."

He smiled. "I shall remedy that. From this moment forth, I will be ever at your side."

"I don't see how, since I'm to go back to Mrs. Treadwell's academy."

He drew away. "No! Your mother said you would be coming to London for the season."

"That is what she would like. But I feel an obligation—"

"To what? Lessons in huswifery? There is no need for them." He stroked her soft hair. "Everything I ever wanted—dreamed of—you already embody. I—" He broke off. Someone had come barging through the doors. Nichola saw with some apprehension that it was Lord Boru, moving awkwardly on his canes.

"**M**ilord!" The detestable little dandy in his tight coat and breeches rose from the wall as Brian approached. "Permit me to tell you how greatly I appreciate your instructions to Miss Hainesworth in fencing! We were only just now discussing—"

"I'd have a word with my pupil," Brian growled. Wallingford blinked.

"Perhaps, Anthony," the girl said tentatively, "you might fetch me some champagne?"

He looked at her, and then at Brian. "Of course, Valkyrie. If that is what you'd like." He hurried back into the ballroom. Brian swung himself awkwardly over to the wall.

"Valkyrie?" he echoed, taken aback at the restrained fury in his own voice.

"I'm a bit surprised," she said coolly, "to see you risen from your chair."

"How *dare* you," he said, so fiercely that she recoiled from him. "How *dare* you let him beat you?"

"What would you know of it?" she retorted. "You weren't even there."

"I know what I heard. He was ahead eight points to five when you—turned your ankle." His voice dripped sarcasm as he looked down at it.

Embarrassed, she tucked it beneath her skirt. "He is a really quite a fine—"

He cut her off with a whirl of one cane. "He is *absymal* on the strip!"

"Then why didn't you tell me so ahead of time?"

"I *did*!" he roared. "I advised against the match!"

"But you didn't say why," she argued. "I thought it was because you were so sure he would best me!"

"Best *you*? That mincing little fop?"

"Now, see here," she declared heatedly.

"And regardless of that," he went on, brushing right past her protest, "it is beneath your dignity—your *honor*—to throw him the match!"

"What else was I to do?" she demanded. "He clearly hadn't the wherewithal to defeat me! I could not let him suffer such—such an indignity in full view of all his friends!"

"Why the hell not?"

"Because he is a *man*!"

Brian knew all about suffering indignities in public. It was her delicate tact in ensuring Wallingford *wouldn't* that had made him so wroth, propelled him out to the terrace after her and her beau. Why should she be so concerned with Wallingford's bloody *suffering*? What about *his*? "A *sort* of man," he said very nastily.

"A good man! A gentleman! A man who adores me!"

"A man you have to lie for—deny your own abilities for."

"Oh, for God's sake! Who set you up as arbiter of what is right and what is wrong?"

"This—*this*—is wrong!" He poked with his cane at her supposedly wounded ankle. "Do you think I worked with you so long and so hard for such an ignominious result?"

"It was you yourself told me I'd be a fool to go and fight on the Continent. What the hell am I to use fencing for otherwise?" Her gaze went beyond his shoulder. Brian turned and saw Wallingford with two glasses of champagne, his nose pressed to the doors. He scowled at the suitor, who hurriedly retreated.

"Your little puppy," he grunted. "So obedient."

"*You* told me it was *all* a fencing match!" she cried bitterly. "And then you paid him off to court me!"

Brian stared. "I *what*?"

"Oh, come now, Lord Boru. He even echoed your words—'the most beautiful girl I have ever seen.'"

"You think I somehow instigated him?" He laughed, so roundly that the girl flushed. "Christ! I said a *worthy* opponent, did I not? There is nothing the least bit worthy in him!"

"But—but—if you didn't—then—why on earth would he have singled out me?"

"Obviously, because he aspires to better his family line."

"He's the duke of Strafford's son!"

"He's a fly on the ass of England."

"You go too far, sir!"

"Oh, I could go farther! But you'd not listen, clearly; you've fallen victim to his heady manners and his murmured endearments. 'Valkyrie' indeed! Go on!" He swung a cane violently toward the doors. "Invite him back! Cuddle with him all you like. I wash my hands of you. What you did this afternoon was beneath contempt."

"All I did," she said evenly, "was attempt to repay his remarkable kindess to me. I see no dishonor in that. And while we are on the subject of dishonor, where in your catalogue of offenses does—does *exposing* oneself to innocent young ladies fall?"

Brian's fury abruptly subsided; he glanced away. It was a very good question. What in God's name had possessed him, that morning in the river? This English girl meant nothing to him; she was—well, not young enough to be his daughter, as Hayden had charged. But far too young to evoke the sensations she had as he'd stared at her across the sparkling water. In that moment, in that solitude, some madness had seized him. It had become monstrously vital that she know, that she *see,* what he once had been. . . .

But would never be again. "I—ought not to have done that," he admitted haltingly. "Forgive me."

"The devil I will! Were I to mention it to Wallingford, he would tan your hide."

His sneer returned, redoubled. "I would like to see him try."

"You." She took in with a pointed gaze the canes he leaned on. "You are hardly what I would call a worthy opponent yourself these days." She brushed past him, heading for the doors. And against all odds, he found he could not bear to see her go. To let her go . . .

"I am what I am!" he shouted at her back. "Damn you! Don't—don't leave me!"

She whirled to him. "Why not? Do you require some assistance?"

He stared at her, saw the glow of the moon ignite the streaks of shimmering gold in her eyes. God, but she was lovely! Lovely and whole and vital and rife with possibility. He'd lied to her. He'd looked on from a window of Yarlborough House that morning, had seen the way she attacked Wallingford, the grace and grandeur of her every movement—right up until the moment when, clear as day, she'd decided to throw it in. And for what? A dandified duke's son, a man who'd only ever seen the Continent on the obligatory six-month whirlwind I-am-out-of-Oxford tour. What right had Wallingford to such a prize?

Ah, but this was what Christiane had wanted. *I was only ever the means to this end,* he recognized. The girl knew it. And so should he.

"No," he said, with a wealth of bitterness. "No, thank you. I can manage on my own."

"I am glad to hear it," she declared, with a toss of her sheeny hair. Brian watched as she flounced back inside, to Wallingford, to her bright, happy future with him.

Chapter
Sixteen

"Well, Nichola!" Madame said at the breakfast table on their first morning back at the academy after the holiday. "How went your visit to the countess of Yarlborough's?"

"It was fine," said Nichola, and took a bite of egg.

Bessie nearly gagged on her toast. "*Fine*? Is that all you can say, Nick—*fine*?"

Madame raised a brow at Bess. "What word, pray tell, would you use to describe it?"

"I should have to use a great many of them. Extraordinary, for one, and marvelous, and exciting, and wonderful, and splendiferous, and—"

"Whoa!" Madame laughed, holding up her hand.

"And I wasn't even the one who caught myself a beau!"

"Someone has got a beau? Let me guess." Madame pursed her lips, surveying the upper-form girls seated around her. "Katherine?"

"I *might* have," Katherine spat out, "if another certain young lady hadn't been making such a positive *spectacle* of herself!"

"Oh, dear, dear," Madame murmured. "Who in the world did that?"

"*She* did." Katherine glared at Nichola. "She fenced a man in public. In breeches!"

"Goodness! Did you, Nichola?" The countess's dark eyes glittered. "And did you win?"

There was a moment of pregnant silence. Then, "No," Nichola said briefly. Bess started to speak up, but Nichola managed for once to quell her, with a dartlike glance.

"With whom did you fence?"

"Wallingford," Bess put in, before Nichola could even answer. "He's her beau. He is absolutely *smitten* with her. Never left her side."

"He is ever so kind and nice," Gwen added shyly.

"Wallingford—that would be Strafford's son, no?" Madame inquired.

"Do you know him?" Nichola asked quickly.

"I knew his parents, once upon a time. Lovely people. Very refined. The duke, as I recall, was quite a tulip of fashion."

"So is the son," Bess said eagerly. "The most exquisite manners and clothes! And he dances like a dream."

"Did you dance with him, Nichola?" Madame asked, and she nodded.

"They danced *all the time*!" Bess clarified. "When they weren't kissing on the terrace, that is."

"Bess!" Nichola cried, going scarlet.

Madame chuckled into her teacup. "It seems, Nichola, you have made quite a capture. Your mother must have been pleased."

"There were *three* letters from him already waiting for her last night," irrepressible Bess informed the table.

"Mother *was* pleased," Nichola told Madame. "She said ever so many mammas asked about the academy.

You'll be pleased to know she was singing Mrs. Treadwell's praises to the sky."

"He has *millions* of friends," Bess burbled on. "And he introduced all of them to Gwen and me. You might ask Gwen about Lord Botheringly."

"Really?" Madame glanced at Gwen. "It seems to have been an extraordinarily successful holiday for you all!"

"Not for me," Katherine noted bluntly. "I was *mortified* by Nichola's disreputable behavior. As, I might add, were the young ladies of quality present."

"Nearly all," Madame amended. "That reminds me, Nichola. Will you see me in my office after Mrs. Caldburn's lecture? There's a package has come for you."

"Likely a diamond from Lord Wallingford," Bess teased.

"It's rather too large for that."

"Perhaps he's posted himself to her," Gwen suggested slyly.

"Good heavens, I hope not!" Madame said with a smile. "It arrived some days past."

"More likely it is linens from Mother—already embroidered with W's," Nichola noted with rue.

"Or the wedding invitations," said Bess.

Nichola laughed along with her friends. It was a new and very pleasant sensation, to be teased about a suitor. Still, there was a strange heaviness far down in her heart, though she could not think why.

Then she remembered how she'd wakened at dawn, in her room upstairs, and started up from bed to don her pads and mask and hurry down to the courtyard—before realizing that of course Lord Boru would not be there. She wished she had not been so cruel to him there on the terrace at Yarlborough House. But the way he had belittled Wallingford was infuriating! And she'd said things she didn't really mean in response—and then so had he—

Well, it was too late now. She'd heard he'd left Yarlborough House early the next morning. Wherever he'd headed, she was quite sure it wasn't back here, to take up

fencing lessons with her again—which, when she thought
about it, was just as well. She didn't know how she would
have gone on with that after the scene in the forest. Odd
how seeing him that way had affected her. The image
popped into her head at the strangest times. And it was
always so clear and exact—the sunlight, the sparkling water
sluicing down from his body, the taut hardness of his muscles, and his rod standing boldly upright, proud and erect
as a pennant on a castle's tower. . . .

"Look at her." Bess's giggle scattered the image, like a
rock thrown into a reflecting pool. "She is thinking of him
now! See how dreamy-eyed she is!"

Nichola jerked back to earth. "I was doing no such
thing," she said hotly.

"Liar! You are as red as a cherry!"

"Leave her be," Madame said gently, pouring herself
more tea. "You have had your holiday; now it is back to
work for you all! I trust you comprehend after this expo-
sure to society why Mrs. Treadwell and I have been such
harsh taskmasters. Nichola, you won't forget to come to my
office?" Nichola shook her head slowly. "But, girls, you
must tell me all the *on-dit* about everyone—everyone *besides* poor Nichola! What were the fashions like? How
were the gentlemen wearing their cravats, and the ladies
their hair?"

Nichola knocked at the door of the tiny antechamber
Madame had for her office. "Come in!" that French-tinged
voice sang out. Nichola pushed open the portal. Madame
was at her desk, a quill in her hand. She turned to smile.
"And how was Mrs. Caldburn this morning?"

"Deadly as ever. This one was on silver-polishing, if
you can believe it. Two entire hours devoted to the secrets
of shiny forks and knives."

Madame laughed. "Does Lord Wallingford know of
your aversion to housework?"

"Bess and Gwen made it a point to inform him. He doesn't seem to care in the least."

"I don't wonder, with the Strafford fortune. The girl who marries him will never have to lift a finger." She set the quill aside. "I've spoken to Mrs. Treadwell, and she is *beaming* with pride in you, Nichola. She showed me a glowing letter of recommendation on behalf of the academy your mother passed on to her. How did it feel, then, to make such a success?"

"Very peculiar, frankly. I didn't do a thing to earn it. Wallingford simply attached himself to me. And once he did, the rest all flowed from there."

Madame gestured her to a seat on the small settee. "You like him?"

"Very much. But I am extremely puzzled as to why he likes *me*."

"Love is like that sometimes. No rhyme or reason to it. Mrs. Treadwell also told me you insisted on returning to finish out the session, rather than going on to London with your mother."

"Yes. I—I'm not certain I am ready for London. Everything happened so fast. . . ."

"Perhaps you simply needed a bit of a breather." Nichola nodded gratefully. Those dark eyes glinted. "First kiss, eh?" Nichola flushed. "What did you think of it?"

"It was *marvelous*," she admitted.

"Oh, I am so happy for you! That's just as it should be." Madame crossed her hands in her lap. "I'm sorry to tell you, I've had a letter from Lord Boru. He writes he cannot continue with your fencing instruction."

"I . . . expected as much," Nichola said in a small voice.

"Did something happen between you?"

What had happened between them, exactly? Nichola tried to find words. "He—he opposed my fencing match with Lord Wallingford. I went against his opinion. Then, afterward, we . . . quarrelled."

"I regret to hear it. I believe your lessons meant much to him."

"He was an utter *bastard* about Wallingford. And about a great many other things."

"Dear me. It sounds a dreadful scene. He always did have a terrible temper." Nichola was reminded suddenly of all the times she'd been jealous of Madame in Lord Boru's presence. How she longed to know precisely what had gone on between them! But what did that matter now? She would likely never see the man again, except in passing, with her on Wallingford's arm.

"I know," she said apologetically, "you had hoped teaching me fencing might restore him . . . physically. But really, he is so—so bound up in *anger* at anyone with two good legs. . . ."

"Yes," Madame said with a heavy sigh. "You are quite right about that. Oh, Nichola. If just once you might have seen him as he was. . . ."

But I have, Nichola thought. *There in the river, he was virile and whole and shining—*

Madame shrugged. "We did the best we could, didn't we, Nichola?"

"Yes. I believe we did."

"He sent you that." Madame nodded toward the sideboard, which bore a very long, narrow package wrapped up in brown paper. "It came with his letter."

"Sent it to *me*?" Wonderingly, Nichola moved to the sideboard, saw the bold, printed letters: MISS NICHOLA HAINESWORTH, MRS. TREADWELL'S ACADEMY.

"Aren't you going to open it?"

"Yes. Of course I am." Nichola untied the string. Her fingers were trembling. Inside the paper lay a gleaming wooden box. She unfastened the latches and lifted the lid. "Oh," she whispered, as the sunlight from the window glinted on the bright metal within. Gingerly she lifted out the gift—a saber, its basket handle a mass of intricate tracery, its blade a great length of glorious steel. "He never said I was ready for the saber," she murmured in wonder.

"He must think you are now. What exactly went on at that fencing match with Wallingford?" But Nichola couldn't answer. She swallowed hard, weighing the gorgeous weapon in her hand.

"May I see that for a moment?" Madame asked. Nichola brought it to her, and the older woman examined it closely. "I thought as much. It's his regimental sword."

"Oh, no!" Nichola cried. "Not that! I couldn't possibly accept it."

"He knows he will never use it again."

The sword with which Lord Brian Boru had attacked the French, the edge slicing through who knew how many enemy breasts . . . Nichola recoiled a little, then advanced, staring at the blade. Did he mean he wished she had gone to the Continent? That even that would be preferable to seeing her in Wallingford's arms?

"I can't accept it," she said once more.

"But you must! Such an invaluable keepsake . . . it only goes to prove how right I was. Your lessons *did* mean much to him."

"You don't understand. I *cannot* accept it!" Nichola felt that too-ready blush. "He sent it as a rebuke."

"Surely you can't think *he* was offended that you fenced with Wallingford! After the outrages to propriety he has committed?"

"It isn't that," Nichola said miserably.

Madame was looking thoughtful. "Yet you did say he'd advised against the match. I wonder why?"

"Because he *knew*," she whispered.

"Dear child, he knew *what*?"

"He knew I was the better fencer!" And then the dam broke, and she poured out the entire sorry saga—how Bess had brought the subject up in the first place, and how excited Wallingford had been, and how the gentlemen had all laid wagers, and then how Wallingford had applied to Lord Boru for his opinion. . . . "And I took his objection all wrong," Nichola confessed. "I thought he meant I didn't have a chance. But if that was so, I couldn't comprehend why had he spent all that time with me! Had he only been lying when he said how fine a fencer I was? And so I defied him. I accepted the challenge. But practically from the first stroke, I realized Wallingford didn't know the least thing about the sport! Oh, he looked the part, in his fancy clothes, with his handsome foil. But he couldn't fence. He couldn't fence at all!" She paused for breath.

In the breach, Madame said, "I don't understand. You told me that you lost the match."

"I . . . allowed Wallingford to win it."

"*Oh*," said Madame, and her shrewd gaze glinted. "I quite see, now. But, Nichola, why?"

Nichola turned away, paced across the tiny room and then back. "Because . . . he'd been so very kind to me," she tried to explain. "Because of how much I like him. He'd asked me to dance! He made me dance—like an angel. And he'd kissed me! How could I possibly shame him in front of his friends? Why, he'd be scoffed at for the rest of his days!" She affected a taunting tone. " 'Lost a fencing bout to a *girl*!' "

"And that's all there was to it?"

Nichola slammed down gracelessly onto the settee again. "No. There was also Mother. I . . . she . . . at the ball, when Wallingford first took a fancy to me . . ." She swallowed; her throat was tight. "I saw her looking at me . . . the way she has *always* looked at Tommy and Spence and all my brothers. I'd never once made my mother proud of me. Not in all my life. I . . . was afraid. If I beat Wallingford, I knew she'd tell me I was hopeless. That I'd ruined my one chance for happiness. And so I just . . . let him win."

"Did you tell Lord Boru that? About your mother?"

"Of course not! It is none of his business! Besides, he was far too busy being *beastly* about Wallingford! Called him a little fop. And all manner of other ghastly names!" She looked up plaintively. "Why *does* he have to be so—so boorish?"

"Well." Madame sat with the saber in her hands,

weighing its gleaming blade. "I understand now why you think the gift is a rebuke. Considered, however, in a more charitable light, is it not possible Lord Boru meant it as an apology? An effort at . . . reconciliation?"

"Him? Oh, really. Don't be absurd."

"If you don't mean to keep it, what will you do with it?"

"Send it back to him, of course. With—with a note." God, what would she say?

"You might return it to him in person."

Nichola shook her head. "I've no idea where he is."

"He's put up at the White Fox, in the village. He has been ever since he came to teach you."

It had never once occurred to Nichola to wonder where he was living. She had simply assumed he was staying with friends. "At that miserable small tavern?" she asked, aghast.

"I told him the Davenports would be delighted to have him. But he has an aversion to imposing on folk. I think he makes too much of it, frankly. A symptom of his pride."

Nichola's mind formed the most morose picture of him ensconced in a horrid let-out room for all these months, eating bad food, drinking bad whiskey—and all for what? To teach her to fence. Christ, no wonder he'd been furious when she had thrown that match! But the prospect of seeing him again was just too daunting. "I'd prefer to send a note."

Madame caught the saber up by its hilt, made a few bold strokes. "If you think that is the best way to set things to right," she observed mildly.

"Besides," Nichola hurried on, "it would be tremendously improper of me to call on him there, wouldn't it? At a common tavern?"

"Ordinarily, I would agree. But considering the circumstances—his injury, not to mention that indefatigable Scottish guardian of his—the rules might well be relaxed." Madame saw the reluctance on Nichola's face. "I could accompany you as your chaperone, if you'd like."

"I'd like that very much," Nichola stammered. "Though, actually, I still think a note, conscientiously worded—"

"Nichola. Have you any notion whatsoever how much a soldier's sword means to him? How infinitely Lord Boru has honored you in sending you this?"

She did. Still, she could not help her misgivings. Perhaps she ought to tell Madame what had happened on that morning of the hunt, in the forest, by the river. But—no. She could not bring herself to speak of that moment, that revelation, to anyone. She would go there with Madame. She would give him back the saber, apologize graciously for having disappointed him and be done. It was not really so hard a thing. She could get through that.

"When?" she asked, and was appalled to hear how her voice shook.

"He told me in his letter he was leaving here on the seventeenth. The day after tomorrow."

"Tomorrow, then," Nichola said more firmly. "Is that convenient to you?"

"I believe I can make time in my schedule. But not until after supper. Shall we say seven o'clock?"

"If you like."

Madame rose and laid the saber back in its box. "You will be glad in the end," she said softly, "that you made the effort. Now, haven't you a lesson in embroidery to take?"

Chapter
Seventeen

Nichola had only ever seen the White Fox in passing, while riding with Mr. Saliston and, of course, on her way to the academy with her mother. The baroness had pointed out the low-slung, whitewashed building set right up to the road and noted it was precisely why they had stopped for luncheon elsewhere. "The sort of place where all manner of ruffians no doubt collect," she'd said with a sniff. "And I can only imagine the bill of fare!" Nichola was somewhat astonished, then, when the postboy in the courtyard behind the inn greeted Madame with a warm, familiar grin as their carriage drove up. "William!" Madame cried, evidently equally glad to see him. "How is your mamma's catarrh?"

"Better, thank yer kindly fer askin'! Cissie's caught it, though. Mum was only just sayin' at breakfast how she wished she had more o' that medicinal yer gave her."

"I shall see that she gets it. A bit of water is all the team needs, William. We won't be long." Madame handed him the reins and climbed down. Nichola followed tentatively,

balancing the long saber case she had carried on her lap.
"Is Lord Boru still here?"

"Aye, m'lady. But busy packin' up to go. Mum'll be
right sorry to see him leave. So will we all."

It suddenly dawned on Nichola why Madame should
be so well acquainted with the boy and his family. She must
have been to visit Lord Boru here—many times, from the
sound of things. She glanced at the woman, who was still
chatting away with towheaded William. Had she spent
nights here? The girls often did not see her after supper
had ended. A curdle of resentment soured in Nichola's
craw. Though she always had suspected Madame and Boru
had been lovers once, it never had occurred to her they
might still be. But the supposition, now that she considered
it, made absolute sense. Impossible to conceive that His
Lordship would have stayed on in this wretched little inn
merely to give an awkward girl fencing lessons. It was much
more likely he'd put up with the squalid surroundings in
order to share stolen moments with Madame. Still, that *she,*
with her continental worldliness, would have been content
to make this their love nest . . . her estimation of her
mentor slipped several notches even as Madame beckoned
to her gaily: "Come along, Nichola!"

They went in through the back door, like common
tradesmen. A fat, sweating woman was just sliding loaves of
bread from the oven in the kitchen; when she glimpsed
Madame, her broad face brightened. "Ah, Countess!" she
cried, dusting flour from her hands. *Countess?* Nichola reg-
istered, as Madame and the woman exchanged hugs. Really,
there was such a thing as too much familiarity with the
help!

"I am so glad to see you up and about!" Madame
declared, gazing about the kitchen. 'And as busy as always!"

"Aye, well, when yer livelihood depends upon waitin'
on others, what choice d'yer have? But it was that potion o'
yers set me to rights again. Though I be sad to report Cissie's come down with the blasted bug."

"William already told me. Mrs. Wickers, this is Miss
Hainesworth, one of the students at the academy."

"Ever so pleased to meet yer," the woman said warmly,
dropping a curtsy. Nichola inclined her head—barely—and
then recognized with a flush that she was behaving exactly
the way Katherine would.

"We've come to call on Lord Boru," Madame noted.

"Have yer, then? See if yer can talk him out o' leavin'.
Such a splendid gentleman he is—a good influence on the
rest o' the squatters in this place!"

"I'm afraid he's made up his mind to go," Madame
said with a frown. "We merely came to wish him good-
bye."

"Well, yer know the room!" Mrs. Wickers announced,
which left Nichola in no doubt as to the substance of Madame's relationship with the crippled lord. Madame did not
seem a bit taken aback at the revelation, however; she simply smiled and went through the kitchen into a dim, dingy
hall.

"Mrs. Wickers was kind enough to give over her front
parlor to Lord Boru, in consideration of the difficulty he
has with stairs," she confided over her shoulder. Nichola,
noting the moldy hunting prints on the walls and the mothy
carpet, shuddered a little. The common room to their left
was filled with rowdy drinkers finished with their days in
the fields; she winced as they turned to watch her and Madame progress along the corridor. *He must have gotten very
little sleep these past months*, she realized, *what with his
rooms on this floor, and waking before dawn to come and
fence with me. . . .*

Madame knocked at a door on their right. A burst of
noise from the common room obliterated the sound, so she
did so again. "Brian?"

"Is that you, Christiane?" There was a lengthy pause,
while Nichola glanced anxiously over her shoulder at the
carousing drinkers, who were staring back at her.

"It's taking rather long," Madame noted idly. "I wonder—"

Just then the door opened, to Lord Boru himself, on his canes. "Sorry for the delay," he said with a grin. "Hayden's gone to—" He glimpsed Nichola in the shadows behind the countess, and his welcoming expression changed. "Christ, Christiane," he muttered. "What in God's name possessed you to bring *her* here?"

Madame bustled past him. "Hayden has gone where?"

"To—to London," Boru said, moving aside as Nichola reluctantly followed Madame into the room. She noticed he was jacketless, with his white linen shirt open at the throat. "To fetch the wagon-train. Such a bother, packing up."

"Don't I know it," Madame said with feeling, settling into a chair and pulling off her gloves. "I never, ever in my life intend to move again."

Nichola glanced about dubiously. The room was spacious and surprisingly clean, except for stacks of books lying everywhere. Besides the chair Madame had taken, there was a small settee, upholstered in bedraggled red velvet, and in the far corner, under the windows, a bed that did not look nearly long enough for His Lordship. On the mantel above the hearth were a mismatch of cups and wineglasses, most of them sticky. The windows were covered with outrageously gaudy fringed drapes.

Lord Boru was frowning at her—or, rather, at the box she held awkwardly in her arms. "What's that?" he demanded.

"You know perfectly well what it is, Brian," said Madame, nodding at Nichola to have a seat. Instead she stayed rooted, irritated at being exposed to this evidence of how Lord Boru had lived for the past months.

"Miss Hainesworth appears taken aback at my accommodations," he noted dryly. "Did you not forewarn her that to a soldier, a roof alone is counted luxury?"

"Do you mean that Tommy—" Nichola stopped, aware she sounded idiotic. Why had she never thought how cramped and miserable those tents that gleamed in her imagination must be?

"Is far worse off than this," His Lordship confirmed.

"Did you not consider that, Miss Hainesworth, when you made your plans to sojourn abroad?"

She could have kicked him for bringing that up. "I'm only too aware," she retorted, "how childish my thoughts of joining a regiment were."

"Spoken like a true belle of the *ton*," he told her. "How is Wallingford?"

"Quite well, thank you."

"She's been deluged with letters from him," the countess put in.

"Bully for her."

"I say, Brian. Is there anything to drink?"

He smiled tautly. "In a commonhouse? Of course there is, my sweet. Only tell me what you'd like."

"Whiskey and water, I think."

Nichola stared at her. What woman drank whiskey and water? "And for you, Miss Hainesworth?" Lord Boru drawled.

"Nothing, thank you!"

He threw open the door and shouted, in a voice that cut straight through the common-room clamor, "Two whiskeys with water, Bert! And a claret!"

"Comin' right up, m'lord!" came an answering shout.

"I *said*—" Nichola began.

"Oh, I know what you said. But you need relaxing. You may as well sit, you know. There aren't too many spiders or roaches. And I've altogether eliminated the snakes." Nichola fought off an urge to make a face at him and perched very gingerly on the edge of the settee.

"Where are you headed, Brian?" Madame inquired, just as Bert, the barman, came in with an affable grin and a tray.

"Whiskeys and water here and here. Claret *there*," Boru noted with a grimace at Nichola. He remained on his feet, too, on his canes, because the only open seat was next to Nichola on the settee. He moved to the mantelpiece and leaned against it, so he could grasp the cup Bert set there for him. The barman's grin turned shy as he put Nichola's wineglass into her hand.

"Hope yer'll find the vintage suitable, mum," he murmured.

"I'm sure I will," she replied, with no intention whatsoever of drinking out of any container in that place.

"Strathclyde, Christiane," said Lord Boru, returning to her question. "Hayden is pushing for it. And frankly, I'm played out."

"How is the knee?"

"The knee is gone. The knee is a thing of the past."

"You needn't jump down my throat," Madame chastised him gently. "Dr. Cohen says—"

"Cohen's a bloody fool." He jerked his gaze back to Nichola, who still held the saber case on her lap. "What did you bring that back for?"

She stared at the floor. "Because I cannot accept it."

"That's for me to decide."

"You mean it as—as some sort of reproof. For what happened with Lord Wallingford."

He considered her for a moment. "No," he said then. "I meant it as encouragement. To keep what happened with Wallingford from ever happening again."

"What exactly do you think happened with Wallingford, Brian, pray tell?" asked Madame.

"She threw the bout," Lord Boru said in disgust. "She found him an unworthy opponent."

"*Would* you stop harping on that?" Nichola demanded, and without thinking took a sip of the claret. The savor of the wine—smooth, warm, rich—made her forget the argument to stare at the glass in her hand. "Gracious!"

"I travel with my own cellar," Boru informed her, his upper lip curling. "It's the main reason Hayden had to go and fetch the wagon-train."

"I should have thought you'd have drunk most of it by now," Madame said dryly.

"I have the whiskey as well." Boru sipped deeply from his own cup. Nichola watched his Adam's apple move up and down, was reminded of the river water splashing down his chest, and quickly looked away.

"Goodness, I nearly forgot," Madame declared, starting up from her seat. "I must go and tell Mrs. Wickers the receipt for that medicine I gave her. William tells me Cissie is now ill."

"I'll go with you," Nichola said abruptly.

Madame's fine, dark eyes considered her. "I rather think," she said softly, "you must explain to Lord Boru why you can't accept his gift. And having guests in her kitchen who put on airs makes Mrs. Wickers very nervous."

"I? Put on airs?" Nichola stammered helplessly. Madame gave a little shrug and went out. Nichola started to follow, but Lord Boru went and shut the door.

"You heard her," he told her. "I should not want my final meals with Mrs. Wickers disrupted. She is an exceedingly fine cook."

Nichola sank back onto the settee. Lord Boru moved awkwardly toward the chair Madame had vacated and let himself fall into it, casting the canes aside. Nichola recognized with glee that now he could not stop her leaving even if he chose to. She also recognized, somewhat less happily, that he'd left his whiskey atop the mantel. He followed her gaze. "It would be too much, I expect, to hope that you might bring that to me."

"Of course I will. You must not think, Lord Boru, that simply because of our disagreement regarding Wallingford, I am any less . . . indebted to you for all you've done for me."

"I'm not at all sure what I've done for you." He took the glass from her hand. Their fingers brushed. Nichola rushed back to the settee for another gulp of claret.

"I admit," she said then, somewhat haltingly, "it is difficult to comprehend. I know this, though: My mother is proud of me for the first time in my life. The other girls at the academy envy me. And Wallingford—seems to be in love with me." Her voice was tinged with wonder.

Lord Boru leaned back in his seat. "And that is what you look for in life."

"It is a great deal more than I ever expected," Nichola said hotly. "How would you ever understand? You are a man—and a great hero to boot!"

"Ah, yes. Lord Boru, the great war hero. I would hate to tell you, Miss Hainesworth, how short a time the natural interest in a great war hero is sustained amongst the *ton*."

"The *ton* are idiots."

"Well. We are in agreement there." He reached up, patting his chest. "Dammit all. I've left my cigars on the mantel as well. Might I bother you to bring them?"

Nichola got up. The mantel was so cluttered with debris that it took her some moments to ascertain his cigar case wasn't there. "I'm sorry. I—"

"On my desk, then."

She started toward it and glimpsed the case, with great relief. She quickly brought him the cigars. He selected one, nicked off the tip. "Mind if I smoke?"

"It's your room," she retorted. Then her resentment gained the upper hand, and she demanded, "What is it about Wallingford, exactly, that sticks in your craw?"

He'd struck a match and lighted up; now he leaned back in the chair, exhaling a slow plume of smoke. "Doesn't really matter what I say," he noted idly, "since you'll put it down to jealousy of his having two good legs." She winced; that *was* what she had told Madame. "But so long as you ask—he is, as noted, an able-bodied fellow, reasonably hardy. Why do you suppose he is not abroad?"

Nichola was taken aback. "I—I never thought about it. He's very young."

"He's twenty-five damned years old."

"I suppose you are going to tell me next he is a sympathizer with Napoleon's cause!"

"Not at all. At least, not that I know of. I've heard him make any number of stirring supper-table speeches against the man."

Now that Nicola considered it, so had she. "Perhaps he has . . . some physical imperfection?"

"I think it more likely his rich papa has paid someone to take his place. But as for physical imperfections, you would know far better than I."

"See here!" she cried. "There's no cause for you to make such insinuations! I don't understand why you must be so bloody *horrid* about him! I am going to find Madame." She started for the door—only to find her way blocked by a cane that he'd retrieved from the floor with astonishing quickness. She whirled to him, staring.

"Perhaps," he said heavily, slowly, "it is because he has had that which I have only dreamed of." The crook of the cane had hooked around her thigh. He gave a tug, like a fisherman playing his prey. Nichola stumbled toward him, wide-eyed.

"What in God's name do you think you are doing?"

"Not permitting you to walk out of my life again." He tugged harder, drawing her closer, pulling her all the way into his lap. She landed off balance, with a thud that left her breathless. He threw the cane aside and put his two hands to the sides of her face. Then he kissed her, with a hard, intent purposefulness as unlike Wallingford's tender embrace as the night was from day. His lips forced themselves onto hers, bruising in their brute power, for such a long time that she grew dizzy. She sought to push him away, but he was far too strong.

"Go on and fight me, Valkyrie," he whispered hoarsely.

"Oh! You!" Infuriated, she slapped at him. He blocked her hand readily, catching it in his own. "How dare you jest at him?"

"I don't. Idiot though he be, the term he chose is apt. Handmaiden to the gods . . ." His mouth sought hers again, with that same wild fury. As he pressed against her, he brought his right hand to her breast, covering it, encircling it. And where his mouth was bruising, his touch through the muslin was as delicate as soft spring wind. His

thumb flicked against her nipple. Nichola felt the most remarkable flurry deep in her belly, like carriage-sickness,
when the floor of the coach seemed to drop away and leave
one dangling in air. She sought to raise her head, drink in
air, clear her tangled brain. But he would not allow it; he
only followed with his insistent kisses, letting his lips slip
downward to her chin and then her throat. *I must get out of
here*, Nichola thought. *I must find Madame. . . .*

In a sudden swift motion, he curled his fingers in the
edge of her bodice and the corset beneath, yanking them
downward, baring her breasts. His breath escaped in a
long, slow sigh as he put his mouth to her flesh, drawing at
her with all the desperation of a starved man confronted
with sustenance. His need was so unexpected, so staggering, that unconsciously she wrapped her arms around his
neck and gathered him in.

Instantly, horrified, she recognized her mistake. He
raised his head for a brief moment, his wide smile blazing.
Then he renewed his assault, and this time, his hands were
hovering at her skirts as she lay splayed on his lap. But the
sweetness of his tongue caressing her breasts, moving from
one to the other, was so lulling, so soothing. "Ah," he
sighed, sounding not at all like himself, sounding helpless
and enthralled. "Oh, Nichola. You are . . . sweet as rain."

The odd, quaint endearment made her shiver. "Lord
Boru. Please," she managed to muster.

"Please what?" He sucked hard at the tip of her breast.
Her emotions puddled.

"Please God," she whispered.

"Or the handmaiden to him." He licked a long line
between her nipples. Her skin burned.

"Wallingford never—" she began.

"His loss," he broke in impatiently. " 'To the victor
belong the spoils.' " His huge hands molded her shoulders,
pushing the sleeves of her gown away.

"But," said Nichola. "But—" Then she could no
longer speak. He'd put his mouth to her again. His tongue
circled the taut bud of her nipple relentlessly, setting off a

tingling rush of sensation so devastating that she forgot entirely what her protest had been.

"Speak my name," he challenged her, raising his head to stare into her tiger's eyes as he stroked her, enticed her.

"Lord Boru—"

"My *name*."

"Brian," she whispered, and he smiled just before bowing to her breasts once more. "Brian," she said again, haltingly. "No. Please. Don't—"

To her complete astonishment, he drew away. "I'll not have you say I forced you," he told her softly. "I would not want you . . . if you did not want me as well."

God. What did she want at that moment? She wanted for him to go on touching her forever with his feathery hands and his silken tongue. The very certainty of the realization gave her pause. "Madame," she said haltingly.

"The door is locked." His blue eyes were as well, locked on hers.

"My—my reputation."

"Can only be enhanced. A kind academy girl, come to give comfort to the cripple . . ." There was a bulge against Nichola's side that only reinforced how absurd the label was.

"If you are a cripple, I am the queen of Sheba."

He laughed. "Now that you know my secret, I'm afraid I have no choice but to . . . swear you to silence." He pressed his mouth to hers. That hard rod thrusting at her side reminded Nichola of the way he'd looked in the river, raising himself up by his arm, the water abandoning him, flowing from him, while his manhood pointed to the sky. . . .

"Why?" she breathed.

Against all reason, he had followed her train of thought. "Because I want you to know . . . I am not just an object of pity."

"I never pitied you," she told him helplessly.

"Liar."

"Well—not for long, anyway."

He lifted her into the air effortlessly, settling her more comfortably across his lap, and she was reminded of how she'd had to pull herself into the saddle when Wallingford had given her his hands. She'd thought her diminutive suitor's kisses were wondrous. What, then, to call this man's, that dissolved all knowledge of right and wrong, left her welcoming his scandalous embraces, caused her to allow him liberties she would not have imagined only moments before? True, Boru's kisses held little of sweetness. But their wild, reckless hunger was a revelation. *I could never again be satisfied with Wallingford's embraces,* she realized, and shivered at the admission.

"What is it?" he murmured, his tongue tracing the curves of her ear.

"I am afraid," she confessed. "Lord Boru, I must go. I must go *now*."

"Before you do something you will regret?"

"I have already done much that I regret!"

He leaned back in the chair, nonchalant and grinning, his splendid red-gold hair working loose of its queue. "I'll let you leave if you kiss me."

"I *did* kiss you."

"No. I kissed *you*."

"Kiss you where?" she asked suspiciously, trying to tug up her disheveled bodice.

He raised his brows in innocence. "Here." He pointed with a finger to his lips.

"And what if I refuse?"

"I'll hold you here until you do." The immense strength of his arms proved he could, and readily. With all that had gone on between them by now, what could one kiss cost her? She leaned forward gingerly, to press her mouth to his.

It cost her her innocence. He stretched flat beneath her, his hand coming to rest on her buttocks, drawing her hard against him, so that his manhood pressed between her thighs through her tangled skirts. Then he held her there as he ground his loins against her, his movements tantalizing and slow. Her breasts were crushed to his shirt; his palm was pressing, pressuring her, holding her fast there. Nichola gasped as her belly convulsed in a rush of sweet fire. "Oh," she breathed.

"*Oh,*" he echoed softly, still clasping her to him. She heard his own breath coming in quick, short gasps. "Oh. Christ. Nichola—" He was moving against her in a frenzy, drawing her up and down, faster and faster, his hard manhood pushing at her furiously, desperately. Straight through the tangle of muslin and linen and crinoline, she could feel its hungry force, and his need became her need, his longing her longing, as they danced together this strange, wild dance. She caught her hands in his shirt, pulling it open, fighting with the buttons to lay his broad chest bare. When she succeeded, when her breasts brushed his naked skin, he laughed and brought his mouth up to kiss her neck with passionate intensity. "Oh, Nichola! You naughty girl!"

"I don't care," she whispered, manuevering higher so that he could suck at her nipple again. He claimed it with a ferocity that made her head spin. God, but it felt fine, what he was doing to her—his mouth, his hands, his eager, thrusting groin! All she wanted at that moment was for this ecstasy *never* to end. His arms slid downward, over her buttocks to her knees, and then grasped at her skirts, drawing them upward as he gathered them in his fists. He tucked them up at her waist, then ran his hands down over her thighs, the backs of her knees. He snapped the garter of her stocking, and she let out a cry of chagrin that he swallowed, his tongue pushing between her lips. He tasted of whiskey and want. He smoothed her drawers down hard against her buttocks. The sheer batiste was scarcely any barrier at all. Her skirts had become bunched between them in the front, though.

"Blasted bloody clothes," he grunted. "What I'd give to see you without them!"

As she had already seen him. But he was beautiful. A god. And she . . . was only Nichola Hainesworth, graceless and oversized. She— "What are you doing?" she asked in alarm.

"Unfastening your ribbons."

"Oh, no!" she protested, clutching at muslin. "You don't—you wouldn't—I'm not—oh. Please. Don't." He ignored her blithely, pulling the gown up over her head and flinging it to the floor. She recoiled, pushing away from him to stand clad in only her corset and pettiskirts. He caught her by the waist, fingers unfastening hooks and clasps with astonishing adeptness. *I am not the first woman he has ever undressed,* Nichola thought fleetingly, wistfully. There went her drawers. He was the first man who had ever seen her . . . like this.

She turned her head away, blushing. He tipped it back with a gentle finger. She gathered her arms across her breasts, reconsidered, and let them fall to shield her privates instead. His hands dropped from her, and she *knew,* she *knew* what he was thinking—or thinking better of. God. Why had she—

"Nichola."

"I had better go." She bent to gather her discarded clothes.

"Nichola. Look at me. Please," he added, in a voice utterly unlike his, tentative and beseeching. Slowly she raised her gaze—and saw his blue eyes shining brightly. He reached out to her, stroked her waist, the curve of her hip. "You are . . . so beautiful," he said haltingly.

"Oh, no. Not I. I am—"

"Don't you tell me otherwise! I have seen enough naked women to know when I am confronted with beauty!"

"I cannot imagine what I was thinking," she stammered, "to allow you to—"

"Come here."

She edged forward. He touched her breast with his fingertips, let them slide down to her belly and then lower, to the thatch of blond curls between her thighs. He let out his breath in a long, slow sigh. "Beautiful," he whispered. He was fondling her there, caressing her, fingers moving down through the curls, reaching, probing, exploring. They struck wet, warm softness, hesitated, withdrew. Nichola's hips followed, all of their own volition. He smiled, his free hand unbuttoning his breeches. Nichola did stop him then—to pull off his shirt. When that was done, she knelt and drew off his boots. "You do that better than Hayden," he observed, watching her through narrowed eyes.

"I have more cause," she said softly.

He laughed and raised himself up from the settee on one elbow, yanking his breeches down to his thighs. There he paused. "It is not," he noted, "terribly pretty. This next part. You might want to—"

Still kneeling, she pulled his left leg free of the broadcloth, then bared his right, his injured knee. She caught her breath at the sight of the long, jagged scars that encircled it, the new flesh still raised and red and oddly smooth, like a baby's skin. "Oh. Oh, Brian," she whispered. "I had no idea. . . ."

"Perhaps you ought to put out the lamps," he said shortly.

Instead she bent and kissed him, put her mouth to those terrible wounds, traced them with her tongue.

He flinched from her touch. "God, Nichola. Don't."

"They are part of you, are they not?"

"The worst part. My ruin."

She raised her head then. "Without them," she asked softly, "would you ever have looked twice at me?"

His blue eyes, dark in the flickering light, met hers. "You are very . . . blunt. Likely not. But the loss—oh, the loss would have been all mine!" Satisfied—she could not have *borne* it if he'd lied—she smiled and rose, to climb into his lap again. But something sad had come over his face; he held her at arm's length, drinking in the sight of her for a long moment before dropping his gaze. "No. I cannot," he said, and his voice was shaking. "I was wrong. This is wrong. How can I ask this of you? I have nothing to offer. I am—the shell of a man."

"Rather a hardy shell," she remarked, looking steadily back at him. "Like a giant clam."

He tried to laugh but couldn't. "You don't know . . . what you are missing. What *I* am missing."

"I see plain enough what is there."

"Dammit, I'm not jesting! You deserve better than me. You deserve—"

"Wallingford?"

"If he can dance with you, and ride with you, and walk with you down—by God, yes!"

"I have kissed Wallingford," Nichola began thoughtfully.

"Don't you think I know it?" he demanded, scowling.

"Doing so never aroused in me the least inclination to do anything more than . . . go on kissing. Whereas you . . ." She tilted her head at him, glanced down ruefully at her bared limbs. "See what kissing *you* has done?" He started to say more. She laid a finger against his lips. "I'll not have it said that I forced you. I would not want you . . . if you did not want me as well."

And at her echo of his earlier words, he suddenly burst out laughing, laughed so long and hard that she thought they must hear him in the common room beyond, nay, back at the abbey. Then he gripped her waist and drew her onto him, planting a kiss on her mouth. "*Touché.* I surrender, Miss Hainesworth. Totally and utterly. For I *do* want you. As I have never wanted anyone or anything on this earth." His kisses covered her cheeks, her throat, her eyes and ears. He put his hands to her buttocks, settling her atop him, and the feel of his naked flesh against hers, the whole length of it, made her shiver with pleasure. His hard rod was between her thighs, urgent and demanding. He stroked her with his hands, caressing the small of her back. "How tall are you?" he demanded suddenly.

"I—don't know. Mamma stopped measuring me when I was eleven. Out of despair, I believe."

"I shall measure you now." He shifted her again, drawing her downward until their toes met, then raising his palm to the top of her head. She reached all the way to his mouth. "Not quite six feet," he said with satisfaction. "A perfect size."

"For what?" Nichola wondered.

"For this." He lifted her with his hands—so very easily he moved her!—and tilted her backward. Then he slid the whole length of his great rod inside her, sinking it to the hilt with a sigh of such immense satisfaction that Nichola neglected to observe that she had just relinquished her virginity. "Ahhh," he murmured, his mouth at her ear, his fingers holding her tight against him. The sensation was astonishing—like a hand going into a glove, like a root reaching into the earth, like mountains pushing up against the sky. Nichola licked her lips, which had suddenly gone dry. He noticed and obligingly wet them with his tongue before kissing her again. He spread his knees so that hers parted as well, so that she straddled his loins. "Oh. God," he whispered, fingers catching in the hair that cascaded down her back. "Nichola. Nichola—" He began to move, slowly, delectably, hips thrusting at her and then pulling away, that long rod sliding deeper, withdrawing, sliding deeper again, while he pressed his mouth to hers hungrily. Nichola mimicked his motions with her own, kneeling up on the settee as he drew back from her, descending when he thrust in, lost in the dazzling bright heat his every movement evoked, oblivious to everything but their wondrous dance. In and out and in again, like some wild, lustful quadrille—but rather than their feet treading the steps, their entire bodies were engaging. Her breasts smacked into his chest, rose in the air between them. He caught the tip of one in his mouth and sucked at it hard, making her cry out with longing. His manhood was a saber, piercing and bright, and she was the scabbard it sought, fitting him perfectly, a sublime match. He smoothed his palms over her buttocks, pulling her closer yet, sinking ever deeper within her, moving faster and faster, until—

Nichola screamed, and his hand clapped across her mouth, gently and firmly. But she could not help herself;

the fire in her belly had flared like a forge. She leaned downward, so that he sank into her again. "Oh, oh, oh!" she moaned.

He held her so close that only their hips were moving, up and down, his mouth hard to hers to swallow her ecstatic cries. "Oh," he agreed, the word coming out halting and breathless. "Oh, Nichola. Nichola—"

She tucked her knees tighter around his waist, riding him astride, going hell-for-leather, and he matched her motions with his own, bucking like a stallion, a great frantic beast. And just when she thought she could not bear the pleasure any longer, thought she must go mad if he did not stop, she ceased thinking altogether, her conscious mind shutting down, reaching beyond reason into some glorious stretch of blinding white light that stretched above them, an enveloping angel folding them in its wings. She strained onto him; he thrust back, hands splayed across her buttocks; the heat and the light joined in a blistering flash that jolted her eyes open, then spread out in slow, lingering waves. She stared down at him. He reached up to kiss her, his eyes as wide as her own. In their bright circles she saw the shimmering reflection of the passion throbbing through her, bathing the dismal room, the shabby inn, the whole of Kent—nay, the world and the universe—in its amazing glow. Then the waves of flame slowly receded. She bowed her head to his chest, scarcely able to breathe, while he held her tightly, his hands caught in her tangled hair.

She felt incapable of speech or motion. She never had imagined, never had any inkling whatsoever, that her body had the capacity for that. She was awestruck by what they had shared, wondered if he had felt anything like what she had, if anyone in the history of mankind ever had. Then she colored a little. He would have, of course. He was no virgin. He'd had scores of lovers. She was no different from the others—except, no doubt, less adept.

Something touched her hair, close by her temple. Christ. A bedbug. Then another, and another—she roused herself, pushing up on her elbows against his chest, tossing her hair impatiently. Then she caught sight of his face, saw the gleam of tears at the edges of his blue eyes, saw another bright drop fall, and she froze. "Oh, Lord Boru," she whispered. "Please, don't cry."

"I never . . . cry," he said haltingly, as the tear coursed slowly down his cheek. "Great heroes never cry."

She bent and licked the salt drop away. "Don't," he warned, "or you'll reduce me to jelly. As though you haven't already." He sat up on the settee, drew her around so that she lay in his lap. "And don't call me Lord Boru, for Christ's sake." His voice was falsely gruff.

"Brian," she corrected herself. She stretched her arm out for his whiskey and water, held it to his mouth.

"Am I so pale as that?"

"More pale."

"Well," he acknowledged, taking a swallow, "it has been quite a while." She started to stiffen—so! It was only the long period of drought his injury had effected. . . . But even before she could fully form her fury, he had kissed her and finished: "My whole life, in fact."

"Liar," she countered, unconvinced. "How many women have you had?"

"Many. But only one worthy opponent." He caressed her cheek. "Everything else was only practice for this bout."

"You would know what to say."

"I would," he agreed readily. "You, on the other hand, you babe in arms—what would *you* know of passion?"

"I know what I feel," Nichola said stubbornly. "What I *felt*."

"Which was?"

She shook her head. "Indescribable."

"My sentiments exactly. They do say true passion is tongue-tied." He drew her closer. She nestled against him, almost satisfied.

"But surely," she began.

"Umm?" He nuzzled her bare shoulder, brought his fingertips up to the tip of her breast. Nichola caught her breath as a half-recollection of ecstasy constricted her belly, shivered her womb.

"Surely one woman is much like another," she finished, even as he brought his mouth to her nipple, let his tongue slide over its taut bud.

He glanced up, meeting her dubious gaze. "They always were until now," he told her, and lowered his head to her breast once more.

Chapter Eighteen

"I really must go."

Nichola had been lying on the floor of Lord Boru's room, atop the rug she'd so disdained when she'd entered, for what seemed like hours, dozing against her lover's chest, reveling in the marvelous sensation of his bare skin touching hers. At some point he'd suggested moving to the bed, but she'd noted it was scarcely big enough for him alone, much less accompanied—holding to herself the reservation that such translocation would have involved him using his canes and thus again exposing his weakness. She did not care for her own part, but she had the intuition that what had happened between them had done more for his fragile self-credit than all their fencing lessons, and she did not want him reminded of the reason why he'd tried to forestall it. And so, when the settee had grown cramped, she'd simply gotten up and fetched the quilt from his bed and lain down at his feet. He'd tumbled down beside her

with awkward gratefulness and promptly made love to her
again.

Now, though, the last dawdlers in the common room
had headed home, calling their farewells from the courtyard, and the moon had risen beyond the curtained windows, so bright and full that it cast shadows straight
through the cloth, and heaven alone knew where Madame
was or what she must be thinking. . . . "I really *must* go,"
she said again, and reached for her discarded clothes.

"Don't," he murmured into her hair. "Stay."

"I can't. It must be nigh on midnight! I cannot fathom
what Madame meant by leaving us alone together all this
time."

"Christiane knew just what she was doing." He kissed
her throat, began to stroke her breasts with those long,
gentle fingers—

But Nichola drew back. "Surely you don't mean—"

"She has always had her own plan for restoring me to
my former glory. I imagine this was part of that."

She stiffened despite his winning caresses. "You make
her sound like a—a procuress! And me like a common
tart!"

"There's nothing common about you," he protested
drowsily. "Stay with me. Sleep with me."

But that old, nagging jealousy—what had the two of
them meant to one another, once upon a time in Paris?—
had reared its head. She turned from him. He was not the
sort of man, she felt certain, who'd take kindly to prying
questions. Still, now that *this* had occurred, surely she deserved some explanation, some clarification of the facts.

"Brian?" It came out so breathless that he did not hear
her. She swallowed, tried again: "Brian?"

"Mm?" He moved closer to her beneath the quilt,
tucking up against her, his knees fitting behind hers just so,
his arms curled tight around her. In the silence of the de-
serted inn, she could hear his heartbeat, his every slow
breath.

Did it matter, whatever he and Madame had once

shared? He wasn't with Madame *now*—he was with her.
He had cried for *her,* told her *she* was the only true lover
he'd ever had. Damn. She needed time and space to think
on all of this, and he was affording her neither; sleepy
though he might be, she felt his manhood surging to hardness at her back.

He felt it as well, and mumbled in apology: "Sorry."
He shifted so it was not as obvious. "You must be sore by
now. But I can't stop wanting you." He nuzzled the nape of
her neck.

Nichola *was* sore; she felt as though she'd been riding
astride for days on end. It was a most delectable soreness,
though. . . . She let her hand wander back to his thigh,
smoothed the wiry hair there—

"I thought you had to be going."

"I do," she said, with such dejection that he laughed.

"Tell you what," he proposed. "I'll have you back by
dawn. For a lesson in the courtyard."

"Katherine and Gwen and Bess—"

"Are sound asleep by now," he murmured into her ear,
tracing its curves with his tongue.

"I haven't got my pads. My mask."

"You can borrow my extra set."

"My foil—"

"You have a saber," he reminded her. "Mine."

"I can't accept your saber."

"You already have. More than once." She giggled as he
slid his hard rod between her buttocks.

"You know what I mean."

"It was only ever a symbol. Of what I longed to do
with you. Oh, Nichola." He was pushing against her from
behind, the smooth tip of his manhood seeking out her
sheath. When he thrust that way, the sensation was entirely
different but no less magical. He covered her breasts with
his big hands, pinching her nipples with gentle insistence,
and she sighed happily and surrendered to another storm of
frantic ecstasy. When it had passed, when he'd brought her

once more to quivering, shivering fulfillment, he kissed her cheek with infinite sweetness and fell soundly asleep.

She lay beneath the heavy, welcome weight of his thigh, watching the slow passage of the moon across the curtained windows. To leave now was unthinkable; he might conclude that she regretted what they'd shared. And she did not, could not, harbor regrets, whatever might be the consequences, for she loved him—how long *have* I loved him, she wondered? Forever? For always?—with a ferocity that was breathtaking. The tawdry chamber that had so dismayed her had taken on a gilded glow, the moonlight turning every bit of furniture and scrap of fabric to enchantment, like a fairy bower.

For a moment, her practical mind fought to enumerate obstacles. His age. His background and character. His injury, and all the damage it had wreaked on his soul . . . But practicality had no force against that moonbeam magic, against the argent sheen of his promises and whispers and tears.

"I love you, Brian Boru," she told him, told the insensate mass of him that cradled her closely. "And I will love you straight up until the end of time." He stirred, his arms tightening around her, almost as though he had heard her. And perhaps he had, she thought wearily, happily, tugging the edges of the quilt to her heart.

Chapter
Nineteen

Full-flush spring had come to the abbey, the ivy sprouting thousands of new tendrils along the ancient walls, robins and wrens splashing once more in the mossy water of the antique fountain, the grass in the courtyard growing lush and green beneath the pointed toes of Nichola's boots. She nicked a swath across it with the edge of Brian's—her—saber, drinking in the sweet new-mown scent as she watched grim-faced Hayden plying a shovel against the soft earth.

"A wee bit deeper, I think," Brian instructed him from his chair. His aide-de-camp grunted and set his shoulder to it, muttering under his breath.

"I should think you might tell me what it is you are doing," Nichola noted, her mask tilted back on her head as she observed the mysterious preparations. "After all, I shall have to explain to Mrs. Treadwell why you are putting a trench straight through that patch of chamomile."

"All in good time," Brian retorted, his smile sly and

teasing. "And now, Hayden, if you would just fetch what is in the back of the carriage, I'd be much obliged." The manservant straightened—stretching his back rather more, Nichola thought, than was necessary, considering that his labors hadn't been all *that* strenuous—and made a show of hobbling toward the doors as though he'd just cleansed the stables of Augeas singlehandedly.

"Are all Scotsmen so remarkably averse to physical exertion?" Nichola wondered aloud.

Her lover made a mock scowl. "Saucy thing. I don't see you digging."

"I could have done it in half the time—and with a deal less grumbling."

"Hayden doesn't approve of you."

She let her eyes go wide. "He *doesn't*? Lord, I'd never have guessed as much. Why ever not?"

"I have no idea—unless it is because he'd no sooner come with the wagon-train from London last month than I sent him back with it once more."

"I wish you'd send him again for it now. Or, better, to fetch tea from China."

Brian lit up a cigar and tossed the match aside. "He'd defy the order, I believe. He's determined to protect me from you."

"Is he so possessive against all your . . . friends?"

That made him snort. "Hardly. He seems to find you especially formidable."

"I can't imagine why."

His gaze, blue as the cloudless morning sky above them, met hers, and the fire burning there sent a quiver shooting straight to her belly. "He sees the changes you have wrought in me," he said quietly, intently, and put the cigar to his lips, his tongue caressing the tip in precisely the way, only an hour before, he had been suckling her breasts. She watched in fascination, taking a step toward him without even realizing she had. Only the sudden brief shake of his head warned her off; lacking it, she would have climbed into his lap then and there.

She might have anyway except that Hayden had appeared again, dragging a great length of iron pipe across the courtyard. His excavations had attracted an audience: Gwen and Bess were on the balcony, their heads close together, whispering avidly. "Is it a Maypole, Lord Boru?" Bess called down gaily.

"Nay," he thundered back at her, "a stake for burning overcurious young virgins." Nichola's two friends dissolved in shocked giggles. "You, at least, are safe," Lord Boru added sotto voce to Nichola, making her blush to her toes. "Put it in the hole, then, Hayden," he went on briskly. "Good and deep—aye, that's the way. Thrust harder . . . work it in well. Aye, aye—and now mound the earth up about it. Something amiss, Miss Hainesworth?"

"No," she managed in a strangled voice. God, everything he did reminded her of their nights together! Then she caught the sly twinkle in his eye and stuck her tongue out at him. He made an O of his mouth and drew his breath in as though meeting her tongue with his. Nichola burst out laughing. "Oh, you are incorrigible!"

"So they tell me," he said complacently, and blew a smoke ring into the air.

Bess's voice called out again. "If it is for hanging laundry—"

"Nothing so base, I assure you!" Lord Boru retorted with an affect of injured pride. "Have you a guess to hazard, Miss Carstairs?"

"All I can deduce," she threw back at him, "is that you have concluded that without your stalwart presence on the Continent, Napoleon's forces are sure to invade us, and so you have precipitated the installment of fortifications."

Nichola held her breath, wondering if Gwen's jest might lie too close to home. To her great relief, Brian took it in stride: "Let me assure you, I have already sent word to our generals that should the Corsican be so brash as to assay England's shores, he must by all means possible be enticed to visit Mrs. Treadwell's academy. Not even he

would stand a chance against the charms of the young ladies here."

Bessie let out a delighted sigh. "Are there more like
you at home in Scotland, Lord Boru? For if there are, I
fully intend to take up residence there."

In the midst of laughing, Nichola paused, seeing that
Katherine Devereaux had appeared on the balcony as well.
"What the devil is all this hubbub at this ungodly hour?"
she demanded crossly, with a toss of her golden ringlets.

"Oh, don't be such a damp rag, Katherine," Bessie told
her. "Lord Boru is rigging up some sort of mystery in the
garden. Ask her has she a guess, Lord Boru."

But Brian recognized readily enough that one resident
of the academy lay beyond his power to enthrall. "I beg
your pardon, Lady Devereaux," he apologized, "for disturbing your sleep. We are nearly finished. Tamp that
ground down firmly, Hayden, if you please." The servant
obliged, stomping with such vigor that Nichola imagined he
was pretending *she* was the loam. She saw from the corner
of her eye that Madame had come to the kitchen doorway,
a steaming cup of tea in her hand, and was taking in the
proceedings with an air of bemusement. A bevy of the
lower-form girls had gathered on the balcony opposite
Gwen and Katherine and Bess as well. And here came Mrs.
Treadwell, her cap and pinafore spotless as always, her
mien as placid as though it were an everyday occurrence to
have a member of the nobility directing the digging of holes
between her flower beds. "Is it too close to your primroses,
Mrs. Treadwell?" Brian inquired politely.

"Oh, I don't believe so. Though that will depend, of
course, on what it is *for*."

He stubbed his cigar out beneath his boot heel and
rose up in his chair. "Time to reveal all, I suppose. My
mask, Hayden, if you would?"

"I still say, m'laird, this will prove far too taxin'. Dinna
Dr. Cohen tell ye—"

"My mask, Hayden," Brian reiterated in quite a different voice, one that promptly brought the item requested,

albeit with a sullen lack of grace. "And the canes." Nichola
watched, perplexed, as Brian used the crutches to propel
himself straight up to the pole, then clapped his mask down
over his face. He hooked his left arm around the stout pipe
and hesitated for a moment; she thought she heard him
draw in his breath. Then he tossed the canes over his back
into the thick grass and stood hanging on to the pole. With
his right hand, he drew out his saber. "Miss Hainesworth.
En garde."

"Oh, Bri—oh, Lord Boru," she corrected herself
quickly, aware of Katherine looking on avidly, and the goggling younger girls. "You mustn't . . ." But something in
his stance, in the fierce pride he exuded at standing on his
own feet to face her, silenced her abruptly. She glanced
uncertainly at Madame, who shot her a quick nod.

"You have gone beyond what I can teach you from a
chair," Brian told her, with a slash of his blade.

"Dr. Cohen says," hapless Hayden tried again to protest.

Lord Boru whirled on him with astonishing swiftness.
"Dr. Cohen says I can do whatever I believe I can. I believe
I can do this. Miss Hainesworth?" She approached gingerly. "Your left hand," he noted with familiar disdain, "is
dangling." She swiftly drew it up. "That's better. Now let's
have at it, shall we? And if you do not defeat me, I warn
you, I shall cut off your head."

The lower-form girls let out a collective gasp. From
beyond her shoulder, Nichola heard Katherine's voice, low
and bored: "What a silly charade. A cripple versus a dolt."

That whipped her on as nothing Brian himself might
have said could have. How *dare* she call him a cripple in his
hearing? She lunged ferociously, clashing her blade against
his with a crash that made the little girls scream. Beneath
the uproar, she heard Brian's voice, low in her ear: *"Never
let your heart rule your head!"* Then he deflected her saber
so forcefully that he nearly ripped it from her grasp.

Nichola fell back, regrouped, took a firmer grip,
feinted right and then dove left, attempting a diagonal cut.

He swung about on the pole to meet it easily. "Why to the left?" he demanded through his mask. "You know my right will be the weaker side."

"Brian, I—"

"Play to your opponent's faults," he said implacably. "If you go soft on me, let me assure you, I will go soft on you." He made a motion with his sword hand to his groin. Anyone else watching would have thought he was adjusting his padding. But Nichola knew exactly what he meant. And she was far more fearful of wounding his spirit than his body. She set to it, using everything she knew, every advantage he had taught her over these past months. She did not submit, as she had to Lord Wallingford. And she triumphed, ten touches to nine.

When she scored the final point, he tore off his mask. For an instant, she was filled with terror. But only for an instant. He was beaming at her, his blue eyes bright with pride and admiration, his smile wide as the sea. "*There,* Miss Hainesworth!" he declared. "You have earned the right today to be called a fencer!" Gwen and Bess burst into cheers; the younger girls were applauding madly. Mrs. Treadwell nodded in satisfaction, and Madame—Madame's lovely face was positively luminous as she watched Lord Boru whirl around the pole once more and hop to his chair. The sole discordant note amongst the celebration, except for Hayden's glower, came from Katherine, who called out loudly and clearly:

"Even if it was only against a one-legged man!"

"You know," Nichola noted, taking a sip from the winecup she'd just held to his mouth, "I could conclude that *you* went easy on *me.*"

"I? Never!" He raised her up in his lap, shifting her from his right knee to his left. "You'll excuse it, I know, but I have got a cramp."

"I'll rub it for you." She set the cup aside and slipped from the settee to the floor to do so, taking his calf between

her hands, smoothing it with her palms and fingertips until
the coiled muscle loosened at last.

"Mmm," he murmured, leaning forward to kiss her
hair. "Hayden used to do that for me, you know. Only
never so well."

"You might have told me what you were planning."

"What, and have you agonize over whether or not it
would prove acceptable to best me?"

"*Most* men—"

"Are idiots. What shame is there in losing to a woman
when she is superior?"

"I'm not," she countered. "Or wouldn't be. If
you . . ." Her voice trailed into nothingness.

"But I don't, do I?" He winced. "There, that's gone all
tight again."

"You overworked it," she chastised him, pressing the
sore muscle gently.

"I haven't worked it at *all* in nigh on a year. Considering that, it doesn't hurt too badly."

"Stop being so damned brave."

He laughed. "All right. It hurts like hell. But even hurt-
ing is preferable to—to deadness. Dullness." She glanced
away. He saw it, and tipped back her chin with his fingertip. "What is wrong?"

Nichola could not put into words the dreadful thought
that had struck her. If by some miracle he regained the use
of his leg, became what he had been before this—what use
would he have then for her? She counted herself blessed
when there was a knock on the door and Hayden entered
with a tray. "Yer whiskey 'n' water, m'laird."

"Put it here." His Lordship indicated the table beside
the settee. "There will be nothing more for tonight."

Hayden shot a bitter look at Nichola as she knelt on
the floor. "Dr. Cohen recommended peace 'n' rest. I dinna
think—"

"I said there will be nothing more, Hayden," Brian
told him bluntly. "Go on to your bed." The servant withdrew, his black brows in a knot.

"What amazes me," Nichola observed, setting to work again on his leg, ignoring that awful moment of insight, "is that you ever had any lovers at all, with him to watch over you."

"I already told you—he has never been so mother-hennish before. To the contrary, he always proved most encouraging in my escapades."

"I wish he liked me," she said wistfully.

"He doesn't even like *me,* I don't think."

"Why do you keep him on?"

Brian grimaced. "His is a hereditary position. Aide-de-camp to the Boru; that would be me. Ask him. He'll tell you. For four hundred and something-odd years, the eldest of his clan has been the Boru's right-hand man. It went a lot more smoothly, of course, when the Boru was a fiend bent upon destroying England's stranglehold on Scotland. Hayden has had a hard time coming to grips with the consolidation of our respective kingdoms."

Nichola was remembering what Mrs. Treadwell had told her many months ago: that but for a few accidents of fate, Brian Boru would have been king of Scotland and Ireland both. "Haven't you?" she asked in wonder.

"Christ, no. I'm no fan of the Hanovers. But I have nothing but scorn for Scotsmen who'd reverse the course of history. It has always seemed natural to me that England and Scotland should be united. We share such a small space on the globe."

"But—united under the English, rather than under the Scots?"

"We've had our chances to take it. We *did* take it, in a way, if you hark back to James the Fifth. Our blood's still on the throne."

"But not your blood."

"Now you are truly reaching into the dark depths. Have you been meeting secretly with Hayden? Be serious, Nichola. I'm not about to strike a claim to the greatest kingdom on earth because my father's seventeen-times grandfather once ruled the Isles."

"Yet you have king's blood."

"When my family ruled," Brian said shortly, "women wore no underwear, horses were unknown, and men of fashion painted their faces blue. Do you want to know what I'm in favor of? Progress. Britain has made progress. The rest of it can go to hell." He stretched his hand out for the whiskey. Nichola could not restrain a faint grimace. She disliked the taste of Scotch whiskey and always had.

Her reaction did not, of course, escape him. "What is wrong?" he demanded.

"I simply prefer Bordeaux to Scotch."

"Because it costs more." He shot her a mock frown. "Or because there is no stink of peat in your blood. Nonetheless, I'd give it up for you."

"I'd never ask you to," she said, regretting having spoken.

"I drink too much of the bloody stuff anyway." He pushed the glass away.

"But Hayden will—"

"For Christ's sake! He's my aide-de-camp, not my guardian! You make me feel whole, Nichola—as nothing, no one, else ever has. And I don't mean my leg. Give me the winecup." She obliged. He took a long draught.

"Would you like a cigar?" she proposed.

"I'd like to go to my bed. *Our* bed," he corrected himself, with a devilish smile.

She stood and held out her arm for him. He took it now without shame, let her help him to the bed tucked beneath the window, allowed her to undress him, turning away only to use the chamber pot. Then he took his turn undressing her, with such avid pleasure that she blushed and laughed to feel his eager fingertips.

When they both were naked, he eased himself down onto the mattress, pulling her atop him. She lay on his chest and kissed him, her hands caught in his thick hair. When she shifted to kiss his ear, he winced. "What?" she whispered.

"Damned leg again. Ought to cut the bloody thing off."

She reached to rub the aching muscle. "You know what the trouble is? This bed's entirely too small."

"I've been thinking on that. Ah. There, right there." Her fingers had found the knot in his calf. "Mm. Agh! Not so hard!"

"Sorry. What have you concluded?"

"Oh. Just that I've got a lovely large one in the house in London."

"Send Hayden for it," she suggested promptly.

He laughed. "I believe I might. Probably throw him into convulsions."

"Unless . . ."

"Aye?" He'd leaned back, hands behind his head, and was watching her ministrations.

Nichola took a deep breath. "Unless you don't intend to stay for very long, of course."

There was a beat of silence. She stared at his knee, with its smooth furrows of scar.

"I intend to stay for as long as you can stand me," he said at last.

It was the closest they'd come, in the month they'd been lovers, to anything like a discussion of the future. Did she dare press on? How could she bear *not* to? "I'll be leaving here, you know, at the end of the term. For London."

"And the term ends in a matter of weeks. Hardly seems sporting to make poor Hayden drag the bedstead here and then back again."

"Then I will . . . see you in London?" She felt the knot in his calf ball up abruptly. "I mean," she amended quickly, resuming her rubbing, "I know it cannot be like this—"

"Nichola," he started to say.

She rushed on. "Although it could be, in a fashion, I suppose. Men in London have paramours, don't they? There must be some means of managing it. Perhaps I could find a book on the subject in the library at the academy. *Instructions for an Illicit Affair* . . ." Her voice was too bright; she could hear the tears she held back, knew that he must as well. One trembled at the corner of her eye, hung for an instant, then fell, splashing onto his thigh.

"Nichola. I—"

"It doesn't matter," she said swiftly, brushing the salt spot away with her hand. "I should not have spoken of it. Forgive me."

"Once you are in London, you'll have little enough use for me."

Her gaze darted to his face in shock. "How can you say that? How do you *dare* to say that?"

"Because it is true! What part will there be in your life there for a—a dried-up husk of a man?"

"Don't call yourself that? Don't ever, ever—"

"You'll be the belle of the season. You'll have dozens of bright young tulips dancing attendance on you. It is what you deserve."

"It isn't what I want. I want you." And her voice was rock-steady. "I love *you.*"

Oh, God. Now she'd done it. She'd spoken that word she'd *sworn* she'd never say before he did—because, really, what could he reply? Only two things—"I love you, too, Nichola"—or . . . not that. Something less than that. Something that would tear her heart apart forevermore.

She waited, head bowed, heart pounding. In the common room beyond the locked door, someone shouted out a bawdy joke; the crude words hung in the air between them, ballast for that *love* word, dragging it down from the skies to the earth. *It is different for men.* Hadn't her mother told her that, in some rare moment of what passed with the baroness for confidences? *Even the best of them don't feel emotion as we do.*

But she didn't believe that. She'd seen enough of Lord Brian Boru in these past weeks—his lust, his bravery, his humor, his tenderness—to trust that his heart was as bountiful as her own, that he knew passion and fear and hope every bit as fully as she did. The difference lay elsewhere, in what he would allow, permit, himself to acknowledge. And of that, she was not nearly so sure. Or was she deluding herself? Why was he still lying there in silence? Why didn't he say *something*?

Because you have left him nothing to say . . .

Furious with herself—why had she sought to corner him? Wouldn't any red-blooded man shy from such entrapment?—she bent her head even lower, until her mouth touched his injured knee. She kissed him there, then let her lips range upward, putting her mouth to his thigh, the hollow of his groin, the swirls of coarse red hair surrounding his manhood, and finally his rod itself, that had gone unaccustomedly slack.

He spoke at last, his voice rough and tangled. "Nichola. Don't think that you must—" He broke off then, with a gasp. She had taken him into her mouth.

It was a curious sensation, having him there. She drew back, ran her tongue around the smooth, knobbed tip. A glistening pearl of moisture appeared there, and she licked it away. He shuddered beneath her. Slowly she let his rod— it was much longer now, and hard—slide between her lips again, savoring its ridges and veins. He groaned, his entire body gone rigid. "Nichola. There's no need . . ."

But there was—there was *her* need, her desperate urge to prove to him that that word, that wretched *love* word, had been true, and would be for all time. Even if *he* would not speak it, did not feel it, he could not stop her from loving him for all she was worth. She cupped her fingers around his stiff manhood, let it slide as far into her mouth as she could stand, withdrew, her tongue and lips caressing its head, and then pushed down on him again.

"Oh, Christ. Oh, sweet Christ in heaven." His hips were moving beneath her, thrusting up at her, begging for more, imploring her to accept him, take more of him inside her. She obliged, fist sliding up and down with the motions of her mouth. "Oh, Christ! No! Nichola, I can't—"

Too late. His seed burst out in a sudden spurt, a lot of

it, more than she expected. It tasted salty-sweet, fresh like
grass and yet sour like sweat. She rolled it in her mouth,
exploring the savor, and then swallowed. He lay sprawled
beneath her, chest heaving. In her grasp, his manhood
convulsed in constricting waves. His hand lunged toward
her, settled onto her hair.

"You ought not to have done that," he said after a
minute, when he could speak.

"Why not?" she retorted.

"It isn't—proper."

"I enjoyed it."

With some difficulty, he raised his head, saw her shining eyes. "By God, I believe you did. Well, then. See how
you enjoy this." He yanked her down onto the bed beside
him, hauled himself up onto his good knee, and put his
head to the blond curls between her thighs. His tongue
flicked out, its tip caressing her, exploring her, tasting the
love juices set flowing by his own surrender. "So sweet," he
whispered, his head buried against her. His tongue found
the small, tight bud of her desire, circled it slowly, entic-
ingly; then his mouth closed on it, sucking hard. Nichola
gasped at the sensation, at the swell of delight that flooded
her body. Briefly he raised his gaze. "Shall I stop?"

"Don't you dare!"

Laughing, he set to his task with abandon, and did not
let up until she had reached an entirely novel pinnacle of
fulfillment, in which great waves of what was either the
most pleasurable pain in the world or the most torturing
pleasure had swept through her like a midsummer storm,
leaving her limp and dazed. "What is sauce for the goose,"
he murmured as her eyes opened at last, wide and filled
with wonder. "I wonder did they hear your cries at Bert's
bar?" She went crimson. "Nay, nay, I was only jesting. The
door is stout enough. But they were music to *my* ears." He
tweaked the nipple of her breast.

"No one ever told me. . . ."

"What?"

"I mean—that is to say—Mrs. Caldburn has *touched* on the subject. . . ."

"What subject would that be?" he demanded, grinning as he hauled himself up beside her in the narrow bed.

"A woman's duty to her . . ." *Husband.* Another forbidden word. "What goes on between a woman and a man. But she never, ever mentioned—and neither did Mother! Why does no one ever tell you the important things?"

He tucked her head into the curve of his strong arm. "Are you daft? If young ladies had any notion of the delectations of sexual congress, there would be no virgins past the age of thirteen."

"Men, though," she noted, with an edge to her voice. "Men know. They tell each other."

"How would you conclude that?"

"My brothers and their friends. It just occurs to me. This is what all their nudges and winks and ribald puns are about."

"Absolutely."

She pushed herself up on his chest. "Well! Do you think that is fair?"

"I'm not at all sure I follow—"

"All my mother said of intercourse was that it was to be avoided!"

"Advice any young woman would do well to heed."

"*Why* is it to be avoided?"

"There you come down to the great, sad difference between male and female anatomy, my heart. God—or the fates—kindly created men in such a way that intercourse has no lasting repercussions. Whereas for women—"

"Babies," Nichola said succinctly. "Damn. How bloody unfair." Her eyes, brown shot with gold, met his. "That is why you use—those things you use."

"Condoms," he said easily. "Any man with a conscience would."

"Except that first time."

"You caught me off-guard. You'll note you haven't since." He grinned and kissed her. Nichola knew she ought to be grateful for his conscientiousness. But somehow, it made her sad.

He was tired. His eyelids were drooping. He lay back against the pillows, and within moments she heard him start to snore. Nichola got up to turn down the lamp wicks. Her mind was buzzing far too much for sleep. She sat on the settee in the dark, pondering him, his thoughts, what might be going on in his brain. Did he love her? Or was she simply something of convenience for him, the only girl he'd found since he'd been wounded who was willing to overlook his injury, with all its implications? He did not want her bearing his children. He'd made that plain enough. He'd avoided responding to her own declaration. Was that because he did not love her, or because he honestly believed she deserved better than him?

Her heart inclined toward the latter. But then she thought of how Madame's face had shone that afternoon when he'd risen from his chair for fencing, when she'd seen him standing on his own two feet again. Only her acquiesence had allowed their affair to go on as it had; she'd covered for Nichola dozens of times, told Mrs. Treadwell and the upper-form girls that their companion was sleeping in her rooms, to care for her while she had a touch of the grippe, so that Gwen and Bess and Katherine had no reason to question her absence from their quarters at night. And each dawn, Nichola was back in the courtyard with Lord Boru, so that no one was the wiser. Well, no one but Hayden. But he was only a servant—the Boru's aide-de-camp—and bound to hold his tongue.

She was not certain what she'd done to earn Hayden's enmity. It seemed to her he ought to be happy to see his master healing, pushing himself out of that confining chair. It only had to subtract from his duties, didn't it, that she was now undressing His Lordship of nights and seeing him to bed? Her mother's servants always had been grateful for any reduction in their work.

Brian was stirring amidst the blankets, his hand seeking

for her. She slipped into the bed, curling tight against him, and heard him murmur her name.

Her name. Not Madame's, nor that of any of the other women he'd had—how many women had he had? Those were cabinets best left unopened, questions that must stay unasked. For now, she was his, and he was hers. She wrapped her arm more tightly about him, felt the beating of his heart beneath her palm. The dawn, with its new battles and tribulations, would come soon enough. She closed her eyes and willed herself to sleep.

Chapter Twenty

"Mail call!"

The cry rang out over the sodden trenches carved into the rolling plains of Flanders, bringing every soldier in the Crown's Twenty-Fifth Regiment instantly to alert. Tommy Hainesworth sprang up from the ditch in which he and three companions were squatting, packing shell cases and talking, as always, of home.

"Get down, you bloody fool!" Ned Prescott shouted, yanking at Tommy's coat. "Want your head shot off by the blasted frogs?"

"I want a letter. From Nichola, preferably. But I'd take one from my mother."

"The boy'll bring 'em round."

"Can't wait," Tommy announced, and dove out of their ditch into the next one, nearly flattening Bill Simms.

"What the devil—where are you going, Tommy?"

"Mail call!" he sang, clambering over the crouched men.

"Tommy must have himself a lover," George Naylor announced slyly.

"A sister, actually."

The soldiers hooted in derision: "Mail from his sister!" "Can't wait for a letter from Sissy!"

"Shut the hell up," Tommy said goodnaturedly. "My mother's gone and packed her off to some bloody finishing school, if you must know, and Nicky is funny as hell telling about it. Hours and hours spent on bleaching bed linens and sewing up cushion covers for chairs."

James Woffentin, who'd been to Hainesworth Hall often enough, went goggle-eyed. "What? Nicky at finishing school?"

"Who the hell is Nicky?" George demanded, perplexed.

"His *sister,* you bloody arse," Woffentin informed him. "And a livelier bit of goods you never could imagine. Remember that time, Tommy, she beat me swimming the river?"

Tommy laughed. "By two lengths she did!"

"Swimming? Your sister?" Bill Simms echoed in wonder.

"You ought to see her ride to the hounds, m'boy," Woffentin said smugly. "Got a better seat than General Pickering himself, she has. And one hell of a fine shot!"

"She sounds a right ruddy Amazon," another soldier observed.

"That she is," Tommy agreed proudly.

Woffentin was shaking his head. "I just can't picture her pricking away at needlepoint, Tommy."

"Nor can I. She's kept her humor about it, though, I must say." The mussed blond head of the general's boy appeared above the ridge of the ditch.

"Give 'em here, give 'em here," Simms told him, reaching for the packet of letters he was clutching. "All for me, I know, from the host of hearts I left broken—"

"Nothin' for you, sir," said the boy, and the men all laughed.

"Not even a declaration of paternity suit?" he demanded, affronted.

"Who'd claim you as dad to a babe, you miserable cur?" Woffentin gave him a nudge that sent him sprawling into the mud. "A lass'd more likely plead immaculate conception than admit to a tryst with you!"

"Who else is in there?" the boy asked, shuffling through the letters. "Lord Woffentin, sir!"

"Who's it from, then?" they all asked, crowding around him.

"My solicitor, my good men."

"Bah!" Michael Ridpath declared, spitting over the top of the trench. "You can have it and welcome! No such letter ever brings anything but news of accounts past due."

"Mr. Simms, I believe this is yours?"

Bill snatched the missive from the boy's hand, glanced at the penmanship, and gave a happy sigh. "From the wife."

"I'd sooner have a solicitor than a wife," Woffentin said, grinning.

"You don't know my wife."

"Actually, I believe I do."

Bill made as if to tackle him but was blocked by Tommy, who asked plaintively, "Nothing for me, Rufus?"

The boy brushed back his tousled hair. "Aye, so there is." He dangled the letter above Tommy's reach, waving it back and forth under his own nose. "And perfumed, too!"

"Damn," said Tommy. "Mother. Nicky never would do such a thing. Still, it is better than nothing."

"Your mother perfumes her letters?" Woffentin's eyebrows were arched.

"My mother would perfume my boots, given the opportunity. Give it here, Rufus. Don't tease."

The boy relinquished the letter, and Tommy tore it open. The men who had received mail were doing the same; those who hadn't were busy peering over their shoulders, as though just the sight of feminine penmanship was a comfort—which, in fact, it was. "Look there," Michael Ridpath said wistfully, hanging over Simms. "See how neat and clean it is."

"It won't be if you go dripping mud on it," Simms noted darkly.

"Good God," Tommy announced. His cohorts raised their heads expectantly. He was examining the envelope, checking the handwriting. "If I didn't know better, I'd swear one of you sent me this as a jest."

"Why? What does it say?"

"Well, the baroness writes she had a most splendidly enjoyable Easter holiday at Yarlborough House, with the duke and duchess—"

"Simply fascinating," Woffentin drawled.

"No, no. You don't understand. Nicky—my sister—was there as well. And Mother says she was the belle of the ball!"

"Nicky?" Woffentin realized belatedly how rude that had sounded. "Not that I mean—"

"No offense taken, believe me! I can scarcely credit it myself. But listen! 'I am pleased to report that your sister's first official immersion into society proved a grand success. Dear, dear Mrs. Treadwell has done wonders with the girl. Not only did Nichola comport herself like a true lady—she has got herself a beau!'"

"Ooooh!" the soldiers chorused.

"Who's the lucky fellow?" Woffentin asked curiously.

Tommy scanned the page. "Jesus! Lord Wallingford himself!"

"I know him," Bill Simms said promptly.

"Everyone knows Wallingford, you dolt," Ridpath told him fondly.

"He's heir to the bloody duke of Strafford, ain't he?" Woffentin demanded.

"My sister a duchess!" Tommy was in a daze. "Are you sure none of you fellows wrote me this in sport?"

"Where would we get the bloody perfume, eh?" someone growled.

Tommy grinned. "There is that."

"Hell, I always knew your sister was a thoroughbred," Woffentin allowed. "Still, I can't picture her a duchess."

"I'll let that pass," Tommy said mildly, "seeing as I can't either." He read on. "Oh, no. Oh my God."

"Let me guess," Ridpath offered. "King George has named her his heir, and . . ." But something in Tommy's expression made his voice trail off.

"I say," said Woffentin, alarmed. "Bad news, is it?"

"The worst possible," Tommy said grimly, and started climbing out of the ditch.

"Where d'you think you're going, then?" asked Simms, looking up from his own letter with alarm.

"To ask the general for leave."

"Is there a death?"

"If only it were that."

Woffentin grasped him by the collar. "Here, now, Tommy, hold on! Share your troubles with your mates, eh?"

Tommy paused, halfway up the slope. "If you must know—Mother writes that Nick has met Lord Brian Boru. He's been instructing her in . . . well, in something. Mother's not terribly clear."

Woffentin let out a whistle. "Lord-a-mercy. You have my sympathies, mate."

"I've got to get back to England right away."

"Lord Boru?" Michael Ridpath piped up. "Wasn't he with the regiment before I got here? Isn't he the one they call—"

"Shut up, man!" Bill Simms hissed.

But Ridpath blazoned on: " 'Ballocksing Brian Boru'?"

"She's ruined, aye and for sure," one of the soldiers whispered.

"Shut your bloody trap!" Tommy shouted. "If I can just get home—I may not be too late!" He reached the level ground and ran, ducking and weaving a desultory scatter of bullets, for the general's tent.

Ridpath stood on tiptoe to watch him, nonplussed.

"Christ, what a nincompoop! As if the general would grant him leave to go home just on account of that!"

Woffentin wagged his head in mourning. " 'Tis plain enough, Ridpath, you have never met Ballocksing Brian Boru."

Tommy got his leave, and spent the two days before a wagon-train left for Bruges in composing what was no doubt the most difficult letter of his short life—to his mother, in case some happenstance of war should keep him from reaching Mrs. Treadwell's academy. While he did not want to alarm her overmuch, he felt he must impress upon her the absolute necessity of removing his sister from Lord Boru's sphere. It was not, to be sure, that he wasn't fond of Boru—in truth, he'd never known an abler soldier nor a more entertaining companion. But his memories of campaigning for nearly a year in the company of His Lordship could not help but be colored by his recollections of the remarkable number of Flemish beauties who had tumbled to the fiery-haired giant's bed. That Brian Boru was now possessed of only one firm leg made no impression at all upon Tommy, who'd been eyewitness to the havoc the Scot could wreak on female hearts straight through the barriers of language, logic, and the hazards of war. *Oh, Nicky,* he prayed every night as he waited. *Don't be a fool. Don't fall for him.*

He landed at Dover on the twenty-fifth of May, hired a horse, and rode north like a man possessed, having delivered the letter to his mother into the care of a junior officer headed in the direction of Hainesworth Hall. Spring storms had swollen every creek and river between the Downs and Mrs. Treadwell's academy. Tommy tried to ford one anyway, lost his horse, caught a chill, and was delirious for three days. When he came to his senses, he snarled at the kindly tavernkeeper's wife who had tended him, stole a horse from the stables—he'd lost all his money in the river—and rode on without stopping. He asked directions

of a field-worker, got sent in the wrong direction, wasted
three entire hours in which he imagined his sister giving
birth to a whole sequence of bastard babies, got better directions at a tavern in Blayton, and set off once more, in
another blast of rain. He rode through the night without
stopping, reaching the academy gates just as dawn was
breaking over the hills.

The elegant lettering on the sign there gave him pause.
I must look a fair ruddy sight, he thought ruefully, taking off
his hat—he was still in full uniform—and pushing back his
soaked hair. More than likely he'd be shot by the help as an
intruder if he burst in now. The windows were dark; the
girls were all safe abed. Perhaps I ought to find a village
and tavern and straighten up a bit, he mused. Time enough
to . . .

Just then, the unmistakable shimmer of cold steel hitting steel sliced through the quiet air.

The sound sent Tommy's soldier's blood coursing.
Jesus, what could it be? Bandits? The French invading?
Praise God he was here on the spot! More chinks and
clinks, and then a howl, indubitably masculine, of furious
anger—

Tommy leaped from his horse and rushed the gates
with his saber drawn.

He was fortunate they hadn't been locked, or he'd have
knocked himself senseless. They swung open with a shuddering creak, and he hesitated, searching for the source of
the sounds. Hard to believe those inside the place hadn't
raised an alarum. The front doors were securely bolted, he
ascertained from assaying the latch. But the building was a
renovated abbey, he realized, pacing along the exterior,
built with a courtyard inside it. That was where the battle
raged. How to get there? Ducking low to hide himself from
possible sentries, he skirted the ivy-draped walls, seeking a
door. The swordfight had reached a nigh-frenzy of parrying
and thrusting, from the clamor the combatants were making. When he saw another door set into a low archway, he
kicked at it in a fury. It sprang open. The noise of the battle

had faded away. Christ, was he too late? He dashed into the shadows of some sort of arched passage, found the door in the opposite wall, and went careening through.

He emerged, breathing hard, into the inner sanctum, his saber at the ready. *"En garde!"* he screamed out. The two figures on the rain-drenched grass turned to stare. Well—Tommy could only assume they were staring, since they both wore masks. And pads, he recognized slowly. What the hell—was it a duel? He looked more closely. The larger of the men had one arm draped around some sort of pole and the other around his opponent, clutching him hard, as though in a death grip. For an instant, nobody moved.

Then the smaller of the sword-fighters reached up to tip back his mask—*her* mask, Tommy noted, seeing that the motion had unleashed a torrent of pale blond hair. She gaped at him, openmouthed. Finally she said, "Tommy?"

"Great God, it *is*!" the tall fellow burst out. "Tommy Hainesworth!" He slung his mask off into the grass. "Won't I be damned!"

"So you shall, Boru," Tommy growled, flourishing his sword. "Take your bloody paws off my sister!"

"Oh, for heaven's sake, Tommy!" Nichola was laughing. "Don't be such a fool!"

"Here, now, let's not go off half-cocked!" Brian said amiably.

"Don't you talk of cocks to me, miscreant!" And Tommy rushed him with his saber. To his utter astonishment, Nicky stepped between them. For a moment, unable to halt his momentum, he was afraid he'd kill her. Then, coolly, calmly, she met his blade with hers and deflected it with a deft lateral. Caught off balance, he nearly skidded headfirst onto the slick grass.

"Get out of the way, Nicky, damn you!" he roared at her.

"You'll have to come through me to get to him," she countered, clapping her mask down.

Boru was still hanging on to the pole. "Here, now,

Nichola! That's enough of that. I'm sure your brother is simply laboring under some misconception—"

"*I'll* show you misconception!" Tommy launched an attack, but somehow Nicky managed to intrude herself again. She not only met his blows—she beat them off and responded with her own, so forcefully that he found himself fading back.

"Christ, I don't want to fight *you,* Nick!" he shouted. He hadn't much choice, though, seeing as she was still advancing.

"Nichola! That's enough!" Brian Boru announced.

"Are you mad? He'll put that stupid saber straight through you! What has gotten into you, Tommy?" she demanded, even as she executed a *flèche* that nearly decapitated him.

"Jesus, Nick!" Tommy had retreated, panting, toward the courtyard wall. "Where did you ever learn to fence like that?"

"From Lord Boru," she said curtly, not letting down her guard. "What did you imagine we were doing?"

"I bloody well *saw* what you were doing!"

"He was adjusting my stance," Nichola said evenly.

"He was *fondling* you!"

"Well, what if he was? What business is it of *yours?*"

"I know that man." Tommy pointed with his saber. "I know him very well indeed!"

"So do I," said his sister, and the pride in her voice, the way she turned to glance at Boru through her mask, sent Tommy's heart sinking. He *was* too late. Boru had had his way with her.

The realization was devastating. "Damn you, Brian," he muttered. "How bloody dare you? My own sister!" He rushed the pole-bound lord again, in blind rage.

And again Nichola intercepted him, catching his blade with her own. "Get the hell out of my way!" Tommy shouted at her.

"If you hurt him, I will have to kill you." She drove home the threat with a truly breathtaking cut. Tommy attempted a *quinze* parry—and watched as his weapon, diverted by the strength and quickness of her blow, went sailing out of his hand into a thick bed of primroses.

Nichola rushed to put her foot on it, shaking her masked head. "Mrs. Treadwell," she declared, "is going to be very vexed at you for that."

Tommy had, of course, like any good soldier, a dagger tucked in his boot. But the notion of rushing at his twin with that weapon took all the steam out of him. He let his arms sag to his sides. "Oh, Nicky. You idiot. What have you done?"

Brian Boru spoke up, his mask shoved back, his face split in a beaming grin. "Besides learn to fence, you mean? That was magnificent, Nichola! Don't let me ever hear you say again that I am going easy on you!"

"It *was* rather neat, wasn't it?" she acknowledged, pushing up her mask, retrieving Tommy's sword. She held it for a moment by the blade. "We could have at it some more, if you like. But if I'm not mistaken, you have violated the cardinal rule of swordplay: 'Never let your heart overrule your head.' "

Tommy was confused and weary and damp and, above all, disillusioned. "So have you, I'd say. Nick, don't you know what sort of man he is? He has broken more hearts—and left more bastard babies wailing—across Europe than anyone I know!"

"Here, now, that's utterly untrue," Brian said with a hint of anger. "I'd never be so careless as that."

"I think you must be misinformed, Tom. He always uses a condom," Nichola noted reasonably.

"Agghhh!" Tommy rushed at Boru, intending to throttle him. But his sister moved in once more, and put the point of her saber to her twin's throat.

"Don't take a step. Not one single step," she warned, in a tone that made his stomach heave.

"Nicky. Nicky! I only want to spare you. . . ."

What might happened next—whether she really would have cut him, whether Boru would have grabbed her to stop her—none of them would ever know. For at that moment, there came a high, distraught cry from the door Tommy had used to enter the courtyard: "Tommy? Nichola? Great heavens, what is going on?"

Nichola glanced in that direction. Then her head whipped back to her brother. The expression in her eyes was so deadly fierce that he caught his breath. "Oh! You *bastard*!" she snarled at him. "How *dare* you bring her here?"

The baroness of Hainesworth took a tentative step forward. "Your letter, Tommy—I must say, it was quite alarming, if a tad confusing. I gather you feared Nichola was in some sort of *danger*?"

Nichola's brown-gold gaze was still on Tommy, only now it was desperate, pleading. He could hear the words her heart was crying to him: *Don't tell her. Don't tell her, Tommy!* How often had she begged that of him, cajoled that from him, after some childish adventure gone awry? But this was no child's play. Boru had deflowered her, dishonored her—and, by God, dishonored him as well!

His former regiment-mate was still holding to the pole, and he, at least, was cool as cucumber. "Lady Hainesworth! What a delightful surprise! But how early you are up and about!"

"I rode the whole dashed night, if you must know, thanks to Tommy's letter. And what do I find? Nothing at all amiss. I wrote you, Tommy, did I not, that Lord Boru was instructing your sister in fencing?"

"Miss Hainesworth just provided Tom with a sampling of her prowess," Boru said smoothly, then added in a low tone to Nichola, "Fetch my canes, would you, pet?"

Pet. The quaint endearment, the easy familiarity of his words, like a quiet caress. Tommy watched with a wrenching pain in his gullet as Nichola hurried to bring them to him. Christ! The man couldn't even walk! How in God's name had he managed to sweet-talk Nicky into his bed?

But then he glanced again at his sister, saw the glow that suffused her face, the high, proud set of her shoulders.

. . . He had never seen her look more lovely, . . . happier. Until, that is, she turned to their mother, and the familiar slump set in. Tommy was hardly unaware of the baroness's bland cruelty toward her—how could he be, when he and his twin practically shared the same soul? She was nineteen—an adult. Old enough to know her own heart. What right did he have to naysay her?

But *why* did it have to be *Boru*?

He might have spoken up then and told their mother the truth, might have felt, despite his sympathy for Nick, that it was his duty as her brother and protector—except that as Boru gamely hobbled toward the baroness on his canes, she wrinkled her nose, as though his infirmity might be catching. As though—as though he were a leper, instead of the most valiant fighter Tommy had ever seen. Nicky was moving beside him, slowly, watchfully, yet absolutely unobtrusively. For the first time, Tommy took a closer look at Lord Boru. Could a man change? Could a wild, unruly heart like the Scotsman's ever be tamed? Could Nick—his Nick—have done that? Watching them together, he was on the verge of being convinced.

A clatter from the balcony above them made him glance up. A passel of little girls in soft, innocent spring dresses was passing along the stone walk. "Good morning, Nichola!" a few called shyly. "Good morning, Lord Boru!"

His Lordship paused to bow to them, with all the elegance he might have shown to the queen. "Top of the morning to you, ladies!"

"Nichola!" On the opposite balcony, more voices: older girls, his sister's age, one with the most amazing shock of red hair. "Who is that there with you?" A pause. "Good Lord! Is that your mother?"

"Hush, Bess!" a petite brunette said sharply, digging her elbow into the redhead's ribs.

"Mother," Tommy said. "Mother. I don't know how you will ever forgive me. The truth is, I—I—" He recalled his recent experience in the rain-swollen river. "I caught a chill! Yes, that's it! And I was . . . quite delirious when I penned you that letter. Can't imagine what I was thinking now. How could Nicky be in any sort of danger here?"

Oh, the look his sister gave him then! Her gratitude was positively breathtaking. "Oh, Tommy," she whispered. "Thank you. Thank God!"

"A chill?" the baroness echoed in alarm. "Then what in heaven's name are you doing standing here in the rain?"

Tommy laughed. He had the most peculiar sense that what he'd just done was, against all reason, the noblest action he had ever taken.

Then another of the outer doors to the courtyard opened. A dainty figure in an elegant jaconet muslin gown beneath a Berlin silk jacket entered, accompanied by a matronly woman in cambric. The smaller woman called out to Nicky, in a voice with a hint of foreign accent: "Nichola! I thought I heard a carriage! Have we visitors?"

The matron, beaming benignly at the courtyard occupants, suddenly tensed and caught at her companion's arm. "Christiane," she hissed.

Tommy saw his mother turn. He saw her back go stiff. He heard something oddly like a snarl escape her painted lips: "*Christiane . . .*"

The foreign woman's head came up abruptly. She met the baroness's eyes. For an instant, she seemed to flinch. Then she kept coming forward. "Why, Emily! Can that possibly be you?"

His mother turned on the matron. "Mrs. Treadwell! Perhaps you can explain to me what this—this *harlot* is doing here at your academy!"

There was a flutter from the girls on the balcony, a sort of shaking of wings. Nichola was looking from her mother to the foreigner and then back again. "Madame?" she said, in a strange, querulous voice. "Madame, you know my mother?"

"I know *her* all right!" the baroness thundered. "Know her for the shameless slut that she is!"

"Mother!" Nichola cried in shock.

"I think you'd best mind your tongue, milady," Brian

Boru told the baroness, in a tone so frigid that Tommy shivered.

His mother whirled to face the crippled lord. "Her—and you! Oh, Tommy, there was nothing fever-struck in your premonitions! Grave mischief is at work here!"

Tommy managed to rouse himself. "Mother, I haven't any notion at all what you might mean."

"Nichola!" The baroness's voice was like a whip. "Who introduced *His Lordship* to you? Suggested you take fencing lessons from him?"

"Why—it was Madame!" Nichola stammered.

"And what other lessons might he have been plying you with, pray tell?"

Nichola blushed, so wholly that Tommy wished, for her sake, that she might disappear. "I'm sure I haven't any *notion—*"

"Has he made love to you?"

"Oh!" came a chorused gasp from the balconies. And Tommy, looking up, saw one young lady, a very striking girl with glorious gold ringlets, smile with snakish satisfaction. "I *knew* it!" she crowed.

The redhead at her side slapped her lovely face.

"Here, now," Brian Boru said furiously, "that's quite enough of *that* sort of talk!"

The baroness ignored him; her gaze was boring into her daughter's. *"Nichola?"* Her voice would have sliced through glass. Tommy found himself rooting wildly for his sister: *Stand up to her! Show her what you have shown me! Let her see your happiness.* . . .

But Nichola was cringing, the pull of so many years of miserable obeisance proving too strong. Every sinew of her body screamed out her guilt; it was plastered all over her face.

The baroness drew herself up. "We are going," she announced. "We are leaving. Immediately! Go and pack your things, Nichola. On second thought—leave them. I would only burn them anyway."

"Lady Hainesworth." Boru, at least, was standing as straight as he could. "I beg you—"

"*You?* You beg me? After what you have done to her?"

"I won't let you do this!" Boru said stoutly.

She turned on him an expression of the most exquisite disdain. "How do you intend to stop me, pray tell? Crawl over here on your hands and knees?"

"Mother!" Tom had been goaded far enough. "Lord Boru was wounded in defense of his country—*your* country!"

"There are matters here you do not understand, Thomas," his mother said archly. "*He* does, though, well enough! And so does she!" She lowered her finger at Madame. "My daughter—my *only* daughter. God! What a cowardly revenge!"

"Revenge?" Nichola repeated blankly. "For what?"

"Never mind that!" the baroness snapped. "Take her in hand, Tommy! We are leaving this place!"

Seeing as Nichola was still clutching her saber, Tommy hesitated, naturally enough. But she didn't seem wont to use it; she let the blade slip from her hand, and Tommy's sword as well, looking dazed. "Brian?" she whispered fearfully.

"You didn't tell her you and Christiane were lovers?" the baroness demanded.

"That's not true, Emily!" Madame cried out.

The baroness cast her a withering glance. "Oh, come, Christiane! Everyone knows of the affair you had with him in France. It was the talk of the *ton*. When, that is, we were not marveling over your host of *other* indiscretions! You are nothing but a whore, and you always were!"

"Brian?" Nichola whispered brokenly, in anguish. He said nothing; he simply stood balanced on his canes. The eyes of the girls in the gallery were as wide as full moons.

But the baroness wasn't finished. "As for *you*," she declared, stabbing a finger in Mrs. Treadwell's direction, "you may rest assured that I have every intention of letting the families of the other girls you have *lured* here under *false pretenses* know exactly to whom their daughters' care has been entrusted! A school for young ladies, indeed!"

The small dark-haired girl in the gallery cried out suddenly, unexpectedly: "Oh, no, please! Don't tell them! Don't spread gossip about our Madame! We *adore* it here!"

And the redhead echoed her: "Don't let them send us home, Madame, Mrs. Treadwell!"

The baroness shook her head in dismay. "You poor, benighted creatures. Were it only in my power, I would take you *all* with me now, instantly! At least I can make certain that my own daughter does not spend another moment in this—this *hellhole* of iniquity! Take her, Tommy!"

Nicky, though, was backing away toward their mother of her own accord. "Brian?" she said again, so haltingly that Tommy felt his own heart aching. "Brian, what did she mean—revenge?" The baroness grabbed her arm and steered her toward the door. She followed, though her eyes stayed on Lord Boru's face. "Brian?"

His Lordship stood tall and silent. The girls in the gallery were sobbing.

Tommy went to pick up the swords from the soaked spring grass. He sheathed his own, glanced at the other, recognized it as Boru's regimental saber. That decided him. No soldier worthy of the name would bestow his regimental weapon on a lowly girl, however adept at fencing she might be. For once, he had to admit, his mother's instincts had been sound. He'd known that himself, when he'd realized what had gone on between Boru and his sister. Only the— the *glow* to her had made him reconsider. Christ. What if she was with child?

He shot Boru a look of sheer hatred. *Bastard. Filthy Scots bastard.*

Then he followed Nicky and his mother to the carriage waiting at the gates.

Chapter
Twenty-One

"And where are you and Lord Wallingford headed to this evening, Nichola?" the baroness of Hainesworth inquired, pouring out a cup of tea.

"I scarcely know," Nichola said as her mother handed her the cup.

"You are *rattling*," the baroness noted sharply.

"Was I? Ever so sorry." Nichola set the tea down on the table at her side with elegant negligence. Tommy, who'd just made himself a stiff brandy and soda, shot her a worried glance.

"To his parents' house, didn't Anthony tell me that?" he pressed her.

"Perhaps so." She sat on the sofa in a gorgeous pewter-colored satin gown, her pale gold hair in classic twinned knots, a single strand of pearls at her throat.

"Then this may be the night we hear the happy pronouncement," Emily Hainesworth said with relish, stirring sugar into her own cup.

"What pronouncement is that?" Nichola asked idly.

The baroness barked a laugh. "Oh, you know perfectly well what pronouncement I mean!"

Tommy took a deep swallow of his drink, wishing his impulsive request to have his leave from the Continent extended—on account of "compelling family circumstances"—hadn't been granted. He glanced up, relieved at the prospect of visitors, as the butler hurried to the door. But it was only the baron, fresh from whatever coffeehouse or club he'd spent the afternoon holed up in. "Hello, darling," the baroness greeted him as he came in.

"Hrmph! Tommy, Nichola." That was all the hello he gave the lot of them. "What're you drinking, Tommy?"

"Brandy and soda, sir."

"I'll have one of those myself."

"Yes, sir." Tommy hurried to make it for him. "Busy day in the House?"

"Infernal boring, as always."

"Nichola is going to the Straffords' tonight, dear," the baroness said pointedly.

"Is she? Hrmph! I'll take this along to my rooms." He barreled toward the stairs with his drink.

"We were just remarking," the baroness went on, "that this may very well prove the evening of the happy pronouncement."

"What pronouncement is that?" The baron's voice was every bit as disinterested as his daughter's had been. Despite his misery, Tommy almost had to laugh.

"Why, of her betrothal, of course!"

The baron glanced at his daughter. "Hrmph! Well! Fine fellow, Washford."

"*Wallingford*!" the baroness hissed.

"Of course. Of course. Wallingford. Hrmph!" He went out, gathering up the gazettes from the credenza on his way.

The baroness rolled her eyes. "Half pickled again— and us with an invitation to the Regent's! I doubt he even recalls it."

"Don't fret. Everyone else there will be half pickled, too," Tommy said helpfully.

"That's enough of your insolence, young man!" She swept to her feet in a swish of skirts. "I'd best remind him. Nichola, do have Tavendish do something with your hair before you leave. You look a dreadful ragamuffin."

"Yes, Mother," Nichola said agreeably. The baroness headed for the stairs.

"And rub some paint into your cheeks!" she called back as a parting shot. "You are ashy as a ghost!"

"Yes, Mother."

A ghost, thought Tommy. That was precisely what his sister was like—a creature drained of life and yet filled with some dangerous energy. Clutching his brandy, he went to the sofa and plunked down beside her, stretching out his legs. "Nicky. It's time we had a talk. I know that you are angry with me." He waited. She said nothing. "Very well—infuriated."

"I suppose you had your reasons," she noted blandly, "for doing—what you did."

"You are bloody right there! Nick, it has been six weeks! Has he written you? Come to call?"

"Of course he hasn't. How could he, with what Mother said to him?"

"He hasn't," Tommy said patiently, "because he's a cad! Oh, an extremely charming and smooth-tongued cad, but a cad nonetheless. He got—"

"Shut up, Tommy." *There* was a hint of spark.

"What he wanted from you," Tommy pressed on bravely. "Do you think it doesn't pain me to tell you these things? Most men are cads. I'm a cad. Father is a cad."

"Perhaps I ought to join a nunnery."

"That's not what I mean, dammit! If you ask me, you got off lucky from all this."

"Oh, yes. I am extremely lucky." She moved to pick up her teacup. Her hand was steady as rock.

"You've got Wallingford. He's infatuated with you. Christ, I've never seen a man so head-over-heels. *He* is not a cad. He's the real thing, he is. And Mother's had the decency to keep her mouth shut about Mrs. Treadwell's academy—"

"Oh, Tommy. You *are* stupid. The only reason she hasn't screamed the news of Madame from the housetops is that if she told what she knows, any chances I have of making a successful marriage would be shot all to hell."

He looked taken aback. "You think she realizes that?"

"I *told* her that."

"That was smart of you, Nicky. Very smart indeed."

"I'm not the idiot you take me for."

He reached for her hand. "I *don't* think you're an idiot. And I'm sorry I called you one. You simply . . . made a mistake. Plenty of young girls do."

"What exactly was my mistake?" she asked evenly.

"Why—believing what he told you! Believing that he loved you!"

"He never told me that."

"He *didn't*?" Tommy goggled.

"No. I said I loved him, though." There was a wisp of a smile on her face. "I am glad I did."

Tommy tried to regroup. "You heard what Mother told us in the carriage about Madame—the countess d'Oliveri. How she was wild to marry Father even though he was as much as betrothed to Mother, tried to trick him into wedding her so shamelessly that it got her banned from the *ton* and packed off to the Continent. Don't you think the conclusion that she set all this up as her revenge is logical?"

"I think Madame very fortunate not to have married Father."

"Well. I cannot argue with you on that." Tommy drained his glass. This discussion wasn't going at all as he had meant it to. "I've asked about, you know. It's quite true what Mother claimed of Boru and the countess. Dozens of folks know that they were lovers in Paris."

"He and I were lovers. Does that make me a whore?"

"Christ, Nicky! Of course not! You are just what I said—a girl who made a foolish mistake."

Her brown-gold gaze slanted toward him. "Have you had a lot of lovers, Tommy?" He flushed. "Are *you* a whore?"

"A man can't *be* a whore!"

"No. He can't," she agreed thoughtfully.

"She ran a brothel in Paris! I have it on absolute authority!"

"I'm sure it was a very fine one. Have you been to brothels, Tommy?"

"Have I—that is no sort of question for you to ask!"

"I thought you had."

How in God's name, Tommy wondered, had all of this gotten turned upside down? "Now, see here, Nicky—"

"Lord, don't bluster. You sound as stuffy as Father."

"He's ruined you," he said suddenly. "I don't know what he has done to you, exactly—"

"Really?" Nichola murmured coyly, blond brows arched.

"But he *has* ruined you! Or that Madame and Mrs. Treadwell have—I don't know. You have lost your innocence—and I don't mean your bloody maidenhead. There's more to it than that," Tommy said with sudden insight. "You may be mild as milk with Mother, but you've changed. You've no intention whatsoever of marrying Wallingford, have you?"

"Whatever my intentions, I've certainly learned from all this not to confide in *you*."

"Dammit, Nick, I've told you time and again—any man in the regiment would have done the same had he learned his sister had been exposed to Boru!"

"You make it sound as though he were the plague." Nichola finished her tea and stood up, with such unconscious grace that Tommy stared. She had changed in more ways than one. If the—the sparkle had gone out of her, something else, something most disturbing, had taken its place: a cold calculation he had never dreamed his twin possessed. He'd been watching her. He'd seen it with Wallingford, whom she kept dangling like a pet spaniel on the end of a leash. Was it only what she knew—what Boru, damn his black soul, had taught her—about what went on between a man and a woman that made her so formidable? Their mother's rote corrections of her manners and bearing and dress were utterly unnecessary, made only out of habit, and they glanced off her like water from a duck's back. Nichola's social graces were as polished and bright as a regimental saber—and from what he'd witnessed of the scores of young men willing to make asses of themselves paying court to her, just as devastating. Perhaps that was why she hadn't yet committed to marrying Wallingford. Perhaps she was holding out for a beau more to her liking. Though the notion that she could aspire to better than a duke's son was a trifle unnerving. Who *was* there who was preferable to Wallingford? One of the princes, for God's sake?

Still, he found the idea oddly comforting. She'd spent the months at the academy in such isolation—well, except for Boru—that more than likely she was just enjoying testing her wings. But she was sensible, his Nicky. She'd realize sooner or later, when the glitter of the *ton*'s rush wore off, that Wallingford was the best catch.

"You'll excuse me, I trust," she announced, with a devastating curtsy. "I must fetch my hat and my wrap."

"Nicky . . ."

She turned in the doorway, looking so beautiful that he felt he might cry. "Aye?"

"Whatever you are up to . . . be careful. Even Mother is bound to forgive one mistake. But a second—there would be hell to pay."

She flashed him a smile. "Don't fret, brother dear. I *have* learned my lesson."

Tommy only wished he knew what that lesson was.

Wallingford came for her at eight and drove her to his parents' exceedingly grand town home in his sleek, speedy curricle. There was a lavish dinner, followed by a musicale at which Nichola sat beside the duchess and amused her greatly with girlish tales of life at the academy. The duke looked on approvingly from behind his monocle, tapping the toe of his high, spotless boots to the string quartet's beat. Afterward, when drinks and dainties were served on platters of solid gold, Wallingford came to claim her for a stroll in the gardens. She took leave of the duchess with a moue so expertly balanced between regret and anticipation that it would have made Tommy's blood run cold.

Along the parterre, with the night breeze billowing scents of roses and lilies, she let Wallingford lead her to a bench, nestled beside him while his arm tightened around her bared shoulders. "You drive me to distraction," he murmured, tracing her cheek with his finger. Then he kissed her, and she allowed that, too. He tasted of meringues. "You taste of heaven," he whispered. He slipped his hand down to her throat, very tentatively let it range lower. Nichola closed her eyes, picturing a dreary inn in Kent and the scratch of a worn rug beneath her back. . . .

"Oh," Wallingford sighed as he cupped her breast through the shimmering satin. "Oh, Nichola. Do you love me, sweetheart, just a little?"

"Of course I do."

"Marry me," he begged, pressing his lips to hers once more. "Marry me, and I will make you so happy. . . ." He shifted so he could smooth the silk gown over her thigh. Nichola stiffened in his embrace.

Hurriedly he withdrew his hand. "Forgive me, love. It is just that—God, what I would give to have you! To be wed to you now, and have you in my bed—"

"Anthony!" she said in shock.

"Marry me," he entreated her again.

"I have already told you, I need time—"

"For what?" And he dropped to his knees on the bricks. "What man could love you as I do?"

His blue eyes shining as he thrust inside her, arching above her. His hair loose across the pillows. The scent of his skin, the savor of his mouth . . . tobacco and sweat and Bordeaux . . .

She forced herself back to the present moment. Wallingford was reaching into his waistcoat, drawing out a small crimson velvet box. "Nichola. Here." He pressed it on her. She shook her head, pulling away, refusing to take it into her hands.

"Anthony. Please. Not yet."

"Why the dickens not? We are perfect for one another. My mother and father love you as much as I do. If we became betrothed now, we could be married in October. Hunt season. A great huge wedding at the estate. The entire *ton* there. My hounds are howling for you, Nichola! Can't you hear them across the miles?"

All she heard was the swift intake of Brian Boru's breath as he'd entered her, the conviction in his voice as he'd said, *I intend to stay for as long as you can stand me. . . .*

"I believe I do," she managed to reply with a smile. "But surely you have taught them it is not wise to hurry the chase."

"I'm afraid I will lose you," he said abruptly. "That all of this is too good to be true."

"Sweet Anthony." She reached to caress his cheek. "I have told you and *told* you—there is no one in all of London I prefer to you." *Where was he now? Who was he with?*

"Say yes, then, to my proposal. Oh, do, my dear love!"

Love. Why did that word come so readily to him when it had never crossed Brian Boru's lips? And yet Wallingford scarcely knew her—did not know her at *all,* if the truth were reckoned. When had the two of them ever spoken of what mattered to them in life, what they longed for, dreamed of, feared?

A fencing bout, she reminded herself. It was time for a graceful retreat.

"You honor me, Anthony, in your proposal," she told him quietly.

"Accept it, then!"

"I cannot. Not yet."

His fist curled around the little box in disappointment. Then he raised his head, earnest as a child. "Cruel girl! Give me some hope for the future, at least."

Nichola paused, then said—not too carefully, she imagined—"Were I to marry anyone in England at this moment, it would be you." After all, Boru had never come within a mile of proposing. That made the white lie true.

He clutched her fingers, covered them with kisses. "I'll be patient," he vowed. "You'll see. I *will* win you, Nichola Hainesworth. I'll be damned if I don't, in the end." Then, praise God, he rose from the bricks. "We'd best return to the guests. There is sure to be whispering about us." But he looked quite smug at the prospect as he dusted off the knees of his dark breeches, gave her his arm, and started back to the house.

Nichola walked at his side, adjusting her strides to meet his shorter ones. He had his arm around her waist. His head came up to her ear. She thought of how it had been to lie in Boru's arms, to feel small against his great bulk, cherished and protected. . . .

Enough of that.

"What is it?" Wallingford demanded, stopping on the path. She was surprised, frankly, that he had sensed the tensing of her muscles, had not considered him so sensitive. She would have to be more careful; she could not afford at this point to make a mistake.

Oh, not the mistake Tommy had cautioned her against that afternoon. That was hardly likely. But the sort of faux pas that might cause Anthony Wallingford to wonder why a baron's daughter would have any *reason* to refuse his persistent proposals. The kind that could upset her well-laid plans. Tommy had been right on one count: She had no intention whatsoever of marrying her suitor. She was playing for time, stringing him along, waiting for the news that would allow her to tell him exactly what she thought of his professions of love.

She was waiting until Gwen and Bess—Katherine Devereaux could go hang, for all she cared—had found their wings, just as she had. Until Madame and Mrs. Treadwell, God bless their wisdom, had given them the confidence to fight against the *ton*'s ridiculous rules and pretensions. Until her two friends had become secure enough to seek out their futures without the awful, crippling fear of being judged as lacking by a bunch of silly stuffed shirts and lace bodices. Once that happened—once she knew her actions would not cause her mother to tell the world about Madame, and force the academy's closing before Gwen and Bessie were ready—*then* she would be honest with Wallingford, tell him that as kind and nice as he was, she could never marry him.

Because despite all his pretty words, she sensed no passion in him. Boru had taught her about passion. It was different from love, but linked to it as inextricably as warmth to the sun. One could have love without passion, but never, never, passion without love. And once one had tasted passion, mere, common, everyday love was as dry as dust.

Chapter
Twenty-Two

Nichola settled onto the sofa in the parlor and kicked off her kid shoes, unspeakably grateful that her mother was out shopping. She was weary—nay, she was *exhausted*—from the charade she had kept up for more than two months. The tightrope she walked each day and evening with Wallingford—keeping him happy and contented, yet unfulfilled in his dear wish to formalize their betrothal—was taking its toll. It was becoming increasingly difficult to submit to his kisses, his eager fondling, and not tell him the truth—that he hadn't a chance with her, and never would. Dammit, she liked the fellow! She was grateful to him, had never forgotten that his initial attentions to her had set the imprimature of approval on her for all the *ton*. She even enjoyed spending time with him—when he wasn't *after* her—hearing his sly, devastating comments on the Regent's girth, or Lady Preston's hat, or Lord Winthrop's cravat. In some ways, being with him was as warmly comfortable as being with Gwen and Bess; he was a good, funny friend.

But she did not love him. And as the weeks went by and London society began to view them more and more as a couple—it was rare now that they were not paired in invitations, one sent to each of their houses for soirees, balls, supper parties, and her mother had abandoned any pretense of chaperoning—she was more and more stricken with guilt. He really was too nice to be led on this way.

Alas, the news she had from Gwen and Bess at the academy was not encouraging. Her fate seemed to have dealt a severe setback to Madame's influence there. Gwen's first reply to her letter demanding information reported that the countess had taken a leave of absence—and had bemoaned the fact that science experiments and tutorials with Dr. Caplan had gone by the wayside as well, with far more attention in the curriculum to linens and chinaware. A follow-up letter from Bess brought the welcome news that Madame had returned—once, evidently, Nichola's explanation of her mother's continuing silence on the countess's involvement had been received and absorbed. All the same, it did not seem likely either girl would be launched into a debut anytime soon. Even plans for a repeat visit to Mrs. Treadwell's daughter in August had been abandoned, until, Nichola surmised, those concerned could be certain that the baroness would hold her tongue.

I am at an impasse, she recognized abjectly. Only her marriage—marriage to a stalwart soul like Wallingford—could irrevocably keep her mother's mouth shut. And marriage was the one thing she most wanted to avoid. Still . . . *perhaps I am being selfish,* she thought, barely glancing up as Tommy came into the parlor. By sacrificing any chance she herself had for happiness, by agreeing to Wallingford's increasingly insistent pleas for a betrothal, she could still buy Gwen and Bess futures less onerous than her own.

"Nicky?" her brother said tentatively, going to make himself a drink. "There's a world of care written on your forehead."

Quickly she unknotted her brows. "Can't have that,

can we?" she replied blithely. "I was only wondering what to wear tonight to the theater."

"I daresay it doesn't matter. You could go in a loincloth and the *ton* would instantly adopt the fashion. I don't suppose you've noticed how many brunette misses have been blonding up their hair."

"On account of me?" she asked in genuine surprise.

"Well, it isn't on account of Queen Charlotte."

"Fancy that," Nichola murmured. "Silly sheep." If Bess made a splash next season, would they all dye themselves red?

He came and stood with his brandy and soda in one hand, a newspaper tucked in the other. The expression in his eyes, light brown shot through with gold, twins to her own, was tentative, uncertain. Then abruptly he held the paper out to her. "There's something in today's *Gazette* that you ought to see."

"Dear Lord. Don't tell me Anthony's gone ahead and announced our betrothal without my agreement!" But he didn't smile. His solemnity was a little frightening. Nichola reached for the paper he extended, suddenly concerned. Had something happened to Madame? To Mrs. Treadwell? Had one of them died? The academy—had someone else discovered its secret? She unfolded the page, scanned the headlines. Debate on the Corn Laws. Three Luddites executed in Nottingham. Napoleon about to enter Paris. Regent's health in question—again. She glanced up at Tommy in confusion.

"There." He jabbed his finger. Nichola looked down again, at a small item near the bottom of the sheet. "Three Proposed for Order of the Garter, One for Order of the Thistle," the heading read.

"Oh, Tommy. Those ridiculous, antiquated honors? Who pays any attention anymore? I . . . ." Then her gaze caught on a name in the body of the text: His Most Excellent Brian, Lord Boru, Master of Antrim, Seneschal of Strathclyde, Hereditary Keeper in Holding of the Western Isles. . . . The listing ran on and on. "He has got a world of useless titles, hasn't he?" she murmured. "I had no idea." She scanned through to the meat of the matter. " 'To be presented by His Highness, the Prince Regent of Great Britain and Ireland, with the Order of the Thistle for extraordinary service to the Kingdom and exemplary bravery in combat, at a ceremony in London on the eighteenth of July . . .' " A most inelegant snort escaped her. "He won't come."

"For the Order of the Thistle?" Tommy stared. "Of course he will! Who wouldn't?"

"*He* won't. It would mean nothing to him."

"Are you daft? Only twelve men in the entire kingdom are admitted to the Order of the Thistle! It is an extraordinary honor!"

Her gaze, suddenly hard, met his. "It won't give him his leg back, will it?"

"No. But I should think it would take some of the sting!"

Nichola folded up the paper neatly and presented it back to him. "If you believe that, Tommy, you had best take care to keep out of the range of wayward cannonballs."

Tommy had another of those fleeting moments of clarification. "Christ. Nicky. Are you saying—do you think he would have wed you if not for that?"

"I know so," she said calmly.

He was reduced to stammering. "But—but—if that is so . . ." She waited. Nothing more was forthcoming. Finally he shook his head, with a very un-Tommy curl of his lip. "So that's the line he is using these days!"

She stood up and struck him, slapped him hard across the cheek. "You know nothing about him!" she cried in fury. "You think that you know him, but you don't know him at all!"

"I bloody well lived and ate and slept and fought with the man for a year!" Tommy retorted. "What did you have with him? A few fencing lessons and a couple of tumbles in the hay!"

She drew herself up. "By God, I'd challenge you for that—if we didn't both know I'd best you. Get out. Get out of my sight! You have no right to say such things!"

"He *will* come," Tommy said curtly. "He'll come, and you'll see him at the ceremony, and the whole bleeding mess will start up again!"

"What are you so afraid of, Tom?"

"That he has broken your heart! That after him, you will never be satisfied with anything less!"

She smiled suddenly, unexpectedly. It was like the sun bursting through clouds. "You're not so dense as I thought you were, dear brother. I *won't* be satisfied with anything less. And since that discounts every living, breathing male in Great Britain, I have a rather lonely road ahead. But you can rest assured on this point: He won't come here. Not for such meaningless frippery as the Order of the Thistle. Not Brian Boru. Not in a thousand years."

"We'll see," Tommy said tautly.

"Would you care to wager? Fifty pounds? A hundred? A billion?"

"You are so sure of yourself," he said sadly. "So certain of *him*. If you could only have seen the trail of broken hearts and misery that man left behind him . . ."

"That was before," Nichola pronounced.

He broke out laughing. "Before he met you? Oh, you do flatter yourself."

"I meant," she said with such cold finality that even Tommy, with all he knew of Boru's exploits, was shaken, "before he met that cannonball."

Chapter
Twenty-Three

Brian, Lord Boru, had one hand on the nape of a rag-coated deerhound called Kilter and the other curled around the bloom of a snifter of Scotch whiskey—neat, not diluted. He was alternating scratching the hound and sipping from the glass, with an equal share of inattention, while staring into the fire in the grate of his chambers in the ancestral castle known as Tobermaugh. The sun was setting in the west, across the great stretch of the Firth of Clyde that was dotted with small, mist-wreathed isles—the lands peopled by his vassals. Silly concept, really, vassals. Almost as silly as a hereditary aide-de-camp. He had his right leg up on a hassock and was contemplating ringing for his hereditary aide-de-camp to remove his boot.

A knock at the door brought a low growl from Kilter. Brian silenced him with a snarl of his own and called, "Who is there?"

"It be I, Brian."

Damn. His mother. Quickly he shoved the glass beneath the edge of his chair. "Come in."

She pushed the door open and crossed to him, moving slowly. She was plagued by arthritis, and it was a bitter grief to her, curtailing as it did her favored amusements of gardening and riding. At the age of sixty, Maegan Boru was a striking woman, still with the red-gold hair she had bequeathed to her only surviving child—a passel of siblings had never made it through infancy. Her hair, though, now bore brushmarks of gray. Her eyes were as blue as Brian's, but the rest of him—his bulk and his broad-planed, high-boned face—had come from his father. Maegan was a McCullough of Ayr, born of a clan that prided itself on the fierceness of its men and the beauty of its women, and despite her son's reputation for worldliness, in all her life she'd not crossed the Cheviot Hills into England. *Her* world was here, in the wilderness of Strathclyde. They had never understood one another well, Brian and his mother—it was beyond her ken why any Scot would care to go gallivanting about with the English, much less fight their wars for them. But there was between them the indomitable tie, nonetheless, of blood and shared loss and abiding love.

"Growing dark in here," she observed, her hair ignited by the flames of the sunset. "Light the lamps, shall I?"

"No cause for that. But I *was* about to fetch Hayden to take off this boot."

"I'll do that for ye." She eased onto the hassock, her back held straight, and took his leg in her lap. Carefully—nearly as carefully as Nichola had—she eased the stiff leather down, taking heed that she not twist his knee. Kilter came nosing at her skirts; she laughed and tossed him a rind of cheese she had in her apron.

"You spoil that cur," said Brian.

"Bairns and dogs—they were meant to be spoiled." The boot off, she sat back. "Now, then, did not Alaster McCrimmon tell me he'd asked ye to his place this night for supper?"

"He asked me."

"And ye did not go? Too lofty be ye now, Laird I-have-been-to-London-and-Paris-and-Flanders, for yer old mates?"

"That's not it, and you know it."

"Ach, what be it, then?"

"My leg is paining me."

"I do not wonder, seeing as ye have not moved from that chair the whole lifelong day." Her blue eyes were shrewd. "It be not like ye, Bri, to be so slothful."

"I beg your pardon, Mother. What would you have me do? Reshingle the roof for you, perhaps? Dig over the rose beds? Ride out and shoot a stag?"

"I do not ken why ye cannot ride," she noted placidly. "Ye still have yer buttocks, do ye not?"

"I can't ride *properly*," he retorted, exasperated.

She nodded. "Ach, I see. Cannot keep yer pretty London seat, eh?"

"I can't control the bloody horse!" His voice had risen; Kilter looked up from his cheese rind, ears perked.

"Ye might still handle a phaeton, then. Yer arms seem braw enough."

"There's more to driving a team than just sitting on one's arse."

"Well, there be more to life than just sitting on it, too."

Brian was wishing to hell he hadn't stuck the whiskey under his chair; he could have done with a draught of it just then. "You've no idea what it's like," he said sulkily.

"What? Not to be what ye once were? Do ye think I always was so slow and clumsy? That there was not a time when I could dance the night out when yer father, God rest him, had the fiddlers and pipers in?"

"You're old," Brian said bluntly, rudely.

"Ye will not think so when ye be my age," Maegan said with a hint of humor.

He sighed, staring up at the smoke-mottled ceiling, groping beneath his seat. The whiskey was beyond his grasp. "There's a glass," he began.

"Do ye think I did not smell it on ye when I came in?

Here, then. Here bae yer bludy whiskey. Fine company of nights for a man of yer talents." She thrust the snifter into his hand.

"I have you as well, Mother, of course." His voice was dry.

"Bridey Donnaugh is to be married Sunday next. To Angus Rafferty. Will ye come to the wedding?"

"I've already sent a gift. With my regrets."

"Taegus tells me the salmon be running thick as mullet down the river. Says he can get ye close in the carriage, take ye down a path ye can manage with the canes."

Brian's lip curled. "Sounds jolly. I don't think so."

Maegan lost her patience. "Ach, dammit, boy, what be I to do with ye?"

"Take off my boot now and then."

She reached into her apron again. Kilter, noticing, sprang up from the hearth. "Nah, it be not for ye, ye cursed hound—though for all the care he took of it, it might as well be. Tessie found this going through yer laundry."

"Damn. I thought I'd burnt it," Brian said, seeing the vellum she held in her fist.

"Burnt it? *Burnt* it? All ye have given to those bludy English, and now they seek to give ye somewhat back, and ye be wishing ye'd *burnt* it?"

"It's nothing but a sop, Mother, thrown to a useless dog."

"Ooh! If yer father could hear ye talk—I asked Pastor Padraic about this, Bri. He has some knowledge of the English. Such an honor it be, he tells me! Twelve men in all the kingdom only, and a great ceremony in Winchester Cathedral—"

"Westminster Abbey."

"Wherever. And the king himself likely to be there—"

"The king is still suffering from . . . whatever it is that the king suffers from. It would only be the prince regent. And I know well enough your opinion of him."

"A rogue and a scoundrel," Maegan acknowledged

readily. "But the man's own dishonor cannot taint yer repute."

"You only say that because you haven't met him." He swallowed whiskey.

"Dammit, Bri, why will ye not take what they give ye? For the family honor, if not for yer own? Someday ye will have sons. . . ." The muscles in his throat tightened suddenly. Maegan did not miss it; she narrowed her eyes. "Unless, perchance, all that dawdling with the fairy French has made ye averse to women."

"You go too far!" he roared at her.

"And ye go nowhere! Nowhere at all, only sit in that reeking chair, making yerself blind with drink!"

"I can see all too well," he said, with an undercurrent of irony.

"Ye must think of the future, son!"

"What future?" he demanded hotly. "What future have I got?"

"Blast it, ye be a laird! Ye have passing looks, and land, and money—do ye mean to tell me there be no lass in the entire British Isles would wed ye, gamey leg and all?"

"None worth the having," he told her after a moment. In the pause, Maegan's heart had skipped a beat. Something there was in that silence, something grim and dark and unspoken. . . .

"Bri?" Her voice was softer, tender. "Oh, Bri, my braw boy. Be ye disappointed in love? Be that what brought ye here?"

"Ye may be certain nae!" he snapped—but the lapse into his childhood tongue, the one he'd known long before Oxford and London and the Continent set their veneer upon him, was a dead giveaway. He clapped his mouth shut, knowing it as well as she did, then opened it again, for the whiskey glass.

"Who—who be she, Bri?"

"I don't know what you're talking about." He was back to the king's English. "I came home for some bloody

peace and quiet—neither of which, I'll add, I have a chance
at, with all your nattering at me!"

The letters she'd had from him before his return had
come from Kent. But Kent was close enough to London,
wasn't it? She whistled for Kilter and caressed his rough
snout, buying time, thinking hard. He wouldn't go to London for himself, for his own sake. But might he go . . . for
hers?

London. Jesu, what a prospect. English all about, and
she with her quaint speech and manners, not knowing a
single soul . . . what would she wear? How would she
know what was proper? She'd be a fish without water so far
from home.

She glanced at him from beneath lowered lashes, saw
him finish the whiskey and ring the bell defiantly for Hayden, ready to ask for more. Ready to blot out whatever
might have happened that had sent him hightailing it back
to Strathclyde—what the devil *had* happened? He never
would tell her; she knew him well enough to recognize that.
Her only hope was to go there, to the land of the English,
and find out for herself.

The prospect was worse than daunting. But the Mc-
Culloughs of Ayr had never been ones to shy from a fight.

"I have been mulling on this," she said slowly, "ever
since Tessie brought me the letter. Ye must go back there,
Bri. Ye must accept this honor." He started to speak, and
she hurried on: "Yer father would've wanted it so."

"Father?" He burst out laughing. "Father had less use
for the English than you do!"

"Aye, and that be what sent ye off there in the first
place, be it not? Provoking the poor man . . . ye made his
last years a misery, ye ken, with yer gallivanting about, and
the reports we had of ye racing and dueling and wenching—"

"All exaggerated, I assure you."

"Were they? I do not think so, Bri. Ye forget, I have
known ye from a babe. Ye have a wild streak wider than the
Firth of Clyde. But see here—it be not yer father this clos-

est concerns, seeing as he be resting peaceable in his grave. This concerns *me*."

Hayden had come, and was hovering in the doorway. "Another," Brian said briskly, holding out his glass. "I really can't see how, Mother."

"Nah? Let me set it out for ye, then. If serving the damned bludy English has cost ye so much—yer future, and any hope I have of yer marrying and bearing me grandbairns—then, by Jesu, I mean to go and see the regent make ye a knight."

"You? Go to London?" Brian was dumbfounded.

"Aye, right enough!"

Hayden, who'd hesitated in filling his master's order, turned to her. "Beggin' yer pardon, m'lady. But His Laird-ship's physicians specifically endorsed his removal here. Peace 'n' quiet, they told me, war wha' he war needin'.'"

"I be not overmuch concerned with *his* needs," she said sharply. "Go and fetch him that drink!" The man-servant trotted out. "And close the door behind ye!" she added, with a premonition—the McCulloughs of Ayr were prone to them—that he was lurking in the corridor, listening.

"Honestly, Mother," Brian protested. "He's my aide-de-camp, not a spy."

"Never mind that. Just tell me this—be ye taking me to London to see ye so honored?"

"I'm not going to London."

The McCulloughs of Ayr had, as well, a reputation for adept playacting. She wrapped her arms around Kilter, crooning softly, sadly: "And who held him in her grasp, then, when he was no bigger than a flea? Who taught him how to walk, how to talk? Who suckled him—"

"Mother, that's enough!"

"At her breast when he was hungry? Sang him lullabies to keep the dredgies away?"

"A mite melodramatic, aren't you, poor Mother Mae-gan?"

"And here be my recompense for all I have done for
the lad—my dying request turned down flat!"

"You're a long way from dying."

"He cannot ken how I suffer when the weather be
brisk or blighty," she whispered into the dog's ear. "How
my old bones ache, and how I pray for release . . ."

"It means that much to you? An honor given by the
regent you despise?" Brian asked, incredulous.

"My last moment of glory," she murmured to Kilter,
kissing his wet nose. "All I have to look for in this life . . .
and he be turning me down."

"Oh, for Christ's sake," he muttered.

"The Laird in heaven must ken, I have nothing else to
comfort me, since he says he will not be marrying," she
confided to the hound.

Brian threw up his hands. "Damn you, Mother! All
right! All right! I'll go to London. You can see me made a
popinjay knight in Westminster Abbey. But, by God, after
that, I don't want to hear one word, not one *word* from
you, *ever,* about how I choose to live my life."

"Ach, Bri. Ach, my sweet boy." She brought the apron
up to dab at her eyes. "Ye cannot ken how happy ye make
me."

"And ye cannot ken how miserable ye make me," he
told her, laying the Scots on thick.

She put her hand on his leg, still stretched across her
lap. "There, ye always were a good son, laddie. 'Twill prove
the high point of all my days, to see ye wearing that robe
and wreath. God bless ye for this mercy."

"God damn me for an idiot," he retorted, "and you for
one as well!"

But Maegan was complacent as she leaned across the
hassock to kiss his furrowed brow. He could have said no.
He hadn't even put up much of a fight. And to her sharp
mother's mind, that proved one thing: Despite his professed reluctance, there was someone in London with
whom he had unfinished business. "I must see to my wardrobe!" she exclaimed, rising with some difficulty from the

low seat. He reached his arm to aid her, but she shook it off with a gay toss of her head. "Nah, nah, light as a feather I be feeling, now that we be heading off to London Town!" She looked again at the vellum. "The eighteenth of July—scant a month to get there! We must hurry, Bri, if we would be in time!"

Chapter
Twenty-Four

Darkness, and a tangle of sheets. Restless dreams—again—of Brian Boru. Nichola woke before the sun was up, clinging to the last sweet shred. He'd kissed her—there. She tugged her wrinkled nightdress down over her hips. She was in London, London in July. She lay and watched the sky beyond the window slowly brighten. The day dawned damp and hot. At long last, she fell back asleep. In late morning, she roused again and climbed from bed with her hair plastered to her neck and head. She called for a bath, a cool one, and the ladies' maid her mother had engaged for her, a smart little thing named Donleavy, nodded in agreement. "Best to start out fresh," she said cheerily, "for you've a busy day, miss."

"Have I?" Nichola eased out of the clinging nightdress.

"Oh, aye, miss! Luncheon at the duke and duchess's—how could you have forgotten? And then Lady Printon's musicale this afternoon, and supper and the opera—and you'll be heading off somewheres after that, won't you, you and Lord Wallingford?"

"I suppose we shall." Made tired already by the prospect of such a schedule, she sank into the deep copper tub. Donleavy hastened to bring her toiletries.

"What scent for the water, then, miss?"

"I don't know. What have you got?"

Donleavy did not care to see her mistress unhappy and did not understand why she so often was. "Lavender, rose water, jasmine, sandalwood," she recited, pushing through the vials. "Oh, and here's something new I picked up for you at Whitacker's. Heather."

"Heather?"

Donleavy nodded eagerly. "Grows in Scotland, so they tell me. On the high hills there."

Scotland. "Let me smell it." The maid uncorked the bottle and held it to Nichola's nose.

"Nice, eh?" asked Donleavy, taking a whiff of it herself. "Brisk and clean."

"It will do." Nichola watched as the bath oil slipped into the water drop by drop. Home to Scotland was where Brian Boru had gone. Bess had written in her last letter that Madame had told her so. He was on a high hillside there now. She closed her eyes and tried to picture him in that wild land.

"Wash your hair, miss?"

"Go ahead."

The maid's small hands ran through Nichola's heavy blond hanks, scooping up water from the tub. The scent of heather floated through the room. Nichola lay back. The images her mind formed were of Brian with a red-cheeked dairymaid, spreadeagled naked in flowers on a mountaintop. But—he could never get himself up to such a spot, not with his knee. The picture drifted away, dissolving into bubbles. "What's the date, Donleavy?" she asked suddenly.

"Let me think on it. Sunday was my mum's anniversary, and that's the thirteenth. So—must be the fifteenth."

Only three days until the ceremony at Westminster. He

wasn't coming, just as she'd assured Tommy. She wished she had been wrong. Or perhaps she didn't. It would have been damnably awkward for him to make his way down the aisle at the cathedral on those blasted canes . . . .

The maid rinsed her hair and scrubbed her back for her. Nichola did the rest of the washing, at so languid a pace that Donleavy glanced nervously at the clock. "Best hurry, miss. Nigh on noon already."

Noon, and she wasn't even dressed! Why, at the academy, she'd have been up since . . . Safer not to pursue that line of reminiscence. She was glad when Donleavy asked, "What to wear to the luncheon, then?"

Pads and masks. The sharp clash of their swords in the snowy air. His hand firm on his waist as he showed her how to execute the *fleche,* and his breath steaming . . .

Donleavy sighed. "Lord Wallingford is coming for you in less than an hour, miss. What would you like to wear?"

Nothing Anthony liked too much. He was becoming terribly sure of himself. Last night, in the curricle, he'd pulled right off Whitechapel Road and kissed her, where anyone might have seen them. She'd had a hard time restraining his wandering hands. So unlike Brian's hands they were, so small and white and smooth . . .

"Miss?" Donleavy said helplessly.

"The jonquil muslin." Its neckline was virtually finger-proof.

"Hat?"

God, what a bother. "The fern wicker." No. He'd said he admired that particularly. "I mean . . . the chip with the yellow ribbons and the silk larkspur." She opened her eyes, saw Donleavy about to pose more queries. "And the blue kid boots. And the blue silk parasol. There. Does that cover it?"

"Jacket," the maid said briskly.

"Something blue. And light. The saracen." She stepped from the tub. Donleavy wrapped her in a thick length of Turkish toweling, applied another to her hair.

"I'll be hard put to get this dry in time," she muttered

ominously, and went and laid the clothes on the bed. There
was a knock at the door.

"Nichola?" Her mother, sounding dreadfully chipper.
"Lord Wallingford is here!"

Donleavy's eyes widened. She was terrified of the baroness. "You'll have to give him tea, Mother," Nichola
called back. "I am only just out of my bath."

"Oh, for gracious sake! Hurry, you silly chit!" Emily
Hainesworth said in exasperation.

Despite Donleavy's urgings, Nichola took her time. It
was another hour before she descended to the drawing
room, with Donleavy trailing in her wake.

Wallingford was waiting, handsome as ever in his tight
superfine coat and pantaloons. He'd got new Hessians, she
noted, with little gold tassels on them. Frivolous for a man.
Brian Boru would not have been caught dead—

"Nichola!" He jumped up to greet her. "You've worn
the bonnet I love so well!"

Damn. She'd been certain it was the wicker he had
singled out. She smiled, though, as he came and kissed her
cheek. Her mother did the same in the background, but a
little uncertainly. By now, even the baroness was wondering
why this betrothal that seemed so sure had not been made
official. "You ought to take along a hardier wrap," she admonished her daughter. "I'd swear that we are in for rain."

"I'll take good care of her, milady," Wallingford promised, his hand tight on Nichola's arm.

The baroness gave a girlish giggle. "I swear, to see the
two of you together puts me in mind of when the baron and
I were young and courting."

"Is His Lordship here?" Wallingford inquired. "I'd be
pleased to pay my respects. . . ."

"Gone off to Parliament again," the baroness declared,
with an airy wave. "Business of state and all that." More
likely gambling at White's, Nichola thought darkly. For an
instant, she nearly felt pity for her mother's lonely married
life. But then the baroness spoiled the moment by putting

her nose in the air and sniffing. "What's that peculiar odor?"

Donleavy blanched. "I have a new bath oil, Mother," Nichola said smoothly.

"What is it—eau de peat?"

Nichola bit her lip in bemusement. No wonder she had liked the heather—it *did* smell a bit like Scotch whiskey. "Hyacinth," she lied, much to Donleavy's confusion.

"*I* find it utterly charming—just like the wearer," noted Wallingford.

"Well, in that case—do run along, you two lovebirds," the baroness trilled as Nichola hurried Wallingford toward the door. "And keep an eye out for rain!"

The stoop was already splashed with droplets. "Do you want an umbrella?" Wallingford asked anxiously. "I've got one under the seat."

"I daresay it will pass over quickly. Let's just dash between the raindrops, shall we?" Nichola hoisted herself up, careful not to let too much of her weight rest on his aiding hands. He climbed in beside her and giddy-upped the pair. Nichola sat back against the velvet seat and watched those hands as he held the reins. They *were* delicate and pale—all the fashion among the *ton* dandies, who soaked their fingers in almond milk and covered them in silk gloves at the least sign of chill. Boru's hands had been tough and callused and broad, just like the rest of him. Yet his touch had been tender enough.

Wallingford held the reins too loosely, the same way he had held his sword. Yet any passerby would only have remarked his exquisite driving posture. That laxness made Nichola a trifle nervous. The duke's perfectly matched bays were high-spirited, tending to start and shy from other vehicles. She would have taken a far firmer grip.

"We ought to have listened to your mother," Wallingford noted ruefully, glancing up at the sky beneath the fringed carriage top. "Looks as though the rain intends to come down hard."

"You ought to wrap the reins on your wrists," Nichola suggested. "Leather gets slippery when it's wet."

"I can manage the team," he retorted with a sidelong grin. "It is only you I have trouble bending to my will. I talked to Father last night." He leaned to give her a swift kiss. "He offered to build us a new town home here in London when we are married. Something to rival Carlton House."

"Sounds like a deadly lot of linens to keep clean."

"You'll have plenty of staff for that."

Nichola wished he would stop speaking as though their marriage was a foregone conclusion. The rain came pattering down. He moved for the umbrella. "I'll get it," she said sharply.

"Nonsense. It's right here." He groped beneath the seat. "Or it was. I wonder where the devil . . ." He bent down, peering between his legs into the shadows.

"Anthony!" Nichola cried. He'd nearly missed the hard turn onto Hollingsford Road.

He came up grinning, with the umbrella. "Have you so little faith in me, my love?" She took the handle, unfurled the ribs. The rain had become slashing. A sudden gust of wind caught the canvas, ripped it upward. "Damn!" Wallingford said with annoyance. "Just bought the blasted thing!"

The road was filled with pedestrians scurrying for cover. "Forget the umbrella," she told him, teeth gritted. "Mind you watch the way." A far swifter curricle, driven by a steadier pilot, was coming up hard on their left. Nichola wondered if Wallingford saw it and, further, whether he would be provoked should she call it to his attention. While she was still undecided, he veered the horses that way abruptly, to avoid a puddle. "Anthony!" she screamed.

"What?" he answered, perplexed—just as the noses of the team beside them cleared the carriage hood. Nichola saw what was about to happen next, envisioned it all in an instant.

"The *team*," she started to say, as the bays whipped

their matched heads to the side. She watched their eyes roll in unison, going wide. "The *reins*! Wrap them around your—"

Too late. The bays had decided, jointly, that they would not be overtaken. They sprang out with a leap that shuddered the staves. Nichola clutched the rail, her sodden hat snapping back by the ribbons. A thousand pounds of horseflesh took charge, thundering down the rain-soaked road in a frenzy. The noses of the team beside them vanished with sickening suddenness. An apple vendor was right in the curricle's path, toting his cart to the edge of the road with grumbling leisure. Wallingford tried to steer aside.

"Make way!" Nichola screamed for all she was worth. The vendor glanced up in alarm, sprang for safety. The edge of the curricle glanced off his abandoned cart, which went flying in a hail of shining fruit, further alarming the bays.

"I would have held 'em," Wallingford chided, "if you hadn't shouted."

"They are out of control," Nichola said from between gritted teeth.

"Nonsense! They're simply stretching their legs!" The curricle careened around a curve. A flock of sheep was just ahead. Nichola closed her eyes, then opened them again. It wasn't worth dying—or seeing such splendid horses lamed—simply to avoid causing him embarrassment.

"Give me the reins," she told him.

"I'll do no such—" They were plowing through the flock. Nichola reached over and wrested them from him. "What the devil do you think you're—" She twirled them over her wrists with a flap, braced her feet against the footboard, and *hauled*. The bays, unaccustomed to such firmness, flared their nostrils, considering their chances. She tightened her pull. The drover was shaking his fist at them in fury.

"*Whoa!*" she cried in a terrible voice.

Bested and knowing it, the team surrendered, shuddering to a stop. *Now I've done it,* thought Nichola, even as she fumed at Wallingford for his negligence. She whirled on him, prepared to give him a piece of her mind, then paused. He was staring at her with the rain running down his dark hair, looking positively reverent. "Oh, Diana," he murmured. "You *are* splendid!" And he reached over to kiss her again, even as the drover came running up, spouting curses and wrath. "I say, I am sorry," Wallingford apologized, his arm still around Nichola. "This ought to cover the damage." He reached for his purse, pulled out a handful of shillings and dropped them into the man's hands.

On their right, the team that had spooked the bays appeared again, going far more sedately. Big pied coaching stallions, Nichola noted idly, and very sleek indeed. "Anyone harmed?" a voice called from the driver's seat of the phaeton. A voice that was oddly familiar . . . She glanced over and found herself looking into Hayden's grim face.

His eyes met hers. She saw him gather the reins, even as Wallingford called gaily, "Nah, my good man! No harm done!" The aide-de-camp meant to gallop away; Nichola was sure of it; he was already regretting that he'd stopped. . . .

But the glass of the passenger compartment had slid open. Another face, one she'd never seen before but almost recognized, poked through. "Good Laird in heaven, ye gave us a fright!" the woman cried in a rich Scots accent. "Hayden, ye fool! How many times must I tell ye, ye cannot drive in this great mad city as ye do at home?" Then she smiled at Nichola, who caught her breath. She knew that smile, wide and deep as a mountain lake, and those eyes as blue as summer skies. . . .

"Lord Boru?" Wallingford piped up, craning to see into the carriage around Nichola. "Can that possibly be you?"

The figure beside the woman in the coach seemed to hesitate. His gaze was on the curricle reins that Nichola held. She sat perfectly still, the rain streaming down over her, and knew he knew exactly what had happened, and why.

"Friends of yers, Bri, be they?" asked the blue-eyed woman in surprise.

He edged forward on the seat, so that his face loomed up beside hers. "Mother," he said slowly, heavily. "I have the honor to present to you Miss Nichola Hainesworth and Anthony, Lord Wallingford."

"You came," Nichola breathed, all thoughts of her escort driven from her mind by the sight of him. "I did not think you would." They looked at one another, the rain pelting down between them. "I am glad for you," Nichola said.

"Quite an honor, isn't it, that you're to be handed?" Wallingford broke in expansively. "Order of the Thistle! Our congratulations! You must be very proud of him, Lady Boru."

Lady Boru was staring at Nichola, who felt stripped bare beneath that clear blue gaze. "So I be," the Scotswoman said. "Betrothed be ye, the two of ye?"

Wallingford laughed, circling Nichola's drenched shoulders with his arm. "As good as such, milady, I am pleased to say."

She nodded thoughtfully. Her son rapped on the box. "So long as everyone is safe," he announced, "I think it best we all get out of this rain. Good to see you again, Ni— Miss Hainesworth. Wallingford. Hayden, drive on."

The carriage clattered past them. Nichola sat and watched it, clutching the reins so tightly that the leather dug into her skin.

Wallingford pried them gently out of her grasp. "I can take it from here," he said, not a bit chastened. "I must say, you never fail to amaze me, Nichola, my love. That *was* a pretty bit of driving!" He whistled to the cowed bays, who trotted off dutifully.

Chapter
Twenty-Five

The idiot might have gotten her killed.

Brian Boru sat in the suite he'd engaged at the Savoy—why not show his mother the best on her only trip to London?—and stewed on the fact, chewed it, rolled it on his tongue and choked again and again. Horses like that, flightly and high-spirited, wont to startle . . . it ought to be against the *law* for a man with cotton hands to drive such a team! He was so angry, he forgot to sip his whiskey and water. And in the pouring rain—why hadn't the idiot brought a closed carriage? Any fool could tell the weather had been ominous. What if she caught a chill from being soaked to the skin?

Her skin . . . he remembered the way her blue jacket and yellow cotton gown had clung to her, the cloth of her skirts so wet with rain that they'd limned the curves of her thighs. He shook his head, shook off that image and the one he had in his mind of the way the light, the love, had died from her gold-shot eyes in the abbey courtyard. Oh,

God, he ought not to have come here, never should have given in to his mother. He took a long draught of whiskey. And all for what? A bloody knighthood. Would that change anything?

The door to the adjoining room opened a crack, and Lady Boru peeked in. "Bri? Be we going to dinner or not? It be half past—why, ye be not even dressed!" She came into his chamber, frowning at him. "Here I be all got up in my new clothes, ready for my son to treat me to a fine meal. . . ."

"You look lovely," Brian said automatically, then noticed, looking at her again, that she truly did. It would be a pity to disappoint her. Still . . . "If it's just the same with you, I was thinking we could have supper here in our rooms. It's the identical food as down below, without a host of silly blighters making all sorts of noise and bother. I think you'd find it restful. After all, it has been such a busy day."

Lady Boru lowered her red-gold head in its handsome wicker bonnet. "Ach, well. I see how it be." And she smoothed her hands ruefully over her new crimson skirts. "Ashamed of me. Well, I cannot blame ye. I always said to yer dear late father, ye can take a bumpkin out of the country, but ye cannot—"

"For God's sake! Are you daft? Of course I'm not ashamed of you!" Brian told her, aghast.

She held one finger up to hush him. "Say no more. I understand completely. Yer city friends . . . ye would not have them seeing the lowly stock ye came of. In faith, I be naught but a backward Scotswoman—"

"You *have* gone daft, Mother. When did I ever hear you say a Scotswoman, *any* Scotswoman, was not worth ten English princesses?"

Maegan shrugged. "Ach, that was before I saw London Town, so grand and lofty as it be. Order what dinner ye like. I do not care where we eat it. If the truth be told, I'll be glad not to have to fret over makin' missteps at table."

"You have better manners than any *ton* hostess, and

you know it damned well!" Brian was puzzled and aggrieved. "Where in the world would you have gotten the notion I might be ashamed of you?"

"Ye did not seem so eager this afternoon to introduce me to yer friends."

"*What* friends?"

"Why, that nice young couple in the curricle. Lord Wallingford and Miss . . . Miss . . ."

"Hainesworth." Damn. He hadn't thought she'd noticed, with all that had been going on. "But that had nothing to do with you, Mother!"

"So ye say. All I ken be, the first pair of souls in all London we meet that ye have their acquaintance, and ye be loathe even to let them see that ye were in the carriage with me—and then go rushing off like a house afire!"

"It was pouring bloody rain! We hadn't even gotten to our hotel yet." God. What were the chances of that, anyway, that he'd encounter her straight off the bat? The fates were in a quirky humor this day. He downed the whiskey he'd been holding.

"And now ye'd have us eat our supper in our rooms, like a couple of poor mice that nibble scraps in the attic whilst a whole feast be laid in the dining hall—"

"All right! I'll get dressed!" Much as he hated the prospect, Brian could not bear for his mother to harbor the false notion that he might be embarrassed by her. "We'll go downstairs, and I'll ply you with oysters and beefsteak and Bordeaux—hell, we'll have champagne!—and baba au rhum. And afterwards, I'll take you dancing at Vauxhall. I won't be able to squire you myself on the floor, of course, but you'll find partners a-plenty. Will that suit you?"

"A damned sight better than eating here with naught but ye and yer glum face," Lady Boru said frankly. "And do not take too long at dressing. I be half starved to death." She went out, with a cheery wave.

Brian sighed and called for Hayden. "Another whiskey, m'laird?" the manservant asked knowingly.

"I only wish. I need to dress for dinner."

"If ye'll pardon the thought, m'laird, ye hae had a tiring day. Would nae a bite t' eat here in yer rooms suit ye better?"

"It would. But it does not suit Mother." Brian pushed himself out of his chair. "The dark blue coat and the suedes. I'll need a clean shirt as well. I hope you've blacked my boots."

Hayden went pale. "But I hae nae, m'laird! In truth, it ne'er occurred t' me ye might gae out again, wi' such a fatiguin' day already beneath yer belt!"

"Some aide-de-camp you are," Brian said wearily. Then he sighed. "It doesn't matter. I'll wear 'em unblacked." So what if when he staggered in with his canes, every eye in the dining room would be on his legs? Better that than Mother getting it into her stubborn Scots skull that he did not care to be seen publicly with her. *That* consequence would rankle far longer than a bit of wounded pride.

In truth, it went off better than he had expected. Their rooms were on the first story—how it galled him to have to make that request!—and despite the whiskey he had already downed, his arms were steady as he limped across the polished marble floor. The maitre d', having observed his slow progress through the lobby, seated them at a table quite near the doors, so that he wasn't forced to negotiate through a sea of tables and chairs. His mother's eyes were shining as she glanced around the restaurant at the elegant diners. And only two tables away, Lord Burrington, whose cousin was with the Crown's Twenty-Fifth, looked up from a broiled lobster, saw him, and hurried over, making more of a fuss than Brian would have liked. But it *did* give him the opportunity to prove to his mother that his ill manners on Hollingsford Road that afternoon had only been because of the rain. Burrington, bless him—he was somewhat in his cups—made a huge to-do over her, blathering on and on about how he'd be more apt to believe she was Lord

Boru's sister than his mother. Maegan blushed and giggled and then listened avidly as Burrington ran on about her son the hero, and how no man in the Isles deserved a knighthood more than he.

The food was damned good, too, and the wine—he *did* order champagne—even better. Brian was actually feeling rather mellow by the time his mother's baba came. He leaned back in his chair, sipping a brandy, relishing her expression as she had her first taste. "Ooooh," she said, and she smiled hugely. "I must have Cook assay this recipe!"

It was just at this point that Brian became aware of a conversation at the next table. The name "Wallingford" leaped out at him from the muddle of voices there—two young men and two young women, very much of the fashion—and he craned toward them as much as he could without being obvious. ". . . lucky devil," one of the men was saying.

"What?" one of the ladies, a stunning brunette, cried in mock anger. "Do you mean, Charles, you'd prefer me to be blond like her?"

"She hasn't got a penny," the other lady—a rather hard-looking sort, Brian thought—put in thoughtfully.

"She's got a decent settlement," the gentleman who'd spoken first averred.

"But it isn't as though she were an *heiress,*" the hard-boiled one noted.

"Don't matter." He waved his fork in the air, speaking through a mouthful of lamb cutlet. "Not when she's got such style. I was there at Yarlborough House, y' know, last Easter. I *saw* the fencing bout."

"Did you really?" The brunette leaned forward expectantly. "Was she as good as everybody says?"

"Better," he announced succinctly. "She would have beaten me."

"*Imagine* appearing in public in breeches!" The hard one sniffed.

"She wore 'em damned well," her companion retorted. "Damned well indeed. What I can't understand—"

"Bri?" His mother held a bite of baba out to him on her fork. "Ye must try this. Ye truly must! It be—"

"Hush!" he told her sharply. She stared, but he didn't care; he wanted desperately to know what the fellow who had been at the fencing bout didn't understand. Too late, though. Whatever he had said while Brian's mother was talking had sent the table into a burst of laughter. That had better not be at Nichola's expense, he thought furiously, putting his hand to his side, where his sword once would have been.

Then the brunette spoke up again: "Of *course* it is a love match!" she said brightly, reaching for her wine. "They are perfection together, the two of them."

"She makes him look like a dwarf," Hardboil asserted. But she was hooted down soundly by her companions:

"So she's a tad on the tall side!"

"Miranda, you're a dreadful cat!"

"And he's a bit on the short side," the brunette acknowledged. "What of it? Why should she prefer another suitor to Wallingford on such a basis?"

"It isn't natural," Hardboil said stubbornly.

"It seems to be for *them*," her escort retorted. "Anthony told me he has bought a ring—a *huge* thing, from DeBeers. Diamond surrounded by sapphires. Cost him ten thousand pounds."

Oh, no, Brian thought. *Not sapphires and diamonds. Not for her. A cat's-eye, or citrine, or amber—aye, amber, brown shot through with gold. That's what I would have bought. . . .*

"Well, I for one," Hardboil announced, "will be glad when she takes it, so you bedazzled men will remember the rest of us!"

"I must admit," the brunette sighed, "it does become tedious being compared to an Amazon and found lacking. If I learned to fence, Charles, would you like me more?"

"I couldn't possibly like you more than I do," her companion assured her, his hand covering hers. Brian, looking on, felt a pang in his heart. If the *on-dit* had been that he, instead of Wallingford, were to claim Nichola, how would they have reacted? If they felt pity for Wallingford, a duke's son and heir, for his diminutive stature, how would they look upon a man who couldn't stand on his own two feet? *I did the right thing in letting her go,* he told himself. *No one would have envied her—or even* discussed *her—if she were marrying me.*

Lady Boru had excellent hearing. She hadn't missed her son's sudden attention to the neighboring table, and her ears had pricked as well as his. All the time she was savoring the baba so lovingly, she was watching Brian's face across the table, seeing it change like quicksilver from avid curiosity to wrath—he'd even made a move as though to draw a sword!—to the wretched resignation he now wore. Her interrupting offer of a taste was only meant to make absolutely certain his attention was as riveted as it seemed.

So. Now she knew. Miss Hainesworth, for whom Lord Wallingford had bought a ring, was the reason they had come to London. Not much to go on, but more than she'd have learned had they stayed in Strathclyde.

"Forgive me, Mother," Brian said quietly, "for that rudeness just then. I was . . . thinking on something."

"Faith, I be sorry to have intruded on yer thoughts." Maegan was thinking herself. She hadn't anticipated approving of whatever English lass Brian had lost his heart to; she had only sought to see her son's unhappiness relieved. But Miss Hainesworth wasn't what she had expected. She'd seemed remarkably . . . solid. Down-to-earth. Unflustered by the rain and her curricle having come within an inch of crashing—and Maegan hadn't missed the fact that it had been *her* hands on the reins when the horses finally came under control.

So. A girl who didn't mind having her fancy clothes doused and drenched. A lovely girl, with winsome brown-gold eyes. Young, too! And not yet married! Maegan had been very much afraid her headstrong son might be pining for another man's wife—or, worse, for some loose actress type. *Ach, such bairns the two of them would have together,* she mused, envisioning it all in a moment: Tobermaugh filled to the towers with grandchildren and hounds and kittens, muddy footprints on the floors, hand-marks on the banisters, she combing and plaiting the girls' hair in front of the fire on chill winter nights. . . .

"Mother?"

"Aye?"

"You look so . . . happy."

She drew back to reality. The thing was a long way from settled yet. There was Wallingford, that the lass was as good as betrothed to. And there was Brian's bloody pride as well—no underestimating that obstacle! Not to mention that she hadn't much time . . . "Why should I not be happy?" she replied. "When my son has given me my heart's desire?"

"What—a trip to London? You could have come to be with me here years ago, if you'd ever said you wanted to." Though that, of course, was a lie. There wouldn't have been a place for her in his whirlwind life in the city before . . . before the cannonball. Odd, wasn't it, how being forced to sit still could alter one's point of view? Maegan was far better company than most of the girls he'd wined and dined—just as Nichola was worth twenty of the simpering misses and dissatisfied wives and elegant courtesans he'd so eagerly pursued. Is this what growing up is? he wondered vaguely. Discovering that what matters more than dash and flash is simple happiness?

God, she had made him happy. Even remembering how happy they'd been was a comfort of sorts.

And then he had a disquieting thought: *Would she be happy with Wallingford?*

Of course she would, he answered himself briskly. Why shouldn't she be? The little fop loved her, didn't he? He'd bought her that ring.

Sapphires and diamonds. Brian squeezed his eyes shut, picturing it. Perhaps this very night she would accept his proposal. Perhaps, even now, they were celebrating together, the damned thing glittering on her hand. How had Wallingford phrased his plea? What had he said? *I love you.* She'd said that to him. Why hadn't he said it back?

He forced his eyes open again, looked across to his mother. She'd finished her dessert and was sipping her coffee, waiting patiently. Brian roused himself. "I beg your pardon. I am dreadful company, aren't I? I promised I would take you to Vauxhall. To watch the dancing."

"Do ye ken, I feel too tired for such goings-on this evening," she admitted. "Must be my age catching up to me."

"Well. If you are sure, then—"

"I be."

He signaled for the check. When he'd made his way up the single flight of stairs to their suite, he kissed his mother good night at her door. Hayden was waiting for him with a whiskey and soda. He accepted it gratefully.

"Too rough a day fer ye," the manservant observed, easing off his master's right boot.

"It has been a long one," Lord Boru admitted.

He fell asleep in his chair and dreamed of nights in a cheap Kentish inn, her soft hair across his pillow, her breast in his hand.

"Nichola," Wallingford whispered beneath the cover of the music. "Come out to the terrace."

Nichola was feeling tired and cross and not one whit like submitting to his kisses. "I am enjoying the program," she told him.

"I know something you'll enjoy even more." He winked. She was hard put to keep from yawning. For some reason, on this night she did not care to permit his fondling, pretend his caresses aroused her when they did not at all.

Gwen and Bessie, she reminded herself sternly. But even that strong spur could not overcome her revulsion.

She stared at his soft white hands, remembering the curricle ride, his blithe obliviousness to their danger—

"Come *on*," he hissed impatiently, drawing a bemused, doting glance from the duchess.

"Oh, very well." What choice did she have, really? She never had refused him before; to do so today might seem peculiar. Although he had no way of knowing anything about Lord Boru . . . damn, now she'd gone and thought of him, when she'd *sworn* she would not! Penitently she permitted Wallingford to lead her away from the circle of listeners and through the French doors.

"Ah, what a night!" He drew in a deep breath on the balcony, staring up at the sky. Nichola followed his gaze. So many stars . . . why should there not be a single one lucky for her? He planted himself against the wall, beckoned to her with a finger. "Come here, my sweet." She dragged her feet going forward, tense as a drawn bow. He gathered her in his arms, pressed his lips to her forehead. "I love you so, Nichola. . . ." There it was again—that word *love*. What the devil did he mean by it? In all the time they spent with one another, they never discussed anything more than whatever divertissement they were attending, or the other attendees' clothes, or who was courting whom, or what young men were to be sent overseas, or—on his part, at least—how splendid life would be when they were married. And though their conversations were comfortable enough, she could not shake her sense that she might as well be chatting with a schoolmate rather than a man who professed to be in love with her.

Something pricked at her memory. "Anthony?"

"Aye?" He was nibbling her earlobe.

"Why did you not go into the army?"

He pulled back from her, surprised. "Why should I have?"

"I don't know. I've heard you talk often enough about the threat Napoleon poses to English freedoms."

He had the grace to look uncomfortable. "The plain

truth is, sweetheart, I wouldn't be suited for it. That life . . . mudholes and tents and bad food . . ."

"Did you pay someone to take your place?"

He winced. "Father did so. But plenty of fond daddies do. I *am* an only child." So was Brian Boru. "I suppose you think I am a coward," he continued rather stiffly.

"No! No. That isn't it at all. I only wondered."

He stared up at the stars again. "I *would* have gone," he said then, faintly. "I was more than willing. But Father said—and it was hard to argue with him—that I wouldn't prove much good. I'm not . . . sturdy. I never have been, from a child. I've tried to—to exercise, build myself up. But I'm not—not *naturally* good at stuff like boxing and fighting. I haven't got the stomach for it. Nor the heart."

Nichola wished to hell she hadn't brought up the subject. There was a pain in his voice that was awful to hear. "We all have got different talents," she began, and realized that he was broaching matters they had never discussed, baring his soul to her, just as she'd longed for. Why, then, did she feel so awkward?

"I cannot think what mine might be," Wallingford said wryly.

"You are a very good friend," she told him, without realizing how that would sound.

"Friend." He pronounced the word with a shudder.

"Oh, Anthony." She reached out to him, took his hands in hers. "You have so many fine qualities. Your dancing. Your—your elegance. The way you set folk at ease. The way you set *me* at ease, that first night you saw me—"

"I thought you were a dream," he said with a smile.

"You'll never know how much it meant to me," she told him honestly, "your asking me to dance. It—it changed my life forever."

"Well. That is something to hold on to, I suppose." He sighed. "But not enough for you to marry me."

She stared down at the stones beneath their feet. "I've told you time and again—it isn't *you*. I'm just not ready to marry."

"Not ready to marry *me*."

"There isn't anyone else!"

"What about Lord Boru?" he asked shrewdly.

Her gaze flew up to his. "What do you know about . . . Lord Boru?"

"What all the *ton* does. That he's a dissipate, a scoundrel."

"So he is," Nichola echoed emphatically.

"That hasn't stopped any number of women from submitting to his charms."

"But all that's in the past, isn't it?" she retorted. "He is nothing more now than . . ." How had Brian phrased it? "An empty shell."

"I am glad to hear you say so." Wallingford appeared heartened. "When we saw him today, on the Hollingsford Road, I rather thought—"

"Any woman in her right mind," Nichola said decisively, "would avoid Brian Boru like the plague."

Wallingford was reaching into his waistcoat. "In that case," he began, "perhaps tonight you'll finally accept this." And he held out the crimson velvet box. Nichola caught her breath. *He hadn't even wanted to show himself,* she thought. *He tried to hide in the carriage. He ducked his head, and then only came forward because he had to, because his mother forced it. And he was off like a shot once the niceties were over. Not one hint, one breath of all that had gone on between us . . . You bloody stupid fool, what were you hoping for?*

She looked at Anthony as he stood before her, looked long and hard. You could do far worse, she reminded herself. He *is* a good man. And tonight he'd shown himself every bit as dissatisfied with the lot he'd drawn in life as she was. She thought of every rebuke her mother had ever addressed to her, imagined them, reversed, addressed to him by his father. They would always have *that* to share, that basic sense of unworthiness.

And it would settle the futures of Gwen and Bess, assure that they would make their entries into society untainted by any whiff of scandal surrounding the academy.

He loves me! she thought wildly. Why do I hesitate?

Passion. The fire in his eyes as he'd held her. The way he caught his breath as he entered her. His touch where no one ever had touched her—his seal set on her for life.

Her mother's expectations. Tommy's horror of Lord Boru.

The lie she would have to live . . .

The lie that she was living now.

Wallingford had withdrawn his hand, was tucking the box back inside his waistcoat. "I'll wait," he said, with a wealth of resignation that tore at her heart. "I'll wait until you are ready. But I *can* make you happy, Nichola. I know that I can."

The rain pouring down between them, like a curtain that could not be parted . . .

She put her hand over his, took a breath. "I'll marry you, Anthony."

His eyes met hers in disbelief. "You *will?*" She nodded, and could not help but smile at the joy on his face. He threw his arms around her, kissed her hair, her nose, her mouth. "Oh, Nichola! Oh, Nichola, you have made me the happiest man on all the earth!" He caught her by the arm, tugged her back to the house, burst in through the doors. "I have an announcement!" he proclaimed, causing the startled musicians to falter. His mother and father turned to him, alarmed. "Miss Hainesworth has accepted my proposal of marriage!" Belatedly he recalled the ring, took it out of the box, slid it onto her finger. It did not go past the first joint. "Oh. Damn," he muttered. "I'll have it enlarged tomorrow."

But the moment was lost in the general rejoicing, as the duke and duchess and their guests swarmed forward. "Welcome to the family, my dear," the duchess said with feeling.

And her husband embraced Nichola, kissing both her cheeks. "We are so happy for you!"

Nichola accepted all the felicitations, smiled as was expected, thought, briefly, of how pleased her mother would be at the news. And Tommy would be happy. His worst fears would be unrealized—his fears that her heart still clung to Brian Boru.

Who, of course, was in London. And who, of course, would surely hear the news, too. But it would make no impression on him, surely. He hadn't loved her. He'd never said he loved her. Oh, God, if only once he had said that he loved her. . . .

"Nichola?" Anthony cried gaily, pulling her toward the dance floor. "This one is ours, I believe."

She let him lead her through a quadrille. She did not miss a step. She kept the smile on her face. No one in the company could have told how her heart was breaking.

At least Bess and Gwen will be safe now forever, she thought plaintively.

Chapter
Twenty-Six

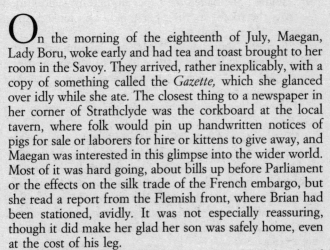

On the morning of the eighteenth of July, Maegan, Lady Boru, woke early and had tea and toast brought to her room in the Savoy. They arrived, rather inexplicably, with a copy of something called the *Gazette,* which she glanced over idly while she ate. The closest thing to a newspaper in her corner of Strathclyde was the corkboard at the local tavern, where folk would pin up handwritten notices of pigs for sale or laborers for hire or kittens to give away, and Maegan was interested in this glimpse into the wider world. Most of it was hard going, about bills up before Parliament or the effects on the silk trade of the French embargo, but she read a report from the Flemish front, where Brian had been stationed, avidly. It was not especially reassuring, though it did make her glad her son was safely home, even at the cost of his leg.

Near the bottom of the first page was a black-bordered box with the heading TOWN TATTLE. Really, Maegan thought with a sniff. Only the shameless English would lay their gossip right out for the world to read! About to turn the page, she stopped, her gaze arrested by the sight of a name in the very first paragraph. *Miss Nichola Hainesworth . . .* She held the page closer to the window to catch the light. *It is official at last,* the block of type began. *The duke of Strafford has confirmed the oft-rumored betrothal of his son and heir, Anthony, Lord Wallingford, to the incomparable Miss Nichola Hainesworth. No date has yet been set, but that sound in the distance is the shattering of brittle male hearts everywhere—or could it be the relieved sighs of the season's other debutantes, who are sure to embrace the news with glee?*

Maegan sat very still, her mind racing furiously as she stared at the words. It couldn't—it must not—be! Not after she had come all this way! Not after fate had been so kind as to allow her to find and pinpoint the object of Brian's longing with such ease! Oh, the devil had a hand in this, sure enough! She balled the paper up in a fury and hurled it across the room, startling her maid, who looked up in surprise. "Mum?" she said.

"I needs must dress," Maegan announced. "And quickly, too—do not stand there like a ruddy statue! Bring the striped morning gown and my paisley shawl, then get started on my hair."

"Where be we off to, then?" the girl asked, hurrying to comply.

"Ye be staying here. Mind ye find Hayden and tell him this, on yer life—His Lairdship must not see the gazettes and newspapers today. Do ye understand, lass?" The girl bobbed her head. "Now hurry, for the love of Christ!" The maid rushed her into the dress, did up the ribbons, fetched stockings and boots. Maegan tapped her foot impatiently for the long minutes it took to arrange her hair and set her hat in place.

"Shall I send for the carriage, mum?" the increasingly curious maid wanted to know.

"No time for that. I'll take one of them that be for hire

outside." Maegan caught up her reticule. "Mind ye tell Hayden—no newspapers!"

"Aye, mum," the girl said dazedly as her mistress strode purposefully to the door. "Yer shawl, mum!"

Maegan slung the thing around her shoulders. She'd been nervy at first at this prospect, but now she felt very calm. She was doing what she must do, for Bri, for the empty corridors of Tobermaugh Castle, that cried out for small footsteps and handprints on the walls. She marched down the single flight of stairs and across the grand marbled lobby. "I need a carriage," she announced to the smartly uniformed young man who held the doors open for her.

"Very good, mum." He signaled with his gloved hand, and the first in the row of the black coaches along the street rolled up to the entranceway.

"Where to, mum?" the driver asked as the doorman handed her in.

"Where to—Christ Almighty, I do not ken!" She turned to the doorman, wild-eyed. "I needs must find a girl. Her name be Hainesworth—Nichola Hainesworth."

"Hank?" The doorman appealed to the driver, who was leaning to listen.

"Hainesworth . . ." He thought a moment, shook his head. "You got me."

"There must be some way of findin' her!" Maegen said desperately.

"It's a big city, mum," the doorman told her, not unkindly.

"Ye do not understand! This be a matter of—" What *was* it a matter of? "Life and death," she finished firmly. And it was, wasn't it?

"If you don't have any address, mum, there's no way of telling—"

"Hold on, hold on," Hank announced, hopping down from the box. He ran back along the row of coaches. Maegan hung from the window, watching, as he called up to his fellow drivers. At the fourth coach he paused, listened for a moment, then held his thumbs up in a signal as he trotted back.

"Fifteen Crescent Street," he said rather breathlessly as he swung up to the box again.

"Thank the Laird in heaven," Maegan murmured, pressing shillings on the doorman in her gratitude.

" 'Tis Hank you ought to be thanking," he observed, closing the hansom door for her.

"Oh, so I shall!" she vowed. "Fifteen Crescent Street, then, as fast as ye can go!"

Hank took her at her word, setting out with a lurch that hurtled her back against the seat cushions. She laughed—it was a sign, wasn't it, that he should have found the address so quickly?—and held her hat on with her hands. Life and death . . . some folk, she knew, would have concluded that the *Gazette*'s announcement put an end to the matter. But some folk weren't Maegan Boru.

Tommy Hainesworth awoke on the eighteenth of July feeling happier than he had since before that mud-drenched morning in Flanders when he'd opened his mother's letter, despite a somewhat heavy head thanks to champagne downed the night before. It was settled, at long last. Nicky's betrothal to Wallingford was fact. He'd penned the notice to the Town Tattler column himself just after midnight, hoping to make the morning edition of the *Gazette*. He sent his man for the paper now, and read the words with overwhelming satisfaction. He felt so chipper, in fact, that he went downstairs for breakfast at the un-heard-of hour of eight.

He had the dining room to himself. Over eggs and sirloin with béarnaise sauce, he read the notice again and again, with a grin he couldn't hide. The maid who waited on him, too, was all smiles. "So glad we all are, sir, for your sister," she said shyly as she poured his coffee. "Such a lovely gentleman, Lord Wallingford. 'Tis certain she'll be happy."

A little crack broke through Tommy's complacency, then instantly healed over. She *would* be happy, dammit. She'd done the right thing. And their mother—Christ, the baroness had been out of her mind with joy when Wallingford brought Nicky home the night before and made the announcement. Even Lord Hainesworth had been pried out of his study to proffer his congratulations. Granted, he'd looked a bit dazed, but who wouldn't be? For Nicky to have landed the greatest catch in all of England . . . Tommy shook his head in bemusement. He could go back to war now with a clear conscience. The future shone very bright.

The door knocker sounded. Both the maid and Tommy glanced in surprise at the clock on the mantel. "Not even half after eight," the girl murmured, disapproving. Then she brightened. "Likely flowers for Miss Hainesworth, from Lord Wallingford. Cheeky tradesmen should know better than to come to the front door!" Simmonds, the butler, his cravat only half tied, was hurrying down the stairs. Tommy felt a tug of sympathy for him; he'd been up long after two in the morning, popping celebratory corks. The maid was already headed to the kitchens for a vase.

Tommy took a huge bite of egg and chewed, still staring at the black-and-white proof of Nichola's splendid future. He was so lost in self-congratulation—really, none of this would have come about if he hadn't talked sense into the chit—it only dawned on him very slowly that the butler and the visitor were engaged in quite a heated exchange. He laid the paper down and listened, hearing a female voice interspersed with Simmonds's. It wasn't overloud, but it was exceedingly firm. Curious, he stood and went to the dining-room entrance, where he had a view of the front hall.

"I am telling you, mum, that Miss Hainesworth is still abed."

"And I be telling *ye,* sir, that I would have ye wake her!"

"That's quite impossible," the butler said stiffly.

"Simmonds?" Tommy stepped out into the hall. "Is there a problem?"

The butler glanced his way with a telling roll of his eyes. "This . . . lady, sir, is insisting that I awaken Miss Hainesworth. She says she must have a word with her."

Tommy hadn't failed to note that slight hesitation before the word *lady*. He came forward to see the visitor, a very handsome older woman, simply but elegantly dressed. Only her Scots accent could account for Simmonds's disdain. There was no snob in all the world, Tommy reflected, smiling at the woman, like an English servant. She smiled back. He saw the red-gold hair beneath her chip-hat and caught his breath. "You . . . you are?" he stammered, knowing he was being rude as well, but even worse, knowing the answer to the question.

"Lady Boru, sir. Maegan, Lady Boru."

"Brian Boru's mother."

She brightened. It was easy to see where Boru got his looks. "Do ye ken my son?"

"Very well," Tommy said slowly. "We served in Flanders together."

"Did ye, now? Fancy that. Ach, it be a small world, be it not?"

She was still on the threshold. Tommy wished to hell he could leave her there. But politeness demanded . . . "It is true my sister hasn't yet risen," he told her. "She—we all . . . had a rather late night."

She nodded easily. "Ach, so I can imagine! Saw the announcement of her betrothal in the *Gazette,* I did. Ye must be right proud."

"We are." Simmonds had his eyebrows lifted. Tommy glared at him. "I was just having my breakfast. Perhaps you'd care to join me?"

"How very kind of ye, Mr. Hainesworth." She stepped into the house and curled her hand over his extended arm, with a withering glare at Simmonds that made Tommy smile despite himself. Plain enough where Boru had got his cockiness as well!

She let him lead her into the dining room. The maid was standing there with a vase in her hands. "Set another place for Lady Boru," Tommy instructed. "Tea? Coffee? Chocolate?"

"Tea, if ye please." He held out the chair across from his, and she settled into it a little stiffly. "Arthritis," she explained. "Bane of my existence."

"I am so sorry to hear that." He took his own place, waiting until the maid had brought a plate and napkin and utensils and tea. "May I ask, Lady Boru, what brings you to call on Nichola?"

"Ye may." She stirred sugar into her tea. "But what I have to say be between yer sister and me." The maid offered toast and eggs. She took the former, declined the latter, and spread jam thickly across the bread.

Tommy was suddenly more than a little nervous. He forced a laugh. "I do hope, Lady Boru, you have no intentions of attempting to . . . to overthrow Nichola's happiness."

"To the contrary! Her happiness be my sole concern." She took a bite of the toast. "Well—that and Bri's, of course."

Tommy felt the need to interject. "Lady Boru. Believe me. Having served with your son, I am exceedingly aware of all his many outstanding qualities. I have never in my life met a braver, finer, more . . . congenial man. He—"

"What be this Wallingford like, then?" she demanded abruptly.

"Anthony? Why, he is very . . . very . . ." Jesus. What the hell *was* Wallingford like?

"Rich?" the woman across from him said shrewdly.

"I suppose he is."

"Ye suppose he be."

"And very debonair!" Tommy said. "Very dapper! Witty! An excellent dancer!"

Her mouth, which was wide and full, just like her son's, curled in disdain—just like her son's. "What every girl must long for in a husband—an excellent dancer."

Tommy's hackles rose. "At least he isn't a dissolute!"

She didn't take offense; she merely nodded thoughtfully. "My Bri does have a dreadful reputation, I suppose."

"Deservedly," Tommy said curtly. "Believe me. I know."

She dipped the spoon into the jam jar again. "So did his father, heaven ken. Ach, a great one for the wenching and gambling and carousing, he was."

"Then you must understand why . . . why . . ."

"Until he met me," Maegan Boru said complacently. "The right woman—that be all it takes to turn a wayward man about."

"With all due respect, Lady Boru," Tommy said from between his teeth, "I'd not have my sister serve as proving ground for such a theory. Your son, whether you know it or not, has already seduced her. Stolen her maidenhead."

Her red-gold brows rose up. "Do ye suppose Laird Wallingford be aware of that?"

Tommy cursed himself for not keeping his mouth shut. "Of course he isn't," he snapped. "And if you've any notion of telling him—well! I can't imagine what sort of woman you might be."

She set her elbows on the table, those blue eyes trained straight at him. "Ye said yer sister be happy. That be all I would ask of her. If I hear that from her own lips, I'll be gone from here."

"Of course she is happy!" Tommy burst out. "Why the devil shouldn't she be? What more could any girl like her ask than to be married to a duke's son?"

Maegan Boru shrugged. "Why will ye not let me ask yer sister, then?"

"Ask me what?"

Tommy's head jerked up like a marionette's. His sister stood in the doorway, clad in a dressing gown, her long hair loose over her shoulders. "Nicky." He swallowed. "This is—"

"I know who she is. We have been introduced. Lady

Boru." Nichola made a curtsy. "How very remarkable to find you here. What is it that you wanted to ask me?"

"Nicky," Tommy started to say. She was paying no attention to him, though; her gaze was locked on Lady Boru, who was looking her over slowly, up and down.

"Ach, ye be lovely enough," she murmured thoughtfully. "Still, he has had a host of lovely women. What be it, do ye suppose, has made him—"

"You said one question only!" Tommy interjected sharply.

"I was but musing to myself. So, child! Ye be betrothed to marry!"

Nichola nodded, not entirely trusting herself to speak. Why *did* she have to resemble him so—or, rather, he her? It was like looking at Brian Boru in miniature, to gaze into Lady Boru's blue eyes. Then she realized how offended he would have been by that notion, and bit her lip to keep from laughing. No comparison in *miniature* could suit a man so large of life.

Lady Boru dabbed a spot of jam from her lip with her napkin. "Yer brother here tells me ye have given yer maidenhead to my son."

"Tommy!"

He flushed bright red. "I was only . . . remonstrating with her, Nicky. Telling her she must not interfere now that you are . . ." *Happy.* Why could he not get the word out? "Betrothed to Wallingford," he finished, and knew how lame it must sound.

Nichola had recovered her composure. She sat at the head of the table, quite a distance from either of them. "I'll have coffee," she told the goggle-eyed maid, who left reluctantly. When she was gone, Nichola dared look again at Lady Boru. "From what he told me himself, that fact does not place me in particularly exclusive company."

Lady Boru sucked in breath. "Ach, ye be so angry at him! What has he done, pray tell, to make ye that way?"

"I think," Tommy blustered in, "the mere fact of—of what we all acknowledge has—"

"Shut up, Tommy," said his sister, then trained her gaze on Brian's mother. "He lied to me. And he used me."

"Used ye how?"

"Nicky," Tommy began again, "you have no need, no need *whatsoever,* to explain—"

"*Will* you shut up? I'm not a child anymore. He was . . . in cahoots with a woman at the academy, Lady Boru. A woman who . . ." What? Was wronged by? Had wronged? "Once knew my mother," she finished uncertainly. "She brought Bri—Lord Boru—there to . . ." To seduce her? But who had seduced whom? Where had it all started? Hadn't he tried to stop what went on, and hadn't she insisted? *I would not want you if you did not want me.*

"To see her ruined," Tommy said abruptly. "And so he has!"

"Really?" Lady Boru drawled. "I cannot for the life of me understand how. Ye be engaged to marry this great muckety-muck now, be ye not, Miss Hainesworth?" Nichola and Tommy stared at her in silence. "I cannot comprehend what offense ye might put to Bri in such circumstances."

"He *seduced* her," Tommy barked, finally finding his tongue.

"And kept his counsel about it, did he not?"

"You've been posing a hell of a lot of questions," he said angrily, "for someone who came claiming she'd ask only one!"

"In all fairness, Lady Boru," Nichola began.

"Now *you* shut up, Nicky!"

"It is solely thanks to your son," she continued relentlessly, "that I am . . . where I am today."

"Where *ye* be." The Scotswoman seemed on a low simmer, and about to boil over. "Where *ye* be? And what about *him?*"

"He—"

"Nicky . . ."

"He never spoke to me of marriage!" she burst out,

glad to have that burden off her chest. "He never made me an honorable offer! He—he—"

"He took from her what he could," Tommy put in coldly. "Just as he did with so many other women."

"He loves ye," Lady Boru told Nichola bluntly.

"Nonsense," she said after a moment.

"Lass, he loves ye so, it be tearing him apart! And the damned bludy fool does not realize it himself!"

Tommy felt a desperate need to take charge of this unseemly situation. "Now, see here, Lady Boru. It is all well and good for you to tell us your opinion. But the fact remains—Nicky, you told me yourself he never said he loved you! And even if he had, what has he got to offer?" He regretted *that* as soon as he spoke it. Lady Boru's brows drew together above blue eyes that were icy cold.

"Granted, he may not be so rich as some . . ."

"I didn't mean his money!" Tommy protested.

"Nor the heir to a duke," Lady Boru went on relentlessly.

"Nicky. Nicky, for God's sake. *You* tell her. You explain it!"

His sister was sitting with her chin on her hand. "What makes you think he is in love with me?"

"Oh, Christ!" Tommy swore, and hurled the saltcellar across the room, causing both women to turn to him. "You said one question *only*!" he reminded Lady Boru in desperation. "Ask the one bloody question!"

She trained those blue eyes straight at Nichola, with an intensity that was breathtaking. "Be ye happy?" she said.

Tommy swore and kicked the leg of the table. "Stuff and nonsense! Is she happy? She's betrothed to the finest catch in England!"

"Be ye happy with yer choice, lass?" Brian Boru's mother asked again. "If ye be, I swear to ye, I'll up and leave this instant, and no more will ye hear of me for so long as ye live."

Nichola closed her eyes and sat in silence. When she opened them again and spoke, she sounded weary, like an old, old woman, so that Tommy winced to hear. "I am—satisfied, Lady Boru, with the choice I have made. And the fact is, I don't believe many women are happy in this life." There were so many images reeling through her mind: Mrs. Treadwell announcing curtly to Vanessa, "I think the heralds are a bit de trop!" Gwen blushing at Lord Botheringly's sotted attentions. Madame saying earnestly of Lord Boru, "Oh, if only you might have known him, Nichola, when he was whole and himself!" The—the *awe* in her mother's eyes last night, when she and Wallingford had announced their betrothal. But the picture she could not shake off was of Brian Boru on that morning he'd been swimming in the river, rising out of the water with his hair slicked back, the sun gleaming on his naked skin. *I loved him from that moment,* she realized, and raised her hand to brush away tears.

Tommy was staring at her, aghast. "God, Nick! What a thing to say! Why *shouldn't* women be happy? *They* don't have to go off to war! They don't have to fret about making a living! All they have to do is—is look pretty, be polite and gracious. Get married! Have children! Take care of their households and husbands—what's so damned difficult about that?"

Lady Boru, however, was rising from her seat, gathering her gloves. "Fair enough," she declared. "I *could* say—but I will not. I trust ye'll be attending the ceremonies at Westminster this evening?"

"Of course *I* will," Tommy declared. "I'm from Brian's regiment. You must know, we are all of us there extraordinarily proud of him."

"And ye, Miss Hainesworth?"

It was on the tip of Tommy's tongue to protest yet another question, but Nichola spoke up before he could: "I—I'm really not certain what plans Lord Wallingford has laid." Then she glanced suddenly at their guest. "You must be furious with me."

"No, no, lass. Ye have yer reasons, no doubt, for denying yer heart. It be no place of mine to ask what they might be."

"Just what," Tommy began hotly, "makes you so certain she is . . ." But then his voice trailed away as he looked at his twin. Of course she was denying her heart. Of course she loved Boru, loved him with such breadth and strength that it terrified him. He'd known that from the first time he'd seen them together, fencing in the abbey yard. "I'll—I'll see you to the door, Lady Boru," he said much more quietly. She waved him off, though:

"I'll see myself, thank ye kindly. Give me the chance, it will, to root yer snooty butler in the balls." Tommy nearly choked. Nichola, however, burst out laughing.

"See that you do, Lady Boru. Simmonds is an insufferable snob. I wonder. . . ."

"Aye, lass?"

Nichola shook her head, her loose hair flinging shards of morning sunlight from the windows. "Only . . . what I would have thought of Scotland."

"Ye would have taken to Scotland," Lady Boru said ruefully, "like a cow to corn." She went out. Just before the door closed, there was a muffled gasp from Simmonds. Nichola swallowed a smile.

"Nicky," Tommy said suddenly. "See here. If you're not . . . contented with Wallingford—"

"It's rather too late for all that now, isn't it?" She took a sip of her coffee, wrinkled her nose. "Gone cold." She set the cup down and left him. He watched her go, with a horrible misgiving in his heart.

Chapter
Twenty-Seven

"I really think, Anthony, I'd prefer just to be alone with you tonight," Nichola noted as he wheeled the curricle onto Whitehall, merging with the long line of carriages there.

"Nonsense, my sweet! This is where all the *ton* will be—and where we should be, too! I intend to revel extravagantly in the congratulations." And he leaned over to steal a swift kiss.

"But there's sure to be an awful crush," she argued, fidgeting. The bays were stamping and snorting while he edged them into the queue, and she had a sudden wish: Perhaps they'd bolt again, bolt so far that they'd never get back to Westminster in time. Her betrothed, however, seemed to have learned his lesson; he had the reins curled round his fists and was holding them fast.

"A crush of your admirers," he said with complacence. "I shall enjoy observing their envy of me. Did you get my flowers?"

"You already asked," she said softly. "And I already told you—yes. They are magnificent."

"So you did. Mother suggested lilies, but I thought roses suited you better."

"I'm very fond of roses."

"Of course you are. All well-bred young ladies are."

What I really would have liked, Nichola thought, *was a great huge bouquet of heather.* She'd grown fond of its scent, had sent Donleavy back for more of the bath oil. But heather was too unruly and coarse for the fiancée of a duke's son.

"Wallingford!" The driver of another curricle, joining the line from the Westminster Bridge, stood in his seat to hail them, raising up a flask in a toast. "You finally did it, old man!"

Wallingford tucked an arm around Nichola's shoulder. "Of course I did, Botheringly! Was there ever any doubt?"

"My felicitations, Miss Hainesworth!" Botheringly called. She nodded and waved. "When's the wedding to be, then?"

"I—"

"October," Wallingford interjected. "At Wentworth Hall. Hunt season, don't you know."

"Anthony," Nichola whispered, "we hadn't yet set a date!"

He glanced at her, surprised. "We most certainly did. I distinctly recall discussing it. The wedding, then a hunt, and a great huge breakfast—did you have some objection to October?"

"It's so soon," she said without thinking, and then hastily amended: "There is so much yet to do! Mother tells me it takes at least a *year* to make all the plans."

"I don't intend to wait that long," Wallingford said simply. He grinned at her. "And anyway, what is money for if not to hasten matters along?"

She had no reply to that, so she held her peace. October or December or a year or two years from now—what difference did it make? Her fate was sealed.

"Nichola!" A girl in yet another curricle coalescing into the mass headed for Westminster raised a white-gloved arm to her. Nichola recognized her: Cecilia Farnweather, a dainty brunette—she, at least, had not joined the rush to dye herself blond—who had always been exceedingly kind to her. Wallingford glanced her way, and the reins in his hands suddenly went slack. If Nichola hadn't nudged him, the bays certainly would have made for Land's End. He brought them under control. Cecilia was riding with her brother, one of Wallingford's cronies, who winked broadly as he fell into the line:

"Congratulations to the both of you!"

"Thanks, John. Thanks, Cecilia," Wallingford said, and then was uncharacteristically silent. Cecilia hurried to fill the awkward space:

"I am so happy for you, Nichola. And for you, of course, Anthony. You are perfect together. Everyone knew it from the first time you danced with one another, at the duke and duchess of Yarlborough's Easter weekend."

"Fancy your saying that, Cecilia!" Nichola exclaimed in astonishment.

"Oh, how could I forget? It was the very next day that you had your infamous duel."

"But you weren't there," Nichola observed.

A faint flush appeared on Cecilia's pretty cheeks. "Wasn't I? Well—John always reports to me in such detail, I sometimes imagine that I am!"

"Set a date for the wedding?" John boomed.

Surprisingly, this time, Wallingford said nothing. Nichola realized he must be waiting for *her* to confirm what he'd already told Botheringly. "In October," she said, thinking to please him, atone for her former faux pas.

"As soon as that," Cecilia marveled.

Where the devil was Anthony's tongue? "Hunt season," Nichola explained. Then the line lurched forward, taking the Farnweathers' curricle ahead of theirs. On the warm summer wind, Cecilia's voice wisped back toward them:

"I trust you'll be very happy!"

Nichola, for her part, was growing sick to death of that word.

But there were many such good wishes sent their way as the queue crawled slowly toward Westminster Abbey. She accepted them graciously. Wallingford seemed to be concentrating on controlling the team, which, all in all, she considered a good thing. Finally they reached the gates, and a boy ran to take the reins. Her fiancé came to help Nichola down, and there was the usual awkward moment when she felt she had to accept his support without crushing him with her weight. He set her down with a bit of a grunt, and she knew this time, she'd failed.

John Farnweather, in the curricle ahead, lifted his petite sister with a flourish that sent her skirts whirling. She blushed, with a covert glance at Wallingford's coach, and admonished him.

Wallingford took Nichola's arm, his grip very tight. "Shall we go in?" he said, a little grimly, she thought. No doubt Farnweather's carelessness of his sister's repute had offended him. He *was* a bit of a prude, Nichola reflected; even last night, with their betrothal finalized, he hadn't done more than kiss her and make a few swipes at her breasts. What would it be like to be made love to by him? She had a sudden awful premonition that it might very well be like having him help her out of a carriage—she fearful she would strain him, always mindful of the distinction in their size. With Brian, she had never . . .

She dipped her fingers into the holy water at the portal, made the sign of the cross, willing all such thoughts away.

They took their seats. Wallingford had insisted on departing early, so they were well up in the nave, perhaps a dozen rows from the front. Lord and Lady Hester, next to them, leaned over to proffer their congratulations, and the earl and countess of Somerleigh, in the pew behind them, did the same. Nichola sat with her hands in her lap, contemplating the glory of the abbey—the radiating chapels of the choir, the soaring roof, an exquisite censing angel carved into the arch to her left. She was glad when a burst of trumpets and a murmur of the crowd announced the entrance of the regent. She stood with the rest, and curtsied when he passed their pew, staring at him from beneath her lashes. *There* was a man who would make any woman feel petite! He looked fleshy and soft, though he carried himself with great dignity. More, really, than he had claim to. She'd been presented to him on several occasions, and his roving eye and lewd jocularity always set her on edge. Brian would have made a better ruler, she thought briefly.

"Why are you scowling so?" Wallingford demanded.

"Was I?" she whispered back. "I—I hadn't much sleep."

"Nor had I." And he winked. "Contemplating the future."

The future. This great vault that held so much of England's past at least lent some perspective. In the end, she and Anthony were no more than wisps of the wind.

The regent had taken his seat on the altar, beside the archbishop of Canterbury, and the host of dignitaries who trailed in his wake took their places as well. A bell tolled somewhere, and the voices of the boys in the choir rose in a swell of spine-tingling beauty. Nichola bowed her head, letting the soothing, ancient words of the service lull her sore heart to rest. The three candidates for the Order of the Garter strode grandly down the aisle. Nichola knew one of them, Lord Winnerley, by acquaintance. He was a friend of Wallingford's, and from what she had gathered from dinner-table conversations, his foremost qualification for the honor to be bestowed on him today was a speech he'd given in the House of Lords that convinced the peers to increase the regent's yearly allowance. As for the other two, Lord Stallings and Lord Kulp, *on-dit* said the former had purchased this honor with a sizeable loan to the regent's coffers and the latter by holding his tongue after Prinnie got his wife with child. Odd company for Boru to be in. Perhaps he was meant, she thought wryly, to lend the proceedings *some* air of gravitas.

The three new knights accepted their garters and collars and ribbons and stars from the regent, then turned and saluted the audience. Again the voices of the boys soared. Then the knights moved aside, Winnerley and Stallings, at least, grinning broadly. As the last notes of the canticle died away, Nichola heard another sound from the rear of the nave, a slow, alternating thump and drag. She could not resist turning. Lord Boru was making his way up the aisle on his canes.

God, he looked magnificent. He was all in black—a piquant contrast to the gaudy recipients of the Garter—and bareheaded; his gold-red hair gleamed in the light of the tapers. Nichola suppressed a shiver, remembering the feel of that sleek head against her breasts. His chin was held high; he did not glance to either side, but stalked straight onward, eyes trained on the altar before him. What it must be costing him, Nichola thought, to display himself this way! Why had he ever agreed to come? She knew how little respect he held for the regent. What could have made him submit to such a charade?

He passed her pew. She stared at his broad-planed face, the unwavering blue eyes, and felt such a stir of pride in him that she had to bite her lip to keep from crying. Then, above the heads of the hushed onlookers in the pews before her, she saw another gleam of red-gold—Lady Boru, also in dignified black, her smile blazing. *He came for her,* she realized, a lump rising in her throat. *He came because she wanted this. Because she asked him to.* And the knowledge that the great, randy warrior Brian Boru would endure this public spectacle for the sake of his mother brought her tears spilling over. In the pew beside her, Wallingford frowned and offered his handkerchief.

She scarcely noticed that she took it, pressed it to her eyes. He was standing before the regent and archbishop now, balancing on the canes. "Let us pray," the archbishop intoned, and Lord Boru, with wrenching care, managed to lower himself to his knees. Nichola's clenched fist came up to her throat. Oh, Lord. How would he ever get up again?

The archbishop laid his hand atop Boru's head and began to drone. She was watching in horrified terror, waiting for the awful moment when Lord Boru would be called on to rise. The archbishop gave a stirring rendition of the candidate's heroism in battle, the lives he had saved through his selfless actions, and Nichola hoped the poseurs who'd been honored with the Order of the Garter were thoroughly ashamed.

She was. For as she listened, her heart seemed pinched in a vise. She was suddenly aware that of all the misdeeds laid at Brian's doorstep, dishonor had never been among them. To the contrary—all the outrageous acts her brother had so eagerly catalogued had been those of a man desperate for repute, starving for recognition, driven by a sense that Britain's nobleness had been cast aside by the regent and his cronies. He was like—like Lancelot, on fire from within, a foreigner sent to remind his adopted nation what honor should be. He showed it now, in his arrow-straight shoulders as he knelt, in his solemn stateliness, so in contrast to the regent coming forward to nick his shoulders with the sword and gild him with the star and collar and badge. *"Nemo me impune lacessit,"* the archbishop intoned, raising his quavering hand over Boru's rock-solid figure. It was, she knew, the motto of the Order of the Thistle, and also of Scotland: *No one attacks me with impunity*.

And yet, she had. She had accepted her mother's assignment of the most vile motives to his seduction of her, had questioned his honor so starkly in her shocked appeals to him in the abbey courtyard—and he had never spoken a word in his defense. In her wretched confusion, she'd assumed his silence proved him guilty. But all it proved, she knew now, knew with a certainty as hard as tempered steel, was that he would not debase himself by answering those charges—for the sake of his own dignity, yes, but for Madame's as well.

Oh, Brian, how I wronged you! she thought desperately. Were he the sort of man her brother and mother assumed him to be, why would he have held his tongue about what had gone on between them? Why wouldn't he have told the world that he'd deflowered Lord Wallingford's intended, that the belle of the *ton* wasn't the innocent she pretended to be?

Tommy and the baroness were a few rows ahead of her in the church. She saw her brother turn now, glancing over his shoulder, and his eyes were full of a strange unsettledness.

The moment came for the newest member of the Order of the Thistle to stand. Nichola saw Hayden, who had been hovering in the wings, start toward him. But Brian waved him off, reached on his own for his canes. For a long moment, in which the entire abbey seemed to hold its breath, he struggled uncertainly. The archbishop put out a hand, and even Prinnie took a step toward him. Lord Boru, however, struggled to his feet of his own accord. Then he turned. He looked out over the assembled nobles and ladies, and Nichola saw the slightest curl to his wide upper lip. He glanced at his mother, and his mouth softened, smiled. The choir exploded in a frenzy of rejoicing. The regent, looking a tad unsettled, proceeded back down the aisle. He was followed by the three now thoroughly disgruntled new knights of the Order of the Garter and then by Brian Boru, moving very slowly with the aid of his canes.

The buzz in the nave in their wake was raucous, like a clattering of crickets. "Dreadful notion of Prinnie's," Nichola heard Lord Asterton mutter to his wife, "setting Boru up against those sycophants." She would have lingered to hear more, but Wallingford was pulling at her sleeve.

"Let's go," he said briefly, and tugged her into the flow of congregants heading for the exits. Nichola submitted with unaccustomed meekness. She felt she'd lost all claim to protest.

He was glum and silent as they waited for the curricle. Nichola saw Tommy start toward her through the crowd, but just as he approached, their carriage was brought around, and Wallingford seemed in a rush to be away.

Once on the road, though, Nichola was determined to speak out. "Anthony," she began.

"Do you mind?" he responded abruptly. "I am occupied with keeping the team under control."

There was, Nichola knew, to be a reception at Carlton House for the new-made knights. She half expected Wallingford to produce some excuse for not attending, but to her surprise he drove grimly in the long line of vehicles headed for St. James's and then onto Bond Street. "Anthony," Nichola said again, as they reached the gates and a boy ran to take the reins. Wallingford came around the coach and held out his arms. His handsome face was strained.

"Let's wait," he proposed, "until we have a space of peace and quiet. We'll talk then."

Peace and quiet? Carlton House was the wrong place for any such thing.

Still, she felt relieved to have the discussion postponed. What she had to say to him would not be easy. And it was *not,* she told herself, as they entered through the torchlit portico among the swell of guests, that she had any hopes of marrying Brian Boru. It was only that, with what she'd just witnessed, she could never marry Anthony Wallingford. She was not at all certain, though, how she would explain that to him.

There was, of course, a receiving line for the new knights—quite an immense line. Nichola and Wallingford joined it and snaked slowly forward. She was trying to imagine what she might say when the moment came for her to curtsy to Lord Boru, and despite the lengthy wait, she arrived at no conclusion at all. By the time they reached the regent, her mind was a muddle of longings and regrets.

"Wallingford!" Prinnie exclaimed happily, as her fiancé made his bow. "Splendid news about your betrothal! My utmost congratulations! Though, of course, I am sorry to see Miss Hainesworth removed from the eligibles list." He winked at Nichola and took the opportunity to pinch her as she curtsied. Wallingford thanked him and progressed down the line through the three new Knights of the Garter, who at least kept their hands to themselves.

Lord Boru was last. Wallingford bowed to him, smiling. "No man deserves the honor more," he said stoutly, and motioned Nichola forward. "You have heard our happy news?"

That damned word again. Nichola forced herself to look up, meet that blue gaze. "Lord Boru."

"Miss Hainesworth." He kissed her hand, very swiftly. "My best wishes to you on your engagement."

"And mine to you, on your new honor." God, the stifling politeness of it all! What she wanted, what she longed to say . . . but the crush was already carrying her past him. She glanced back over her shoulder as Wallingford led her on. "Your mother," she began.

Those wondrous blue eyes flickered toward her. "Yes?" he asked, almost breathlessly.

Wallingford's grip was tight on her elbow. She saw her own mother and father, a few places behind her, and the baroness's face was watchful, tight. *Says that you love me.* But what did it matter, really, what his mother said? "Is a most charming woman," she finished.

He smiled at her one last time, that huge, blazing smile she loved so. "Thank you, Nichola." His use of her first name propelled Wallingford to yank her firmly away.

Considering that, she was surprised when, once they'd reached the main ballroom, he promptly vanished from her side. "Going to fetch us some wine," he murmured, pressing a kiss to her forehead. "Wait for me here." With nothing else to do, she stood against a marble pillar, observing the crowd. It was oddly subdued for one of Prinnie's spectacles, though Lord and Lady Ashton were doing their best to organize a dance. The new knights came through the crowd, the receiving line finished, and ranged themselves behind the regent on a dais at the front of the crystal-lit chamber. Prinnie had his sister-in-law, the duchess of York, at his side. By standing on her tiptoes, Nichola could see above the mass of heads. Lord Boru was being ignored by his fellow knights; he sat solitary and silent on his gilded chair.

"Nichola!" Tommy's voice—and she was grateful to hear it. He waved to her above the throng, but then got caught up in a sudden rush to the opposite direction, as the dancing began. She wondered where on earth Wallingford had got to. It wasn't like him to abandon her for so long in a public place.

Then he popped up at her shoulder, with two glasses in his hands. "We need to talk, Nichola," he announced.

"I—I believe we do, Anthony."

He gazed about at the mad crush. "This isn't the place. Come out to the gardens?" She nodded gratefully. He gave one glass to her, gulped down his own, and set it on the tray of a passing waiter. Then he grasped her hand tightly and led her across the packed room toward the open French doors.

He seemed, Nichola thought, to be moving with unusual purposefulness. Just as they gained the balcony, she caught a glimpse of Lady Boru, looking somewhat lost amongst the foreign throng, and would have stopped to speak to her except that Anthony hurried her on. Lords Turlington and Botheringly were lounging at the head of the stairway to the garden. She expected Anthony to pause to speak to his friends, but he barely nodded to the pair before plunging down the stairs and onto the calm, quiet pathways below.

Then, at last, she had the chance to catch her breath and sip from her champagne glass. His abrupt pace slowed, and once or twice he glanced back over her shoulder as though he expected someone might be following them— Boru, perhaps. Nichola thought of mentioning just how long it would have taken His Lordship to traverse those stone steps.

He stopped within a grove of willows. A stone bench lay within the sheltering branches, and she sank onto it gratefully, glad not to have to tower above him when she spoke her piece and thus add insult to injury. He hovered over her, pacing back and forth in his exquisite fawn breeches and forest-green superfine coat, his Hessians polished to such a gleam that they reflected the faint rays of a crescent moon. "Well, Nichola," he said then. "You have something to tell me?"

"Anthony. My dear, dear Anthony." She twisted her skirts in her hands. "Yesterday, when I agreed to your proposal of marriage . . . there was something I did not tell you. Something that, had you known, would surely have kept you from voicing it."

"That you were Boru's lover."

Nichola's head jerked up. It was the last response she had expected. "You . . . *knew*?" she said in disbelief.

He thrust his hands into his waistcoat. "I suspected. All that time he took with you, teaching you fencing . . . well. He's not the sort, is he, to offer something for nothing?"

"It wasn't like that at all," she protested.

"No? What was it like, then, exactly?"

Like coming out of fog into stark, bright sunshine. Like finding one's footing in a desperate mire. Like . . . Enough of that. "Under the circumstances, Anthony," she managed to say, "I cannot comprehend why you continued to pursue me."

"As I said, I only suspected. Today, at Westminster, I knew. You looked at him . . ." His voice was strained, aggrieved. "As though he were a bloody Titan."

"I'd hoped . . . I was not so transparent as that."

"Well, you were!" he said peevishly. "And it did not suit me at all to have my just-announced fiancée goggling at another man!"

"I am sorry. I—ought to have told you before now."

"That's neither here nor there," he announced, so briskly that she was taken aback. "What matters now is that I marry you as soon as possible and keep you well away from him."

"But, Anthony. That is what I wanted to tell you. I—" Before she could finish, Wallingford clasped her hands.

"Listen to me," he said intently. "The past is over and done. We must look to the future, you and I."

"But, Anthony—"

"You're not so foolish as to imagine *he* will marry you, are you? He's had scads—dozens—hundreds of women!"

"No," she said very firmly. "No. I don't imagine he will. But I am just as certain that wedding you would prove a mistake. *Not,*" she added hastily, seeing his backbone stiffen, "because you are not wonderful. I have told you before how much I appreciate all that you did for me— singling me out at the Yarlboroughs', taking me under your wing. . . ."

"Gratitude," he interjected, "is a perfectly sound basis for marriage."

"No! No! I mean—some folk may think it is. But . . . marriage is *forever,* Anthony! Marriage requires love!"

"Nonsense," he retorted. "Marriage merely requires the best interests of the parties involved. *I* am in your best interest."

"So you are," she said ruefully. "Mother and Tommy tell me so all the time. But really, you cannot convince me that you want to marry me now. I am . . ." She swallowed. "Soiled goods. Not the virgin you thought me."

"I'm not a virgin either," he noted—with, she could have sworn, a touch of pride. "That didn't keep you from accepting my proposal."

Nichola was trying desperately to collect her scattered thoughts. "That's expected in a man."

"That's why I went ahead and did it."

She stared at him. "Because it was *expected*?"

He nodded. "Father took me. On my eighteenth birth-day. To a brothel."

She shuddered. "How terribly paternal."

"What I am *trying* to say," he noted with impatience, "is that our situations are entirely comparable."

Nichola flushed. "I don't think so! That you have had intercourse with a prostitute, and I have made love to Bri— to Lord Boru—"

" 'Made *love* to,' " he echoed nastily. "I don't see *him* asking that you marry him!" She had no response to that. But she rose from the bench.

"Anthony." She drew a breath. "As I have said, I am *extremely* grateful for all that you have done for me."

"I could undo it just as readily."

Nichola paused. "What do you mean?"

"I could break off our engagement. Announce to the world that you and Boru were lovers. You'd be driven from the *ton*. Any hopes you ever had of a decent marriage would go down in flames. You would be like—like that pitiful countess d'Oliveri."

"What do you know of Madame?" Nichola asked, aghast.

He smiled—a smile of terrible complacence. "I knew very little—until Lord Boru's manservant approached me this evening and whispered into my ear. Sterling fellow, that Hardin."

"Hayden," she breathed.

"Whatever. What he told me was enough to more than seal your fate."

"Which is?"

"To wed me, Nichola Hainesworth."

"I will *not*!"

His smile deepened in satisfaction. "Oh, dear Nichola, you will. After tonight, you see, you have no choice."

"I don't care what you tell the *ton* about me! I don't *care* if you tell them Brian and I made love!"

"I don't intend to tell them that," he said flatly. "I intend to tell them that you and I have."

She stared at him. "And I'll deny it!"

"No one will believe you. Because, you see, it will be true." With a sudden movement, he tried to gather her up in his arms. The effort did not prove successful.

"For heaven's sake, Anthony! Whatever are you doing?"

"Abducting you," he grunted, and tried again.

She pushed him away as he came at her—not so hard

as she might have, but forcefully enough that he staggered backward. "Don't be ridiculous!"

"I intend to make it true, Nichola. You may as well submit."

He came at her once more, his face taut with concentration. This time he managed to grab her by the waist. She elbowed him sharply in the rib cage. "Dash it all!" he cried. "I don't want to hurt you—"

The notion was so absurd that Nichola nearly laughed—and yet she didn't dare. His expression was too determined; he would never see the humor in this. She made her voice soft, placating. "Anthony, please! Can't we discuss this like two civilized people?"

"The time for discussion is long past. I mean to have you, Nichola." He lunged at her. She came down hard with her heel on the instep of his left boot. He let out a sharp yowl of pain, then quickly clamped his mouth shut. Nichola backed away, her hands up, cocked in fists. She was starting to lose patience with him.

"I'll scream if you come near me again," she threatened.

"Go ahead. Scream your head off. No one inside will hear you—and these gardens are all too accustomed to the outraged cries of women." He ran at her. She sidestepped him adeptly, and he plunged into the tangle of willow branches. She started to flee back to Carlton House, but he caught her from behind and held on ferociously.

"Anthony, you are making an ass of yourself!" she told him, still moving toward the palace with him clinging to her shoulders. She pushed his hands off, fairly sure she could outrun him even in her skirts. But he'd caught hold of those now, in her wake, and if she broke for it, she fully expected the sheer fabric to tear. Ridiculous situation! She whirled around on the path. "I am warning you for the last time— let go of me!"

"Never!" he vowed.

"In that case—" She drew back and cold-cocked him with a single punch.

He dropped to the ground like a dead man. Nichola nibbled her lip in contrition. She hadn't thought she'd hit him *that* hard. "Oh, Anthony. You utter fool," she whispered. His nose was bleeding. It would get all over his impeccable white shirt. She found she still had his handkerchief in her reticule and knelt over him; she could at least make certain he didn't have to go back into Carlton House looking as if he'd been slapped about by Fleet Street hooligans.

Just as she reached to stanch the crimson flow, a twig snapped in the darkness behind her. She started to her feet in alarm, but before she could turn, a net of silken black settled over her head, was abruptly drawn tight. She twisted, lashing out in alarm with her nails bared, but someone very strong had got her arms clasped behind her back and was twisting them so savagely that she gasped and dropped back to her knees in pain.

"*He* may not have wanted to hurt you," a male voice hissed in her ear, "but I have no such compunctions."

Nichola screamed for all she was worth. The cord binding the domino at her throat drew tight with a yank, choking off her cry.

"Come along nice and easy," the voice purred again, "and I'll give you air enough to breathe. Otherwise . . ." She kicked backward, aiming for his groin, and had the satisfaction of hearing him groan. His grip on her slackened, and she darted from his grasp, trying to tear the hood away. Before she could, however, she stumbled blindly into another man's arms. He caught the cord and tugged it tight.

"He *is* a fool," the second man agreed, "but not an utter fool. He did allow for this contingency." Then something hard and cold came down with a thud against Nichola's forehead, and she crumpled in a heap.

Chapter
Twenty-Eight

Brian had been wanting to leave Carlton House for quite some time now, but, inexplicably, Hayden, faithful Hayden, had been absent from his accustomed post at His Lordship's shoulder. And Brian was not about to stagger up in front of all that grand company and hop around to find his canes. Where the devil had the fellow got to? Brian stretched up in his chair, scanning the masses of lords and ladies, and finally spotted him, making his way back across the room from the entrance to the gardens. He noted absently that little Lord Wallingford was just coming in through the doors as well, and heading for Nichola, who'd been standing, looking lost and abandoned, against a pillar on the side of the room for a full half hour. *Were she mine,* Brian thought, *I'd not leave her alone for one instant in this den of vipers.* But Wallingford was pushing toward her now, murmuring polite apologies as he elbowed his way along, snagging two flutes of champagne from a waiter going by. And here, thank God, was Hayden, climbing up to the dais to assume his usual position. Wallingford was talking to Nichola quietly, intently. She nodded; he took her arm and led her toward the gardens. The sight further blackened Brian's dark mood. "Where the devil have you been?" he demanded of his aide-de-camp.

"Dinnae I e'er mention t' Yer Lairdship that my aunt's husband's second cousin works in th' kitchens here?" Hayden said apologetically. "I only slipped off t' hae a word wi' him."

"Well, I am ready to leave—and have been for quite some time."

Hayden's gloom-stricken face looked almost cheerful as he reached for the canes. "Very gude, m'laird. Dreadful sorry fer th' inconvenience. But Auntie ne'er would hae forgiven me had I nae passed him her gude wishes."

In more than a decade of service by his aide-de-camp, Brian had never heard him mention any relatives in England. Against his will, he watched Nichola and Wallingford disappear through the garden doors into the darkness outside. "Go and tell my mother we are leaving."

"Bound t' bae disappointed, she bae."

Disappointed. No one could be so *disappointed* as he.

But what the devil had he hoped for? he thought irritably, taking his canes from Hayden. Why should Nichola care what became of him, when she believed he'd betrayed her so shamelessly? Her mother's deduction regarding the countess d'Oliveri's procuring of him for her fencing instructor had been perfectly logical, on the face of it. One would have to know Christiane as well as he did to recognize its foolishness. Granted, it *looked* terrible—that he'd seduced Nichola the way he'd seduced so many young women. But, dammit, it hadn't been at all the same. *There's* the curse in being a rake, he pondered. You turn out like the boy who cried wolf. When love finally strikes, nobody believes you—and with just cause.

Hayden had found Brian's mother, and the two of them were inching toward the dais through the throng.

Maegan's face was a study in regret. "I hear ye be wanting to leave," she announced.

"I don't see any point in staying."

Maegan's keen blue gaze hadn't missed the exodus of Nichola Hainesworth and her betrothed. In fact, just before Hayden came for her, she'd been reflecting that the two of them had made a nervous-looking pair. Was it possible that something had gone awry with the wedding plans? She fully intended sticking about to see them come back in. "It be such a treat, Bri, to look at all the swells and ladies. . . ."

"Look your fill, by all means. But I am going back to the hotel."

Maegan's shoulders slumped. "If that be what ye want, then—"

"It is. And first thing in the morning, I am heading for Tobermaugh."

So fine and proud he'd looked there in the abbey. So— so *alive*. And now he wore that awful stamp of defeat again. "Bri," she said hesitantly. "If ye would care to go out to the gardens, Hayden could—"

"Why the devil would I want to go out to the gardens?"

He'd given up. That was plain enough. "No reason," she said sadly. "I may as lief come along with ye." The hallways at Tobermaugh still empty and silent, the woodwork free of small handprints . . . *What did I ever do so wrong*, Maegan thought plaintively, *to be deserving of this?*

Hayden went ahead, to summon the carriage. Maegan stayed at her son's side as he moved awkwardly through the pressing crowds. Here and there, a hand reached out to clap his shoulder; a voice wished him well. But all in all, London seemed as ready to be quit of him as he was of it. And no wonder, she considered darkly, taking in the lush spectacle, the women in their filmy, revealing gowns, the men got up like popinjays, the champagne flowing like water. Perhaps he is right. A man such as he is a fish out of water here. And the devil take Nichola Hainesworth, if all she wanted in life was a wee strutting fool of a fellow in a silly cravat!

Back at the Savoy, she climbed glumly to their suite, with Brian clumping behind her. He may get over her yet, she thought hopefully, then saw the grim expression on his face as he kissed her good night. Before the door even closed behind him, she heard him ordering Hayden: "Whiskey. A tall one."

My darling son.

But what could she do, except undress and go to bed?

She might have been gratified to know that the whiskey Hayden brought his master went nearly untouched. Brian sat in a chair by the window overlooking the street, idly smoking a cigar, while the valet removed his boots. He was remembering how Nichola Hainesworth—soon to be Nichola, Lady Wallingford—had looked that evening at Carlton House, tall and lithe and glorious in a gown of midnight blue shot through with gilt threads that caught the gold in her eyes. Her hair had been sleeked back in a chignon that bared her long throat and ears. . . . He could recall so clearly the taste of her ears, the sensation of trailing his tongue along their intricate curves while she shivered in anticipation beneath him, just before he thrust into her. . . .

"Will there bae anythin' else, m'laird?" Hayden inquired, straightening up from the floor.

Yanked back to reality, Brian stubbed out the cigar. "No, Hayden. Good night."

Uncharacteristically, the aide-de-camp lingered. "Another drink, mayhaps?"

Brian glanced at his glass with the uncomfortable knowledge that there wasn't enough whiskey in Scotland to drown this sorrow. He shook his head. Still Hayden did not withdraw to his small adjoining room; he shifted his weight from one foot to the other until Brian said irritably, "Did *you* require something else?"

"I only wanted t' say, m'laird—ye bae better off wi'out her."

Brian's weary head jerked up in surprise. "Without whom?"

"That lass. Miss Hainesworth."

He'd come to dire straits, Brian reflected, when dreary Hayden advised him on his love life! "What makes you say that?" he inquired curiously.

"*Sasenach*," Hayden declared with distaste. "Ye cannae trust 'em. Do ye wrong at every turn, they will."

"The common opinion," Brian reflected, "would be that I did *her* wrong."

"Nae more'n she deserved. Like all th' rest of 'em. Payin' 'em back, were ye nae, fer all th' wrongs they 'n' theirs done t' Scotland, eh?"

"*Who* did?" asked Brian, increasingly perplexed.

"Why, their menfolk, m'laird. Th' women wha' ye had yer way wi'. *Sasenach* duchesses 'n' heiresses 'n' such."

"Miss Hainesworth's brothers," Brian said after a moment to digest this, "are on the Continent, fighting against Napoleon."

His aide-de-camp grimaced. "Only fer sae lang as he distracts 'em. Soon eno' they'll bae back t' plantin' their bludy sheep on our hills, transplantin' us t' Australia, th' Americas, settin' their mark on wha' by rights belongs t' th' Scots."

"Why, Hayden. In all the time you have served me, I never knew you were political."

The man straightened. "La, m'laird, ye cannae fool me! We may hae lost at Culloden, but there bae more'n one way t' skin th' cat." And then he grinned hugely, conspiratorially. "Plant eno' Scots bastards in English lairds' beds, 'n' who can sae who bae conquered by whom?"

It was on the tip of Brian's tongue to mention that he always had employed condoms. He was too bedazzled, however, by his valet's bizarre view of his behavior over the past decade or so. Could the man be right? Was it possible that in some unexamined corner of his soul, in all his seductions and strivings, he'd been reenacting Scotland's battles against England? "You're daft, Hayden," he said dismissively.

"It should bae *ye*," the valet responded, not a whit offended, "sittin' on that stinkin' regent's throne."

Brian bit off laughter. "God, who'd want the filthy job? Go to bed, Hayden. We leave for Tobermaugh tomorrow."

Hayden nodded approval. "It bae time ye found yerself a gude, true Scots lass to wed." He went out, leaving Brian to muse on how you could live with a fellow for years without ever knowing what he was like at heart. Hayden's image of him as a sort of randy Bonnie Prince Charlie, conquering the English one bed at a time, was really very quaint.

It would have seemed more amusing, of course, if the future didn't loom so bleak. He lit a last cigar and smoked it, watching the hansoms come and go on the street below on his final night in London Town.

He must have fallen asleep in his chair; he awoke a long time later to the thunder of artillery in the distance. The sound brought him instantly to attention; he reached for his sword and instead knocked over the table holding his whiskey glass. "What the hell . . ." Dimly he realized he wasn't in Flanders at all, though someone, somewhere, was shouting his name with military urgency: "Boru! Open up, Boru!" That explained the gunfire. Whoever was shouting was pounding on his door.

Where were his bloody canes? He groped in the darkness but felt nothing. "Boru! Damn you, open up at once!" the voice roared again.

"Hayden!" Brian bellowed. Where had that idiot left his canes? Whoever was out in the corridor was going to rouse the entire hotel. When the valet failed to appear, Brian cursed beneath his breath, fumbled into his boots, and pushed himself up in the chair. "I am coming!" he shouted back irritably. "You needn't wake the dead!"

The uproar went away briefly. Brian stood on his two feet and hopped to the door, arriving just as the clamor started up again: "Open up, Boru, you miscreant, or by God, I'll—"

Brian threw the door open. "You'll what?"

Tommy Hainesworth stood on the threshold, a pistol in his hands. He clamped his mouth shut on the last of his shout, then thrust past with rude force, so that Brian had to grab the jamb to keep his balance. "Where is she?" Tommy demanded.

"Where is who?" Brian inquired politely.

"My sister, dammit!"

"Have you looked in the Carlton House gardens? The last time I saw her, she was headed there."

Tommy was blundering about the room, pulling the draperies aside, yanking open the wardrobe, even ducking to peer under the bed. "I know she's here, Boru, and I mean to find her."

"If you should," Brian drawled, "no one would be more surprised than I. There's a lamp on the table there— oh, no. I knocked it to the floor coming to answer your summons. What time is it, exactly?"

Tommy found the lamp, struck a match, and lit it. The golden cast fell over his taut, exhausted face. "Two o'clock." He checked behind the chair. "Dammit, she's *got* to be here!"

"It's the last place *I'd* think of looking for her," Brian observed. "Have you tried Lord Wallingford's residence?"

"She's not there."

Brian arched a brow, shutting the door and hopping over to his canes, which he'd finally spotted in the lamp's glow. "Are you certain? Did you search the water closets?"

Tommy turned on him. "It's just like you to make light of this! My sister is gone missing, I tell you!"

"Two in the morning's not so very late for a newly betrothed pair of lovebirds. Perhaps they went to Vauxhall. Or to a card party somewhere." Tommy had wrenched open the window and was craning to see out onto the sill. "For God's sake, man! I tell you, she's not here!"

"What's through that door?"

"My mother's rooms."

"And that one?"

"My valet. At least, I thought he was. Hayden!" Brian bellowed again. "Fellow sleeps like the ruddy dead! *Hayden!*" Still no answer. Tommy was moving toward Maegan's door. "Oh, go in if you like," Brian invited, "but she'll likely stab you with a hairpin."

"Are you in there, Nicky?" Tommy shouted through the closed portal.

After a moment's pause, the door flew open, to reveal a sleepy-eyed Maegan in her nightdress and cap, her red-gold hair in a braid over her shoulder. "What the devil be all this fuss?" she asked irritably.

"I don't believe, Mother," Brian announced, "you have made the acquaintance of the Honorable Mr.—"

But it seemed she had. *"Ye!"* she declared, her eyes going wide. "What be *ye* doing here?"

"My sister's gone missing," Tommy said briefly.

"More than likely, gone dancing," Brian put in squelchingly.

"She went to the gardens at the regent's reception," Tommy went on, addressing Lady Boru, "and she never came out."

"How can ye be so sure of that?" Maegan demanded.

"The boys at the doors told me so."

"Ach, in all that crush, 'twould be easy enough for them to have missed her."

"Nicky's hard to miss," Tommy said grimly, and Brian thought—*God. So she is.*

"What about Lord Wallingford, then?" Maegan wanted to know.

"They didn't see him come in, either."

She pursed her mouth thoughtfully. "Well. *He'd* not make so much of an impression." Brian bit off a smile. Nothing like a mother's resentment! How on earth had she guessed? And where had she met Tommy? "What I cannot understand," she went on, "be why ye thought to look for her here."

"You know why. You know damned well why," Tommy said bitterly. "Because she is in love with him." He yanked his thumb toward Brian, who blinked.

"In love with—"

"Aye, so she be, ye big bludy fool," his mother said, her voice scathing.

"But she is marrying Wallingford!"

Tommy, at least, had no patience for chitchat. "If she's not here . . ." He pushed back his hair, shook his head. "God! I don't know *where* she might be!"

"Vauxhall," Brian suggested again.

Nichola's brother scarcely seemed to hear him. "She's in trouble," he announced. "She's in terrible trouble. And I just—I *assumed* that meant she was with you, Boru!"

Brian clumbered toward him on the canes. "You've gone off the deep end, Tommy. Honestly you have. You ought to ask for a leave from the army."

"I'm *on* leave from the army!"

"What," Maegan interjected, "makes ye so certain that she be in trouble, lad?"

Tommy looked straight at her. His hand came up to his chest. "I—I can feel it. Here."

"Oh, for Christ's sake." Brian rolled his eyes. But his mother's expression was suddenly concerned.

"Close be ye then, ye and she?"

"We're twins," Tommy told her. "Born within minutes. Of course we are close!"

"Ach, twins! Well, then, ye have the second sight, eh? One of ye to the other?"

"Mother, don't get started on that superstitious rigmarole."

Maegan paid her son no heed; her attention was riveted on Tommy.

"I—I don't know that I would call it that," he said hesitantly. "But I *do* know when she needs me. I can *sense* when she needs me. And she needs me now! I just can't find where she is!"

"Ye have been to Lord Wallingford's?"

Tommy nodded, seeming relieved to have someone take his fears seriously. "The butler wouldn't let me in the door. It didn't matter, though. She wasn't there. I knew she wasn't there."

"Was *he* there?"

"The butler said not. Said he hadn't come home yet."

"Ye believed him?"

Tommy paused again. "I knew he spoke the truth."

"Felt it in your heart, I suppose," Brian noted dryly. "You know who truly has gone missing? Hayden. I could use a bloody drink. Hayden!" He stomped toward the aide-de-camp's door.

"Has she friends, lad?" Maegan inquired. "Someone she might hae gone to see?"

"Not here in town. At the academy, yes."

"Well! Perhaps she be gone back there! Though that would not explain why the boys at the doors to the gardens—"

"No," said Tommy. "It would not."

"What on earth made ye think she might be here?"

"I—I saw her today. At the ceremony. The knighting. I saw her face. And I knew she had decided not to marry Wallingford. That she *couldn't* marry him. It was as plain as day."

"The two of you," Brian announced, "sound like a pair of spooked Strathclyde fishwives. The second sight, indeed! Hayden!" He yanked the door open. The aide-de-camp nearly fell into his arms; it was clear that far from sleeping, he'd been eavesdropping. "Fetch me a whiskey!" Brian snapped. "I can't deal with these fools clearheaded!"

"Aye, m'laird." Hayden whirled about. Brian lunged abruptly for the fellow's collar. He might not believe in the second sight, but by God, he'd glimpsed something in his faithful aide's expression that gave him pause.

"Hold on, hold on," he murmured, the gist of their

earlier conversation coming back to him. *Ye bae better off
wi'out her.* . . . Tommy Hainesworth and his mother were
still wrangling it out about where Nichola might have gone.
"Be still a moment, would you?" he snapped at them. They
looked to him in surprise.

"I'll just fetch ye that whiskey," Hayden murmured,
trying to squirm from his master's grasp. But Brian held
tight to the nightshirt.

"*You* wouldn't have any notion of Miss Hainesworth's
whereabouts, Hayden, would you?"

"I, m'laird? Why should I?"

Brian shrugged his massive shoulders. "Because she is
a *Sasenach,* perhaps? Because she wouldn't suit for me?"

He hadn't been mistaken. Hayden's gloomy eyes
glinted. "Nae doubt she bae carousin' wi' that prissy wee
laird she bae fixin' t' marry. Nae soldiers t' fret about
comin' fro' that match."

Tommy had never seen a man move so fast as Brian
Boru did, to crook his arm around the manservant's throat.
"What mischief have you been up to?" he growled. Hay-
den's choked face was going red. Brian tightened his grip.
"What the devil have you been up to?"

"Ye must not murder him, Bri," Maegan Boru said in
fascination. Hayden's tongue was lolling out of his mouth.

"Is he right?" Brian demanded, ratcheting his forearm.
"Is she in danger?"

"Nae . . . nae danger!" the aide-de-camp gasped out.

"You know where she is?"

"Nae!" Another tightening.

"But you might have an idea," Brian suggested. "Was
it only coincidence that you came in from those gardens
tonight only a hair ahead of Wallingford?"

"I think he's going to pass out," Tommy noted nervously.

"Oh, Scots are tough." Brian increased the pressure.
Hayden's eyes were bulging. A droplet of spittle curled out
of his mouth; he clawed at his master's arm. Abruptly Brian

let go his hold—just long enough to let his victim gasp a breath. "Anything to say to me, Hayden?" The hereditary follower shook his head. "You're quite sure?" Brian wrenched him around, so he could see his eyes. "You've no notion whatsoever where Miss Hainesworth might be?"

Hayden's forehead had gone blue. "Hayden," Maegan interjected. "Ye ken ye have a duty to yer master! Ye must tell the truth!"

"I dinna—I dinna—"

"What in hell did ye do?"

"By God," Tommy announced, coming toward him, "I'll kill him myself!" And he drew out the pistol. The sight of its gleaming barrel made Hayden go limp. Brian released him, and the aide-de-camp collapsed in a heap on the floor.

Brian would have kicked him senseless if he hadn't needed his good leg to stand on. "Your aunt's husband's second cousin," he sneered. "Do you reach the kitchens through the gardens? You *were* with Wallingford, weren't you?"

"I dinna ken nae Walling—" Tommy had cocked the gun. Hayden curled into a ball, hands covering his face. "Christ in heaven, dinna let him murder me!"

"One last chance, Hayden. What do you know?"

"Nothin'! I swear it!"

"Kill him, Tommy," Brian said briefly.

"Oh, Bri," Maegan murmured, "I really do not think . . ."

But Tommy aimed the pistol straight at the man's head. "Very well!" Hayden screamed out. "Mayhaps I did hae a word wi' th' man—"

"What exactly did you say?"

"I said—I said—all I told th' little fop war, if he would hae Miss Hainesworth t' his wife, he had best take her now, this night, or she would bae back t' her auld ways wi' ye!" All of them—Brian, Maegan, Tommy—stared at him. " 'N' sae she would hae been, too," Hayden said in a wounded tone.

"What the hell difference does it make to *him*?" Tommy demanded in puzzlement.

"Hayden," Brian explained, "is my hereditary aide-de-camp, and as such is unwilling that I should marry an Englishwoman. He thinks instead that I should raise up an army of Scotsmen and claim Prinnie's throne."

Maegan gasped. "I have never in my *life* heard such an outrageous notion! Hayden, what *could* ye be thinking?"

"Would *ye*," Hayden appealed desperately to Her Ladyship, "hae him wed a *Sasenach*?"

"I would have him wed a two-headed sheep, ye ruddy fool, if it would set him at peace!"

Tommy was working it through. "So. He told Wallingford the time to strike was now if he wanted to marry Nicky. But what's become of them, then? God, you don't think they've gone off to Gretna Green!"

"You're the one with the second sight," Brian noted edgily.

Tommy shook his head. "She'd not have gone with him of her own accord. Not after . . . I tell you, I saw at the abbey: Her mind was set. She wasn't marrying him."

"But they went out to the gardens together," Maegan put in worriedly.

"And never came back." Tommy's voice was grim. "She must have told him there that she wouldn't have him. I think he's abducted her, Boru. Straight out of those gardens."

Brian couldn't help it; he laughed. "There's a sight I'd like to see! Why, she would have flattened him if he'd tried such a trick!"

"But if he had help! He isn't stupid. He would have known he stood no chance against her."

"I really think you're spinning this out too far, Tommy," Brian said gently. "A conspiracy of felons lurking in the shrubberies?"

"They wouldn't have to be felons! They might just be his friends!"

"What man with any self-respect would be party to such dastardliness?"

Tommy didn't answer. He had his eyes clenched shut, was trying to picture in his mind what he'd seen as his sister headed out to the gardens with Wallingford. Two tall, shadowy figures lounging idly beside the regent's potted palms . . . He groaned. "Turlington. And Botheringly. They were there at the doors to the terrace. And they were reeking drunk. They'd been sipping from their flasks at Westminster, for Christ's sake."

"I'd still lay odds on Nichola, with all three of them against her." But a memory was pricking Brian's mind as well. Turlington had served as umpire in Nichola's fencing bout against Wallingford at Yarlborough House. The man was an extremely fine fencer; Brian had gone up against him twice and been hard put to beat him. *He* would not have been fooled by Wallingford's theatrics. He would have known exactly what had gone on in that match. It seemed, on the face of it, a most peculiar spur to convince a man to kidnap. Yet the English did like to keep their women in their place. . . . And if he *had* been drunk . . .

"Hayden." Brian's voice came out hoarse; he tried again. "What did Wallingford say, exactly, when you told him—what you told him?"

The valet had apparently decided no one was going to kill him; he had a stubborn look on. "I dinna ken wha' ye mean, m'laird."

Despite the canes, Brian leaned down and hauled him to his feet, held him dangling in the air. "What did Wallingford *say*? It is a plain enough question! Where's your bloody pistol, Tommy?" Tommy already had it aimed.

"Ye wuld nae," Hayden said uncertainly.

"Don't try me," Tommy grunted, and pulled the hammer back with a click.

Hayden swallowed. "He said—he said—ach, it dinna make nae sense, wha' he said!"

"What did he say?"

"He said he'd take a page out o' her mamma's book."

"The fellow must be daft," Maegan murmured in sympathy. "Why, yer mother be a fine lady, be she not, Mr. Hainesworth? What could she ever have had to do with kidnapping?"

The blood had drained from Tommy's face. "The countess d'Oliveri," he whispered. "I *knew* there was something amiss in that tale Mother told!"

"Wha' tale?" Maegan demanded.

Brian knew it, had heard it from Christiane herself, a lifetime ago, in Paris. How Emily Madden had been on the shelf for three seasons with no sign of a serious suitor. How Harold Hainesworth smiled at her at a dance, had her on the floor for two sets, and how she'd sworn he was hers. Their romance had deepened. Emily Madden had been distracted with joy. And then . . . and then . . .

Then Hainesworth caught sight of Christiane at her very first *ton* ball and was smitten by her. Emily let it be known amongst her circle how much this displeased her, made wild threats against her rival. And a man whom Christiane had spurned as a suitor, a wastrel named Farley Weatherston, came to Emily's aid. Weatherston approached Christiane one evening at a ball and told her Lord Hainesworth was desperate to elope with her. She, most foolishly, accompanied him to the inn where he claimed Hainesworth was waiting to meet her. Once they arrived, though, her supposed husband-to-be was nowhere in sight. Weatherston convinced Christiane to come inside, upstairs with him, to wait. Then he tried his best to rape her in that squalid little room. She fought him off—but it proved to be of little use. He bruited it about to all the *ton* that she *had* given in to him, even produced witnesses from the taproom below, and the barmaid herself, a brazen, surly sort to whom Weatherston had passed five quid right under Christiane's gaze that awful night. . . .

"You're right, Tommy. She has been abducted," he said quietly. But abducted where? What was the name of that inn? Christiane had told him; Brian was certain of it.

She had recalled every detail of the humiliating ordeal. He clenched his eyes shut, thinking back.

Kent. It had been in Kent, he remembered that much. And a color in the name. An animal as well. Christ, that only described half the inns in England! He was so unspeakably furious with Wallingford that he could not think straight. *Don't let your heart overrule your head,* he told himself. *Nichola is in danger. You have to remember!*

A dark color. Blue. No. Black. And the animal—

"Stallion," he announced abruptly. "The Black Stallion. On the through road to Kent. That's where he's taken her."

"How do you know?" Tommy asked, sounding dubious.

"That's where Weatherston took Christiane. The countess d'Oliveri. At your mother's instigation. She set up what happened to Christiane, Tommy. She was determined to have your father. Just as Wallingford is set on having your sister."

"I'll send for the carriage," Maegan declared, moving for the door.

"There isn't time for that. How did you get here, Tommy?"

"I rode, of course."

"They'll have taken a carriage. On horseback, we have a chance of catching up to them."

"Ach, nae, m'laird," Hayden declared decisively. "Ye cannae ride nae horse—nae wi' yer rum knee."

"I'll ride," Brian said with grim determination, "until I fall out of the bloody saddle. And after that, I'll crawl." He stumped toward the door with his canes. On the threshold, he paused. "You know what, Hayden? Here's your penance for such mischief. Had you not spoken to Wallingford tonight, I'd have gone home to Scotland resigned to never seeing her again. None of this would have happened. And you likely would have gotten your wish—that I wed some nice Scots girl."

The aide-de-camp went moon-pale. Then he roused

himself, with an air of defiance. "Ye'll bae too late, m'laird. They'll bae lang since married."

"If they are," said Brian, shrugging into the coat that Maegan held for him, "I'll come back here and shoot you dead myself."

Chapter
Twenty-Nine

Nichola came to her senses with a splitting headache and a definite sense that she was suffocating. She was in a carriage, a closed one; she could tell by the clack of wheels and the absence of wind. The domino was still over her head, and when she reached up to remove it, she found her hands had been bound in front of her. She felt helpless and cold and very frightened. "Please," she whispered through the black cloth. "Please. Is someone there?"

"Told you I didn't hit her so hard as all that," said a slurred voice from beside her. And in the emptiness, another man laughed raucously:

"Not so hard as she hit him! Well, what is it, spitfire?"

"I can't breathe," Nichola gasped out.

"Good. Helps make up for the blow you gave my bloody balls."

"No, I mean it! I cannot catch my breath!"

"Here, now," the man beside her said with a hint of inebriated worry. "We don't want her dead."

"Speak for yourself," his companion muttered.

Seized with inspiration, Nichola pretended to swoon. The offending domino was swiftly snatched away. She lay perfectly still, though, slumped against the side of the seat, until she sensed the man beside her was leaning over her. Then she brought her trussed hands up against his chin so hard that his teeth snapped. "Jesus! You're worse than Gentleman Jackson in the ring, aren't you?" he muttered, rubbing his jaw. Nichola tried kicking him and found her legs were bound as well.

"That's enough of that," the man across from her growled, "unless you want another egg on your head." She wished she could see them, but the inside of the carriage was too dark. Their voices, though, were those of gentlemen, not cutthroats, and she took some scant comfort in that.

"I don't know who you are," she said pleadingly, "but I beg you—have mercy on me. For the sakes of your own mothers, your sisters, your wives . . ."

"Like to see my mother throw a punch like that one you dealt Wallingford," the man across from her noted with a snicker.

"Botheringly?" She'd suddenly recognized Anthony's friend's voice. "That is you, isn't it?" She turned to the man at her side. "You must be Lord Turlington, then." She felt a flood of relief. "For heaven's sake, let's put an end to this nonsense! You are gentlemen, are you not? You'd not aid in a lady's abduction!"

"That would depend on the lady in question. If you ask me, Miss Hainesworth, you deserve to be forced into submission."

"Why?" she cried in astonishment.

"You're too damned good at fencing."

"Oh, dear God. What has that to do with anything?"

"Dangerous notion, teaching women to wield weapons," Turlington observed, and she heard again the whiskey, loud in his belligerent tone. "Might make 'em get to thinking."

"Thinking *what*?" Nichola demanded.

"Oh, all manner of things. A woman's place is in the home, serving her husband's whims, not knocking about on the fencing strip."

"Aye," Botheringly agreed, pulling out a flask and taking a gulp, "and he has got the right to knock *her* about if she displeases him. Which could prove a mite hard to do if she's armed." He passed the flask to Turlington, who took it eagerly, then glared at Nichola with unfocused eyes.

"So you'll stay tied up nice and tight, Miss Hainesworth, right up until the parson has declared you and poor Wallingford there man and wife. Though why he'd want such a hellion for his life's partner is beyond my ken." Nichola, straining to see through the shadows, realized there was a fourth figure in the coach, curled up next to Botheringly. Anthony. Of course. And he was still out cold.

She sat, wracking her brain for some appeal that might soften her captors. "Listen to me, both of you," she said finally. "I don't think you realize what you are doing. This is—this is kidnapping, for God's sake! You'll go to prison!"

"No we won't," Botheringly promptly retorted. "All we're doing is helping out our friend."

"I hardly think seeing me married to Wallingford is worth the scandal you'll cause!"

Turlington waved an airy hand. "What scandal?" he slurred. "You're already betrothed, aren't you? We're just helping to move things along." He let out a belch.

"My father will kill you," Nichola threatened. But even she knew how hollow *that* rang.

"If he can tear himself away from the tables at White's," Botheringly noted with disdain.

"My brothers, then!"

"D'you know, I had a talk with Tommy on the subject of your marriage tonight." Botheringly took another gulp from the flask. "If you ask me, no man in England wants to see you hitched to Wallingford more than he."

She scavenged for more arguments, but none that

might deter her inebriated kidnappers leapt to mind. Clearly Turlington had been hankering to pay her back for the prowess she'd displayed in her duel against Wallingford months and months ago. And Botheringly had made his views on upstart women more than plain. Of course, they couldn't marry her off to Anthony until the little blighter came to. If she stretched, she thought, and made her move sudden, she could manage a swift two-footed kick to his head. That would buy her time. She was just about to try when the carriage made an abrupt turn from the road. "We're here," Turlington announced with satisfaction. "Which one do you want?"

"I'll take Wallingford. He's a hell of a lot less trouble. And he weighs less, too."

Nichola was peering through the carriage window. They were at some sort of roadside inn, she realized, and the thought gave her hope. They couldn't possibly get her in there without her raising a devil of a ruckus. Somebody, surely, would come to her aid! An innocent girl being toted by two drunken louts—she drew in breath, preparing to scream the instant the door opened. But as she opened her mouth, Botheringly stuffed a wad of cloth inside. She gagged, trying to spit it out, but he promptly tied another length around her head to hold it in place.

"Eru," she choked out. "Eru wan—"

"Shut up unless you want that second lump." Botheringly climbed past her, lifting Wallingford's limp body in his arms and staggering with him toward the inn. Turlington hauled Nichola to her feet, tried lifting her, found he couldn't, and dragged her from the carriage with his hands beneath her arms. She dug her heels into the gravel of the drive, rolled her eyes helplessly above the gag at the driver, who was looking on avidly. "Hmrw!" she tried to cry to him—"Help me!"

Turlington observed her efforts with bemusement. "He works for His Lordship," he noted with a giggle. "No sense appealing to him."

Oh, this was impossible! Nichola struggled as best she

could as she was pulled toward the inn, but Turlington was a good deal more robust than Wallingford. They entered through a back door, and the stout woman washing up pots in the kitchen did not seem one whit surprised by her new guests. "T' the left at the top o' the stairs," she said briefly, handing Botheringly, who was less burdened, a key. Nichola stared back at her as she was dragged away.

She thought she might have a chance on the staircase. But Botheringly stumbled up with Wallingford in his arms, then returned to help his partner in crime, taking her feet, so that no matter how she struggled, she could not get free. She did, however, deliver several kicks, not to mention a knock of her head to Turlington's chest that made him curse violently. When they'd reached the room—a wretched little space with no more in it than a bed and a table—they dumped her unceremoniously on the floor. Wallingford, she saw with dismay, was stirring on the bed.

"Who's going for the parson, then?" Turlington demanded, wiping sweat from his forehead.

"I need a drink. Several drinks. You go."

"I could use a dram or two as well. Let's dend the shriver—I mean, send the driver," Turlington proposed.

"Excellent thinking, my good man." Botheringly clapped him on the shoulder. Nichola was glad to see Turlington wince. She'd *thought* she'd bruised his ribs.

They went out, slamming the door and then locking it. Nichola instantly began testing the ropes that bound her hands, seeking slack.

"Uhhhh—" A groan from the bed arrested her attention. Wallingford was struggling to sit up, his palm over his nose. He took his hand away, saw blood on it, and went ashen. He looked about the room wildly, noticed Nichola on the floor, and grimaced. "You didn't need to do that," he muttered.

"Nmrwdfgh!" she answered through the gag.

"They didn't hurt you, did they?" he asked anxiously. "Is that a bruise on your forehead? Dammit, I distinctly told them they were not to hurt you!" Above the cloth, her eyes were sparking gold. "You—you're angry with me, aren't you?" She nodded emphatically. "I didn't want that, either. But dammit, Nichola, you would not listen to reason!"

"Grrr!" she said, and that, at least, came through clearly. He raised himself up and came toward her gingerly, the way a handler might approach a wild beast.

"You are going to have to trust me," he said earnestly. "You agreed to marry me. All I am doing is moving up the date a bit. The fact is, I can't bear the thought of losing you. But I am sorry that it had to be this way."

Nichola had decided to hold her breath until she went blue. She only reached a sort of robust pink, though, before he paled and knelt beside her, hands tugging at the gag. "You won't scream if I take this off?"

She shook her head. He loosened it.

She screamed like a banshee from hell.

He clapped his hand to her mouth. "Here, now, you promised!" he exclaimed, sounding wounded.

"You bloody bastard!" she spat at him around his fist.

"There's no need for *that* sort of talk!" he said in shock. She stared at him. Then all of it—the terror of the ride, the throbbing in her head, the helplessness of being trussed like a chicken—rolled in on her, and she started to cry. "Oh, Nichola," he murmured. "Oh, no. Please don't. Not you. Not you. You mustn't." He cradled her shoulders, pulling her toward him, rocking her in his arms. She was so taken aback at his sudden tenderness that her tears broke off. "That's better," he announced briskly. "There's the Nichola I love!"

"How—" She shook her head furiously, to throw off his hand. "How can you say you love me? After *this*—after doing *this* to me? Finagling those two drunken *beasts* into kidnapping me—"

"I only have our best interests in mind."

"It is hardly in *my* best interest to be dragged to the altar bound and gagged! And for your information, Anthony Wallingford, no force on heaven or earth could *possibly* convince me to marry you now!"

"You're distraught."

"You're bloody right I'm distraught! How could you even want to marry a girl who doesn't love you?"

"I need you," he told her.

"Need me? For *what*?"

"I need for you to have my children."

It was the last answer Nichola expected. She gaped at him. He sank back onto his haunches at her side. "Why?" she managed to say.

He glanced away. "You couldn't know—you *couldn't*—what it is like . . . to be what I am. A—a weakling. Inept. The runt of the litter."

Against all reason, Nichola felt a pang of pity for him. "How can you say that?" she protested. "You are the greatest catch in all of England! Tommy tells that to me thrice a day!"

"I'm a miserable specimen of a man," he said quietly.

"You are no such thing!"

"*You* don't want to marry me!" he said in an accusing tone.

"But not because—it has nothing to do with . . ." It did, though, of course. She found herself floundering. "That is to say—you would make a positively *splendid* husband for any number of girls!"

"Petite ones." He winced. "And what sort of sons would they give me? Midgets like me."

A dim sort of understanding was dawning on Nichola. "You want to marry me because you want big, strapping sons?"

He nodded. "And they will be *marvelous* fencers as well," he said with mounting excitement. "Soldier-stuff. They'll be just like you, Nichola. They will never be timid or afraid."

"Anthony, I am afraid all the time!"

"Of what?"

"Of—of breaking china! Of blundering into people!

Every time you help me out from a carriage, I am consumed with terror that you'll rupture yourself!"

"You see what I mean?" he said bitterly. "You despise me, just the same as Father. He is always *at* me: 'When are you going to grow into a *man,* Anthony, and cease being a fop? When will you be good for something more than pirouettes and natty dress?' And he wouldn't *let* me be a soldier. When I begged and begged, he told me I'd trip over the first musket ball aimed at me."

"You ought to have told him you'd pirouette out of the way."

"God, you're right. I should have. There, that's what I mean, Nichola! That's why I've got to have you! You always know what to say, what to do. You're a wonder at all the things I wish I could be good at—shooting, riding, hunting. You are a *lioness.*"

"You ought to speak to my mother," Nichola said ruefully. "According to her, I am a hopeless case. I really only agreed to marry you to please her. Or to tweak her—I'm not certain. I only know, she never expected me to fare so well on the marriage market. It was like—like a dream come true when you asked me to dance that first time. You made me feel so . . . lovely. Graceful." Just the memory made her smile.

"I can make you feel that way for the rest of your life," he promised earnestly.

Nichola smiled at him. "Dear Anthony. I believe that you would try your best. Tell me this, though—and tell me honestly. It will help make up for your having frightened me out of my wits tonight. Do you *enjoy* hunting?" He hesitated. "*Honestly,*" she reminded him.

"Well . . . I don't much care for guns. They're so devilishly *loud.*"

"Riding?"

"I never have liked horses. Big bloody beasts."

"Do you swim?" He shook his head. "Enjoy fencing?"

His gaze fell to the floor. "You have seen how poor I am at that."

She took his hands in her bound ones. "Anthony. What exactly is it, then, that you imagine we will *do* together for the rest of our lives?"

His chin jutted out stubbornly. "I intend to wed you, Nichola, and have sons just like you—strong and lusty and athletic. *They,* at least, won't grow up to be little twits who make their mark on life by inventing new dance steps and cravat ties. *They* will be the sort of men I've always longed to be."

"You can't marry a girl just for her looks!"

"Why not? Men do it all the time!"

"They are fools if they do. What you must look for in a wife is someone who shares your interests, loves the things you do." He started to protest again, and she wagged her head at him. "Tell me this. If you hadn't this notion of procuring yourself a bracing batch of sons, what sort of girl would you be attracted to?"

"Well . . ." He raised his gaze. "You know Cecilia Farnweather?"

She nodded encouragingly. "Lovely lit—lovely creature! Ever so good-natured, isn't she? Always dressed in the *pink* of fashion. Marvelous dancer, too. And pretty as a picture."

"Oh," Wallingford said fervently, "I think she is the prettiest creature on the face of the earth." He paused. "Except for you."

"I saw her watching you today at the abbey. I think she loves you, Anthony. I think she'd wed you in a minute."

"But she's so damnably *petite*!"

"You know," said Nichola, scrunching her nose, "life is a very uncertain thing. What if you and I had only daughters? Big, ungainly daughters?"

"God. I hadn't thought of daughters. Cecilia *would* make lovely daughters." His brow cleared, then furrowed. "But that begs the question, doesn't it? What would become of our sons?"

"I should hope they would grow up to be as kind and wonderful as you."

"If I'm so damned kind and wonderful, why won't you wed me?"

"Because I don't love you," Nichola said simply. "And I don't believe that you love me. You are in love with some sort of *image* that you have of me. But not with me, myself. Why, you hardly even know me!"

"We could grow to know one another," he said desperately. "Grow to *love* one another!"

"Perhaps," she conceded. "But perhaps not. Perhaps we'd grow, instead, to recognize that we are utterly unsuited for one another. Like—like my mother and father. Nothing to share, nothing to reach for and move toward together, only two distinct lonelinesses moving in two separate spheres. Oh, Anthony." There were tears shining in her eyes. "We only have this one chance at life. This sole shot at happiness. Are you truly willing to say, once and for all, that I am what you want out of it?"

"You . . . you . . . I . . ." But he did not meet her gaze; he took a deep breath that sounded like a sob. "I would not hurt you for the world, Nichola. You must believe that."

"I do," she told him. "And that is why you are going to untie my hands and my feet, and let me go home."

"Untie your—yes. Of course. I'm so terribly sorry. I don't know what I was thinking of." He fumbled for the ropes, loosened the knots with some difficulty. Nichola rubbed her sore wrists and ankles briskly, to get her blood moving again. He raised his eyes at last. "God. You must think me such an awful fool."

"Not at all," she assured him. "If you hadn't untied me, I might have. But not now. It's a rare man, I think, who is willing to listen to his heart above the clamor of the *ton*." He looked so forlorn that she leaned up on her knees to hug him. His arms closed around her, and his mouth brushed her forehead.

"Cecilia would accept me?" he asked hesitantly. "You really think so?"

"I *know* so," said Nichola, and pecked his cheek.

"Devil of a thing to do to a man who's just ruined your reputation," he said ruefully. It was at that moment that a shudder like an earthquake rocked the room. They clung to one another in dismay. "Jesus!" Wallingford cried out, and Nichola screamed. There was a momentary pause, and then another blast. The door burst open on its hinges, crashing to the floor. Wallingford scrambled backward, shielding Nichola. In the gaping hole that had been the doorway, two figures appeared, both with pistols cocked. Nichola recognized them in an instant: her brother Tommy and, of all people, Lord Brian Boru.

Brian rushed over the threshold, his pistol aimed straight at Wallingford's head. "I never touched her!" her abductor cried out. "I swear it on my life!" And he hastily pulled his arms from around Nichola.

"Bloody liar!" Brian growled.

"It was all a mistake—just a dreadful mistake!" Wallingford insisted.

"It was a mistake all right! And one for which you'll pay!"

"Brian," Nichola spoke up, "do stop posturing—and you as well, Tommy! Put those guns down at once! There is no need for violence. Anthony and I have passed a most enlightening evening together."

"Enlightening evening?" Brian burst out. "He kidnapped you!"

"Actually," Wallingford noted, with a small, hiccuped giggle, "I didn't, you know."

"But not for want of trying," Nichola said, with a reassuring pat to his shoulder.

Brian's brows shot skyward. "You came with him willingly?"

"Not unless you consider being gagged and trussed like a chicken willing," she retorted. "Tommy, put that gun *down*! You are making me nervous."

"Are you married to him or not?" her brother demanded.

"I'm not even *betrothed* to him any longer. At least—I don't think I am. Anthony?"

"Oh, no. Not a bit. You convinced me, my dear."

Brian put a hand out to the bed rail, to steady himself. He felt curiously deflated. *Whatever* had gone on in this room, it was plain that Nichola hadn't required rescuing at all; she'd managed that on her own. He might have known. She didn't need a hero—certainly didn't need him. He looked at her. Her straw-gold hair had worked loose from its chignon; her midnight-blue gown was crumpled and hanging off one creamy shoulder, and on her right temple, she had a nasty bruise. She had never been more beautiful.

Tommy was befuddled. "You were in danger, Nick! I could feel that you were!"

She got up from the floor, dusting off her hands. "Well, I *was,* I suppose. Back at Carlton House, when I told Anthony that I wouldn't marry him after all, he became quite . . . agitated."

"Oh, say it straight out," Wallingford advised cheerily. "I made an utter ass of myself. Tried to spirit her away. Only of course I couldn't, seeing as she is as strong as two of me put together—maybe even stronger."

"You may not be the most muscular man in England," Nichola agreed, giggling as she remembered the scene. "Still, you had it well planned out. Having Turlington and Botheringly there, I mean, to come to your aid."

"A gentleman always knows his own limitations," Wallingford said modestly. "Though I am *infuriated* with whichever one hit you. I shall never speak to him again." He straightened his rumpled lace cuffs. "I wonder where they have got to, by the by. They were supposed to go and fetch the clergyman."

"They're flat on the floor of the taproom downstairs," Tommy informed him. "Unless they've come to by now. Brian took 'em out with one punch each. I don't think they even knew what hit them."

"Really?" Wallingford was impressed. "Thanks ever so much, old chap!" He moved as if to shake Brian's hand, saw his lowering expression, and thought better of it. "Well! All's well that ends well, as they say. I wonder what the time is? Must be devilish late—or early, rather. I'd best get back to the city. Ever so sorry, Nichola, for the—the inconvenience. And everything else. I'll just be . . ."

"Not so fast." Brian caught him by coat as he edged by. "I've got a little something for you, too, as a memento of the evening." He swung his fist back, just as Nichola suddenly spoke up:

"Brian? Where are your canes?"

He stopped the blow in midair, looking down at his hand. "I . . . don't know. Must have left 'em in the stables back in London. We were in such a rush to get here. . . ."

"How did you get up the stairs, then?"

He thought about it. "Can't remember. Tommy must have helped me."

"Not I," Tommy demurred. "I followed *you* up."

"And how is it you are standing there on your two legs?"

Brian's gaze traveled down to his boots in wonder. His right knee buckled a little, and he clutched the bed rail again.

"Must be something like the rush of energy men sometimes get in battle," Tommy suggested. "You know—where they can fight all day and night without stopping, in a sort of frenzy?"

"But if your knee could get you up a staircase once," Nichola said slowly, "it ought to be able to do so again."

"Seems a fair assumption," Wallingford put in. Then, abruptly, he clapped a hand to his head. "Bloody Christ! The *Gazette*!" They stared at him, except for Brian, who, aware of how his knee was aching, was plunking himself onto the bed.

"What about the *Gazette*?" Nichola asked with trepidation.

"You are going to be furious with me." His dark eyes were full of chagrin. "I went ahead and wrote out an announcement for the morning edition. Sent it there in care of Lord Upton."

"An announcement of *what*?"

"Of our elopement, of course."

"Oh, Anthony. There is such a thing as planning *too* far ahead!"

"I'll ride back and withdraw it," he offered. "I'll go straight away!"

"Too late." Tommy had consulted his pocket watch. "It's nearly four in the morning. You couldn't get there before five, not even on a winged horse. It'll be on every newstand in London by then."

Nichola nibbled her lip. "There will be an awful stink. And Mother—what about Mother?" As the weight of the repercussions began to sink in, a hesitant knock sounded on the jamb of the broken-down door.

A round-faced fellow in a clerical collar was standing there, a prayer book in his hands. He cleared his throat. "Would this be . . . Lord Wallingford's party? I'm Father Dugan. Dreadfully sorry to be so late in coming. I had a parishioner who required last rites."

"Might as well say 'em here, too," Tommy mumbled.

The priest brightened, smiled. "I shouldn't mind, if they had so efficacious an effect as they did on the last recipient. Much to our astonishment, he sat up in the midst of them and called for a pint of ale. A most miraculous recovery! I left him digging into a rasher of bacon and a pair of boiled eggs."

"Imagine that!" Wallingford marveled. "A sort of resurrection." He reached for his purse. "But I'm sorry to tell you, Father Dugan, that your services won't be required here after all. There's been a change in plans. Needless to say, I'll pay you for your trouble . . ."

"Newspapers make mistakes," Brian said, seemingly apropos of nothing, from the bed where he sat.

Only Father Dugan took the non sequitur in stride, stepping toward him across the fallen door. "Oh, you're quite right there, sir. In my opinion, they do so all the time. They get the facts wrong, get the names wrong—"

"My point exactly," said Brian.

"Am I missing something here?" Tommy wondered aloud.

"And all they do *when* they do," Father Dugan went on, with a hint of indignation, "is to print a retraction. But that's no remedy, is it, when an innocent soul's been dragged through the mud?"

"It is better than nothing," said Brian. He looked at Nichola. "This isn't exactly how I would have liked it to be. But . . ." He slid down from the bed, landing with a thump on his knees.

"Brian, you'll hurt yourself!" she cried in dismay.

"If I can kneel for that fool regent, I can kneel for you. Will you marry me, Nichola?"

"Oh, I say!" Father Dugan was tickled. "I've been present at plenty of nuptials, of course, but never at a proposal!"

"Do shut up," Tommy hissed at him. "I mean—please do shut up, Father." He was appalled to see that his sister was shaking her head.

"That's very . . . very kind of you, Brian," she whispered. "To try and salvage my reputation. But—"

"Blast your reputation!" he thundered from the floor. "I love you, and I want to spend the rest of my life with you. Now, will you marry me or nay?"

"Oh, Brian." Nichola's face had gone radiant; her eyes shone with tears. "You finally said it."

"Said it and meant it," he told her gruffly. "Ought to have said it long ago. Wish I had. Sorry I didn't. Said it to too many girls without meaning it, I guess. Was wishing there was another word—one I could have saved just for you. So—what do *you* say?"

"I say yes, of course!" She threw herself at him, nearly knocking him over; only the bed at his back saved him. "Yes, yes, yes, yes, yes!" He grinned and took her in his arms, kissing her with such abandon that Father Dugan politely averted his gaze. Wallingford, looking on, murmured something that to Tommy sounded like, "Hmm. Passion."

Brian broke away from Nichola just long enough to say, "Hold on, there, Father. It seems we'll require your services after all."

"Very good, sir." The priest bustled forward, secure in this familiar routine. "You'll need the ring and the license."

"License?" Brian and Nichola echoed blankly.

"Aye, the special license. To permit the marriage without the required banns."

"I have the license!" Wallingford announced, searching through his pockets. "Or, rather, I have *a* license. A blank one. Turlington gave it to me. Said he always keeps it on his person. Comes in handy when sedu—well, never mind that."

"I do wonder about your friends, Anthony," Nichola told him.

"As do I, after tonight."

"A *blank* license." The priest was frowning. "I'm not altogether certain . . ."

Tommy drew him aside by the elbow. "See here, Father. There's something you may not be aware of. If you *don't* marry my sister to that gentleman, they'll be in that bed together anyway the instant the door closes behind you. As a man of God, surely you can't want that."

"Certainly not! Fornication is a grave sin!" He turned back to the couple. "Very well, then. Let's have the license filled in. Perhaps the innkeeper has pen and ink?"

Wallingford rushed down the stairs and quickly returned with the writing materials. Tommy scratched the names down on the license: Nichola Jane Marie Hainesworth and Brian . . . "Have you middle names, Boru?"

"Brian Bruce O'Neill Wallace James MacDonald Charles Boru," His Lordship said distractedly, probing the bruise on Nichola's forehead with a gentle fingertip.

"Were there any Scots heroes your mother left out?" she inquired, laughing.

"There isn't enough room," Tommy noted, grinning as he scribbled away.

"Two witnesses," Father Dugan murmured to himself, then glanced up. "What about the ring?"

"Got that, too." Wallingford produced one from his breast pocket. "Though perhaps you won't want to use it. Under the circumstances, I mean."

"Has it got your name and hers engraved on it?" Brian asked, frowning.

"No, no. There wasn't time for that."

"We'll take it, then. You must let me pay you for it, though."

"Not at all. Think of it as a wedding gift." He pressed it into Brian's hand. Nichola craned to see it—a simple gold band.

"Oh, it's lovely, Anthony!" she said gratefully.

"And bigger than the last one I gave you." He grinned as she took off the sapphire-and-diamond betrothal ring and tucked it into his fist.

"Well, then!" Father Dugan declared, clearing his throat with a harrumph. "Are we ready to begin?"

"More than ready," Brian told him, clutching Nichola's hand.

"You stand in the beginning," the priest informed them, "and only kneel when it is time to pray."

Brian sighed and started to heave himself to his feet. Nichola tugged him back down. "It wouldn't *invalidate* anything, would it, Father, if we just stayed where we are?"

"I suppose not. Dearly beloved—"

"Oh, Brian, wait!" Nichola cried suddenly.

"What? Changed your mind already?"

"Of course not, silly. But your mother—don't you think we ought to wait to have the marriage until she can be there?"

"Nichola. Trust me. My mother will be so giddy with joy when she hears this news, she won't care a bit."

"You think so?"

"I *know* so. Do go on, Father. Please."

Father Dugan did. "Dearly beloved," he began again, "we are gathered here together. . . ."

The rising sun broke through the window just as Brian slipped the ring on Nichola's finger. It seemed, thought Tommy, looking at the kneeling couple drenched in the new light of morning, an opportune sign.

Chapter
Thirty

"Much obliged to you, Father." Still kneeling, Brian produced two five-pound notes and pressed them into the clergyman's hand.

"Glad to be of help, sir. I'll record the marriage in the parish books, of course. It's St. Ninian's, Boswell, Kent. Just so you know."

Tommy had come forward to embrace his sister. "I'm so happy for you, Nick."

"Are you really?" she asked, searching his face.

"Absolutely. You were right all along, and I was wrong."

"Congratulations, old man!" Wallingford clapped Brian on the back. "No hard feelings?"

"Actually," Brian murmured to Nichola, "some *very* hard feelings. Would you care to share them?" She blushed. Tommy overheard, dropped his sister a wink, and shepherded Father Dugan and Wallingford toward the door—or, rather, the doorway, since the door was still flat on the floor.

"I'll go on ahead and break the news to Mother," he told Nichola with a wince. "I only hope to God she hasn't seen the *Gazette* before I get there. To go from the ecstatic heights of Lord Wallingford as a son-in-law to Ballocksing Brian Boru all in one day will give her apoplexy."

"Thanks ever so much," Brian noted dryly.

"Don't mention it," said Tommy, grinning.

"Good-bye, Anthony!" Nichola called. "Thank you very much for kidnapping me!"

"You're very much welcome," Wallingford said, causing Father Dugan to blink as he left them. Tommy paused on the threshold, examining the burst-in door. Then he shouldered it up and carefully fitted it back into the frame from the outside.

"That ought to do," they heard him say, "so long as they don't ring for breakfast in bed."

Nichola giggled. "Are you hungry?" she asked Brian, who was still kneeling beside her.

"Only for you, wife." He did haul himself to his feet then, with the help of the rail. His blue eyes were shining. "Let's to bed."

"Seems rather shameless to be going to bed just as the sun is rising," she said breathlessly.

"I'll show you shameless," he promised, in a voice that made her quiver inside.

He sat on the bed to undress her, proceeding ever so slowly. His hands lingered on the nape of her neck as he untied her ribbons, caressed her shoulders as he drew her sleeves away, traced the hollows of her throat while he pulled her bodice down. He leaned in to kiss her breast as the midnight-blue fabric tumbled to the floor. She twined her arms around his neck, holding him close. He inhaled her sweet scent, nuzzled her nipple, pulled at it gently, teasingly. She melted against him, pushing him down beneath her on the crude bed.

"Do that some more," she begged, reaching for his shirt buttons.

"Gladly." He rolled her onto her back and did, his fingers kneading her soft flesh, his tongue flicking against her until she thought she would faint with pleasure.

"Oh, Brian. I was so afraid that you would never hold me again."

"As was I." He sat up to ease off his jacket and shirt. Nichola, lying beside him, suddenly started.

"I must get your boots!"

"I can take off my own bloody boots." And he did, as slowly and proudly as a three-year-old just learning to undress.

"Does your knee hurt terribly?" she asked, chewing her lip.

"Like the devil."

"I can't believe you climbed those stairs!"

"I couldn't stand the thought of him having you. Touching you."

"He's really a very decent fellow, you know." Abruptly, she giggled. "How odd to think that it was *he* who abducted me, and *you,* the greatest rogue in all of Europe, that saved me."

"Just goes to show—you cannot rely upon the *ton*'s opinion." He had the boots off and flung them triumphantly to the ground. Then he paused, for the first time seeming to take in their squalid surroundings—the tawdry room, the creaking bed, the dust-mottled floor. "Do you know, one time only, Nichola, I'd like to make love to you someplace other than a cheap roadside inn."

"I'm very fond of cheap roadside inns. So long as I'm with you."

"Sweet," he told her, grinning. "Fond of bedbugs as well?" He plucked one from the pillow and squashed it between his thumb and forefinger.

Nichola shuddered. "At least the White Fox was clean!" Then she squared her shoulders. "Never mind, though. You will be taking me home to—where exactly is it that you live, anyway?"

"Tobermaugh Castle. In Strathclyde."

"A castle!" Her eyes lit up.

"Actually, it's not all *that* grand. If you wanted a rich man, you ought to have gone through with it with Wallingford."

"I have the man I wanted. The *only* man I've ever wanted," she said with reproach.

"I don't know why you would."

"Because . . ." She gave a tug to his breeches. "No one else has ever made me feel the way that you do."

"You lack experience," he grunted, but rose on his elbows so that she could slide them off.

"Because you are so personable, then."

"Hah! Minx!" He turned on her, yanking her drawers down. "I ought to—ought to—" But the sight of her bared thighs, the thatch of corn-gold curls between them, made him catch his breath. "Oh, wife!"

"Oh, husband." She smiled, drawing him down with her onto the lumpen bedstraw.

Their naked bodies pressed together; she could feel his manhood, erect and urgent, pushing against her. He arched above her, kissed each of her eyelids tenderly, and then her mouth, with much more force, and then her breasts, with such bruising eagerness that she laughed out loud. "I can't wait," he whispered, hovering over her. "Not another minute."

"What about the condom?" she asked hesitantly.

"No more bloody condoms. There's no need for them now." His fingers tickled her thighs, parted them, reached down into her soft, slick wetness. "Nichola. Nichola. My love . . ."

"Yes," she whispered, his feathery touch awakening the violent rush of sensation she had feared never to feel again. "Yes, Brian. Yes." He had found the bud, the hard, small knot that made her wild with longing, and he was stroking it, rubbing it in a crescendo of fervor. She reached for his buttocks, clutching him to her. "Now. Oh, Brian, now—"

His manhood pressed against her, slid slowly back and forth in the warm, welcoming dew of her desire, its knob gliding over that sweet bud, while he rocked her in his arms, murmuring into her ear. "Love you," he told her.

"Love *you*," she answered.

He thrust inside her, deep, deep down into her tingling sheath. His breath escaped in a rush. "Oh, God. Oh, God—" He pulled back, pushed in again. The bed was rocking crazily beneath them.

Nichola had her eyes clenched shut, was holding to him with all her might, pulling him farther in with each desperate plunge. She felt as though she would explode with the weight of her love for him, as though she could not get enough of him, as though the world might spin to an end with him deep inside her and she would not care. He brought his hands up under her buttocks, hiking her forward, tilting her toward him as he pushed down into her— and then they were moving together in a fury of ecstasy, perfectly matched, timed, aligned, so that nothing existed in all the world but that moment, and the moment seemed to stretch on forever, and forever was a mad blaze of wild white heat. She cried out—something, his name, her love, her need—and he answered with his own cry, guttural and triumphant, as his seed burst into her in a rush of fire. Still his loins moved against her, hitching and hard, while he poured himself into her, drained his love into her, forced every drop of his semen into her until he ran dry. Then he collapsed atop her, fell onto her like a dead man, while she clung to him with tears in her eyes.

Slowly, slowly, his manhood shrank inside her. She felt her muscles tighten around it, smiled at the sensation of her body not wanting to release him, wanting to hold him there for all eternity. And so she would. . . .

"Flesh of my flesh," he said suddenly.

Nichola opened her eyes. He was looking straight at her, and he was crying, though he did not seem to notice it

at all. The sight of his tears made her feel at once puissant
and awed. "Flesh of my flesh," he whispered again. "And
the two are made one. . . ."

"Forever and ever," she told him, kissing the tears
away. "Amen."

He slept for a little while after that, but Nichola lay
staring at the cracked, water-stained ceiling, his arm tight
around her, the scent of their lovemaking filling the room—
a wondrous, musky smell. When he awoke, she suggested
breakfast. He turned down the offer and instead took her
again, in a rather more leisurely fashion. Then they both
slept, curled together, beneath the scratchy blankets. The
next time she opened her eyes, the sky beyond the window
was dark.

He was sitting up in the bed, his hand stroking
her hair. She turned her head to kiss his fingers. "You
aren't . . . sorry, then?" he said quietly.

"Brian! How could I ever be sorry?"

"I only thought—I might have rushed you a bit. That
you might have liked a real wedding. Westminster Abbey.
A load of attendants. Flowers. All that."

She shuddered. "I would have been terrified to trip
over my train. No. This is just what I wanted. Well—not
precisely. I would have preferred it had you said you loved
me three months ago. It would have spared much pain."
She reconsidered and said charitably, "But perhaps you
didn't love me then."

"I loved you. . . ." He sighed and stretched luxuri-
ously, pulling her into his lap. "From the first moment I
saw you. Or, rather, from the first words you spoke to me."

"How can you say that? I was *horrid* to you! Accusing
you of laziness, of shirking—"

"You were right, though. I was. Lazy, I mean. So busy
feeling sorry for myself—"

"With reason."

"Plenty of good men have died fighting Napoleon," he
said soberly. "I have no cause to complain—though I
thought I did, then."

"I cannot believe that you rode here," she whispered. "To rescue me."

"*I* can believe it. My rear end aches like the devil." Just then, his stomach rumbled. "And I am hungry, too. Starved."

"Poor baby," she teased, reaching up to kiss him. "Shall I dress and go downstairs, to see what the special of the evening might be?"

"Truth to tell, I want to get the hell out of England. Take you home to Strathclyde. Show you the sea, and the islands . . ." His arm tightened around her. "Get you with child."

"I'd like that," she told him. "But—before we go, there is something I must do. Someone I must apologize to."

He looked into her gold-sparked eyes. "She'd understand anyway."

"I know. But I want to say it."

He roused himself, reaching for his shirt. "Well. We're already in Kent; it won't cost us much time. And we can get a decent meal from Mrs. Wickers at the White Fox, thank God!"

Chapter
Thirty-One

The *Gazette* always arrived at the academy from London a day late, on the post carriage through to Dover. Mrs. Treadwell made a ritual of perusing it throughly with her evening sherry, to keep abreast of the town news. She was in her parlor unwrapping it now, while the countess sat at her desk, paying out tradesmen's bills. "It never fails to astound me," Madame noted, dipping her quill, "how much young girls can eat. Did you see this latest tab from the butcher? Thirty-eight pounds!"

"Happy girls are hungry girls," Mrs. Treadwell said idly. "And the food bills have gone down noticeably ever since Nichola left. It's so much quieter, too. I declare, I even miss that clanging steel in the courtyard at dawn." Her voice had gone wistful.

Madame had paused in her writing. "I'm sure she's doing well, Evelyn. Nichola was blessed with great resourcefulness. Look how cleverly she managed to convince the baroness not to shout to the world that I was back in England—and educating the daughters of the gentry."

"That *was* thoughtful of her, wasn't it? Although I can't help but worry. . . . She seemed so forlorn in the courtyard that last morning. So very young. And wounded." She hesitated. "Was it true what her mother said of you and Boru, Christiane? Were you lovers in Paris?"

"Never. Not in Paris or anyplace else. Oh, I will not lie and say the thought never crossed my mind, Evelyn. He has such puissance, doesn't he? But when we met, I'd only just lost Jean-Baptiste. And he was so terribly gallant. He went out of his way to occupy me, escort me places, try to assuage my grief. Yet he never so much as kissed me. It was then that I realized how terribly special he was—and that I determined to someday find the right woman for him."

"You thought Nichola—"

"I truly did."

"He isn't much of a catch," Mrs. Treadwell said dubiously. "At least, not now."

"Oh, but he is. Unless, of course, you only hold to *ton* opinions, and think that fancy dancing matters more than a stalwart, honest soul."

"But he has had so many women. . . ."

"He was only looking all along for the one he could love. And let me remind you, he never was accused of dallying with anyone who was not ready to dally with *him*."

"All those dissatisfied wives," Mrs. Treadwell murmured. "Why did they flock to him?"

"Because he knows how to make a woman feel special—feel appreciated and adored. Oh, Nichola would have been lucky to have him!" The countess stared into space, then roused herself with a start. "We did the best we could for her. For them."

"If only we had had more time . . ." Mrs. Treadwell sighed and flapped open the *Gazette,* her eye turning first, as always, to the Town Tattle column. Then she let out a shriek.

"Evelyn?" Madame whirled in her chair, the quill clattering to the floor. "Whatever is the matter?"

Mrs. Treadwell rose, the *Gazette* clenched in her fist. She spread it on the desk before the countess, stabbing with her finger, too overcome to speak. Madame stared down at the page, read the words there: *It is official at last. The duke of Strafford has confirmed the oft-rumored betrothal of his son and heir, Anthony, Lord Wallingford, to the incomparable Miss Nichola Hainesworth. No date has yet been set, but that sound in the distance is the shattering of brittle male hearts everywhere—or could it be the relieved sighs of the season's other debutantes, who are sure to embrace the news with glee?*

"Well!" declared the countess. "What marvelous news!"

"Yes. Isn't it marvelous."

"The greatest catch in all of England going to our Nichola!"

"The greatest catch," Mrs. Treadwell echoed.

"You had best prepare yourself for a *deluge* of applications, Evelyn! This is certain to greatly enhance the academy's reputation!"

"Greatly. No doubt."

"Not to mention," the countess noted shrewdly, "forever sealing Emily Hainesworth's lips regarding my presence here."

"Most likely," Mrs. Treadwell agreed.

"Didn't I always say Nichola was bound to prove one of our grand successes?"

"So you did," said Mrs. Treadwell—and burst into tears.

"Evelyn!" Madame stared. "What is wrong?"

Mrs. Treadwell had reached for her handkerchief, balled it up to her mouth. "She—she—she—"

"Get a grip on yourself, Evelyn," the countess said sternly.

"She will turn out just like Vanessa! You know and I

know she doesn't love him! Why in heaven's name is she marrying him?"

"We also both know the answer to that question. Because she can't marry Brian Boru."

"Of course she can't," Mrs. Treadwell agreed tearfully, twisting the handkerchief in knots. Then she paused. "Why can't she?"

"Evelyn!" The countess's dark brows nearly climbed off her forehead. "You are the last person in the world I would expect to pose that question! Marry a crippled rake with a hopelessly black reputation—and a Scotsman at that? The girl would have to be daft."

"I don't see why," Mrs. Treadwell said plaintively. "You said the entire purpose of the academy was to strengthen our students enough to withstand the buffets of the *ton*. Make then proud and secure in themselves— 'Whatever they need,' isn't that what you told me, 'to achieve their potential in life'?"

"Wedding the heir of a duke isn't exactly small potatoes."

"It most certainly *is,* if she doesn't love him!"

Unexpectedly, Madame smiled. "Dear Evelyn. I am so proud of you."

"Of *me*?" Mrs. Treadwell was flustered. "I cannot think whatever for!"

The countess went and embraced her. "For feeling as you do. I wasn't at all sure, you know, that when push came to shove, you wouldn't crumple. Give in to the temptation. Find the draw of the *ton*'s admiration irresistible. But you are stronger even than I imagined. And that gives me great hope for the future."

"The future . . ."

"Yes. We may have failed with Nichola, the poor child. The combination of Boru's stubbornness and the baroness's venom simply proved too formidable. But, Evelyn, we have a school full of girls who are relying on us. Who may yet have a chance at true happiness. We must not allow this dreadful circumstance to defeat us. We must forge on."

"Forge on." Mrs. Treadwell sniffed back a sob, squared her plump shoulders. "Yes. So we must, Christiane. You are quite correct. And so we shall." But her gaze trailed back toward the *Gazette,* and her tears began to flow again. "Oh, dear. And to think I had such hopes for that one."

Madame's eyes had a faraway look to them. *"Mon Dieu,* so did I."

Mrs. Treadwell sopped at her tear-swollen face with the kerchief. Then a small giggle escaped her. "Evelyn? You aren't going hysterical on me, are you?" Madame demanded.

"No, no. I am reconciled. We cannot expect, I suppose, one hundred percent success. I was only thinking . . ." The giggle returned, burgeoned. "How very *peculiar* it is," she managed to gasp out, "to view this as a defeat!"

After a momentary pause, Madame's glum mouth curled upward. "He *is,"* she agreed, "only the greatest catch in all of England!" And they clutched one another, giddy as girls, laughing helplessly.

At long last, Mrs. Treadwell paused, caught her breath. "It's really no laughing matter," she noted more soberly. "Not when poor Nichola is condemned to a loveless marriage. She——" There was a clatter of carriage wheels in the quiet night air. The headmistress glanced at the clock. "Half past eleven. Rather late for visitors . . ." The clatter broke off abruptly. After a moment's pause, the door knocker sounded. "Oh, dear. I hope it isn't *more* trouble. You don't suppose that beastly Katherine has finally convinced the duke and duchess to rescue her from us at last?"

"You mustn't refer to the girls as 'beastly,' " the countess chastized her. "Even when they are. I'll go and answer."

"I'll come with you. There is safety in numbers." Arm in arm, they headed for the door.

It opened onto the last face they expected: that of Emily Madden Hainesworth. The baroness's mouth was an angry, twisted slit; her peak-of-fashion bonnet was askew, as though she'd jammed it on without thinking, and her hard eyes were blazing. In her hand, she clenched a copy of the *Gazette*. "Lady Hainesworth?" Mrs. Treadwell said dubiously.

"You!" The baroness lunged for the countess, fingernails first. "You—you thoroughgoing *bitch*!"

"Now, now, milady!" Mrs. Treadwell tried her best to intervene, but there appeared to be no stopping their guest. She knocked the headmistress aside with a blow of her forearm and sprang at the countess again.

"I warned Nichola!" she screeched, clawing for Christiane's eyes. "I told her the sort of woman you were! I curse the day I ever brought her to this ill-begotten place! You have ruined her! The two of you have ruined her!"

Mrs. Treadwell stared, dumbfounded, while the countess did her best to ward off her attacker. "I cannot see, Emily, what you have to complain of," Madame noted reasonably, catching hold of the baroness's fists. "Why, I should think you'd be ecstatic!"

"Ecstatic!" That, apparently, was enough to deflate even Lady Hainesworth's rage; she sagged backward, nearly collapsing. "Clearly you have not seen the *Gazette*!"

"Oh, but we have," Mrs. Treadwell assured her. "We were just now perusing it. And really, I must say, Nichola is a great credit to the academy. We are . . . so very proud."

"*Proud?* God, you are too monstrous for words! That you should *gloat* at this—this abomination!" The baroness groped in her reticule, drew out hartshorn, took a long, deep whiff.

"I really cannot comprehend your objection," Mrs. Treadwell said nervously. "He *is* the greatest catch in all of England."

"The greatest—the greatest—oh!" Words failed the baroness. "You are mad, both of you. I'll see this academy closed down if it's the last thing I do! I will tell every mother in England that to send their daughters here is to seal their doom! I'll—I'll—" Again she inhaled hartshorn.

"Am I to understand, Emily, that this marriage displeases you?" the countess inquired.

"Displeases me? It *appalls* me! As it would any mother in her right mind!"

"I don't see on what grounds," Mrs. Treadwell noted, feeling more sure of herself. "He comes from estimable stock. He has an enviable fortune. He is considered good-looking. He—"

"He's a bloody Scotsman!" the baroness wailed.

Mrs. Treadwell blinked. "Lord Wallingford is Scottish?"

"Wallingford? What has Wallingford to do with anything?"

"Why—Nichola is wedding him."

"She *can't,*" wailed the baroness.

"Why not?"

"Because she's already married!" Emily Hainesworth spat out. "You *said* you'd seen the *Gazette!*"

"Which reported," the countess put in, slowly and distinctly, as if speaking to a nitwit, "that she is at last betrothed to Lord Wallingford."

"That was *yesterday's* news!" The baroness thrust out the newspaper she clutched, with a shudder. "This—*this* is today's!"

For the second time that evening, Mrs. Treadwell scanned the front page. Nichola's mother was poking at the Town Tattler column. It featured, as it had the previous day, Nichola Hainesworth's name. But . . .

"Christiane," Mrs. Treadwell whispered. "Do look at this."

"Today's issue." Madame had noted the date. Then she blanched, seeing the column. *Astounding revelation!* it began. *The report made in yesterday's edition of the betrothal between Miss Nichola Hainesworth and Anthony, Lord Wallingford, appears to have been premature. We have it on impeccable authority that the young lady in question was wed last night to the newest member of the Order of the Thistle,*

Brian, Lord Boru. She glanced up, her dark eyes wide as saucers. "Can it be true?"

"Tommy was there himself," the baroness snapped. "He came and told me this morning. Wed—and consummated—in a miserable roadside inn. Oh, you will suffer for this, Christiane—and you as well, Evelyn! I will make you pay if it's the last thing I do!"

"Christiane!" Mrs. Treadwell could not restrain herself; she hopped a little dance. "She *did* it! She went ahead and *did* it!"

"And so did he." The countess's face was aglow.

The baroness was verging on apoplexy. *Her* face was beet-red, and her eyes were popping out of her head. "You are *happy* about this. I *knew* you were behind it! Just when her future seemed so splendid, so assured, to have this happen—why, I shall never be able to hold my head up in public again!"

Mrs. Treadwell bristled. She drew herself up to her rather negligible height, bosom quaking, pale eyes flashing fire. "Now, see here, Emily Madden Hainesworth. I've had about enough of your bluster. Lord Wallingford may be a very nice man, and a very rich man, and even in line to be a duke. But you may take it from me—none of that meant a fig to your Nichola. Because she has her head screwed on straight, and she always has—despite everything *you* did to try and squelch her." The baroness opened her mouth in shocked protest. Mrs. Treadwell wagged a finger at her. "Just you let me finish! If Nichola *has* married Lord Boru, she did so because she loves him. Nothing else matters but that. If she were *my* daughter, I'd be shouting from the rooftops about her good sense. So go ahead and run back to your gossiping friends and dish out all the tittle-tattle you like about Christiane and me. Close down the academy! Go on! I dare you to. At least the countess and I will have the satisfaction of knowing we helped one remarkable young lady to find true happiness. *That* is worth any amount of scandal you might choose to spread." And she crossed her arms firmly over her heaving breasts.

"Why, Evelyn," the countess said in admiration. "How very well put!"

"I should say so," echoed a deep, masculine voice from the gates. In all the commotion, none of the women on the portico had even heard the horse arrive. Their heads whipped around, and they stared into the darkness.

"Brian?" the countess said tentatively. "Brian, is that you?"

"The one and only," Brian Boru declared as the figure in the saddle before him slipped to the ground and held her hands up to him. He dismounted awkwardly, with Nichola bearing the brunt of his weight. Then they walked slowly toward the abbey, his arm around her shoulders for support.

The baroness took in her daughter's bedraggled ballgown and carelessly pinned-up hair and shuddered. "My God, Nichola! You look—"

"Ravishing," the countess interrupted, smiling. "Radiant. And look at you, Boru! On a horse! On your own two feet!"

"More or less," he said modestly.

"He has made great strides," Nichola declared, smiling up at him. Then she looked to the baroness, very tentatively. "Mother. What a surprise to see you here. I don't suppose . . . you came to thank Madame and Mrs. Treadwell." The baroness was speechless. Mrs. Treadwell considerately answered for her:

"I would not say that exactly, Nichola. More to swear her eternal revenge."

Nichola took a faltering step toward her mother. "I pray you, don't be angry. I know this wasn't what you wanted for me. . . ."

"I shall never be able to hold my head up in public again!" the baroness cried.

"In public . . . oh, Mamma." How long had it been since she'd called her mother that? "Mamma," she said again. "What difference does it make what everyone else thinks, if you are not satisfied at night, in your bed?"

"How dare you speak to me so . . . so pruriently?" the baroness demanded in shock.

"I didn't mean it that way!"

"What goes on in bed fades," her mother said briskly. "Believe me. I know."

"But does it *have* to? *Always*? I was willing to marry Wallingford, Mamma! And do you know why? Not for me—for *you*. All my life, I've wanted so much to please you, make you proud of me." Nichola drew in breath. "I thought that if I could only make you proud of me, perhaps you would be . . . happy."

"And so I would have been!"

"Oh, Mamma. Would you really have? Would my marrying the heir to a duke have put things right between Father and you?"

The baroness's brows drew together in fury. "It's not your place to preach to *me* about my marriage! Not when your own is such a wretched disgrace!"

"Disgrace to *whom*?" Nichola asked plaintively. "Do you want to know what I learned from these ladies, these wonderful, these splendid ladies? I cannot depend on you to make me happy, Mamma. And you cannot depend on me. We all, each of us, are responsible for our own happiness in this life. Agreed, my marrying Wallingford might have cemented your reputation amongst the *ton*. But your reputation there is assured enough already, isn't it? It is at home, with Father, that you are miserable."

"How *dare*," began the baroness, then faltered. She started for her hartshorn, let it fall, cast in the reticule for her handkerchief. "I . . . I . . ."

"If it is any consolation to you, Emily," the countess noted quietly, "I hold no grudge against you. I never have."

"And little wonder!" Emily Hainesworth cried out. "He is the most *infuriating* man! Didn't I give him everything he might have asked for? *Five sons!* Not to mention you, of course, Nichola. Haven't I always maintained the household in perfect order? Kept myself trim and up to fashion? But does he ever take notice? *Does he ever pay me any mind?*"

"It might interest you to know," Mrs. Treadwell murmured, "it was just that sort of marriage Christiane and I had in mind when we formed our academy."

The baroness drew herself up. "You said nothing about *that* in the literature you sent me!"

"We most certainly did," Christiane protested. "We laid it out quite plainly: 'The purpose of the academy is to enable the young ladies of England to achieve their true potential.' "

"Well, yes. But I assumed that meant . . ." The baroness glanced at her daughter, standing straight and tall and shining, Lord Boru's arm about her waist. "Oh, dear."

"Can you imagine, Mamma," Nichola said softly, "anything more wondrous than a man and a woman sharing this world's pleasures and pains together as equals, as partners, as lovers *and* friends? Wallingford understood that, at the last. Why, he gave us our wedding ring!" She held it out, and her headmistress oohed and ahhed appropriately. "That is why we, at least, came here tonight—so I could thank Madame and Mrs. Treadwell from the bottom of my heart. Madame, I am so very sorry for doubting you. Can you ever forgive me?"

"Oh, *chérie*. Of course I do. You know that I do." The countess's eyes were suspiciously bright, and Mrs. Treadwell was weeping openly. Nichola stepped forward to hug them, first one and then the other, while Brian beamed at her, leaning on the gate.

Mrs. Treadwell sniffed into her handkerchief. "Where are you headed now?" she inquired.

"Strathclyde," Brian told her. "The ancestral castle—what there is of it."

"Stop teasing." Nichola elbowed him. "It sounds absolutely marvelous. Overlooking the Firth—he says the swimming is quite splendid! Deer to hunt, horses to ride, and great huge dogs that sleep with him in bed. It will be paradise." Her mother had blanched. Nichola noticed and laughed. "Oh, Mamma, for goodness sake! It will be heaven, for me!"

"Let's have some tea, shall we?" Mrs. Treadwell proposed, mindful that they'd been rather long on the portico.

"Don't suppose you've got claret?" Brian asked. "Not to mention a cigar. I've been dying for a cigar. Rushed out without mine last night."

"I have claret *and* cigars," Madame assured him as they headed inside.

"Praise God!"

The baroness was left standing by the door. Mrs. Treadwell recollected herself. "Lady Hainesworth, do come and join us in a nuptial toast," she invited warmly. "Despite our difference of opinion, surely we can all be civilized. After all, what is done is done."

The baroness darted a glance to be certain the others were out of hearing. "Just between you and me, Mrs. Treadwell, I am inclined to believe this is all for the best. May I confide in you?" Mrs. Treadwell nodded encouragingly. "Well! Tommy told me that when Wallingford attempted to . . . to force Nichola to elope with him, she flattened him with one punch! He *never* would have been able to curb that girl."

"No," Mrs. Treadwell agreed.

"And she is so *impossibly* headstrong—consider if she had gone through with the elopement, then thought better of it! Why, I wouldn't put it past her to run away from him, back to Lord Boru again! And just think of the scandal *that* would have made!"

"I hadn't contemplated that," said Mrs. Treadwell, "but you do have a point. Better one infamy than a lifelong series of them

"My view exactly. Still, what I cannot *imagine*," the baroness went on plaintively, "is how I am to explain all of this to the *ton*!"

"Well." Mrs. Treadwell tucked the baroness's arm into hers, gave it a reassuring pat. "I've always found truth is best in such a situation. Were I in your place, I would

simply say that Nichola, despite her betrothal to Lord Wallingford, found that her heart lay elsewhere and followed it
accordingly."

"Followed her *heart*? But nobody does that!"

"You forget—Nichola's reputation as an original is already secured. Her first notice by society, after all, came
when she accepted Lord Wallingford's challenge to a duel.
Why, the *ton* worships an original, and always has."

"Hmm . . ."

"And there *is* the fact that Wallingford himself gave
them the wedding ring. My guess is that anything you
choose to say will be certified by him."

"I went to see him before I headed here," the baroness
noted. "To my astonishment, he was not at all angry or
resentful. On the contrary, he seemed *relieved*. Kept bab-
bling on about Cecilia Farnweather."

"What, Veronica Farnweather's daughter? She's a
lovely little thing, isn't she? Much more Wallingford's
speed. Wouldn't it be splendid if they made a match of it!
Veronica will be eternally grateful to you for Nichola's bowing out."

"She will be, won't she?" the baroness mused. "Now
that I think of it, any number of other mothers will be glad,
too, to have Nichola off the scene."

"Of course," Mrs. Treadwell added, steering her guest
toward the parlor, "what with the hubbub sure to arise
from the elopement—people *will* talk, won't they, even
when they haven't the slightest notion of the truth?—I'd be
extremely careful to guard against any further blights to
Nichola's reputation."

The baroness stopped dead in the hall. "Such as
what?"

"Well . . . such as mentioning Christiane, perhaps, in
connection with the academy."

After a moment, the baroness laughed. "Why, Mrs.
Treadwell. You ought to be in charge of negotiating peace
on the Continent. You are twice the statesman Lord
Castleneagh is."

"It is interesting to reflect, is it not, on what we women might achieve were we not consigned to our present roles in society?" Mrs. Treadwell said thoughtfully. They'd reached the parlor doors. Brian was stretched out in an armchair with Nichola on his good knee. He had a cigar in his hand, and the newlyweds were sharing sips from one glass. They were laughing. The baroness looked at them, and the wistfulness broke through.

"I wish to *God* I'd let Christiane take Harold when she wanted him," she muttered.

"Have a drink," Mrs. Treadwell urged her, going to the sideboard for sherry.

"Perhaps just a small one," the baroness acquiesced. The headmistress brought her a glass.

"To Nichola and Brian," Mrs. Treadwell announced, raising her own sherry.

"To Nichola and Brian!" Madame echoed.

"To you, Nichola," the baroness said slowly, "and to your . . . husband. I'd wish you happiness, but it's plain enough you've got that in abundance."

"That we do," said Brian Boru, holding tight to his wife. "That, milady, we do."

I̶t wasn't dawn when Gwen awoke the following morning, but it *was* exceedingly early. She lay and stared through the window above the bed Nichola had once occupied at a glorious blue sky, remembering the long-ago night when her form-mate had dressed in her brother's clothes to go off soldiering. Now, Mrs. Treadwell said, Nichola was the belle of society, and set to marry Lord Wallingford. Gwen knew she ought to be glad for her friend. But somehow . . .

"Gwen?" Bess's voice was a whisper. "Are you awake?"

"No."

"I thought so. What are you doing?"

"Just . . . thinking."

"About Nichola. I am, too. I miss her. I hope she is happy."

"Why shouldn't she be?" Gwen asked reasonably. "Wouldn't you be, if you had the world on a string?"

"I'd hoped all along that she would marry Lord Boru," Bess confessed. "They seemed much more suited to one another, don't you think, than she and Wallingford?"

"They made a handsome couple," Gwen agreed. "But she would have to be so terribly strong to go against that dragon of a mother." Katherine was stirring beneath her covers. The two girls waited, breath bated, until she flounced over and settled down. Then Gwen asked very quietly, "Would you ever marry a cripple?"

"I shall have to marry whoever first asks me," Bess said ruefully, "lest no one else ever does."

"I suppose if Nichola *does* marry Wallingford, it will make it easier for us to catch ourselves beaux," mused Gwen. "She is certain to look after us. Invite us to her soirees and balls and what-not."

"Most likely. Though to tell you the truth—and you must not ever repeat this to her, Gwen—I never did much care for his friends."

"No. Nor did I. A lot of flash without much substance. And that Botheringly was a positive sot. What sort of man would you like to marry, Bess?"

Bess sat with her face screwed up tight, her red plaits hanging over her shoulders. "I really can't imagine anyone will ever want me. But . . . in my dreams?" Gwen nodded. "Well, then. Someone dark and handsome, who loves words as much as I do. Maybe a poet."

"Lord Byron?" Gwen suggested.

"Heavens, no. No soul so tortured as that. Besides, he wouldn't be faithful. I *do* want someone faithful."

"Would the two of you," Katherine said acerbically, fluffing up her pillow, "kindly take your conversation elsewhere? I have better things to do than listen to your prattle. It would be one of the greatest miracles of God's creation if either of you *ever* got a suitor."

Bess stuck out her tongue at her. "I haven't noticed you being besieged by beaux, *Lady* Katherine."

"No. And do you know why? Because I am sequestered away at this useless excuse for a finishing school with losers such as—oh!" Katherine clapped her hands to her ears at a sudden clangor from the courtyard. "That damnable fencing!"

"Fencing?" Both Bess and Gwen started up from their beds, wide-eyed. "Can it be . . . ?" Barefoot, still in their nightdresses, they ran for the door, burst out into the corridor and then through to the balcony. Sure enough, two figures in white pads and masks were squared off against each other in the bright summer sunlight below.

"Nichola!" Bess shouted, nearly tumbling off the balcony in her excitement. "Nichola, is that you?" The shorter of the figures tilted back her mask and grinned. "Whatever are you doing here?" Bess rushed on. "You are supposed to be in London, getting betrothed to Lord Wallingford!"

"Something," Nichola noted, "interrupted that plan."

"What?" Gwen demanded.

The other fencer raised his mask, and Bess gasped. "My marriage to Lord Boru," Nichola said calmly.

"Marriage?" Bessie shrieked. "You and he are *married?"*

"We surely are," Nichola confirmed, and fought off a desultory advance from her husband. "Brian, you will have to do better than that if you expect me to take you at all seriously."

"Still getting used to fencing on two legs," he apologized, wobbling a bit as he stood on the grass. "Come at me again."

"Again and again and again," she promised, letting her foil drop and going to him for a kiss.

"Ooh!" On the opposite side of the balcony, a cluster of the younger girls appeared, wide-eyed and giggling. "Nichola is kissing Lord Boru!" And Bessie sighed with delight as she saw Lord Boru return the kiss with soul-stirring passion.

Gwen, more practical, leaned over the balustrade. "But—how, Nichola? When? Where?"

"Two days past," Nichola told her, arm tight around Brian's waist. "We eloped."

"God, it is so romantic!" Bess squealed.

"*What* is?" demanded Katherine Devereaux, who, roused by all the fuss, had come through the doorway behind her.

"Nichola is married to Lord Boru! They eloped!" Bess told her in a fever of excitement.

"Oh, Jesus!" Katherine clapped a hand to her forehead. "That does it. Mother and Father can plead no excuse now. They will *have* to come and remove me from this dreadful place!"

"We appreciate your congratulations, Lady Devereaux," Brian said gravely from the courtyard, making Nichola giggle against his chest.

"Ladies!" Mrs. Treadwell called sharply from the kitchen doorway. "I am pleased to say that Lord and Lady Boru will be joining us for breakfast. You may ask your questions of them then. For now, would you kindly all get dressed? It is most unseemly to have you tottering about in your nightgowns. Where is your sense of decorum?"

"Where is hers?" Katherine asked darkly. "Where is anyone's in this madhouse of an academy? She was supposed to marry *Wallingford*! Then, at least, the rest of us would have a chance!"

"Oh, you will have a chance," Nichola assured her, with her brown-gold eyes aglow. "You will all have a chance. You must be careful, though, that you do not miss it, let it fly right past you. Love, true love, is a slippery thing." Brian smiled a huge smile and bent his mouth to hers again, with such ardor that Bess nearly swooned.

"Ladies," Mrs. Treadwell said warningly.

Reluctantly, Bess and Gwen turned back to their room. Oddly enough, it was Katherine who lingered, looking down into the courtyard at the radiantly joyous couple still embracing there.

Epilogue

In the master chamber at Tobermaugh Castle, Brian was dreaming he was suffocating, being shoved downward into darkness, farther and farther, beneath a huge pressing weight. In his sleep he struggled valiantly, fighting the oppressive force, heaving with all his muscle to throw off the deadly, inexorable burden, but to no avail. He made one last noble stab before the shadows swallowed him whole—and felt a huge wet tongue lap across his forehead. "Dammit, Kilter!" he muttered, snapping wide awake. "You cannot lie on my head!" The deerhound gave him another loving lick and promptly curled up with his withers planted squarely across Brian's shoulders again.

Brian sighed and sat up, pushing the dog from the bed. He bounded back up eagerly, ready to play. "Stop that!" Brian hissed at him. "You are going to wake her!"

"I'm already awake," Nichola murmured from the cocoon of covers. She rolled over to face him, and Kilter, tail wagging, covered her cheeks and nose with slathering kisses. Brian elbowed him aside and leaned over to do the same. Nichola started laughing.

"What is it?" Brian demanded, offended.

"I was trying to imagine Wallingford kissing me after a deerhound had just done so."

Brian snorted, then pulled his face straight. "Here, none of that. I won't have you thinking of that twit in our bed. Kilter, do get down. Here." He reached to the floor for a discarded stocking, hurled it across the room. The deerhound leaped down, making the windows rattle alarmingly. Brian pulled Nichola into his arms before the dog could insinuate himself between them. Her hair was wild and loose in the pale light of dawn, and she smelled of him—his peat fire, his dog, his bed, his sweat and seed. Beneath the thin scrim of linen nightdress, her breasts were heavy and lush. He stroked them softly, saw her nipples tighten, and desire flashed through him with an intensity five months of marriage had not dulled one whit. She smiled and stretched her arms above her head, negligently graceful. The movement arched her back, brought those tantalizing breasts to the fore. "Temptress," he told her, and fell on her, yanking the ribbon at her throat, drawing the linen down, burying his mouth against her sweet, yielding flesh.

Kilter had retrieved the stocking. He paused with his forelegs on Nichola's pillow, dark brown gaze taking in his master's avid ministrations. Then he dropped the toy and withdrew to the hearth rug, licking clean his left thigh.

"Amazingly intelligent animal, the deerhound," Nichola whispered. "Or did you train him to do that?"

"Stop bringing up my sordid past," Brian grunted, heaving his thigh over hers so that she felt his manhood hard against her belly. He drew the forest of quilts up to his shoulders, to shield her from the chill November air. Then he raised her nightdress to her waist, big hands following the curves of her thighs, catching behind her buttocks. Nichola let her hand slide over his waist to his groin, slow and caressing. Her fingers closed on his thick rod, and he let out a heartfelt sigh. "Oh. Mmm. My love . . ." He redoubled his attention to her breasts, sucking and teasing with his tongue, until her free hand drew him up by his hair, brought his mouth to hers. "Already?" he demanded, feigning surprise. "There was so much I had in mind to do to you yet!"

"Such as?" she whispered, staring up into his amazing blue eyes.

"This." He put his fingers to her mound of Venus.

"Oh," said Nichola. *"That."*

Smiling down at her, he reached inside her, into her warm, wet sheath. Nichola shuddered as the tip of his finger brushed across the taut bud of her desire, slipped into her, withdrew, moving back and forth with maddening quickness. Her hands tightened on his shoulders, ran down his back, pulling him to her. The fire had awakened in her belly, was flickering brighter at his every stroke. Impatiently she grasped his manhood in her fist to guide it into place. Still he held back, arching above her while that hard tip teased her, made her quiver and moan and sigh and finally erupt in impatience:

"For God's sake, Brian!"

"Oh, very well." He thrust deep into her, grinning. But the grin dissolved as he felt anew the sensation of her body swallowing his, welcoming him into a shared wealth of passion. Her arms were strong and sure about him; she was not tentative or coy. She took what she wanted, his Nichola, and what she wanted was his rod surging into her, hard and fast, over and over again. There was an athleticism to their lovemaking that took it far beyond anything he had ever experienced with any other woman. She would not be crushed or subdued; she came at him as his equal, demanding as much as she gave. And she gave him . . . everything. From the first time, she had.

Her hands were clutching his buttocks now; her mouth was open in a heightening sequence of cries. He could feel her walls tightening, contracting in sharp waves, and the sudden surge of sweet moisture. Still he held back, wanting to prolong her pleasure, lengthen it, intensify it—though the effort made him bite his lip. But she wanted him *now*. She showed it, tilting back her hips so that his rod thrust into her to its hilt. "Nichola," he warned.

"Oh, Brian, please!"

Vanquished, he surrendered, released his seed in a hot rush that made her cry his name and hold him to her and shudder in a long, rippling sigh. Love puddled and flowed between them, joined them body and soul, until she fell back against the pillows and he flopped beside her, potent and drained. "Ahh," she whispered, shifting to curl against him. "You are so *good* at that!"

"I am, am I not?" He grinned again as she kneed him. "But then, so are you."

"Everything I know, you taught me," she said primly, pulling down her nightdress, reaching to tie up the ribbons. He stayed her hands.

"Wait. I may not be done with you yet."

"Oh! I hope not!"

He arched a brow at her. "*You* were the one begging for conclusion!"

"What I love about lovemaking is having more than one conclusion."

"You insatiable creature." He laughed and kissed her, full on the mouth. "We shall have to do something today besides loll in bed, though."

"Why?" she asked, pouting.

"Mother will insist on it. She isn't fond of sloth."

"This isn't sloth. This is hard work." She caught her fingers in the hair of his chest, twining the curls. "Isn't it?"

"It is on my part."

"I'll be on top this time."

"If you insist," he said airily. And so she was.

After that, they dozed, with Kilter having reclaimed a stretch of bed between them. They did not rouse until near noon, when Maegan knocked and then came in, followed by a maid with an overburdened tray. "Breakfast," Brian's mother announced. "Or luncheon. Whatever ye choose to call it."

Nichola sat up eagerly. "Do you know, I am starving!" Brian laughed and drew the ribbons of her bodice together to cover her breasts.

"Shameless, isn't she, Mother?"

"No more so than ye." But her smile was indulgent. "There be a package come for ye, Nichola. From the academy."

"Another one?" she said in disbelief.

"Aye. More 'broidered linens, no doubt." Maegan snapped her fingers at Hayden, who was waiting in the hall. He came in with a huge paper-wrapped parcel, his expression typically grim.

"Lord, they have already outfitted me with enough towels and sheets to last three lifetimes," Nichola noted wryly.

"Well, love, they know you aren't likely to furnish up the closets of Tobermaugh on your own." Brian's blue eyes danced.

"Just for that, instead of riding with you this afternoon, I shall spend the time at work on tea towels."

"The bloody hell you will," he countered fiercely. Smiling with satisfaction, Nichola untied the parcel strings and tore the paper away.

There was a note atop the box. She slit it open with her finger. "Well?" Brian demanded. "Who is it from?"

"Gwen. But she writes that the gifts are from everyone." Curious, she lifted the lid and pawed through a sea of tissue paper, then lifted out a tiny white shirt covered with embroidery. "Oh!" she exclaimed. "How lovely!"

"A tad small for me, though," Brian noted.

"It's for your son, you idiot."

"My daughter, you mean." He caressed the smooth, wide bulge of her belly.

"Your son," Nichola repeated, and reached farther down into the box. She came up with a square of white linen, its edges turned and stitched with exquisite neatness.

"But here's a handkerchief for you! No, wait—a dozen handkerchiefs!"

Maegan burst out laughing. "La, luv, they be clouties!"

"They are what?"

Brian's mother looked to her son. "Nappies," he clarified. It was at that point that Hayden, disgusted beyond bearing, bowed and withdrew. "Poor soul," said Brian. "I'll wager he's the one now bemoaning that his is a hereditary post."

Nichola grinned at him, then pulled a gorgeous minuscule jumper from the tissue paper. "Mrs. Treadwell must have made this. Not even Katherine can knit decently. Oh, and Brian, look!" She held up a little white batiste jacket thick with seed pearls and French knots. "There's a note attached—from Bess. Says she expects you to display it to every Scotsman you know, as evidence of her fitness as a huswife."

"Scots babies don't wear such things," he scoffed.

"This one will."

"I hope to hell it *is* a girl, then." But he could not help running his finger over the intricate embroidery work. "This must have taken her ages to make!"

Nichola reached in again, drew out a square wooden box, and laughed as she saw the engraving on it. "This *is* for you, I know that much. From Madame."

"Cigars!" He fell on it happily, slitting open the seal. "Cubanos, God bless her. Wait, there's a note on this, too." He unfolded it, read, and his face fell.

"What's amiss?" Nichola inquired.

"She says they're to hand out when the baby is born, dash it all."

"I think you might smoke one or two while we're waiting, don't you, milady?"

"It be Maegan, plain Maegan," Brian's mother reminded her gently. "And aye. I do."

"No time like the present," Brian declared, and promptly lit up—then stared as Nichola turned faintly green.

"Before breakfast, love?"

"Terribly sorry. I forgot. Bring that tray here, Elspeth."
He stubbed out the cigar, and Elspeth did so, smiling as she
uncovered the platters:

"Eggs the way ye likes 'em, mum, 'n' bacon 'n' toast 'n'
haggis . . ."

"That's *my* haggis," Brian announced.

"We'll share it." Nichola sliced the sausage in half.

Brian looked to his mother. "She must be Scots, don't
you think? No *Sasenach* ever had a taste for haggis."

"Yer wife be an unusual *Sasenach*. Be there be no more
in the box, Nichola?"

"I don't think so."

"Nothing from Lady Katherine?" Brian teased.

Nichola, mouth full of egg, was riffling through the
tissue paper. "Oh, wait! There is something more." She
drew it out, drew in her breath. "God! It *is* from Katherine!"

"Let me guess. Poisoned apricots," Brian posited, grinning.

"No, no!" Nichola had shaken out the gift from its
wrappings. She held it up by its ribbons, turned it over,
turned it back again. "It's a . . . I haven't any notion what
it is."

"I *think* it be a cap," Maegan proposed, examining the
present. "Nay—it be a bib."

"Naturally," said Brian.

Nichola was giggling, perusing the attached note. "It *is*
a bib. She says so. And she adds, 'It will no doubt be an
uphill climb to teach a Scotsman's child table manners. Perhaps this will help in the effort.' "

"I'd like to take that stuck-up duke's daughter," Brian
growled, "and put her in a crofter's hut atop Ben Nevis
with a dozen stout Scots lads for the winter. She badly
needs taming."

"What she needs is loving," Nichola said absently. "I
wonder will she ever be so lucky?"

"I doubt it," her husband sniffed. Nichola had put the

emptied box aside and was digging into breakfast raven-
ously. "Do you mind if I have just a little?" Brian asked.

"You can have the bacon," she offered. "I don't feel
much like bacon."

"Very generous of you." Brian took a slice and
crunched it between his teeth.

"Ach, I near forgot." Maegan reached into her apron.
"A letter came for ye as well, Nichola."

"Not from Mother?" She'd paused in mid-bite. "She *is*
threatening to come here, you know, for the laying-in."

"Nay, nay. From yer brother."

"From Tommy!" The meal forgotten, Nichola shot out
her hand. "Oh, let me have it, please!" She slit the seal with
the jam-knife, somewhat to Brian's consternation.

"Nichola, my sweet. You've covered it with raspberry
preserves."

"I've been waiting ages for this, Brian. I need to find
out—" She scanned the letter quickly, knitted her brows.
"I don't understand."

"What, love?" Brian had taken advantage of her momentary distraction to fork some of the breakfast onto his
own plate.

"Well . . . I had written to him, you know, because
there is one thing about that night when Wallingford abducted me that never has made sense."

"And what is that?"

"Don't you dare touch that egg," she warned. "I am
eating for your heir."

"Seems to me you are eating for all Strathclyde." She
stuck her tongue out. "But what is it that puzzles you?"

"The announcement in the *Gazette* of our elopement. I
didn't think either Tommy or Wallingford got back to London in time to change Wallingford's name to yours. I already wrote to Wallingford, and he told me he'd tried his
best, but the paper was already being printed by the time
he arrived. Now Tommy writes the same thing. So how do
you suppose Wallingford's name got replaced by yours?"

Maegan let out a small snort. "You ought just to have asked *me,* love," Brian remonstrated.

"What could you know of the matter? You were with me at the Black Stallion—and then we went straight on to the academy!"

"Ah, but I had left a representative in London."

"Hayden?" she demanded in shock.

"No, no. One who was on your side."

"But the only other person in London . . ." Nichola broke off, stared at her mother-in-law. *"You?"* Maegan nodded, smiling. "That's impossible! All you knew was that I'd been kidnapped by Wallingford! You didn't know for certain where I'd been taken, whether Brian and Tommy would find me—much less that when they did, I'd want to marry your son!"

"I'll admit, when I got to the offices and found Wallingford had left his own announcement, I had a devil of a time convincing the editor that a mistake had been made," Maegan acknowledged modestly. "It was only my being Bri's mother, I believe, that made him yield in the end."

"You took an awful chance!" Nichola cried. "If they hadn't found me in time—if I'd been wed instead to Wallingford—and then if I hadn't married Brian that night—" She could not repress a shiver at the prospect of the devastating chaos that would have ensued.

"Not so much chance as that," Maegan said easily. "Bri may be slow to rouse at times. But when his mind be made up, he gets what he seeks."

"She won't tell you so herself," Brian whispered into Nichola's ear, "but she has the second sight."

"She *must* have," she answered in wonder, just as the babe in her stomach gave a fearsome kick. "So, tell me then, milady—Maegan. This grandchild of yours—is it to be boy or girl?"

Maegan smiled as mysteriously as a Druid priestess. "I would not count on one or the other. Enjoy yer breakfast!" She beckoned to the servants, who followed her out.

"Would not count on one nor the other . . ." Nichola

screwed up her face. "Now, what in heaven can that signify?"

Brian had paused with a forkful of haggis halfway to his mouth. "Oh, God help us."

"Brian?" His jaw had fallen open. "What is it, Brian?"

"Only one thing it can be—or two, rather," he managed to say.

"You don't mean—"

"Aye. Twins."

Joan Johnston

"Joan Johnston continually gives us everything we want . . . fabulous details and atmosphere, memorable characters, and lots of tension and sensuality."

—*Romantic Times*

☐	23470-0	*The Bridegroom*	$6.99
☐	22380-6	*The Cowboy*	$6.99
☐	22377-6	*The Bodyguard*	$6.50
☐	22201-X	*After The Kiss*	$5.99
☐	21129-8	*The Barefoot Bride*	$5.99
☐	21280-4	*Kid Calhoun*	$5.99
☐	20561-1	*Sweetwater Seduction*	$5.99
☐	21278-2	*Outlaw's Bride*	$5.99
☐	21759-8	*The Inheritance*	$5.99
☐	21762-8	*Maverick Heart*	$5.99
☐	22200-1	*Captive*	$5.99